MIDNIGHT DYNASTY

THE HOUSE OF CRIMSON & CLOVER VOLUME V

SARAH M. CRADIT

Cover Design by Sarah M. Cradit
Editing by Shaner Media Creations

First Edition
ISBN: 1500700185
ISBN-13: 978-1500700188

Publisher Contact:
sarah@sarahmcradit.com
www.sarahmcradit.com

FOREWORD

The secretive, ancient, powerful world of the Deschanels and Sullivans is about to change forever, because the Deschanel Curse is back...

You'll find a Curse Timeline in the back of this book as a companion guide, which you can also find on my website: www.sarahmcradit.com. Also on the site are detailed family trees in the Bonus Materials section (which you may find useful, as *Midnight Dynasty* has a much larger cast of characters), and other fun rabbit holes to fall down.

In *Bound,* we left the Deschanels on the verge of a tumultuous phase in understanding their Empyrean heritage. Nicolas is adjusting to both domestic life and new responsibilities, with Mercy at his side. Ana, Aidrik, and Finn await the birth of their child, in Wales.

Reader, please trust I'm nurturing these storylines. However, for the moment, our New Orleans Deschanels are about to face even bigger challenges, as the Curse is back... and it's *hungry*...

1970

1972

1973

1974

1975

1976

1980

∾

Vampires of the Merovingi Series
The Island

∾

Crimson & Clover Lagniappes (Bonus Stories)
Lagniappes are standalone stories that can be read in any order.
St. Charles at Dusk: The Story of Oz and Adrienne
Flourish: The Story of Anne Fontaine
Surrender: The Story of Oz and Ana
Shame: The Story of Jonathan St. Andrews
Fire & Ice: The Story of Remy & Fleur
Dark Blessing: The Landry Triplets
Pandora's Box: The Story of Jasper & Pandora
The Menagerie: Oriana's Den of Iniquities
A Band of Heather: The Story of Colleen and Noah
The Ephemeral: The Story of Autumn & Gabriel
Banshee: The Story of Giselle Deschanel

For more information, and exciting bonus material, visit www.

sarahmcradit.com

PART I
MALEDICTION

APRIL 2006

"A man who lives fully is prepared to die at any time."

Mark Twain

ELIZABETH

*E*lizabeth woke abruptly, sweat pooling at her brow. Her dreams only grew to levels this vivid when their reality was imminent.

Beside her, Connor lay snoring, undisturbed. He had never, not in nearly three decades of marriage, had trouble sleeping through his wife's episodes. She could wake screaming at the top of her lungs and he'd continue on in uninterrupted, restful bliss.

As a seer, Elizabeth often saw glimpses of the future. When awake, her visions were unreliable. She was only given snippets, with much of what she saw open to interpretation. When dreaming, however, they were painfully lucid. She could see the future in all its terror or glory, with no filter to help ease the burden.

Of course, as a Deschanel, this ability was not wholly unique. Her relatives were healers, empaths, and other powerfully "gifted" individuals. But the rest of them experienced things *in the now*. They laid their hands on someone sick and that person was healed. They sensed disquiet in another and helped soothe it. Elizabeth only ever saw what was to come. And, whether it

4

came to her in a dream or otherwise, it always, without fail, came to pass.

She glanced at the clock: two in the morning. Connor would be waking in a few hours to head in to the law firm. Tristan, her son, would be dead to the world until lunchtime.

Though Tristan didn't figure into her dream—thank God, she couldn't lose another child to this wretched Curse—she still had a pressing urge to check on him. Since he was born, nearly twenty-one years ago to the day, she'd always feared he would stop breathing in his sleep. Some nights, even now, she sat at his bedside and watched his chest rise and fall. She'd done the same thing for Danielle too, but now Danielle was gone.

This was the life Elizabeth Sullivan led day in and day out: one of dread. Fear the Deschanel Curse would continue to strike those she loved. Terror it might take Tristan, as it had Danielle.

Tristan lay askew in his old childhood bed, long legs dangling out from the side of his sheets. Elizabeth released the sigh she'd been holding in, and sat quietly on the pine chest beside his bed. Once filled with toys and plush friends, now it lay stuffed with forgotten sports gear and a messy stack of dog-eared video game magazines.

He wasn't in the vision. He was safe, she kept telling herself. But years later, she was still unable to get the sight of her only daughter, lying broken in the street, out of her head. Eyes open, closed, it didn't matter. That image was burned in her heart and mind for all of time. It was a wound that would never heal, a grief she would never recover from.

Though Tristan was safe, for now, there were others in the family, people she loved, who were not. Nieces and nephews she watched grow up. Children who never would.

And there was nothing—not one thing—Elizabeth could do to stop it. It was going to happen. The only unknown was *when.*

TRISTAN

*T*ristan finished cleaning up the dinner mess. His father was working late at the firm, as he often did, and while Tristan knew his mother wouldn't eat, he fixed her dinner anyway. After eating alone, he checked on her, and she was just as he'd left her an hour before: curled-up in a living room chair, head pillowed on one upholstered armrest, vacant gaze fixed on the wall beside her. He considered moving her, ultimately deciding it unnecessary. Elizabeth had her own bedroom for times like this, although when she was "present," she stayed with her husband. In any case, she wouldn't even realize Tristan was gone. She never did.

Tristan drove down to the Quarter. Entering the Desire Oyster Bar, he waited at the small, isolated table in the corner while he listened to the endless drone of tourists around him. He would have to deal with it, as he had for the past year. He chose the tourist traps for her sake. In a room full of locals, the risk of someone recognizing her would be too great.

She was usually a few minutes late. Tristan checked his watch anyway, neurotically every few minutes, as if simply having a grasp on the time might cause her to materialize.

About twenty minutes after the hour she finally arrived, rushing toward him in a great frenzy, an attempt to project her tardiness was the result of some comedy of errors, and not the norm.

Emily was not exactly beautiful, at least not in any traditional sense. She had pretty, apple-shaped cheeks, and soft, but not shiny, brown hair. Her height and figure were equally average, and unremarkable. It was really her smile that caught Tristan's heart the day he met her. Her face was rather ordinary without expression, but when she smiled her entire presence transformed, blossoming with hints of the beauty she must have possessed in her youth.

Emily. He'd been seeing her for over a year now. He couldn't even really call it dating. She was fifteen years older, but more to the point, married to someone else. Her husband remained perpetually buried in his work, and she was looking for more. Tristan happened to be present and available when she realized her need. And although he felt guilty about her situation, it was the safest kind of relationship for Tristan: enjoyable, but without any risk of long-term commitment.

If he'd been born into another family, with different genes, his possibilities would've been limitless. But he was Tristan Sullivan, of the Deschanel clan, and family was not an option. His mother had spent twenty-one years driving this unfortunate point into his head with dogged determination. Because of her emphatic insistence, he was among those who really, truly believed in the Deschanel Curse. His young life—if you could call it that—revolved around this conviction.

He made a vow, with his cousins Amelia, Katja, and Markus, to never, ever have children. Solemnly, they swore to set aside selfish desires, and to never be responsible for bringing more anguish to their family. *We will always have each other,* they'd promised, confident that would be enough. As if the day would never come when they'd realize all they were giving up, for something they had no control over.

There were cousins who disregarded the warnings and started families. Not a day went by that Tristan didn't worry about their safety.

On the other hand, he never let himself get too attached to them, either.

"Hi," Emily greeted, beaming down at him. Her smile was even more ethereal than usual. In fact, she appeared to be very nearly glowing. "Sorry I'm late."

"You're always late," Tristan teased, crossing his arms over his chest in feigned vexation. "Sometimes I'm tempted to change the meeting time to thirty minutes earlier, just so you'll arrive on time."

She wrinkled her nose and frowned, but knew he was teasing. Leaning forward, she planted a soft kiss against his mouth, and he began to relax, remembering this was his escape. It was his time to allow the endless worries to fade away, and let her soothing presence take over.

Rather than asking how her day went, Tristan waited for her to share. Emily had a rather uneventful life. She was a schoolteacher, and didn't get out much. Evenings were spent either with Tristan, or at the school helping students. Her husband was an executive in some banking company downtown—which one exactly, Tristan never wanted to know, just as he didn't really want to know Emily's last name—and worked late into the evenings, leaving his wife to her own devices. He apparently never wondered or cared where his wife invested her time. Tristan suspected Mr. Emily probably had his own fun on the side.

"The Canal Streetcar was packed," she lamented, as if her lateness had nothing to do with her own lack of time management. She drew a deep sip of the long-melted ice water. "Oh, did you hear about the shooting down on Derbigny?"

"No," Tristan replied, not bothering to add that gun violence in New Orleans wasn't exactly front-page news. With nothing polite or interesting to contribute, he decided to break his own rule. "How were the kids today? Any more crazy science experiments?"

Emily brightened at his asking, and started in with a story about something funny one of her third graders did involving the class hamster, George Washington. Tristan smiled and laughed at the right moments, but his mind was elsewhere, despite having resolved to set aside his worry.

He was at a complete loss about his mother.

On one hand, she was right to worry about the Curse. Tristan himself believed in it. And not solely because of his mother, but because the two aunts he respected most also gave it credence. Colleen and Evangeline were both women of science. Colleen was a brain surgeon, and Evie a damned nuclear physicist, for god's sake. They believed, as did most of their children. Amelia, Colleen's daughter, was basically Tristan's hero. He admired her intelligence and kindness, and she took after her mother in many ways. Colleen's son, Ashley, didn't put much stock in the Curse, but he was a good man who Tristan could look up to in other ways. Markus and Katja, Evangeline's kids, were ridiculously smart, too. Markus was one of Tristan's best friends.

Amelia, Markus, and Katja, along with their parents, believed in the Curse on an intellectual level. They saw it through the lens of something that did not necessarily have a logical explanation, but was nonetheless irrefutable.

Tristan's mother, though… her belief in the Curse was different. She viewed it far more personally than anyone else in the family, especially after the shocking death of her daughter. Tristan overheard his Uncle Augustus once say Elizabeth was "afraid of her own shadow, for the love of god." He accused her of still believing in monsters under her bed, and boogeymen lurking in the woods. He meant it as a joke, but as with all well-aimed humor, a great deal of truth interlaced his words. These beliefs of things that went bump in the night were slowly undoing her. Tristan wondered how much longer she could function.

Connor was a decent husband and father. In fact, if not for Connor, Tristan might not have survived childhood. His mother often forgot when summer was nearing end and that the kids needed clothes, but Connor remembered. He would give Colleen or Maureen some money to take Tristan, and his sister Danielle, along when they did the shopping for their own kids. Then there were nights Elizabeth would get so caught up in writing her memoirs she'd forget the kids needed dinner. Or going further back, their diapers changed. Connor took care of everything, and in a lot of ways, he was a parent to three, not two. He coddled Elizabeth in a manner that suggested their marriage was less equal, more that of caregiver and patient.

But in the last year or so, his father had seemingly given up. It had been a slow decline, starting with Danielle's death, but recently he appeared to have lost all hope. Tristan thought it was because he'd begun to really feel the burden of his wasted efforts and came to realize he couldn't save his wife, just as he hadn't been able to save his daughter. He escaped to the office more, seeing as though Tristan was now an adult and could look after himself. Tristan didn't blame him, but it only reinforced the sinking dismay as his mother faded further into melancholy.

Tristan tried talking to his father about this subject many times, but Connor's protective nature would minimize the issue. *Your mother has always been this way. You know that.*

But his mother was drowning in her tortured daydreams, and his father would rather disappear into his work than address it. The Sullivans came from a good, solid family. Irishmen. They understood hard work might bear fruit, and sometimes it could result in famine. A part of Connor accepted his wife was slipping further away, but that same practicality understood there was nothing to be done about it.

Stop it. This isn't the time to be thinking about this. This is your escape, you stupid fool.

Emily eventually realized Tristan was not all there. "Am I boring you?"

"No," he said honestly, but not confidently. Her face fell. "It isn't you. I've had a rough day."

"Your mom again?" she asked as her expression softened to disproportionate concern. He imagined it was the look she gave her students when they scraped their knee on the playground, right before they erupted into world-ending hysterics.

He nodded in confirmation, but didn't offer anything else. Tristan, of course, had never told her about the Deschanel Curse or his mother's mania, but he had relayed some half-truths. It had been enough to say his mother was ill, and he worried for her.

And while he didn't want to talk about it, in acknowledging the upset, he would both be truthful and get her to not press the matter. Emily knew it was a touchy subject and empathy was one of her finest traits. Predictably, she offered more of her exaggerated concern, and covered his hand with a gentle pat. In spite of himself, he enjoyed this tenderness, but continued to keep the wall between them, so as not to ever feel too much around her. The barrier of her marriage, and the Curse, kept his mind focused where it belonged.

While measured empathy felt nice, Emily was working herself into full-on pity, which he detested. In an effort to redirect her compassionate efforts, he suggested, "If you have some time, we could go to Ana's."

Emily immediately brightened at the suggestion they retire to their usual spot. Tristan's cousin, Anasofiya, had been over-seas for months, on business only the Deschanel Magi Collective knew the specifics of, and had given him permission to use her apartment on Chartres. He and Emily couldn't exactly escape to *her* house, and bringing any female to his would raise all sorts of questions he wasn't prepared to answer.

"I would *love* that," Emily exclaimed, eyes twinkling. She placed her napkin on the table, and stood, leading the way as if any hesitation might cause Tristan to change his mind. Tristan left some money for the water and bread, and followed her.

They took his car, and he parked in Ana's spot, ushering Emily back through the wrought-iron gate and into the brightly foliaged courtyard. The sound of jazz from Jackson Square, a block away, filled their ears. He twisted the key in the lock, and as the door swung open, her arms were already around his neck, landing kisses across the hollow under his jaw, and the dimpled cleft of his chin. With practiced dexterity, she had his pants off before he could kick the door closed.

Tristan lost himself in her fervor, unsure of where his usually reserved Emily had gone, but certainly not raising any complaints. Forcibly setting confusion aside, he pressed her up against the secretary.

The first time was quick. With her so ardent, there was no chance of him lasting. But then he let her lead him to the guest bedroom wearing only her Cheshire-cat smile. He followed behind her nude figure, admiring how, even in her late-thirties, her ass was still firm and high, her skin smooth and unlined. *I am so unbelievably fortunate to have a beautiful woman who gives so much to me without asking for anything real in return.*

She climbed atop him as he settled against the satin sheets. Under her tender ministrations, Tristan blissfully escaped into the slow rhythmic movements pulling him further, and further, away from his troubles at home.

After their release, Emily hesitated, looking down at him with wide glistening eyes. At first Tristan was alarmed, worrying he'd hurt her in some way. But then her brown eyes turned glassy as she opened her mouth, and with a great, soft sigh whispered, "I love you, Tristan."

I love you. Words Tristan had avoided, and dared not say to anyone outside his family. Words he never expected having to say in this arrangement. *Words that could not ever be unsaid.*

He was entirely lost for response and, in his horror, flipped her off on to the bed beside him and stumbled out of the room. Instinctively, he knew she was hurt, unsure, and probably many other things he'd caused with such an insensitive reaction. He hated himself for it. But in his panic, he didn't stop.

Why was I such a gentleman about my telepathy around her... why didn't I sense this... how could I have not seen this coming... I am such an idiot!

With the door locked behind him, Tristan dropped to his knees and slid to the floor, cold sweat beading up all over him as the uncontrollable shaking began.

AMELIA

*A*melia closed the manila folder after making her final notes, ending her day in the office. The last patient, a man with borderline personality disorder, was especially troubling. Not so much what he'd said in his therapy session, but more so what he had not.

As an empath, it was difficult not to let her natural abilities seep into her sessions. Newly a doctor of psychology, she had already learned many patients, despite their honest attempts at reaching out for help, often lied about their problems. Instead, they crafted a world more palatable, where they could feel safe. It was Amelia's job to gently deconstruct this illusion, providing reassurance while helping them peacefully accept reality.

Aside from her nagging worry, in all she'd sensed from Jeremy Boudreaux, she did not suspect he would harm himself, so there was little she could do beyond continuing to work with him. And as Jacob would gently remind her, she couldn't always take these emotions home. Allowing them to bleed over into her world was exhausting, and unhealthy. *And potentially fatal,* her mother's words added.

Jacob. Even his name summoned a smile to her lips. Jacob

Donnelly was the only man who'd ever brought a blush to Amelia Jameson's pale cheeks. And, she suspected, the only one who ever would.

She observed Jacob's handsomeness as charming, and completely unintentional. His short black hair flashed here and there in adorable spikes, but not from any great effort on his part. His eyes sparkled emerald green, with a gaze so intense people often looked away without realizing why. But this was a misleading trait, for those who knew Jacob gravitated toward his playful nature. He especially loved to make others laugh. And where Amelia was concerned, Jacob never failed in that.

Amelia knew she should marry him. He had, after all, insisted up and down he could live without having children, as long as he had her. But this wretched Curse didn't exactly come with a manual, and she couldn't be sure bringing him into the family wouldn't put him in harm's way.

As if sensing she was thinking of him, Jacob called. "*Mi bruja blanca*, I don't have to be a damn psychic Deschanel to know you're still sitting at your desk, dwelling," he good-naturedly teased, from across town in the Garden District home they shared. "Besides, I did what we both know you cannot, and concocted a killer jambalaya. I make no promises as to its future if you're not home in thirty minutes."

Amelia smiled. *Mi bruja blanca. My white witch.* He'd called her that for years. Her hair was so light it was very nearly white, almost devoid of pigment. This, combined with Amelia's sky blue eyes and Nordic skin tone, often produced a startling effect on people when they first met her.

"Donnelly, we both know you don't enjoy sleeping on the couch, so why make idle threats?" she bantered back.

"Don't test me, woman. I'll take my jambalaya in the bedroom and lock the door."

"Hmph," she replied, with a short laugh. "You're right, there's not an entire locksmith in all of New Orleans. Whatever will I do?"

"You mean none of your relatives can open a lock with their mind yet? Amateurs."

They could spar like this for hours, but she'd rather do it in person. "I'll be home in a few. Try not to annihilate the jambalaya before I get there."

"Effort promised. Results uncertain," he replied. She could see his wide smile through the phone, as he added, "Love you, *Blanca*." Connected to him on a much deeper level, her empathic senses also felt his pure happiness, a feeling she shared with equal intensity. How he could still make her feel tingly inside, after all these years, was simultaneously baffling and reassuring.

Still smiling, Amelia locked her office and walked a few blocks to the streetcar stop. In tandem with the low rumble of the Canal Streetcar, a ripple of deep pain seized her, shattering her smile as she picked up the agony of someone dear to her. This was not her empathic touch, this was the other ability she had. A seer, some called her, but she was nowhere near as powerful, or precise, as her Aunt Elizabeth. Amelia's felt more like vague premonitions. Loose and unfocused, hinging instead on the emotional impact rather than the physical. A perfect and terrible match for her empathic nature.

Amelia closed her eyes for a moment, trying to solidify any details her mind would allow. Someone close to her, but who? Not Jacob, no. And not just one individual, either. Two. Tristan. And Aunt Elizabeth. With both, it was a feeling of intense foreboding, on the scale of life-changing.

Amelia gripped the streetcar sign as a wave of nausea and lightheadedness overtook her. A man rushed to her side to help, but she waved him away. Regretting the need to be rude in the face of his kindness, the feeling only grew worse when others interfered.

And then, as quickly as the dread had assaulted her, the forewarning was gone. She felt the light breeze from the approaching streetcar and focused on the sounds of wheels and cables crunching, trying to ignore the way her blood coursed feverishly through her veins, whispering of unfathomable agony.

ONCE SAFELY SEATED, AMELIA TRIED TO MAKE SENSE OF WHAT she'd felt. Elizabeth existed in a constant state of emotional turmoil, so she often featured in Amelia's premonitions. But Tristan. This was new. And, oh, was it powerful. His raw, acute pain overwhelmed her so greatly her knees had buckled, and her lunch threatened to overturn. *Please God, not Tristan. I can't lose another cousin.*

Amelia forced herself to disregard the omen, at least for the time being. Unlike her empathic skills, her abilities as a seer were not specific enough to ever be useful. And if she didn't clear her head, Jacob would sense her disquiet and worry for days. Neither voiced it, but the reality she could fall victim to the Deschanel Curse, as many others had, hung over them. She would not add further worries to his already troubled mind.

Sometimes she felt her love for Jacob was incredibly selfish, given her circumstances. Before she met him, she'd always been careful to keep romance at arm's length. It was Amelia who taught Tristan about dating "safe." Until Jacob came into her life, she'd found comfort with older men. Much older men, with age differences that startled her mother. Colleen often remarked, *I don't know which is better, Amelia. Safely dating men twice your age, or taking your chances with someone who might actually speak to your heart.* Even so, her mother understood Amelia needed companionship. Perhaps even more acutely than others, Amelia craved a safe haven in her raging sea of emotions. After watching her brother, Ben, fall victim to the Curse, Amelia couldn't take any chances.

Unlike Tristan, she'd never dated people who were married. She wanted her arrangements to hurt no one. Mostly, she'd gravitated toward old bachelors, or widowed businessmen who wanted no more than she did: simple companionship. None were her type, but this was by design, as she could never risk becoming attached. Ever. Thanks to Colleen's investigative watchfulness, and her empathic abilities, she understood, even if Tristan did not, he was already attached to Emily. Amelia feared it wouldn't end well for either of them.

Maybe that's what I'm sensing.

The streetcar screeched to a halt at Carondelet, and she disembarked, switching to the St. Charles line, as she pushed through throngs of tourists gathering at the edge of the Quarter. Finding a seat near the back, she closed her eyes.

The closer she moved toward home, the keener her sense of Jacob.

They'd gone to high school together. Amelia never had much choice in her social circle, as Deschanels were "old money," and local celebrities for reasons both philanthropic and unseemly. Jacob, on the other hand, fell among the kids who were not exactly popular, but well-tolerated. Sharp-witted, he was funny, and people were drawn to him. Amelia had always been on the verge of striking up a conversation with Jacob, but circumstances never aligned until the day he showed up at Tulane, right as she was entering graduate school.

Amelia smiled, leaning back against the flat wooden seat as she allowed herself to get lost in the one memory that always helped calm her fears, and steady her heart.

AMELIA WANDERED INTO THE COLLEGE PUB, LOOKING TO SEE IF anyone she knew was hanging out. Then she saw him: Jacob Donnelly, that goofball from her high school, who had enough of an Irish accent to sound like he didn't belong here. He wore a baby-blue collared shirt, first two buttons undone and one flap defiantly pulled free of his waistband. The belt cinched at his waist struggled valiantly to keep his trousers on. Black spiky hair atop his head pointed in twelve directions, as it always had, but his facial features had matured into a finer definition. His trademark goofy smile had evolved charmingly, giving an expression bordering on arrogance, but speaking more to his innocence.

Amelia's heart caught in her chest as his appearance produced a completely unexpected reaction. Why is it she never noticed how beautiful he was? Or how that softly-grooved cleft on his chin invited her fingertip's touch?

Jacob was off in his own world, eyes closed, lost to an enthusiastic air drum solo of The Foo Fighters' "Everlong." He mouthed the words as his hands swung with every wild-yet-precise drumbeat, oblivious to the gathering crowd. When the song ended, he finished off his beer accompanied by applause from a handful of college kids. He offered them an exaggerated bow, and as he came back up, his eyes fell on Amelia, who shamelessly stared at him in dumbfounded awe.

"Miss Amelia Jameson! Princess of Prytania, Goddess of the Garden District," he intoned, a great big smile spreading across his face as he sauntered over to her. His dimples appeared, accented by a light touch of facial hair. "You know it's customary to tip when you enjoy the show."

"I have no idea what you're talking about," she protested, flustered. Worse than the lie was that she couldn't figure out why she was telling it. Playing coy had never been her thing, and she was certain he saw right through her. "I didn't know you went to Tulane," she added, attempting to veer the conversation away from her mortification.

The mischievous glint in his green eyes told her exactly what he thought of her falsehood. She half-expected him to flat out accuse her of gawking, when instead he asked, "Have you eaten? I was planning to take the streetcar into Carrollton and grab a burger at Camellia Grill. We can catch up along the way, and if you actually have something interesting to say, I might even buy your burger, too."

Amelia had been too surprised to say anything but yes. And too smitten to recognize how dangerous being around him could be for her heart.

This was 1997, the year after the Deschanel Curse last struck the family, taking more than a half-dozen of Amelia's relatives. Beyond the deaths, her cousin Adrienne went missing, and was still missing in 1997. Amelia's grief was still raw and unchecked, and she hadn't realized, until Jacob came into her life, how much she needed someone to brighten her gloomy world. Someone who was not a Deschanel.

They became fast friends, surprised at how much they had in common. Amelia found herself inadvertently looking for Jacob between classes, and caught him doing the same. She warned him she wasn't looking for a relationship, and he assured her, with a twinkle in his eye, "Blanca, you couldn't pin me down if you dropped your house on me." The friendship blossomed.

On weekends, they'd explore the city like a couple of adventurers, born of Jacob's offhand comment that visitors likely knew more about the city than residents. This resulted in the two of them trying to "outdo" each other with their New Orleans facts. Amelia had a slight advantage because of her family's rich past and connections to the area, but it quickly became apparent Jacob's stubborn insistence on being right would lead them to an inevitable stalemate. Mere debate unsatisfactory, they took their conversations outdoors, determined to find new experiences.

They started in the Quarter, eating at a different restaurant each night after classes, bringing their historical notes with them. Often proprietors would eagerly share colorful stories beyond the dry historical accounts. Napoleon House was an especially fun experience, even though the legend about Emperor Napoleon plotting there in subterfuge was not actually true.

They branched out into the Garden District, where Amelia's family —and many other Deschanels—lived. Jacob's family lived closer to the river, near the wharves, but he told Amelia he spent many hours wandering the avenues as a boy, sketching some of his favorite homes.

He would write stories about the people inside the houses, imagining what their lives must have been like.

"Tedious," Amelia told him. "Mystery solved."

"Easy for you to say." Jacob reached over to her mouth and mocked wiping something away. "Sorry, you had a silver spoon still stuck to your lip."

She rolled her eyes, but was smiling. "Calling me ignorant of my situation doesn't make you somehow an expert," she said. "But who cares about that, I want to see these sketches and stories!"

Jacob's face flushed bright red. Embarrassment was not an emotion he showed very often, preferring to cover his awkward discomfort with dry humor. "They're dumb. I wasn't any good at it. Why do you think I'm going to medical school?"

"You don't have to be good at something for it to be interesting. I love photography, but my mom and brother always tease me about how blurry the photos are. Do I care what they think?" She shrugged indifferently, as he gazed skeptically, eyebrow cocked. "Well, maybe a little," she admitted.

"You don't talk about your family much," Jacob ventured. They had been sitting on a bench in Audubon Park, watching the geese play in the pond. It was spring and a light breeze formed off remnants of an earlier rainstorm, but it was an otherwise beautiful day.

"I don't remember hearing your complete family history either, Donnelly," she argued.

"I don't recall you ever asking."

"Well, I don't recall you ever asking, either."

"I just did," Jacob teased. He leaned back, against the tree behind the bench, staring at her with that startlingly intense gaze of his.

"Well, my family history is well-documented," Amelia responded with a dismissive wave, looking away to hide her unease. "Most of it is pretty simple to look up."

"Do I look like I enjoy research?" he asked, leaning back on one elbow. When he smiled, his dimples appeared, and disappeared, his

emerald eyes never leaving her. Her heart skipped a beat at how hand-some he was.

Amelia laughed. "Some doctor you're going to make then. Doctor of Bullshit, maybe."

He sat up, feigning offense. "You know how to cut right through the heart, Amelia. Straight. Through. Clean cut." His eyes started twitching and filling up with obviously faked tears. "Hurtful."

"I would say I was sorry, but I don't wish to be disingenuous."

"Clean through the heart again! But I know how you can make it up to me..."

She lifted an eyebrow. "Oh, how?"

His face grew serious. Most of Jacob's "serious" faces were some form of goofball mockery, but she knew his real one and this was it. Her pulse quickened. What if he asked for a kiss? What would she do? Her heart was already softening toward him and she'd been thinking it might be prudent to start spending less time together.

"First, I have to confess something to you," he said. Her eyes widened, but he kept talking. "I actually know quite a bit about your family."

"Then why did you ask me about it?" she demanded. His revelation had the effect of an ice cold shower. Foolish to think he wanted to kiss her! "I don't understand where you're going with this."

"Calm down, Blanca," he said, lightly. "This isn't some silly romantic comedy where you discover the dude you've been hanging out with has an ulterior motive. I didn't plan meeting you on campus, getting closer to you and extorting you for information, only to fall in love with you against my better judgment."

A smile played at the corner of her lips. He was such an ass! She wouldn't give him the satisfaction of a full smile though, until he told her what he was up to.

Jacob raised an impertinent eyebrow. "Not as funny as it sounded in my head? Okay, well, anyway... I know about all of the things that happened to your family last year." He let that sink in.

Amelia's breath caught, but she hid her annoyance. "Everyone does, Jacob, it isn't exactly a secret," she said coolly. *Where was he going with this? Had she misjudged him all along?*

"When your Uncle Charles, and his family, got into that car accident down near Abbeville, we, that is, my family, followed the story closely. We couldn't get over how sad it was, and how horrible it must have been for your cousin, Nicolas... both parents dead, three of his sisters also dead, and one completely missing. I found myself wondering what happened to that family. Like I used to do with the Garden District houses when I was a boy."

He looked for her reaction, saw none yet, and kept going. "I approached Nicolas once but he wasn't very nice to me. I tried to give him my condolences and offered my help in finding his sister. He laughed at me and then told me to go fuck myself."

At this, Amelia chuckled. This was exactly the response she would have expected from Nicolas, especially then. "He's like that with everyone."

"Yeah, he's charming. But I couldn't stop thinking about Adrienne. How does someone disappear? If she had died, there would have been evidence of it."

She interrupted him, wincing. Two years after this discussion, they found Adrienne alive and well. At the time of this otherwise happy memory, Amelia still keenly felt Adrienne had died, primarily because she could no longer sense her younger cousin. None of the empaths or seers in the family could, either. "The police said the... gators probably got to her."

"Amelia, you're a student of biology. You know even if that happened, there would still be some evidence... pieces of her clothes, something. An heir of Charles Deschanel's fortune... completely disappeared." He stopped and his voice took a softer tone. "I'm sorry, I didn't come here to lecture you about your family. Putting my foot in my mouth is not a skill I'm proud of. I know this is still a fresh wound."

She nodded. "It is. Very fresh."

Jacob put his hand over hers. "I am so sorry. This was a bad idea."

Amelia ventured a look up, and in his eyes saw a kindness that gave her comfort unlike anything else had since the tragedies.

She put her other hand over his. "You're fine, Jacob. Really. Go on."

He didn't move his hand, and continued. "So I thought back to earlier in the year and remembered what happened to your brother."

Amelia said nothing. She missed Benjamin every day. Amelia loved both her brothers, but she had loved Ben best.

He gently squeezed her hand as it was sandwiched between his. "And I thought, how can one family go through so much? And then at Christmas..."

"Danielle," she finished. Tristan's sister.

He nodded. "It seemed almost unreal for one family to go through so much in a single year. It was really Adrienne's disappearance that piqued my interest to do more research. I found a lot of information about your family online."

"I can't say I've ever looked," Amelia said, meticulously wiping away a tear that had sprung up. For Amelia, tears could be dangerous, her emotional acuity both a "gift" and potentially her destruction. "But I've never needed to, because my family keeps good records."

"Mine didn't," he said, without elaboration. "So in my digging, I discovered what happened last year was not the first time large-scale tragedy struck your family. Maybe you already know those details."

"I do."

"I figured. But what was interesting to me was a group of archived letters I found on a genealogy website. Someone had posted them anonymously as a contribution to family records, so I don't know where they came from. They were letters between an Ophelia Deschanel and a friend of hers, someone named Edna Wallace. Do those names sound familiar?"

"Edna doesn't, but Ophelia was my mother's great-aunt. She died just before I was born."

"She lived a long time," he agreed. "In the letters, she talks about the stuff that happened through generations of your family, and she specifically states her belief none of it was an accident."

Amelia's heart skipped. She had never seen these letters, and was even more alarmed they were online, for the public to see. She thought she knew where he was going, but was terrified of what he might say next. Would he laugh at the superstitions of her family? What if he asked if she believed in it? Surely he would. What would he think of her if she confessed the truth?

She swallowed. "Go on."

"Amelia, are you aware that some members of your family believe the Deschanels are cursed?*"*

A sensation, not unlike the pressure of being underwater, came over Amelia. The world around her muted unnaturally, and she felt light-headed as her heart attempted to thump clear out of her chest. How was she to answer this question? Honesty was an option, but she might lose him completely if he saw her as a superstitious biddy. She had never wanted to be defined by her belief in this, and she had never, ever shared it outside the family. Amid the swirl of emotions, she also considered perhaps it would be for the best if he did bolt.

Ultimately, Amelia would never deceive anyone. It was not in her to pretend to be someone she wasn't. She always spoke the truth, come what may.

"Yes, Jacob, I am," she declared, head up, shoulders squared.

"Do you believe in it?" he hedged, carefully.

She paused only briefly. If he judged her for it, then so be it. "Yes," she said, "I do."

Jacob nodded slowly, then moved his top hand off hers. She drew in a nervous breath. What had she done? Then he lifted the same hand and gently laid it against the side of her face, in an entirely unexpected tenderness. Amelia closed her eyes and let herself lean into his touch, as he kissed her forehead.

"Does it feel good to finally say it out loud?" he asked.

She nodded, but her throat was too constricted to respond. This was not how she expected this conversation to go, if she were ever to have it. He still hadn't told her what he thought, but his kindness assured her that he wasn't running for the hills. Her emotions warred between relief, and growing fear of her feelings for him.

"I don't know what to think about it Amelia, but I grew to respect your aunt through her writing. And while I don't know your mother all that well, she seems like an incredibly sharp lady. She would have to be to operate on brains all day, right? And obviously, she produced you." Jacob smiled warmly. Her heart rate slowly subsided to normal.

"If three very smart, astute women believe in this, then there's something to it. I don't know what, exactly, but something," he concluded.

When she sat speechless he added, "I didn't plan for you to show up at the pub and ogle me, Amelia. I never expected any of this, but since we're here now, I thought you should know. I don't want secrets between us."

Amelia's eyes welled with more perilous tears as the weight of this discussion pushed her thoughts to more serious matters. "I can never have children."

He processed that for a moment and then nodded. "Okay."

She released a long, slow breath. Jacob didn't think she was crazy. He knew her darkest truths, and he was still sitting beside her.

"Amelia, I don't want children," he said to her, in a tone that suggested he'd been mulling her comment over. "I never have. I didn't have... well, the best childhood growing up. Maybe I'll tell you about it someday. But I want to dedicate my life to helping others. I could live happily with someone amazing by my side. Someone who also accepts children aren't a part of our future."

Their careful tempo established, Jacob allowed her to digest his words.

When she didn't speak, he clarified, "I'm not proposing, you ridiculous girl! I'm not even asking you out."

Amelia drew back in mock offense. "What the hell was all that about then, Donnelly?"

He put his arm around her shoulders and she leaned into him, easily. It felt natural, as if she were with family. "Because I want you to know you're safe with me."

She fell in love with Jacob Donnelly, at precisely that moment. From then on, there was never a chance of protecting her heart, for it already belonged to him, and always would.

With Jacob, she was safe.

AMELIA JUMPED OFF THE STREETCAR AT SEVENTH, AND LET THE memories fade away. When her episodes were especially painful, like the one tonight, she latched on to the moment Jacob offered himself to her, selflessly, and without judgment.

Smiling again, she nearly sprinted the half-mile home, premonitions momentarily forgotten.

COLLEEN

olleen observed her baby sister's ranting with an overwhelming urge to let out a long sigh. Histrionics had always been Elizabeth's specialty, and she was in top form today.

"Liz, it's been nearly a decade," Colleen attempted reasonably, knowing it would do little to quell her sister's tirade. And truthfully, Colleen was wary herself. In spite of her dramatics, Elizabeth's visions were almost always accurate, and always had been, since they were children. But it would do no good to indulge her, or Elizabeth would quickly slip into one of her episodes, and she would be lost for days, if not weeks.

"That doesn't concern you?" Elizabeth cried, pacing before Colleen's marble mantle at The Gardens. "The Curse hasn't had its fill in almost ten years! It's *hungry!*"

"Psh," Colleen replied, but looked away. *Ten years.* Ten years since their brother, Charles, and most of his family, perished in a bayou car accident. Ten years since Elizabeth's daughter, Danielle, was struck by a car in front of their home. Ten years since Colleen's son, Ben, and his young family, died in that horrible house fire.

Had Colleen worried the Deschanel Curse would strike again? Of course. That fear floated in the back of all her thoughts. But she also knew dwelling on something you couldn't change benefitted no one.

Secretly, and with some hope, she also wondered if the Curse was beginning to slow, or dilute itself. The potency had dulled over the last hundred and fifty years. Previously, entire generations were wiped out; the family lived in fear of the line dying off. But August Deschanel's brood had thrived. Seven children, with children and grandchildren of their own. And aside from the horrible cluster of events a decade prior, there'd been no other widespread tragedies to speak of.

And now... well, now they had bigger things to worry about. Revelations the Deschanel abilities were not merely coincidence, but instead a product of mingling with another race of beings. Empyreans. She thought daily of her niece, Anasofiya, who was somewhere in Wales, with her Empyrean mate and human husband. Their child would be born any day, the new Deschanel heir.

Setting aside her own worries, she knew she must deal with her sister's current concerns, which would not go away by ignoring them.

"Colleen, we're fighting a power we have no weapons against," Elizabeth pressed, lowering her voice as she stood before her older sister. "There's not a single ability any of us have that can stop this horror. How are we supposed to live with that?"

"We just do," Colleen said wisely, leaning against the marble hearth. Elizabeth's outbursts were physically exhausting, as well as emotionally. "As we've discussed in the Council, we've already taken cautionary steps. We've gently encouraged our children to reconsider starting families of their own."

Elizabeth snorted. "Yes, a lot of good that did! Your son Ashley has three kids! Maureen's offspring are starting families now, too, and Adrienne has a couple little ones to worry about. And now, Anasofiya! We are *flaunting* our children before Brigitte, begging her to take them from us!"

Colleen eyed her levelly. "Some of the children have listened. My Amelia. Your Tristan. Nicolas. Alain. Evangeline's kids..."

"Yes," Elizabeth agreed, thoughtfully. "Thank God for that. And now, we are flirting with danger, with all this business about Aidrik, and these Empyreans. I still can't believe you sent my son to consort with one, though I suppose he did come back safely from Wales... but that's beside the point! We already had enough to contend with, we didn't need one more thing!"

"It wasn't as though we had much choice. Whether we ignore or address our Empyrean ancestry, it remains a fact. Aidrik's protection will keep us safe, for now," Colleen soothed. "As for your visions..."

Elizabeth shook her head, staring off vacantly. "Colleen, soon there will be more pain for us. I'm going to be ill."

"I wish you would tell me who you saw in your vision. It's really counterintuitive to barge in here and tell me there's a problem, but refuse to give me any details," Colleen accused.

"What would telling you the names do? You can't save them!"

"What is telling me *this* doing, Lizzy! Now I know we have more tragedy ahead, and for all I know, it involves one of my own babies."

Elizabeth dropped her head at this, and Colleen's heart sank. It did. It involved one of her brood. "Tell me, Elizabeth," she ordered in a low, stern voice. "Tell me now."

But Elizabeth was already lost to herself, crying and gazing off into the corner again. Once she slipped into her episodes, there were no words strong enough to pull her out.

Colleen wished she could disregard her sister's warning as dramatics, but she couldn't. The visions were the one thing you couldn't wade through for the truth; they *were* truth. More

Deschanels were going to die to the Curse. At least one of the victims would strike close to Colleen.

And there was nothing anyone could do.

After Tristan escorted his mother home, Colleen sat before the hearth to collect her thoughts.

As magistrate for the Deschanel Magi Collective, it was incumbent upon Colleen to make a decision. Should she call a meeting to discuss the matter? Wait? As Elizabeth pointed out, there was nothing they could do. Was it better then, to stress over something they couldn't control? Best to blindly accept the fate their ancestors had given them?

And it was also true, she was forced to admit, the Empyrean business further complicated things. The truth was, she didn't know what danger awaited from that influence, any more than she knew who the Curse would take next. It was a double-headed dilemma, and they had not the weapons to slay either.

Colleen was tempted to call Amelia. Amelia was reasonable. Level-headed. Of course she was, Colleen had raised her. But Amelia might be the victim Elizabeth saw in her dream, and Colleen couldn't selfishly involve her daughter in a situation with that kind of unknown hanging over them.

But she's in the Collective. You can't call a meeting without including her. Your job isn't to protect the others, but to advise them.

Of course, first she must engage the Collective Council, the seven appointed Deschanel house heads. Debating the issue was an unnecessary formality.

She only wished Elizabeth's vague dramatics weren't clouding the situation further. As painful as it would be to know who was going to meet their fate, not knowing was even worse.

Though the Collective's main focus over the years had been cataloguing and tracking the various Deschanels and their abilities, the Curse also came up from time to time. A century ago, more focus was placed on trying to combat it. A more urgent topic then, as it had obliterated almost the entire Deschanel line. But the Curse had only struck one year in Colleen's lifetime, and only once in her father's. Until Elizabeth's vision, Colleen hopefully assumed it would not strike again for another sixty years or so. Yet it didn't surprise her something they couldn't control was also something they couldn't predict.

The worst part was their limited knowledge about the Curse. Every bit of information they had was passed down, and the story had been diluted over the years. Fiction, and facts as they were, had become a blurred quandary.

The accepted story was this: Charles and Brigitte Deschanel, the couple who in 1844 built the family plantation, *Ophèlie*, managed to escape the Civil War unscathed due to Charles' quick thinking. He turned the vast plantation into housing for an entire company of the Union army, affording his family privileges many of their peers didn't get in that time of turmoil. This meant not only did the house and belongings stay intact, but so did Charles' fortune. To his wife Brigitte's dismay, he also struck up friendships and partnerships with these soldiers from the North, which endured even after the war ended.

Worse than his traitorous associations, Charles would seemingly do anything to keep the men happy. This included turning a blind eye to their treatment of his only daughter, Ophélie, for whom the plantation was named. She ended up pregnant, with no indication of which soldier fathered the baby, and was subsequently found stabbed to death in her bed. Up until that point, Brigitte had grudgingly borne her husband's behavior. But the gruesome death of her daughter sent her over the edge of madness.

Brigitte was known by her slaves to be a practitioner of dark magic. They feared her, and though she was benevolent to those who served well, the staff went out of their way to never cross her. As Brigitte's mind spiraled further toward insanity, she eventually formulated a curse upon her husband, Charles, and all his descendants. She vowed no progeny of Charles Deschanel would ever benefit from his behavior, and their lives would be forfeit. In a final macabre ritual, she took her own life thereby sealing the dark words with her blood.

While most of the family saw her actions as a tragic response to grief, some understood it to be far more. When the Deschanels started dying off, one by one, more started taking her ominous oath seriously.

Coming from a family of witches and warlocks, Colleen had no trouble believing the words of a grieving mother could take down an entire family. But what she had trouble grasping was how any mother would want to curse her own descendants for the crimes of one man. Colleen believed the answer to satisfying the Curse lay somewhere in that sentiment, but she had never come close enough to a solution.

Colleen had already lost one child. She would not lose Amelia or Ashley; she wouldn't allow her grandbabies to suffer.

Colleen picked up the phone and dialed her sister, Evangeline, in Washington, D.C.

EVANGELINE RELEASED A DEEP SIGH, ONE COLLEEN KNEW ALL TOO well. Resignation. "Dearest sister, how did I know you would call?"

"Because your hand was already on the phone, preparing to dial me?" Colleen teased back. This had been the way between them for years. One always sensed when the other was in need, and often their times of need occurred in tandem. But though she'd been lighthearted in her volley, the practiced greeting was superficial. Colleen knew her sister was also disturbed about something.

"All is not well," Evangeline agreed. "And I suspected you had some things on your mind when I overheard Markus talking to Tristan."

"Oh? Something specific?"

"No," Evangeline replied. Colleen heard the sound of her sister's chair scraping the wood flooring as she pitched forward, lowering her voice. "But Markus said Tristan seemed troubled. Something to do with Elizabeth, I'm sure."

"Unfortunately, yes," Colleen replied with a weary-sounding sigh. "But first tell me what's going on there. It's not simply Markus' phone call."

"It's Katja," Evangeline responded. This time, Colleen heard a door close. Whatever it was, Evangeline did not want to have this discussion in the presence of her family. "Leena, she's pregnant."

Colleen was aghast. Katja's young age, nineteen, was the least of her shock. Katja and Markus were two of the most levelheaded children the family had ever produced. Their maturity was unusual, to a degree no one ever worried either would get themselves in any serious trouble.

"I assume you're certain," Colleen said, knowing the answer already but searching for ways to process the news.

"Oh yes," Evangeline confirmed. "Kat refuses to let me go with her to her appointments, and won't even talk to me about it. But I would guess she's roughly three months in. She doesn't even have a boyfriend, Leena. I've seen no signs of anything amiss with her, other than the amount of time she's been spending in her research. But you know Kat, she's always buried herself in her studies."

Colleen made a small sound of agreement, but her mind could not grasp what was happening here, or why. "Nothing amiss at all?"

Evangeline cleared her throat. Colleen could almost see her sister running her hands through her unruly hair as she shook her head. Tension crept into her voice. "Well, maybe you can tell me? She's traveled back to New Orleans four times in the past three months. Has she seemed strange to you?"

Any progress Colleen had made in sorting this mess out was halted with her sister's revelation. "Katja? In New Orleans?"

"Yes, yes! Didn't we talk about this?" Evangeline snapped, lightly. Colleen tsked, and they both knew it was in response to her younger sister's flighty nature. When it came to matters of science, Evangeline measured beyond genius. In most other things, her thoughts were loose, and unattached. It was as if she expended all her energy in the lab and had none left over for the rest of the world.

"No, my dear, we did not," Colleen scolded. "But if she was in New Orleans, I should have known. Are you sure she was coming here? Or, is that merely what she told you?"

"Of course I'm sure," Evangeline replied with a hint of defensiveness. "She stayed with Maureen. Kat and Alain are close, you know, and I guess they've been working on something together."

No, Colleen didn't know this. "You guess? You mean, you don't know?"

"I didn't call for a lecture, Leena!"

"Quite right. I'm the one who called you," Colleen reminded, without reprimand in her voice. Katja was pregnant. She'd been visiting New Orleans for months. And Colleen had somehow known none of this?

"I called Maureen, but I wasn't ready to tell her about Kat's predicament just yet. I only wanted to see if she knew of anything weird, you know? I asked her if Kat had been sneaking off to meet anyone, and she snapped at me, the way she does, saying, 'Do you think I would let my niece go off cavorting around this devil's city?'" Evangeline paused, and released a long, dramatized sigh. "Markus doesn't even know what's going on with her, or who the father is," Evangeline revealed. "Kat tells her brother everything. So if he doesn't know, then what does that tell you?"

That something is very, very wrong. Something well beyond a young woman becoming pregnant far before she's ready. "I think it means there are things going on outside of our purview, and beyond our control. And once I tell you what's going on with Elizabeth, I think you'll agree it's time to consider proposing a Magi Collective meeting to the Council Leaders."

"I'm listening."

Colleen related her conversation with Elizabeth. "And in typical Liz fashion, she won't tell us what, or who, she saw in her vision."

Evangeline was silent for several moments. With a low, near trembling voice, she worried aloud, "Leena, doesn't it feel like our family is headed down a path of destruction? Like we've reached our expiration date, or overstayed our welcome. A midnight dynasty, cursed by Brigitte to fall, and fade into oblivion."

Before Colleen could protest, Evangeline continued, "It's not only this. It's the sum of the past year. I mean, hell, we haven't even processed the news we aren't entirely human!"

"We're as human as we always were," Colleen countered. "An Empyrean in our ancestry hundreds of years ago doesn't change our humanity."

But it did. The Deschanel "gifts" were not merely coincidence, but in fact the product of an ancestor breeding with another race. The Empyreans shared the same core DNA as humans, but certain genes—those relating to speed, strength, cell replenishment, and the propensity for supernatural abilities —lay dormant in humans, but were active in Empyreans. Even diluted over several centuries, the Empyrean blood running through Deschanel veins kept the family powerful, and strong.

And vulnerable. For the group that governed the Empyreans strictly prohibited mating between the races. The ancestor who had impregnated the Deschanel woman years ago placed a protection over the family, shielding them from the Eldre Senetat. This same ancestor, a being over four millennia old, was preparing to walk into danger to defend and protect the family, and his people. If he were to perish, all would be lost.

"Leena, are you listening to me?"

"Sorry," Colleen murmured, mind still drifting, attempting to settle on a solid thought of any kind. "If I'm disregarding the comment, it's because I believe the only way to prevail is if we believe we will."

"Then I'm glad to hear you believe," Evangeline mocked, with a humorless laugh, "because whatever hope I had is fading fast."

TRISTAN

*T*ristan knew eavesdropping was wrong. But was it really eavesdropping when people were yelling from the next room?

Aunt Maureen was in the middle of berating her sister for nearly an hour. The two had never gotten along, but his aunt normally took a more passive-aggressive approach and avoided confrontation. This was one of the only times he had ever heard her yell at anyone. And his mother was taking it, silently, not fighting back.

He wasn't entirely surprised. After years of battling crippling depression, Elizabeth seemed to have lost most of her fight. Even the arguments with Tristan's father were one-sided now. When she didn't check-out physically, she was checked-out mentally. Without even being able to see the now familiar glazed-over look in her eyes, Tristan knew she had retreated.

This only made his aunt madder.

"Are you even hearing me, Liz?" Aunt Maureen demanded. Almost anything Maureen said sounded condescending. She could ask for the milk and you'd be left wondering why you were too dumb to realize she needed it in the first place.

"Of course," his mother said vacantly.

"Of course you are lying to me again!" Tristan heard his aunt's heels clicking on the cypress floorboards. "I am just done, Elizabeth! Done! Augustus is done too! We have tried, Lord knows, to talk some sense into you, but you are even worse than Colleen and Evie with this nonsense. At least they have spent time raising their children and making lives for themselves, instead of pouring every waking hour into dwelling on this so-called family curse! Do you know how ridiculous that sounds, even saying it out loud? Do you even know the difference between fiction and reality anymore? Did you ever?"

Maureen was on quite the rampage. Tristan didn't like his aunt, so he was angry with himself for agreeing with some of what she was saying. Tristan knew his mother loved him, but was well-aware he'd not been adequately nurtured while growing up. His belly was kept full, and clothes were provided, but he acutely felt the lack of maternal tenderness. Tristan wasn't angry, understanding with a mature heart, and in a detached way, that every parent does the best they can.

"It's not ridiculous," his mother said, almost in a whisper.

"What? Say that again? It's not *what*, Elizabeth?"

"Why bother explaining anything when you refuse to listen?" Elizabeth declared, louder this time. "There's no point. I can't convince you, Maureen, and I stopped trying years ago. So, why are you here?"

"As if you didn't know! You have everyone worked up with your latest delusions. You want to stir the family up with lies about people dying? You want a Magi Collective meeting? I'm sorry, but no Liz, this is going to stop, right here and right now!"

His mother sighed. She sounded as if she'd given up trying to reason with a spoiled child. "The meeting was Colleen's idea, not mine. And if you're not interested, don't come."

Maureen laughed disgustedly and her heels clicked more

loudly as she paced the floor in frenzy. "You have *got* to be kidding me, Elizabeth. Obviously I won't come, just as I wouldn't come to any of the silly meetings you called before about this crap, but neither will I allow you to drag your nieces and nephews into it. You are not pulling the kids into this. You. Are. Not."

For a moment, his mother's fight returned. "Maureen, I know it must have been hard for you to be the only one of us born without special abilities. But living in denial only makes you look foolish. It won't discourage the rest of us."

Maureen's heels stopped clicking for a moment. Tristan could very nearly feel her fury through the walls. "You're a delusional bitch who has no idea what she's talking about. And you never did."

"Are we done?" Elizabeth asked.

Tristan almost wished he could see his aunt's face at that moment, but her lack of response, furious heel clicking, and slamming of the door sent the message pretty clearly.

He waited a few minutes to make sure his aunt wasn't coming back and then went to his mother. She stared blankly at the fireplace, emotionless.

"Mama?" he asked. At twenty-one, he still called her nothing else. Maybe because he'd been cheated out of some of those moments as a child. Maybe because there was still a lot of child in him.

"I wish..." his mother started. She stopped and let out a deep sigh. "I wish Maureen was right. God help us all."

"Me too," he said.

He put his arm around her shoulder and her head dropped onto his chest as if she was no longer able to bear the burden. He knew the feeling of her dead weight would come with the absence of her again, for who knew how long this time. It was getting worse and worse, and he didn't know how to help her anymore. Unlike his aunt, Tristan didn't believe his mother was crazy. He knew she was right about the Curse, or his aunts wouldn't be so diligent in educating the family. But they hadn't let it consume them the way it had consumed his mother. Their lives hadn't spiraled further and further into despair. It wasn't killing them, the way it was killing his mother.

And now... now he didn't even have his escape, in Emily. He'd ignored her calls, like an asshole, afraid to tell her the truth, or anything that might lessen the pain he'd left her with.

Tristan felt the tears well in his eyes and he forced them back down before they could overcome him. If they started, they wouldn't stop.

ONCE HE WAS SURE HIS MOTHER WAS ASLEEP, TRISTAN PICKED UP the phone and called his cousin and best friend, Markus. It was late already, but Markus was a night owl. It wasn't unusual for him to be up long enough to watch the sun first set, and then rise again.

"It's Saturday night," Markus said, by way of answering the phone.

"Yeah, and?" Tristan retorted.

"And I'm getting laid," Markus replied.

"As in, right this moment?" Tristan replied, blinking.

"She's in the bathroom, cleaning up," his cousin replied evenly. "But I'm sure she'll want to go again. They always do." There was nothing boastful in his response. Markus spoke as he often did, with facts leading the charge. The child of two scientists, Markus Gehring was neither emotional nor hyperbolic.

There was no point in asking Markus who "she" was, because it was always someone different. Markus dealt with the restrictions of the Curse by sleeping with the most emotionally unavailable women and men he could find, usually acquired from a rave or club, where they were looking for the same thing. Markus' only requirement seemed to be that his partner wouldn't seek a repeat, or a call later.

"I'll let you... get back to it, then," Tristan said awkwardly.

"Everything okay?" Markus asked, apparently sensing Tristan hadn't called for chitchat.

"Yeah, it's all good," Tristan lied. "Wanna play tomorrow?" They both knew he meant World of Warcraft.

"Sure," Markus agreed. "I have a raid tomorrow night, but I could level for a bit, in the afternoon. Your druid, my lock? It'll go quicker if you can tank."

Tristan murmured in agreement, then added, "As long as I don't have to heal. I'm tired of keeping your squishy ass alive while you get to blow shit up."

"Whatever," Markus said with an audible shrug. "She's coming back. Later."

"Later," Tristan belatedly said to the drone of dial tone in his ear. He'd learned long ago Markus' clipped nature of speaking was simply a facet of his personality, and nothing to take with any deep seriousness. He also knew if he'd told Markus he needed to talk, his cousin would have kicked his conquest out without even a second thought. He had the other night, when Tristan called to regurgitate his unfortunate evening with Emily.

But even if Markus had been free to talk, Tristan hadn't formed enough words to describe the scope of his worries.

TRISTAN FLOPPED DOWN ON HIS BED, IN THE ROOM HE'D LIVED IN his whole life. Moving away had never been a serious consideration. It was not that Tristan needed his mother. He believed, to the contrary, she needed him.

Elizabeth had always entertained fanciful notions and theories, but this grew exponentially worse after Danielle died. In fact, his mother's neediness quickly morphed Dani's death from a tragedy they could all rightfully claim, into one that revolved solely around her.

While inadvertent, because of this, Tristan had never properly mourned his big sister. And now, nearly a decade later, he was afraid to try.

But something very interesting had happened to Tristan recently. Something no one saw coming.

Recently, the Collective sent Tristan, and his cousin Anne, on a mission to Wales to track down their cousin Anasofiya, who had run off with their Empyrean benefactor, Aidrik. Aside from the grand adventurous nature of the trip, it was also the first time he'd ever been away from his mother for more than a weekend. The prospect of leaving her was terrifying and exhilarating all at once, and he volunteered before he even had a chance to think about the ramifications.

Are you going to be okay, off by yourself? his father had asked. His mother was so infuriated about the whole thing she refused to say goodbye.

Is she?

Let me worry about your mother. Go do this for yourself, Tristan. It's okay to be excited. You aren't betraying her.

Then why does it feel like I am?

The guilt plagued him only until the plane landed in Wales. And then, a rush of freedom passed over Tristan. The invisible tether was severed, and he saw a future full of endless possibilities. He wanted to go help his cousin, Nicolas, with his plans to shelter Empyrean rebels at *Ophélie*. He wanted to battle for their family, if needed. He wanted to soar. To leave his mark on the world.

He should have known it was too good to be true. That his mother would find a way to re-attach the tether.

Emily had been his only escape, and now that was ruined.

Tristan still hadn't responded to her texts. Anytime he tried, he'd freeze up, paralyzed.

And so his phone remained on top of his dresser, untouched, and life slowly went back to the way it had always been.

But part of Tristan remembered how alive he'd felt across the ocean.

I will find that again. Somehow.

AMELIA

"*A*re you sure?"

"I see no reason for her to make it up."

Amelia was having her weekly lunch date with her mother. They started by discussing benign, everyday topics, but the discussion turned, as it always did, to matters closer to home.

Colleen sipped her espresso, watching her daughter closely. Amelia was assimilating the news that her cousin, Olivia, had become pregnant again. She had one young son, Rory, and it was no secret she and her husband were planning to expand their family further, despite warnings to the contrary. Olivia and her mother, Maureen, not only didn't believe in the family curse, they proudly viewed their actions as intelligent defiance of the backward beliefs held by the rest of the family. Maureen had never been known for subtlety, and her daughter was no different.

"Tristan hasn't been returning my calls," Amelia offered. She was looking out the window at the summer storm. The sound was deafening and she'd slowly been raising her voice to be heard over the ragged percussion as rain thundered upon the metal awning. "It's unlike him."

Colleen nodded. "I wish he would leave home and be more independent but I can't say I'm surprised. For all I've been through, at least I never had to worry my mother was going to jump off a cliff at the first sign of tragedy." She sighed and dropped her spoon into the empty cup. "He's in a difficult situation and there's really no solution."

"No," Amelia said. "I guess not."

"You could stop by," her mother suggested. "He loves seeing you, and it would put your mind at ease."

"Yeah," Amelia said, noncommittally. She didn't like going over to the Sullivan house. It had nothing to do with Tristan. She adored him, maybe above all her cousins. But Elizabeth was always there, and while Amelia loved her aunt, there was a darkness around Elizabeth that felt as if it could spread to anything she touched. Amelia was ashamed of being so weak-minded about it, especially since she didn't have to live with it daily as her younger cousin did, but it didn't change her feelings.

She paused briefly before adding, "I had a premonition the other night. About Elizabeth, but also Tristan."

To this, her mother raised a thin eyebrow. "How strong was it?"

"Strong enough I caused a bit of a scene at the streetcar stop," Amelia answered, with an embarrassed flush. "But it was very brief. And it hasn't come back."

While all Deschanels were trained to guard their thoughts against telepaths, none were capable of protecting their feelings from an empath. Because of this, Amelia could sense her mother was deeply worried, so she said, "Tristan experiences a lot of stress over his mother's fears. And he's playing with fire, sleeping with that married woman. I'm sure that's all it was."

Her mother dropped it, but Amelia knew that didn't mean she'd let it go. "There's more on your mind than Olivia and Tristan," Colleen guessed, sipping her coffee.

"Just tired," Amelia said, lowering her eyes to the coffee before her.

"I may not have your skills at sensing emotion, but I know when my own daughter is troubled."

"It's nothing you can assist with, either way," Amelia replied. "And you have enough going on." Earlier, over salads, Colleen had shared with her daughter the news about Katja, the visit from Elizabeth, and also the slew of calls she'd begun receiving of late from other Council members. Seers, empaths, and telepaths across the family were reporting feelings of foreboding, and called their family representatives within the Collective Council. They were demanding a meeting. They were afraid.

"Consider it a needed distraction, then," her mother replied, smiling. "And in any case, I'm not leaving until you tell me."

Amelia sighed, knowing this to be true. Her mother held it as her personal responsibility to tend to the well-being of all carrying the Deschanel name. This went double for her children. "It's Jacob," Amelia admitted, finally. "He's careful how he says it, but I can tell it's starting to really bother him that there's a limit to what I can share." As a non-Deschanel, Amelia was not allowed to reveal many of the family secrets to him, unless they legalized their union. It was a strict rule of the Deschanel Magi Collective that only spouses could be let into the fold. "And I know it's my fault. If I married him…"

"Why don't you marry him?" Colleen asked. "There's absolutely no evidence the Curse applies to anyone outside of blood relatives."

"Laurel," Amelia said. Ben's wife had died along with him and their son, Colby.

Colleen blanched, but retorted, "I believe Laurel was simply in the wrong place at the wrong time. There exists not a single example of a husband or wife dying independent of their Deschanel spouse."

"That isn't good enough for me," Amelia replied, firmly. "I love him too much to rely on speculation."

"What, precisely, is Jacob's concern? Is he doubting all he's seen and heard? He wants proof?" Colleen asked.

"Jacob is a superstitious Irishman," Amelia countered with a clipped laugh. "There's not much he doesn't believe. I think what he's feeling is hurt, and probably helpless. He can't help what he doesn't understand. And while he doesn't say it, we both know it's my fault, for refusing to marry him."

Colleen watched her daughter, a thoughtful expression spreading across her face. "How long have you been together now, dear?"

Amelia thought about it for a moment, and then smiled in surprise. "Almost ten years."

"There is a codicil in the Collective wherein a non-family member who has spent at least a decade with a member of the Deschanel family can be allowed into the Collective, if all Council members vote in favor of it. It was put in place years ago, for this very reason. You aren't the first Deschanel who refused to marry out of fear."

"Is there a precedent?" Amelia asked, allowing herself to feel hopeful about the possibility. "Do you think they would allow it?"

"I don't know," her mother replied. "But I promise to bring it up with the Council. In fact, I'll call them today. We don't need to call a full Council meeting for this. I should have an answer for you shortly."

Amelia smiled. "Thank you, Mom."

AMELIA TRIED TO FOCUS AFTER THE MEETING WITH HER MOTHER, but her mind and emotions were a whirl, and none of her usual techniques to quell them were working. This was it... the solution to her problem, and one she could live with.

Of course, the beautiful delivery she'd come back to might have contributed to her scattered thoughts. She inhaled the soft, delicate scents of the three dozen white roses sitting on her desk. The spread was so large and full people walking past her office couldn't see her sitting there. *Blanca*, the card read, *I hope these brighten your day. I also hope they get me laid tonight, because it's been a while.*

Donnelly, she texted, *be careful what you wish for. Wear the boxers I like. The ones with the ducks on them.*

She smiled. Focused on her love of Jacob, her thoughts were settled, and her mind back on track.

LATER THAT NIGHT, AMELIA SAT IN THE WICKER ROCKER ON HER front porch, sipping her iced tea beneath the dancing glow of flickering gaslights. One bare foot rocked the old chair back and forth, while the other was tucked under her. Seventh Avenue was wonderfully quiet, and still. The ancient Greek Revival houses around her were dark, their inhabitants sleeping, as she should be, if only she could.

Jacob called to lament he was working late at the University. Disappointing, but a relief, for she was not much in the mood for company. Not after her mother called to inform her the Council denied the request to allow Jacob membership.

Amelia couldn't distance herself from the disillusionment she felt toward her own family. They denied her something that would mean so little to them, in comparison to how much it would mean to her.

That was quick, Amelia had said.

It was really over before it started, her mother replied, her tone heavy with apology. *All but two voted against it. There's so much sensitivity around things now, with all our family has going on after the events from last winter...*

Who was the other yes? Aunt Evie, obviously. I can't believe Aunt Elizabeth wouldn't even vote for me.

Sweetheart, you know I can't tell you the voting record, her mother gently reproved. *Now, clear your mind of this. Don't let it worry you. We will find a solution, as we always do. We are Deschanels.*

Amelia closed her eyes, blocking out all the emotional connections of the day, including her own. Only in the evening, when there were no sounds except the cicadas and the humid breeze whipping through the magnolias, could she truly let go.

She allowed the slow, methodical intake of air, filling her lungs; then, expelled it in a measured release. In. Out. In with the intoxicating scents of gardenia and river breeze. Out with her worries, her fears, and the horror of the unknown.

Amelia remained like this for several long minutes before a wash of light swept over the road, and then a car parked in front of the cottage across the street. Oz Sullivan stepped out of the car and waved at her, briefcase in the other hand.

She offered a wave back. They had been neighbors for several years, but her associations with Oz went back to girl-hood. They'd grown up together. Later, he'd married her cousin Adrienne, making Oz not only her friend but family. Oz, Adrienne, Amelia, and Jacob had spent many evenings together over dinners, barbecues, and poker games.

And then there were nights like these, when Amelia was up with her insomnia, and Oz came in late from work. He would spot her alone, and come to share a single drink with her, before disappearing back into his own life.

"Hey, Amelia," he said lightly, as he joined her on the porch. He looked toward the bench seat next to her, waiting for an invite. With a small smile of amusement, she gestured for him to sit down. Oz, ever the gentleman, never sat without being asked.

"Hey, Oz. It's late," Amelia bantered. It was less a hint to leave, and more her typical bemusement he would choose her company over the comfort of his bed. They'd never really talked about it, and she would never force the matter. But there was no harm in a gentle nudge.

"My mind is wired," Oz replied, as his head fell back and he gazed up toward the night sky. She could smell the light scent of his sweat, mingled with fading cologne. The same one he'd always worn. "One of those days where I don't know how to turn the thoughts off."

"I know the feeling," she admitted, leaning her head back and up in the same direction. There was an easy silence between them, one that came with many years of familiarity. She realized she didn't want to be alone so much as she just didn't want to be around Jacob. Not when she was like this. More for his sake, than hers, though he would admonish her for trying to protect him. *I will always protect him.*

But Oz often reminded her of Jacob, in small ways. There were subtle resemblances, from the Irish green eyes, to their hair like midnight. Both had the look of someone who was concurrently amused and yet also thinking about something deep, and unrelenting. But Oz additionally carried the empty gaze of a man who was broken, and did not yet know it. At times, she was tempted to read him, and to understand it better. Maybe, to even help him. But Oz had spent his whole life around Deschanels, and would smell the intrusion a mile away.

"Would you like a beer?" she asked, but she already knew the answer, and was heading toward the kitchen before he had a chance to say yes. She returned and handed him his, then cradled hers between her knees, as they sat again in silence.

"Jacob at work?" Oz guessed, then took a long swallow.

Amelia nodded. "I don't know how he deals with my late nights so gracefully. Whenever he works late, I end up antsy, and out here, like a neurotic child." She wasn't sure where the admission had come from, but her vulnerabilities didn't scare her, nor did others bearing witness to them.

"That's not weird at all," he teased, lifting an eyebrow and giving her a humoring glance from his peripheral.

"But there it is, anyway."

Oz smiled and took another long drink from his beer, but his thoughts were somewhere else entirely. Without even trying to, Amelia picked up the tension radiating from him, and also the carefully-constructed facade he'd created to hide it. *Well, nothing gets past an empath,* she thought. *Even when they're trying awfully hard to be polite.*

"How's Adrienne? You don't think she's patiently waiting for you to come through the door?" she ventured, as she did any night Oz came for his nightcap. She knew his answer would be deliberately evasive, but it didn't stop the words from leaving her lips.

Oz chuckled and finished his beer. "Is that your graceful way of kicking me off your porch?"

Amelia grinned. "You know it's not. Only putting myself in Adrienne's shoes."

He turned. As he did, the flickering light lit up half his face and all the fine lines appeared like ancient cracks, revealing for a moment skin that was sallow and worn, like tattered parchment. And then he finished turning and he was only Oz again; the handsome Irish kid who once flirted with her years ago, only for her to turn him down because he was just cute enough to get her in trouble.

"She's probably sleeping," he speculated, sitting forward, elbows perched on his knees. He studied his empty beer bottle, spinning it in his fingers with a dexterity learned from his college years. His eyes looked heavy, guilty. "It's a good thing, that work is picking up for me, you know? For my family."

Amelia sensed the trailing sentiments hanging from the

words. It wasn't his guilt at working late eating at him. It was the guilt at not wanting to go home.

She thought, maybe, she understood. Adrienne had never quite been the same after her accident at sixteen. It was as if a critical piece of her stopped growing, and never resumed. Though Adrienne was in her mid-twenties now, she still possessed the girlish indignation that when life wasn't fair, the universe was supposed to correct itself. Adrienne lived in a world where justice was always served, and good steadfastly prevailed. It was a life Oz inadvertently crafted for her, unfailingly coming to her rescue no matter the situation. Meanwhile, her family needed more of her than she was capable of giving.

Amelia recalled the nights, when Adrienne was still missing, where Oz would sit alone on his porch, whiskey in hand, lost to his sorrows. But Adrienne had been home now for almost five years. And yet Oz still found his way to a porch at night, even if it wasn't his.

It was through her "gift" Amelia accurately guessed the Sullivan marriage had cracks in the foundation, but Adrienne had been through so much, as had Oz, and though Amelia's Catholicism was the lapsed kind, she still prayed nightly they would find the peace they'd worked so hard for. *Like Jacob and I have.*

But life didn't always work out the way you wanted it to. Amelia clearly sensed the love Oz had for his wife was familial, and dutiful, but no longer romantic. That realization filled her with such a sudden, gripping sadness, the day's emotional release was undone, and she needed to be alone again.

"I think I'm going to try and get some rest after all," Amelia said with a polite smile, gripping Oz's knee briefly before standing, dismissing him. He paused momentarily before pulling himself up, then gave her hair a light tousle before jogging down her porch and across the street. Halfway across, he turned to give her a brief wave, then ascended the stairs to his own porch.

Amelia watched him until he was safe inside his home, and then went back inside her own.

WELL PAST MIDNIGHT, SHE AWOKE TO THE COMFORTING sensation of Jacob's body sliding in under the covers, behind her, as he enveloped her in his warm embrace. His kisses tickled the back of her neck, and she moaned gently, in relief and submission, as his hands traveled over her back, then hips, sliding her pajamas down. "*Te amo, mi bruja blanca,*" her Irishman breathed in her ear, his Spanish mingled with brogue arousing her in a deeply fundamental way. He snared his fingers in her long hair, kindling every last one of her senses, as he always had.

Amongst their friends they were known as Yin and Yang, for the way their contrasts changed to connection as they embraced.

She remembered this now as he entered her smoothly from behind, their bodies cupped together, the yin and yang perfectly completed.

Whatever worries had plagued her earlier, they were pushed away with his tender affection.

TRISTAN

ristan awoke to the sensation he wasn't alone in his room. When he opened his eyes, his mother sat perched at the end of his bed, rocking, tears streaming down her face.

"Mom?"

"Why... didn't... you... tell... me?" she sobbed. Her hair was affright, full of snarls and snags, eyes rimmed in red. She looked even more unhinged than usual.

He rubbed his eyes, trying to shake away the disorientation he felt at waking to this strange scene. "I have no idea what you're talking about," he mumbled.

"I am... I'm your *mother* and maybe I'm not the best one," she started, then paused to take some great huffing breaths. Tristan realized she was making the transition from being checked-out, to reminiscing about what a horrible parent she was in hopes he would disagree with her. "But why wouldn't you tell me about your girlfriend?"

Had her words not been sufficient explanation, the cell phone in her hand was. She'd been reading texts from Emily. Tristan sighed, all at once understanding this conversation had been inevitable as long as he still lived at home. "It's complicated..."

"No," she said, sitting up straight, wiping her tears away. Her sad eyes took on a manic wildness as she leveled him with her gaze. "No, it's quite simple if you're a Deschanel. You can't risk loving anyone, Tristan."

"I don't love her, Mama. And I'm a Sullivan too, you know. Maybe I'm only half cursed?" he joked, and instantly regretted it. Her eyes seemed to flare wider.

"Do you really want to drag her into this family, into all we've experienced?" she demanded.

Tristan dreaded explaining this to her, but he realized the truth, in this case, was probably better than a lie. "Look, she's married. There's no risk of dragging her into anything. She doesn't want to leave her husband and I don't want her to, either. She's safe." He paused, realizing what he was about to say made him seem like an unbelievable jerk. "It's why I chose her."

His mother pursed her lips together and nodded knowingly, then laughed. "So, curse aside then, you're just using this woman. This *married* woman. I raised you better than to wreck homes! I raised you to—"

He tried to cut her ranting off, but she continued berating him as he talked over her. "Mom, I don't need your opinion or help on this! I have done everything you asked. I've believed in this family curse, I'm not planning to marry, or have children, but I'm fucking *lonely*, don't you understand?"

"... and a baby, Tristan? A baby? When were you going to tell me about that? When you sent the invitations to the baptism?"

"What? Jesus, no, Mama, there won't be any babies, she and I have an understanding—"

She threw his phone down on the bed. "Then what on earth is she talking about?"

The text messages he ignored, for days, were barely visible, blurred words on a screen he wasn't ready to read. Suddenly

Emily's behavior earlier came back to him: her nervousness, her hunger for him. Her whispers of love.

He looked at the phone, but didn't touch it.

"Shall I read?" his mother condescended.

This was the worst conversation ever, and the only way to end it was to let her talk.

"Let's see. 'Tristan, we need to talk about earlier.' Then, 'Tristan, please, I only want to talk.' Obviously you're *ignoring* her, so she sends a few more texts and then this is the best one: 'I wanted to tell you this in person, but if you aren't going to talk to me, I have no other choice. I am pregnant. It's yours.'"

I... am... pregnant. The words bounced around in Tristan's head for a while, as he longed for the moment before he'd heard them. It didn't seem possible. They were so careful. She was on birth control, and he always used protection. Well, not always. Mostly. Usually. Sometimes he forgot to bring it, but he never thought it was truly necessary... sort of like double locking a door, or wearing two sweaters in the cold. Apparently, he was wrong.

His mother put his phone on the dresser. "Speechless, I see." She stood up. Apparently satisfied in his level of attentiveness, she was calmer now, but the look on her face scared him more than her usual one. There was a calm resignation in her demeanor, one that chilled him. He preferred her screaming to this.

Still unable to form words, he struggled to process the news while observing this change that had come over his mother. Neither made any sense. "I'm sorry," was all he could muster, but he wasn't even sure who he was apologizing to. Or for what.

"I am, too," she said solemnly. "I wanted so much to spare you the pain I've felt. The pain nearly all of our family has experienced at some point." She sat back down and put her hand on his shoulder in a way that made him think she was providing comfort. Over the years there'd been very little parental touching, so it felt more stiff and contrived than reassuring.

"You didn't do this Mama, I did," he reminded her.

"I thought you believed, Tristan. I honestly thought you understood everything I was telling you. Everything your aunts have told you, and your cousins. Maybe I was foolish to think talk was enough. Maybe I should have done more." She shook her head, pityingly. He wasn't sure who she pitied more: him or herself.

He wasn't able to comfort her or disagree, and instead offered, "The only person in this family who believes in the Curse as much as you, is me. I deliberately avoided girls growing-up, and most women as an adult. All the normal experiences I should have had, I never got. Emily felt safe. She and I both needed more. I knew she would never leave her husband and I was probably the only guy who would ever be truly okay with that setup." He closed his eyes and bowed his head, still in shock. "I guess I hoped maybe there was still a way for me to have some normalcy. I thought I'd found a way for me to get some human contact, some love, without hurting anyone."

It was her time to deny him pity. "Well, you thought wrong, son. And we've gone far too long without a tragedy in this family."

She patted his shoulder awkwardly and gazed at him one last time before standing up and walking out of the room.

THAT NIGHT, TRISTAN DREAMED OF HIS SISTER, DANIELLE. Tristan rarely dreamt of anything abstract or obscure the way most people did. Many of his dreams were recollections.

Eleven-year old Tristan looked at the bicycle his parents bought him for Christmas. Not just any bicycle. This one was bright blue, and shiny. Even sweeter-looking than the ones his friends rode. But something was missing.

"Where are the extra wheels?" he'd asked, looking up at his parents with wide, fearful eyes.

They exchanged a glance. "You no longer need them, son," his father replied, in a gentle tone. "You're ready for the big-kid's bike now."

"Don't you like it? Don't you want to ride what your friends are riding?" his mother demanded, her emotions quickly rising to a pique, as her husband placed a hand on her knee, cautioning. "You're eleven for the love of Mary!"

"If he's not ready, he's not ready," Connor countered, and then began cleaning the wrapping paper mess. Elizabeth threw her hands up in disgust, clearly affronted by her young son's less than enthusiastic response, and stormed from the room.

Danielle nudged Tristan with her elbow. When he looked up, she was making funny faces at their mother's back. Tristan giggled. Dani was fourteen, but she was never too cool for her little brother.

"Wanna see something neat?" Dani asked, eyes flashing. Tristan frowned, but his sister was undeterred, as she sprinted toward the door, pushing his new bike onto the front porch. "You don't wanna miss this, Tris!"

Young Tristan released a put-upon sigh as he reluctantly followed his sister, waiting at the door in mild annoyance. He was still bruised at his mother's outburst, and wondering what he'd done to upset her this time.

Tristan would not understand until later, and even then not fully, how the very thing his mother was angry about had been her fault all along. As a result of her sheltering him so severely, he was ostracized from his peers. From his own development.

"Watch!" Dani cried, as she wheeled his bike first down the stairs, then through the wrought iron fence, and on to the flagstones. Those cursed flagstones were the reason Tristan wasn't excited about the training wheels being removed. Even with them, his tires would catch. One time he'd flipped clear over the front of his bike, and his mother *had been beside herself, insisting upon taking him to emergency when he'd only been a bit scratched-up.*

"I don't care!" he yelled after Dani, as his sister started riding his bike around in circles, her blonde hair flying in wayward, un-brushed waves behind her. He smiled in spite of his foul mood, at how goofy she looked with her knees up by the handlebars spinning the new bike on its front wheels. The kind of bike Tristan should have been riding five years ago.

"Tristan, come down!" When he refused to turn and look at her, the playfulness slipped from her voice. Danielle's plea was sincere, "Come on, little brother. Let me show you how to do this. I taught myself, you know."

But Tristan had inherited his mother's emotional stubbornness, and instead he pouted in the other direction, listening but refusing to watch his sister's attempt to help him.

So he heard, but did not see, the screeching of the tires. Danielle's clipped screams. The crunching of metal. Felt, but refused to look at, his father flying past him through the front door, at first breathing hard and then moments later making sounds that could not possibly be human. Animal. Guttural.

Tristan's sister died trying to make his life better.

Tristan had never forgotten it.

AMELIA

*A*melia awoke with a violent start, gasping for breath. As the room slowly wove into focus, and she gained her bearings, the first thing she did was check to see if she'd roused Jacob. His light breaths were slow and measured, and she exhaled in relief. He couldn't see her like this. It was the only true deception between them, and she had always justified it—would always justify it—as her need to protect him.

She slipped carefully out of the bed and tiptoed through the room, down the stairs, and then entered the kitchen. Outside, orange hues of the inevitable sunrise peeked over the horizon, lighting the shiny banana leaves outside the window over the sink. *I suppose I may as well stay up now.*

The smell of coffee had the power to rouse Jacob from slumber like nothing else, so she made tea instead. Gripping the ceramic mug in both trembling hands, Amelia tried to make sense of her dream.

This time, her foreboding was about her cousin, Katja. Images flashed of the younger woman screaming in agony, blood on her hands, while a man lay motionless beside her. Amelia couldn't decipher who the male figure was, nor did she have any further insight into the unfolding scene. The scent of betrayal, and death, permeated the hazy moments.

Surely this was fear of what Katja's pregnancy held, as earlier Amelia had been worried for Tristan's relationship with Emily. No matter how much she tried to convince herself to disregard these premonitions, she knew better. Obscure as they were, they held meaning. But what?

"*Blanca,*" Jacob murmured groggily as he padded into the kitchen, eyes half-closed, raven hair mussed. "What are you doing down here at this indecent hour?"

Before she could craft a response, Jacob's eyes opened, then widened at the sight of her exhausted, traumatized face. "You're getting them again," he accused, his tone gruff and concerned. "And… you're down here trying to hide it from me."

"Jacob—"

"Dammit, Amelia!"

She had no words in her defense. He had long ago made it clear protecting him was not a valid argument for hiding anything. "I'm sorry," she said, voice low. "I don't know what else to say."

"Maybe that you won't keep hiding things from me? How many times do we have to do this? I'm your boyfriend, not one of your damn patients."

"You know I don't see you that way. You know why I do it," she replied, shame flushing her cheeks. "I didn't ask to be born with this, Jacob. Do you know how much I'd like to be normal, for us?" She was certain protecting him was right, so why did it feel so much like a betrayal?

"I don't need you to be normal, Amelia. I only need you to be honest."

One word, then more, formed at the back of her throat, but none felt sufficient. He was right. What could she say, other than that? She bowed her head over her tea, her heart heavy.

His initial anger subsiding at the sight of her beaten down,

Jacob sat across from her at the table. "Have you ever asked yourself why I stay here with you?"

Amelia looked up, unsure as to the intent of his question, but fearful of where it was leading. "Sometimes," she admitted.

He smiled sadly, and rubbed his eyes, banishing away the sleepiness. "Well, me too. You're a pretty impossible woman," he declared, and then laughed at her scandalized expression. "One of the things I love most about you, though, for sure."

Amelia said nothing.

"In spite of being obstinate and stubborn, though, you're also my best friend in this whole world," Jacob went on. "And you've never once given me any reason to get jealous. I've never caught you even looking at another dude, and I've seen the way they watch you."

"They do not," she demurred, but realized he wasn't dishing out compliments to be agreeable. There was a point. "I don't look at other men, because they may as well not even exist, for all I care. You're it for me, Donnelly, no matter how impossible you might think I am."

"I'm here with you," he went on, "because I believe whatever causes you to see me in such an undeservedly beautiful way will, one day, propel you to finally let me in fully. Not just half way."

"You know why I can't," she said, with a long sigh. "Really, the more time goes on, and the more I love you, the more marrying you becomes an impossibility."

Once the words were out, the effect of their heavy truth settled over her. She could never, ever marry him. Even if meant giving him up.

The hurt in Jacob's face was like a knife to her heart. "I love you so much I can't even breathe sometimes," he cried, in a choked voice. "But I don't know what else to do, to prove myself to you. To show you I can handle anything you throw at me. Even the crazy shit that goes on in a Deschanel living room." He blew out a controlled breath, regaining his composure, as he straightened in the wooden chair. "If I thought you didn't love me, I could try to move on. But I know better. So, instead, here I am, with the love of my life, who I will only, ever, have half of."

"You have the parts of me that matter most," Amelia tried to reassure him, but the words fell flat. She'd known all along keeping him with her was selfish. Every day over the past decade, she'd justified her secrets so she could find ways of keeping him around, knowing her heart couldn't stand to lose him, while unwilling to bring him in any closer. It was her own fault, and this mess was of her own creation. But what else could she do?

"That's like saying it's okay for me to step out on you, because you have my heart, and she only has my cock," Jacob said, crudely. "You can say it every day for the rest of your life, but it won't make it true, and you know it."

Yes, she did. She'd known better for years, and had chosen this willful ignorance in favor of the truth. Instead of letting Jacob find a woman who could give all of herself to him, she'd cleaved to him in selfish arrogance, knowing deep down this day would come, but doing all she could to prolong its arrival. Over the years, his patience had worn increasingly thin, and now she was watching it snap in two before her. They were at a crossroads, and she could either let him in, or let him go.

Only one of those options would ensure his safety.

Amelia swallowed, drawing from the strength her mother raised her with. "I think you should leave," she whispered, pronouncing each world slowly as if holding on to every syllable would give her a greater control.

"The room?" he replied, with a laugh.

"No..." She ran her tongue across her teeth, tapping her foot lightly under the table. *If you don't do it now, you'll string him along for another decade. He will stay, and give up more of his life, because he loves you* that *much.* "The house. My life."

Jacob's expression changed in a dramatic, but gradual shift; a dark cloud moved before his face, and once past, he appeared to have aged ten years. Briefly, his mouth hung open. His eyes were narrow and watery, but there was a glimmer in them, one which Amelia would never forget. It was a look that said, *I expected this all along. I knew this day would come.*

"I'll leave tomorrow," he said in a low, gravelly voice. He'd removed the bulk of his stronger emotions, compartmentalizing them somewhere safer than the space between them. "Or, later today, I guess," he added, gesturing at the sun rising outside the window. "I'll be gone when you get home from work."

"I think that would be best," Amelia responded firmly, in a voice not her own. Jacob studied her, searching for signs she might take it back; that she might not mean what she'd said. But the same love that kept her from releasing him for all these years, now acted to let him go. It was a sign her love had grown so large it now gave her the strength to do what needed to be done. *For better*, before there was a *for worse.*

"I love you, Amelia," he said, bringing an end to not only the conversation, but also whatever they had shared, for all these years. "Maybe not the way you wanted, but I always loved you well."

Jacob stood and left before either of them could buckle and alter the new course their lives were barreling down.

COLLEEN

*C*olleen spent the morning tending to her colorful garden. It was rare for her to take a day off from the hospital, and even more for it to be on a Wednesday. But Tristan requested her counsel, and she sensed a quick lunch in the hospital cafeteria would not be sufficient for what he needed to say.

Early summer was Colleen's favorite time of year in the South. All the fragrant, exotic subtropical foliage came to life in New Orleans, and her garden boasted samples of nearly every species. From gardenia, to bird of paradise, banana trees, bougainvillea, and more, the scents were rich and consuming. On a bright clear day, with low humidity and a slight breeze nipping the air, Colleen could give her worries a short reprieve.

Kitten and Cocoa ran past her, in hot pursuit of something that caught their attention. Kitten, her Persian male, had been content simply to laze around in the sun until Colleen brought Cocoa home. Now, Kitten frolicked such as he never had in many years, and Cocoa thrived under his tutelage. Cocoa was a stray, before Anasofiya, Colleen's niece, offered her a warm spot on a cold Maine porch. Her life in turmoil, Ana had the fore-thought to ensure Cocoa a permanent home. Colleen wished, more than anything, she could have even one glimpse of where Ana was now. Last time she had news, her niece was about to embark on a mission so dangerous even Elizabeth couldn't pull a vision of the young woman's future.

Colleen worried Elizabeth's visions were becoming compro-mised, as her emotional state grew more fragile. If she were to guess, this was what Tristan wanted to bring up on his visit, though she suspected he wouldn't much like the suggestion she had to offer.

"Miss Colleen," Aria's voice sang from the back door of The Gardens, "your nephew has arrived. I led him to the sitting room."

"Thank you," Colleen acknowledged, smiling and dusting herself off. She made her way back to the towering Italianate manse, nearly tripping over the rambunctious cats playing at her feet. For one very brief, whimsical moment, she longed for the days when her children were still young, and the house rang with their playful laughter. But Amelia and Ashley were long since adults, with lives of their own, and her darling Benjamin now rested in the arms of the Lord. Had Elizabeth predicted *that*, perhaps things could have ended differently.

But that wasn't true, either. Elizabeth had spent her life trying to change the futures from her visions. It wasn't possible.

Colleen entered the sitting room as Aria deposited a tray of sweet tea and biscuits. Tristan didn't seem to notice any of it, sitting hunched over with his hands before him, wringing them in frustrated angst.

He seemed to come around as Colleen's shadow towered over him. Standing, he embraced her, planting the requisite kisses on both cheeks. "Now, sit and drink, darling," she ordered, gently returning him to his seat.

Tristan reached robotically for the tea, pouring them both glasses. But he only stared at the swiftly melting cubes swirling around in the tumbler between his hands.

"You're in a state," Colleen observed. "Your mother?"

"If I'm in a state, it's always because of my mother," Tristan replied drily. "It might be easier if my father could step-up and keep her grounded, but we both know he never will."

"I know it's hard for you to imagine, but Connor has loved your mother since they were children. He saved her life many times. More times, even, than I know about."

"Things have changed," Tristan replied. "Spends all his time at the firm now. I guess I see the appeal. Not an emotion amongst the one of them."

"Sullivans," she agreed, in a tone suggesting that was all she needed to say. "They're practical to the point of a complete loss of sentiment. Present company not included, of course, my dear," she added.

"No, it's true. A bunch of damn stuffy lawyers who refuse to get worked up about anything they can't explain," Tristan concurred, with disdain. It hurt Colleen's heart that Tristan had not one, but two parents, who declined to face reality. Elizabeth, through her delusions, and Connor, through his refusal to acknowledge them.

"You're blossoming into a fine young man," Colleen pointed out sincerely. Though, she often worried about Tristan's tendency to get pulled down by his parents' negativity. He was now out of college, and showing no signs of getting a job, or any other real demonstration of broader responsibility.

"No thanks to them," Tristan muttered, then looked guilty.

"Sometimes we end up in a better place in spite of our parents, not because of them," Colleen said, offering him a reassuring smile. "But tell me what's on your mind."

"Mom is missing," Tristan blurted out. His hands began trembling at the confession, and he quickly set his glass down on the table. "She disappeared last night, and no one has heard from her since."

Colleen drew in a breath, forcing herself to sound sympathetic. "Tristan, we know your mother often goes off on little sojourns." She tried not to inject the disdain she felt at this last. Elizabeth's disappearing acts were selfish and cruel to those who loved her, especially Tristan. There was much Colleen could excuse about her confused younger sister, but this was not one of those things. "And I heard about the spat she had with your Aunt Maureen, which was no doubt unsettling to her. Maureen does love your mother. They were once quite close. But she's always been a touch sensitive about being benign. I think her lack of belief is the extension of her buried jealousy over not feeling special." She reached a hand over and patted Tristan's knee, returning her thoughts to the point at hand. "Your mother will be back, child. Likely in a day or so, if past experiences are anything to go on."

"This is different," Tristan insisted. His expression was so deeply troubled it made Colleen doubt her own certainty. "Her visions lately have been worse than normal, and she's been saying things that are crazy, even for her. And then she learned something about me that upset her to a point she stopped talking altogether."

"Which was?"

Tristan dropped his eyes, and Colleen knew he was ashamed, but mostly fearful what Colleen might think of him after she knew his truth. "Mom always made me swear not to get married, or have children. Because of the Curse."

Colleen nodded. She had not been nearly as insistent with her own children, but she at least tried to educate them on the risks. Ashley and Ben had taken the risk, with Ben paying the consequence for that venture. Amelia found a man who respected her wish to not bring children into the world.

"I tried, I really did," Tristan began his defense before the admission. "But Aunt C, I got so lonely! In the years since Dani died, the house has gotten worse and worse…"

"I understand," Colleen assured.

"I thought maybe if I found someone who had no risk of wanting to be with me, it would be okay. I thought, hell, maybe there's someone out there who's as averse to marriage and babies as I am and we can be a match made in heaven!"

Colleen already knew where he was going with this; she knew nearly everything that happened in this family, and was mildly amused Tristan didn't already realize this. But for his sake, she simply nodded, allowing him the cathartic release of expunging the whole messy affair.

"I met Emily at the park one day. She was taking pictures, and she asked me if I would help her set up her camera. I mean, hell, like I know about cameras?" Tristan laughed. "But she was pretty, and nice, so I helped her. And somehow this led to us walking around the park for hours, talking about our lives. Don't worry, I didn't tell her anything interesting," Tristan said quickly, "but it was nice to talk to someone who had problems, too. She told me she was married, and that she was unhappy."

When Tristan looked down to hide the welling tears, Colleen interjected, "Tristan, darling, I already know. You've been seeing her for a long time now. Perhaps not the wisest decision, but I do understand and sympathize with the sentiment that drove you to it, and can even appreciate the wisdom in finding someone safe."

"You knew?" her nephew asked, but then his eyes narrowed and he laughed. "Of course you knew. Why didn't you try to stop me?"

Colleen sighed, and took a long, deep swallow of Aria's tea. "It's not a fun position to be in, to be a mother in this family. I have to look at my beloved children every day, and realize any love I feel for them is also mixed with regret at my foolishness.

And then it goes further when I think of my pleas to not have their own families; asking them to give up that joy when I didn't. I was so sad for Ben when he met his wife, because it was obvious they were too much in love for Ben to ever turn his back on her. And he paid for that. Then I look at Amelia, and though she has resolved never to have children, she's happy with Jacob, and their arrangement is at least somewhat satisfying. Ashley and his wife, of course, refuse to even acknowledge the Curse exists... but that is neither here nor there," Colleen said with a wave of her hand. "The point is, Tristan, I want you to find happiness. It saddens me you must do so in such a non-traditional way, but I want you to be happy, no matter the path. If Emily brings you this happiness, then I must get past my reservations. I have."

Tristan looked at his aunt with a gratefulness that warmed her heart. But then, as if remembering something important, his face fell once again. "Emily is pregnant," he revealed. "It's mine."

Colleen's eyes widened, eyebrows raised near to her hairline. No, she had not seen this. And she supposed it was not the time to question Tristan about how foolish his girlfriend had to be as a philanderer not on some form of contraception.

"That is not ideal at all," Colleen said, searching for the wisdom he had obviously come here for. "And your mother knows?"

Tristan nodded. "She found out before I did. She was reading my text messages! I swear that woman has no boundaries," Tristan griped. "But once she found out, she was like a completely different person. You know what Mom gets like when she's had a bad vision or when she's in one of her moods. Well, this was like that but a thousand times worse."

"What did she say?"

"She was furious with me," Tristan replied. "She accused me of all the things I expected you to... being foolish, careless, immoral. And, of course, she was even more pissed I kept it from her."

"You have a right to your secrets," Colleen assured him, thinking, but not saying, this was especially true when the other person concerned was Elizabeth. "What are you going to do about the child?"

Tristan shrugged; the gesture reminded her of the noncommittal ones he often gave as a child. Having grown up in a world full of ambiguity, it was no wonder he refused to commit to anything.

"Well, what does Emily want?" Colleen pressed.

Tristan shrugged again. "We haven't talked."

"Tristan Sullivan!" Colleen exclaimed. Now, she was frustrated. "She's carrying your child! Married to another man, and probably terrified. You do not get to just walk away from this!"

"I don't know what to do!" Tristan screamed, knocking the tray of biscuits to the floor as his leg swung downward. "I can't have this child with her!"

"The choice isn't yours to make," Colleen said plainly. "But if she has that child, you *will* be a part of its life, ideal or not. I can't judge your choice of a mate, but make no mistake: it *was* a choice. And you will take accountability for that choice!"

"You're as bad as my mother!"

"I am *nothing* like your mother!" Colleen thundered, showing rare levels of heightened emotion. "I wouldn't abandon you in the moment you needed me the most, simply because I was too weak to handle it! I wouldn't make this about me! And dammit, Tristan, I *will* get you through this!"

Tristan stared at her blankly, with a look bordering between confusion and anger. "I'm sorry," she said, before he could reply. "I shouldn't have said those things."

"They're true," he affirmed, his lower lip trembling slightly. "I wish I could be mad at you, but everything you said was fair. She did abandon me. She always has."

Colleen found herself making excuses for her sister, for Tristan's sake, despite her own beliefs. "She has never been strong, Tristan. When she met Connor, and he was such a healthy balance to her instability, I thought things could be different for her. I was wrong. But she does love you, as much as she has ever known how."

"My mother, and other mothers, have very different ways of showing love," Tristan argued, but the heat dissolved from his words. "I think something bad has happened this time. Something really bad."

As Tristan spoke, Colleen's sense of this had grown keener as well. There were other seers in the family, and she could reach out for their services if needed. "For now, focus on resolving the situation with Emily. It won't get easier by waiting, Tristan, and you can't ignore it. I will do everything I can to locate and help your mother."

Tristan nodded, looking relieved. "You know, when you asked me to join the Magi Collective, I felt it might be good for me. That maybe I'd get to break away from my mom. Instead of being Elizabeth's son, I could be Tristan, and I could be useful for a change, help the family. But I don't feel any different. I still feel like Elizabeth's son, and on days like today, I think I'm drowning in it."

Colleen didn't have the words Tristan needed to hear. But she wrapped her nephew in her arms, and kissed his forehead. As she saw him out, she realized with a sinking sadness, no matter what happened with Elizabeth, Tristan would suffer immensely.

Colleen watched her nephew leave, waiting until he had pulled away from The Gardens and down the block, before she moved to pick up the phone. Dialing her sister Evangeline, she knew once the words were out, she couldn't take them back. She'd been considering saying them even before Tristan's visit. He only sped up the process.

"Evie," she said, as calmly as she could, when her sister answered, "we can't wait any longer. We need to bring the Council together. As quickly as possible."

TRISTAN

The sound of his ringing phone woke Tristan. Heart racing, he bolted upright, for a moment allowing himself to believe it could be his mother, calling to assure him she was okay. When he saw instead it was Markus, Tristan's heart sank.

"Yeah?" Tristan answered.

"You wanted to talk," Markus stated.

"Oh. Yeah." Tristan played it cool for a moment, still unreasonably hurt Markus had blown him off the other night. "You don't have anyone over?"

"It's the middle of the week," Markus said, with a short laugh. "I have classes."

Small talk was not typically something the two young men engaged in, so Tristan came right to the point. "Mark, I got Emily pregnant. And my mom has been gone long enough for me to wonder if she's coming back."

"Shit," Markus said simply. "About Emily, I mean. I knew about your mom, but my mother never mentioned you knocking up your girlfriend. You can tell me more about it when I'm there."

75

"Wait... here? You're coming here?" Tristan's voice took on a note of excitement, but it quickly faded to mild suspicion.

"You didn't know?"

"No," Tristan responded, as the pieces slowly started coming together.

"Ahh. Aunt C is pulling together a Collective meeting. First the Council, but then all members, I believe. About your mom, but there's some other stuff going on. Shit they're keeping top secret. I don't know. She insisted we all come this time."

Tristan realized Aunt Colleen *had* taken him seriously, despite her attempt to downplay his concerns. And if Colleen was worried, then that could only mean...

Markus' tone was unusually comforting on the other end. "Tristan? Hang in there, okay? I'll be there soon. We'll find your mom."

TRISTAN CAME ACROSS THE MAIL PILE LATER THAT EVENING. His father, usually quite regimented about his daily addressing of correspondence, had dumped it in a heap in the hallway, and it appeared to have been untouched for some time. Tristan chalked this up to his father's clear dishevelment since his wife disappeared, but it disconcerted him nonetheless. Not even when Danielle died did Connor Sullivan divert from his routines. *The world keeps on turning, son,* Tristan remembered him saying. *Responsibilities must still be tended to.*

What was Tristan supposed to make of this inattention then?

With nothing else to keep his mind occupied, he decided to take care of the mess himself. No surprise, much of the pile was garbage, which he tossed in the recycling bin or discarded in the paper shredder next to the desk. The bills Tristan placed in the oak tray his father reserved for important correspondence. Finally, near the bottom of the pile, he came upon a large manila envelope.

There was no return address, but he recognized the handwriting immediately: it was his mother's, though not as precise as her usual script. The scrawl was harried, and messy. He turned it over in his hands, not quite sure whether he wanted to open it or not. *Whatever is inside... once you open it, you can't go back.*

The envelope was thick and padded. Heavy. He looked again at the front, and while he could find no return address, there was a postmark: Donaldsonville, Louisiana. Tristan mulled this over in his head, while he lightly shook the package, trying to make sense of it without peeking at the contents.

He didn't know whether to feel relief at a sign of his mother's existence or stressed about what might be inside. If it had been simply been a letter it might have given him comfort; he had received many such letters from her when she was "checked-out," although they'd all come from in town. She stayed at different hotels each time, but always in New Orleans.

This package, however, felt ominous. A nearly tangible sense of finality hung over it.

Donaldsonville. Tristan realized, suddenly, why the name nagged at him. *Ophèlie* was not the only plantation the Deschanels owned. There were several other properties scattered throughout the state, *Vivra Sa Vie* being one of them. It was owned by Tristan's uncle, Augustus, but seldom used, and the modest house sat unoccupied.

No one is ever there. No one would think to look there.

"Are you going to open it?" his father asked from across the room, surprising Tristan so greatly he dropped the package.

"Maybe," Tristan said, distantly. "Why didn't you?" His mind was racing through the many possible outcomes opening the package could bring.

"It's addressed to you," his father answered, in a hollow voice. This wasn't the answer; not the real reason. Tristan did not need to employ his mind reading to know his father was as scared as he was. That he, perhaps, knew something Tristan didn't.

That he'd been waiting for this moment for years.

Vivra sa Vie, Tristan thought. Live your life.

If Tristan was hoping to find courage with his father, he'd come to the wrong place. With a measured breath, he very slowly slid his fingers under the seal. The slight tearing sound from the glue coming undone had a dark, final note to it. He turned the opened package upside down and slipped out two very old, worn leather books that appeared to be journals of some kind.

Finally, there was a letter.

As Connor watched with wide, frightened eyes, Tristan slowly took in the contents of the last letter his mother would ever write. His trembling hands could barely hold on to the paper, and as he read the closing words, *Love, Mom,* he finally released it and it fluttered slowly to the floor.

Tristan rolled his head back toward the sky and screamed. The sound began guttural but then faded to a distant echo, as if miles and miles away. And then the world around him faded to black, and all he could feel, or understand, were his father's strong arms catching him on the way to the floor.

AMELIA

*A*melia turned off all the lights in the house for the night. Without Jacob's big personality to fill it, the rooms seemed empty, the house a shell of its once lively self. The stillness in the air rang loud, and oppressing, pushing on her from all sides, waiting for her to give in.

Somewhere, Jacob was going through similar motions. Perhaps thinking of her, and his own overwhelming loneliness. Or, maybe he'd already hardened his heart to her, to protect it from further damage. *No. If he had, I would know it. The door is not shut tight. A light yet peeks through.*

Absence didn't necessarily make the heart grow fonder. For Amelia, it only reinforced what she already knew, that there was no one in the world she loved or needed the way she did Jacob Donnelly. Tomorrow, she would tell him that. She would swallow her fears and ask him to marry her, and pray he wouldn't turn her down. It would serve her right if he did. But she was confident the time apart was small enough the chasm forming could be closed, and mended. There had been no great wrong committed between them.

Denying yourself a life because of your fears is no life at all, her mother had said, when she stopped by the office earlier to talk some sense into her daughter. *Amelia, we could all perish tomorrow, Curse or no. Deschanel or no. We have no promise of a future. All we have are our choices.*

She was right. It took ten years for the words to sink in and take meaning, but Amelia resolutely decided not to be a victim of her own, misguided choices any longer. She would rather live even one more day with Jacob than decades without him.

Thinking of the plans she made, she pictured the surprise, and joy on Jacob's face once he discovered all she'd done, and all she was willing to do, for them. The plane tickets were purchased, and she'd received a response back from the old priest in Ireland Jacob had once held in such high esteem. Of course he remembered Jacob, he said, and was all too eager to help him find his happiness, agreeing to her request without hesitation.

The enormity of it all frightened her, but every happy moment of the last ten years came forward to push those fears back, and enveloped her in the comfort of knowing this was right. Tomorrow, after telling Jacob, it would be real.

Amelia moved through the quiet house, the only sounds that of the old cottage singing its timeworn song. She was struck, not for the first time, how much different this was than her own upbringing. She'd grown up with two brothers, but she may as well have had a dozen siblings for as much time as she spent with her cousins. There would never be dozens of footfalls in her own home, never be the laughter of children, unless it was from her nieces and nephews visiting. That was one sacrifice she was still unwilling to make.

Sometimes this realization was overwhelming, and even stopped her in her tracks. But for the moment, she simply felt an inexplicable sense of peace. Amelia had protected her own little world, and now she understood what she needed to do to sustain it. She and Jacob had formed a barrier around them, and she stopped thinking of it as a sacrifice and began to see it as the only way she ever wanted to see her life. *Tomorrow. Tomorrow, all will be well again. The universe will be set to rights.*

Outside, the world was still. Inside, her heart beat to the rhythm of her light, creaking steps. She walked slowly through the dark, enjoying the silence. Enjoying, despite her grief, these last moments alone where her thoughts could dance among the oak and cypress.

Amelia stopped near the front door and looked out. The gaslights on her front porch illuminated the pathway and the street in a calm but somehow eerie manner. There seemed to be no one else awake at this hour, but as she glanced across the street, she saw a light on in Oz and Adrienne's house.

She remembered the day the family learned Adrienne had come back. If Adrienne's recovery had proved hard on anyone other than herself, it was Oz whose whole life was flipped up and down, in one tumultuous wave after another. Amelia had once fancied Oz, as had most of the girls in their age group. But once Oz fell for Adrienne, his eyes never strayed, and Jacob made Amelia forget other men even existed. Nicolas had once said to her, *you and Jacob are what Oz and Adrienne could be, if they weren't so royally fucked up.*

If Amelia could wish for any ability, it would be to offer peace to those she loved. She would start with Oz and Adrienne.

As she made her way toward the stairs, Amelia doubled over, gripping the bannister. Sudden, acute anxiety rushed through her, from head to toe, building in concentration with every passing moment. Struggling to breathe, she tried to force her mind to expel the sensation, but this was far more intense, far more powerful, even than the episode at the streetcar stop. Her hands started to slip as her body first began to tremble, and then convulse.

Breathe. Grip. Stand. Amelia repeated these commands to herself, over and over, commands which had always worked for

SARAH M. CRADIT

her before, no matter how severe her attack. But her mind was not her own, and her next recollection was of being on her back, looking at the ceiling as images danced erratically in and out of focus.

She struggled back to her feet, but her knees buckled and she hit the cypress floor with a thud, her sweaty palms failing to prop her up.

And then, all of these sensations rose up in unison. A deafening chorus of sound and pain heralded the realizations which ripped through her. For one brief moment, Amelia could breathe. Could see. Could move. In this moment, she saw an image so heartrending, so exquisitely horrible, her breath caught. The terror unsatisfied, she moved from simply seeing it, to feeling it. She was absorbing the scene, and to absorb it meant to take the horribleness and magnify it to levels unimaginable.

"Tristan!" she managed, in one ragged, choking breath. She was terrified, paralyzed. The invisible hands belonging to the black side of her own ability rose up in the dark house, sliding up, up, up, until they encircled her chest, then neck, promising a brutal end to all her hopes and dreams. There would be no reunion with Jacob. No chance to set her life on a proper course, to right a wrong. There would not even be another sunrise for her. This was it. There was no moment of peace to accompany this clarity regarding her own mortality. No light, no welcoming presence to beckon her. It was only Amelia, and the devastating realization she could do nothing to change the outcome.

"Jacob," she whispered to the empty house as she looked into nothing.

And then, there *was* nothing.

PART II
CONVOCATION

APRIL 2006

"Now is the winter of our discontent."

William Shakespeare

JULIANNE

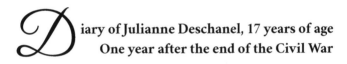

iary of Julianne Deschanel, 17 years of age
One year after the end of the Civil War

AUGUST 18, 1866

ANOTHER EVENING PASSED. MAMAN STILL SLEEPS BY DAY AND WAKES by evening, walking the candle-lit halls. Jean remains vexed with my lack of fruit-bearing. I am becoming irritated as well. His frustrations with my barrenness keep him at arm's length, as if the distance aids in conception. Further, he is closed to any discussion of seeing Ophélie in the halls. Maman's delusions are so strong they have the effect of infectious addiction. I truly wish it was Ophélie in the halls. I wish, more than anything, those horrible things had never happened to that poor girl. That she had never died. That Maman could relax and show us her kind smile again. That there would be other women in this manse whom I could palaver with, and share confidences, instead of being isolated and alone. That Jean would look at me as he used to, with something other than contempt.

Alas, if joys in life were as simple as wishing, no one would go for wanting. I plan to begin reading Crime and Punishment this eve. Edith Bertrand loaned it nearly a fortnight ago and she will be expecting it back.

August 19, 1866

Awoke in the middle of the night to screaming. I smelled smoke and roused Jean, who discovered his mother burning a significant amount of currency. When Jean asked where she found such a sum, she would not be specific, only insisting it was the price of Ophélie's life. No doubt Charles will be horrified when he discovers what his wife has done. For his part, he slept through the whole noisy affair. His apathy lately a standard disposition.

Charles has given up forcing her to eat, so one of the housemaids, Maisie, assumed the role. Maman Brigitte takes up like a feeble-minded child, the food dripping down her chin, allowing it to run errantly all over her garments and the floor. Left to her own devices, she will eat very graveling things such as paper or leftover muslin from patterning. No surprise, she has lost a great deal of weight. When I attempt to engage her, she peers at me as if I am a cloud she can see right through. I do not know if she is unaware I am there, or if she willfully chooses not to see me, but in either case, speaking with her remains beyond my means.

Crime and Punishment is a bit of a disappointment. Was quite challenging to get into. Jean says I should read less about fanciful things and spend more time thinking about why I am such a disappointment. One day soon I may have to tell him my father lied when he signed the marriage contract, and that I have yet to experience my flux. I believe some of the housemaids know. They must. I fear for Jean's reaction if this admission is made, and pray daily for my flux to arrive.

. . .

August 21, 1866

As suspected, Edith requested her copy of Crime and Punishment *back. I can't say I was sorry to return it, although I do regret being untruthful with her about my appreciation of the telling. To say otherwise would have been unmet.*

Once again Jean rebuked me on how useless, not to mention unfashionable, reading is as a hobby for ladies. I can only hope this remains a passing aggravation for him and does not become a more serious matter.

Charles continues to host the Union officers for dinner several nights weekly. Maman is worse on such nights, presumably because they are the same officers who granted immunity to the soldiers who injured poor sweet Ophélie. Charles, by the by, grows increasingly gleeful as he tells us his fortunes have grown since the end of the War of Northern Aggression, but I know that is not true for most of our neighbors and fellow Southerners. One of Maman's few coherent rants is that Charles' fortunes grew at the cost of his daughter's life.

Maman's nightly walks are becoming near unbearable, and make sleep impossible. I gently suggested to Jean that moving to our own home, where I could obtain more sleep in my routine, might lend itself to better fruit-bearing, but I will not be suggesting this again.

August 22, 1866

The heat has become sweltering. Charles laments how it causes inconvenience for his socials, with Northerners not used to such climes. Maman responds Charles should get used to it as it's comparable to what awaits him in the afterlife. Even the breeze from the mighty Mississippi provides no relief. Maisie has been drawing cold baths for me, but the temporary relief is more painful, I think. Maman sits on the gallery overlooking her garden, and stares into the oleander and bird of paradise as if she is having a deep and personal conversation with the foliage. Alarmed by her unusual conduct, the field workers have ceased acknowledging her.

One of the Union officers met with Charles, in his office, for hours. I know not the reason for their conference, but Maman grew more agitated as the evening wore on.

Including an additional note here as something worth writing about has finally happened. I asked Maisie if I could serve Maman her dinner this evening. I brought it to Maman, expecting no different a reaction than every other time, but she was as clear of mind as I had seen her in over two years. She took the plate from my hands and her eyes locked on mine, truly seeing me. Then she started speaking. I came immediately from her side to this diary so I could write what she said, in her exact words:

"Maman?" I asked.

"My child is dead," she responded. I knew she meant Ophélie, but she seemed to forget her two sons.

"Jean is here," I said, touching her shoulder.

She laughed. Then touched my face. "There is a price for everything. All that glitters is not gold. My husband is no partner of mine, and the two men whom I gave life to are no sons to me. There is a price, and they will soon see it is not one worth paying. Soon, but also much later."

I cannot recall the balance of her communication verbatim, but it was along the same line. Her words were uniformly vague, but I gathered her general implication. She was confessing to me having intentionally renounced Charles, and her sons, for their role in her daughter's death and I believe also promising vengeance for it. Beyond that... I cannot decipher her meaning.

Though I shall never forget the last words she spoke. Her face took on a softer look, and she said, "Poor, poor Julianne."

. . .

AUGUST 24, 1866

HOW WAS I TO HAVE KNOWN? AM I A READER OF MINDS? AND EVEN had she told me her intention, could I have put a halt to her actions? I know not, I know not.

I awoke last night, as I do most nights, to the sound of Maman speaking to herself in her sitting room. When I rose to check on her, she was whispering heatedly about the "price of everything," her voice low and feverish. I did not see her, merely heard her, sitting on her balcony overlooking the garden, as she tends to do. Regrettably, I did not hear her climb up onto the white railings and step out to the edge. She did not scream as she jumped.

Ah, but she screamed when she landed. I ran, and ran, faster than I had run since I was a very young girl, and yet it seemed an eternity before I was at her side. There was blood at the corners of her mouth and her limbs were bloody, twisted into unnatural angles. I screamed louder even than she had. Oh, there are not words for such a sight!

But she did not die immediately. First, she told me, "There is a price. Charles and his children will pay it. As will their children, and their children, and all children who attempt to profit from anything Charles has built on the corpse of my daughter. This midnight dynasty will fall, as Ophélie fell, and there will be no more. This I promise, on my mother, and on my beloved Ophélie."

Her hand came up and touched my face again. It was trembling, yet she wiped away my tears. "Poor, poor Julianne," she said, blood foaming at her mouth. Those were her last words.

Oh, Maman. Father have mercy on our wretched souls. I have failed thee.

ADRIENNE

*A*drienne Sullivan switched off the bedside lamp, and closed her eyes, unsuccessfully blocking the wave of emotion that threatened to overcome her in a tidal wave of regret.

In the other room, both of her children—Christian, by her own bearing, Naomi, inherited through her marriage to Oz— slept, safe and sound. She tucked them in, as she did every night, and then went to wait for their father. Oz's recent successes at the firm landed him better clients, but better clients meant longer hours. And longer hours meant many nights where the children were in bed long before their father crossed through the front door, exhausted.

Adrienne did not begrudge him this. She didn't begrudge him anything, really. She couldn't ask for a more caring, doting husband, and if there was a better father in New Orleans, she'd like to meet him. There existed no light brighter than the one in Oz's eyes when he scooped his two little ones into a big, engulfing hug.

It was a light she knew well; one she had seen, many times, when she was still a girl, giving her heart away to a younger, more idealistic, Oz Sullivan. She would do nothing more interesting than enter a room and his entire self would radiate with the joy he felt, simply for knowing her. But all lights eventually fade.

The decline was gradual, as those things go. Once the exhilaration of their tumultuous courtship wore into his relief at finally settling down with her, Oz's subconscious began its work of setting the stage for reality. As excitement and joy wove themselves into a contented pattern, weariness and despair crept into the spaces between those threads.

At first, the spaces were small, entirely dwarfed by brighter, surrounding colors. But over time, the fabric of their relationship grew thinner, and the spaces larger, until one day Oz's love had evolved from a powerful, romantic one to the subtle devotion of a caregiver. While he still lit up—not a bright light as he once had, but a dimmer, encouraging kind—when she had a good day, and was feeling her old self, his resentment at the realization the woman he married was not the fantasy he had molded her into, was a strong one. This subconscious frustration mounted upon realizing he had known all along and somehow ignored it, propelling them forth into a life that was satisfying only on the surface.

One of the few great secrets of their marriage was that Adrienne understood all of this, and Oz did not.

Adrienne rolled over in the bed, tired but far from being able to sleep. There were so many things on her mind, which was churning, churning, churning...

HEADLIGHTS FLOODED THE WINDOW, AND THEN FADED OUT OF SIGHT *again as Oz's car pulled in front of the house. She didn't rise to greet him. He always felt so guilty when she stayed up waiting for him, and she didn't want to be the source of any more worry. Instead, she listened for the familiar sounds: the soft opening and gentle thunk as he closed the front door; the light clang of his keys resting on the secretary; the easy sound of rustling fabric as his suit coat was first removed, and then hung, on the corner rack. Then, his long stretch-and-sigh, where she could picture him looking around the kitchen, wondering if he should bother with supper.*

The garbage, of course. It was garbage night, and this was one of Oz's few chores, which he insisted on doing despite Adrienne's assurance it was no big deal for her to manage. Taking care of the household, and children, had always been her responsibility.

Moments later the back door opened, and closed, then Adrienne heard the familiar rumbling of the can's wheels as he maneuvered it toward the sidewalk. She breathed slowly in and out, counting the seconds until the back door would open, and close, again, as he came back in to heat up his dinner.

But seconds ticked by, and the door did not open. Then minutes, and ultimately Adrienne's curiosity got the best of her. She climbed from bed and moved to the window, peeking out to the street corner, only marginally lit by the gas streetlamp.

Oz was outside with their neighbor, Adrienne's cousin Amelia. Her can had tipped and Oz was helping her shovel the contents back in. Amelia was doubled over in laughter, clutching her stomach as she swatted at the odious garbage with the other hand. Oz laughed with her, as they both unsuccessfully attempted to reload the can. Eventually, both succumbed to their giggles as they fell back on to the upturned sidewalk, lost to their amusement.

Adrienne couldn't hear them, but she didn't need to. She hadn't seen Oz laugh like that in years.

THIS WAS A WEEK AGO. BEFORE AMELIA SLIPPED INTO A COMA SHE might never recover from.

Before Adrienne realized she, too, was dying.

· · ·

ADRIENNE, OF COURSE, KNEW ABOUT OZ'S OCCASIONAL FORAYS TO Amelia's porch, but it didn't bother her. Oz had never so much as feigned flirtation with Amelia. Moreover, Amelia was in love with Jacob to a degree she hardly noticed the existence of other men. And anyway, they were two of the most honorable people Adrienne knew. It wasn't her fear Oz was looking elsewhere which bothered her, though it was jealousy, in a way. Jealousy she couldn't provide the outlet Amelia did.

Adrienne had never been the same since her accident. When she got into that car with her family she'd been an idealistic sixteen-year old girl. Emerging from the debris, she was still a sixteen-year old girl, but a different one. Whoever—whatever—she was when she survived that crash, she remained. Her growth ended when her family died, in an overturned town car drowning in the murky bayou.

Three years she'd lived the life of another person, with no recollection of her former life. As her memory returned, with it came the streaming bits of her past that had included Oz. The forbidden love they'd shared that had threatened to tear their families apart. After a very long wait, and many trials, she brought him a son, and her commitment.

But while Oz had grown into a fine man, Adrienne existed in suspended animation. The intellectually insightful, but artlessly insecure child, who had once loved someone she shouldn't, over one very provocative summer.

Though... that was not entirely true. Something else emerged with her from the swamp that night. Or, maybe more accurately, *awakened*. A series of baffling incidents followed. For years, she didn't realize she was responsible, but her mind eventually pulled these coincidences into a coherent explanation. And after visiting with one of her cousins last year, she even had a name for it: absorption.

"Tis a dangerous ability, absorption," her cousin Jasper had told her, considering his library while running well-manicured fingers over his smooth chin, before he chose and plopped a dusty tome on the counter between them. If anyone would know what afflicted her, it would be Jasper Broussard. His shop, the Soothsayer's Coffer, catered to all things occult, and he was a Council Leader in the Deschanel Magi Collective.

He was also a dash ridiculous, but she wouldn't hold that against him.

"But how do I have it? I thought my father and his children were all benign," Adrienne had countered.

"'Were' is the operative word, my dear," Jasper corrected, giving her a meaningful glance. "We now realize benign was an incorrect assumption about Charles and his children. Dormant, or inactive, might have been a better depiction. At this point, your brother, Nicolas, has almost fully come into his powers. Your sister, Anne, is quite the arborkinetic, as you know. Had your older sisters survived, they might have manifested their own unique abilities. It should be no surprise your gift has awakened."

Adrienne pondered that. "So what does it mean? This absorption? Why is it dangerous?"

"The unpredictability, of course," Jasper explained, leaning forward, with a self-important shrug. "It's a bit like playing roulette. You might absorb someone's common cold, and get a permanent case of consumption. Or, you might get lucky and only be sick for a couple of days. Sometimes when you absorb something from another, it disappears entirely, as if it never existed at all! Other times... pardon me in advance for retelling such a disgusting story, but I recall a man who tried to absorb his wife's hemorrhoids, and turned into one giant blister himself!"

"Gross."

"Indeed," Jasper agreed, as if the offense couldn't have been helped. "The unpredictability is what makes this dangerous, my dear Adrienne. You must use it cautiously, or not at all. For, the other thing I've heard about this ability is that it is sometimes difficult for healers to overcome. There's a sense of *finality* in absorbing something, as if the universe is shaking their finger at your defiance of fate. Our friend who turned into a blister? Even the best healers could not reverse it."

Adrienne considered this, realizing his words didn't constitute her first warning on the matter. Aunt Elizabeth had come to visit her, a week before she died. "I saw you, Ade. I saw others too, but yours... yours is *preventable*! You can avert this, you can, and you must," she insisted, rambling even more than usual in her panic-filled fugue as she dug both hands into Adrienne's shoulders in wide-eyed alarm. "Our family... yours, especially, can't handle your loss!"

Elizabeth's words made no sense until later, but Adrienne had taken Jasper's words to heart. She really had! But how could she turn a blind eye to the suffering of her own children? Over the years, she'd taken colds, sprains, and bruises from Christian and Naomi, and never suffered much more than they would have. So when Naomi started getting those awful headaches, Adrienne had done what she always did, and taken them, too.

Except, they weren't simply headaches. Or maybe they had been when they belonged to Naomi, but they turned into something far darker, and more sinister, after Adrienne absorbed them, just as Jasper cautioned they might. *A mass in the brain. Grade IV Glioblastoma. Inoperable.* Neither doctors, nor the family healers she'd consulted with under sworn secrecy, could fix it, also as Jasper predicted.

Whether this was a product of the Deschanel Curse, or simply an unfortunate turn of events, Adrienne was dying. Soon. Conveniently, the family was converging now, here in New Orleans, and would be consumed with the events surrounding her aunt's death and the tittering of all the seer cousins predicting more on the near horizon. None so far, except the late Elizabeth, had predicted her demise, but it was only a matter of time...

She didn't have the energy to get caught up in any of it. Neither Oz, nor anyone else, knew what was coming, and she would spare them this grief until absolutely necessary.

Adrienne knew what she had to do.

It was not a brilliant plan by any stretch, but neither was dying long before her time. *Or maybe I'm long past my time. Maybe I really died in that car after all, and everything since has been me hanging off a withering strand of fate, waiting for it to finally fray and snap.*

Adrienne hoped the family convocation would give her the diversion she needed to put her plans in motion before it was too late.

TRISTAN

*H*ardly a week had passed since Tristan's mother died. Since then, sleep had become less of an escape and more like descending into hell. Anytime he closed his eyes, he saw his mother flinging herself off the upper belvedere of *Vivra sa Vie,* her broken neck twisted unnaturally to the side, as her wide, lifeless eyes told a story that ended the moment her heart ceased to beat. He imagined her thinking, in her final moments, that this desperate act was to preserve her son. That with her last breath, her heart called out, "For Tristan."

And though Tristan had only read the note once—it was all he could bear to do—the words committed themselves to his memory in a gruesome act of self-torture. The nightmares of this past night had been a recitation of the contents, over, and over, and over…

My Dearest Tristan,

I am dearly sorry for the way we parted. It wasn't what I intended, and if I'd been myself before leaving I would have told you I didn't mean to make you feel badly. I love you above all else in this world, and I always have. Sometimes I think I may have loved you more than your sister even, and so taking her was God's way of punishing me. Of course, I know it's more than that, as do you, but I can't help wondering if her death somehow could have been prevented. If all of our deaths could have been prevented.

I know I have not always done right by you. As a mother, I left a lot to be desired. Don't think for a moment I wasn't aware of my shortcomings. Frequently, I was torn between knowing this, and acknowledging I should never have been your mother in the first place. Sometimes I rationalized I was less to you because I wanted you to hate me for bringing you into this world. Instead, you probably hate me for abandoning you in it.

Before Danielle was taken, I sensed something bad was on the horizon. That same sense of dread has overcome me in the past couple of weeks. I know, without a doubt, more sacrifice is coming. I was wrong to ever believe this Curse was ending; it punished us for those doubts in 1996, and it is going to punish us again.

And here is a confession, as well. I saw Danielle's death when I was still a teenager. I saw my own. But I also saw joy. I saw you. I saw your future as well, Tristan. On that, I'll say no more.

The rules of the Curse are still a complete mystery to me. It strikes several per generation, but how it picks its victims, and the number it will pick, have no pattern I can find. We have had generations where there were no deaths, only tragedy (such as barrenness in some of the women), but your generation has been plenty fruitful. I do believe the more we multiply, the greater our punishment.

Enclosed are the journals of Julianne and Ophélie. I have spent hours in them. Obsessed over them. Given my life to them. I've received little in return, but they were passed to me and I am passing them to you. My solace is belief that through understanding, someone in the family can break this Curse and end the sadness we've all inherited. You are smart enough, and if anyone can, it is you who will accomplish our redemption.

This is a tremendous burden I place on your young shoulders; larger than any I have placed so far, and there have been many. I wish

I could have been more for you. More so, I wish you could have been born into a different family, where circumstances were better and we could enjoy every moment with gladness instead of sleeping with one eye open. But this is not our lot in life, Tristan. At least not now... you may, yet, be able to change this...

You're probably expecting me to tell you to find a way to rid yourself of your unborn child. I could also lecture you about how terrible this situation is, with her being married, but that would be the least of your problems, wouldn't it? However, I believe all life is a gift and no matter the risks, you should do everything you can to see your child born. Ideally, you will be a better parent than I was, but you should choose to be one, even with the risks.

I do not expect forgiveness. You will likely hate me forever, and I wouldn't blame you. Please know I am not doing this to hurt you further, but to hopefully buy you more time—and others in our dear family—to find another way to satisfy Brigitte's hatred. Maybe I can be the last of this generation's victims. I hope that in freely giving my life now, I can spare you and others from this Curse. I am so sorry Tristan. Sorry for many, many things. But know that I have loved you as well as any mother can, and this decision is born out of that love. Do better than I did, and find a way to stop this once and for all.

Love,
Mom

Tristan promptly turned the diaries over to Aunt Colleen without even glancing at them. His mother was right: he couldn't forgive this final abandonment. Not ever. And the crushing feeling in his chest made him wonder if he could even survive it.

Nothing was okay anymore. His mother, gone. His father, completely checked out from reality. Amelia, in a coma she might never emerge from. And Tristan knew this wasn't the end of it. His mother hadn't told him who the Curse was going to take, but he strongly suspected her death didn't stave off anything, as she'd hoped. There was more coming, and none of them could stop it.

Tristan thought her keeping this information to herself was almost more selfish than taking her own life. If they knew who was in danger, the family could band together to protect them. There was so much the Deschanels could do, when they worked together!

But, as Tristan hobbled out of bed, dreading the day, he knew deep down the knowledge she'd possessed would do them no good. When Elizabeth had visions, the results were already carved into the stone of time. Whoever she saw in those visions was already dead.

"Dead man walking," Tristan mumbled, as he grudgingly pulled on his smelly shirt, the same one he'd worn for the past seven days. As he shuffled across the old wood floors, and down the stairs, he tried to focus on how the cold cypress felt on his feet, the way faulty wiring caused the hallway lights to flicker. He took in the musty smell of the old house, holding it in until his lungs burned. As he let it out, his lips began their familiar tremble, and his breaths came out in stilted gasps as he erupted into consuming sobs. He sunk to his knees on the old oriental carpet, and then collapsed into a fetal ball.

His mother was gone. *Gone.* And she'd desperately taken her own life to protect him.

Because he was next. He knew it.

MARKUS

*M*arkus awoke to the sounds of Tiësto thumping through his phone alarm. The girl beside him stirred, grumbling about the early hour. He sat up, pulling the sheet to cover himself, as the first hints of sun fell into his Spartan flat through slatted blinds. Five in the morning. If he wanted to make his flight on time, he would have to get ready now.

"I have to go," he told the girl. He didn't know her name, but then, he hadn't bothered to ask. It was better if he didn't know.

"But we just went to sleep," she muttered groggily, turning over onto her stomach with the pillow pressed over her head. He admired anew the generous round of her ass, two dimples the size of thumbprints neatly punctuating the curves.

"Sorry," Markus said quietly, matter-of-factly. "I have a plane to catch."

She mumbled more annoyance and reluctantly slumped out of his bed, slipping on her tight black beaded dress from the night before. She had looked better out of it, and this contrast was more apparent with the clarity of morning. The dress was at least a size too small, which was what drew him to her in the first place. There were always little "safe" signals he looked for, and that was one of them. So far they had worked. He had yet to meet a girl, or guy, he would have taken home twice, and he'd brought home at least fifty of them.

Fifty. It sounded so horrible when he put it in perspective. But fifty women and men he would forget in a couple of nights was better than someone he might think twice about seeing again. Might develop feelings for.

Markus was twenty-one, tall, slender. Pale skin, pale hair, and strikingly bright blue eyes. His friends said he looked like a Viking, and the same was said of his Swedish father, Johannes, whom he favored. Though, none of the women he picked up knew any of this about him. Markus was an illusionist. He made others see what they most desired. The woman from last night dreamed of finding a young Italian man, so this was precisely what he had given her.

He wasn't in the business of wish fulfillment, though. These glamours were more for his sake than others.

Markus Gehring wanted to be a scientist, like his parents. Evangeline and Johannes were both nuclear physicists. They met while working at CERN, in Switzerland, and now they worked for the Pentagon. Markus had recently graduated from Columbia University, and planned to attend the Massachusetts Institute of Technology for grad school, like his mother. He sought a life modeled after theirs.

Except, even if he did nearly everything the same—same field, same jobs, same career path—he could never truly be like them, could he? Markus could never marry, have kids, or pursue anything like the loving household he grew up in. He and Katja had sworn to do their part in stopping this Curse, by vowing never to bring a child into this world. This family.

And now Katja has broken that promise, and I haven't a clue why.

The events leading to his trip back to New Orleans were enough to satisfy any lingering doubts regarding the Curse's veracity. His aunt Elizabeth was dead, and his cousin Amelia ill with something no doctor had yet been able to identify. It was only a matter of time before one of the others—maybe even him, or God forbid, Katja—took ill or had an accident befall them. While there was no definite pattern, the Curse made a habit of taking a half-dozen or more before it was sated for the next round.

Markus' date gathered items from the floor that had fallen out of her purse in the prior evening's throes of passion. He pulled on his jeans and turtleneck, needing no other preparation. His bag was already packed and in the corner. He'd known he wouldn't be getting much sleep the night before his flight.

She clasped her purse, and then thought better of it, opening it back up and leaving a business card on the small desk by the door. "We can do this again," she offered, and then rushed out before he could respond.

Not the first girl to leave her number. With unusual curiosity, Markus walked over and picked up the thick cardstock, turning it over in his hand. His breath caught as his eyes passed over the embossed letters. Bethany Anderson. Pentagon. *Well, isn't this an interesting turn of events.*

It occurred to him this might be problematic; she worked for the government, and knew where he lived. Obviously he had misread her signals—ill-fitted clothing, tossing back drinks like a college kid, biting her lip before he even walked up to her—or she was good at misdirection. Either way, he'd been wrong, and now, unfortunately, he'd be remembering her, even if there hadn't been any real attraction.

Markus sighed, mulling the situation over. Moments later, his cell phone rang. Katja. "We're downstairs with the cab. You'd better be ready," she said, not bothering with the usual polite formalities.

"Be right down," he replied. He studied the business card again, and then dropped it into the trashcan. Grabbing his duffle bag he made for the door, but as an afterthought, he retrieved the business card and slipped it into the kitchen drawer. He wouldn't be calling her. She was no different than the others, and there was nothing that interested him. But Markus didn't like surprises, and this caught him completely off-guard.

Can't let recent events distract me. I need to keep a clear head for this trip.

MARKUS WAS UNABLE TO SLEEP ON THE PLANE, BUT HE LET HIS eyes close and his mind wander as the thump of his trance beats helped him drift away. Many thought it was disrupting noise, but for Markus it was the exact opposite. It was one of the only things that helped distract him from his overwhelming thoughts. He didn't go to raves to dance or get high, he did it because it was the only moment of the day where he felt himself. Where he felt alive, but mostly importantly, clear.

For as long as Markus could remember, his mind had been like a disjointed racetrack: overflowing with thoughts lacking organization. He tested with a genius IQ at a young age, skipped ahead two grades in middle school, and was then subsequently held back to catch up with his peers when he had trouble with standardized tests. Everyone had varying opinions on why, but none were right. Markus simply could not block out his thoughts long enough to listen. It was his father who introduced him to music as a form of controlling his attention.

Sex served essentially the same purpose. Whether drifting across the beats per minute against the melodic synthesizers, or the rhythmic passage toward release, Markus' thoughts, mercifully, were threaded, even if only temporarily, into something resembling coherent thought.

But intimacy with strangers was a dangerous game if he

couldn't trust his senses. And last night was evidence he might be losing his edge.

Katja knew about his conquests. She found out by accident once when he unknowingly slept with one of her friends. Before then, he'd kept it from her because he was terrified she might get the idea into her head and start following his lead. Best friends or not, she was still his little sister.

Of course, she hadn't judged him. She understood. They were in the same predicament, no? She hadn't found a solution herself—"And don't worry Mark, I have no aspirations of whoring myself out," she reassured him—but she was lonely as well.

But now Katja was pregnant. His beautiful, generous, brilliant sister was going to have a child at nineteen, and there was nothing anyone could do about it. She had kept this secret from him—from all of them—until she could no longer hide it. *As to who the father is, well, I might take that to my grave,* she had told Markus. *If I told you, you'd never understand.*

Katja sat beside him on the plane, drawing atoms all over the back of the in-flight magazine. Her neuroses came in the form of obsessive behaviors, which she channeled through sketching. She had a glazed-over sheen in her eyes and wasn't even looking at the paper.

Johannes called her his "Swedish Princess," and she looked every bit of it, with pale blonde hair, like Markus, and the round blue eyes that resembled northern skies on a very clear day. Unlike her brother, though, she was petite, like her mother. Her light skin had a glow to it, like freshness from a summer day. Now, the glow in her cheeks came from the life growing inside of her.

Katja looked up at him. His face must have betrayed his thoughts. "What's wrong?"

Markus sighed, unwilling to cause her discomfort by admitting she had been the source of his worry. "I fucked a Pentagon chick last night."

Katja's eyes grew wide, but her pen kept moving. "That was a lot of information in one sentence. And this is bad because she might figure out you're an international terrorist?"

His eyes narrowed as he smacked the pen out of her hand. It went rolling down the aisle ahead. "We're on a plane for the love of God, Kat."

She snickered. "Maybe the Homeland Security officer will be hot and you can round out your public service experience."

"Very funny."

"Lighten up! I'd tell you that you need to get laid, but..."

This time Markus did laugh and she joined him. In moments like this, he could almost forget she was about to give up her entire future. He could overlook the dark circles growing daily under her eyes, and the troubled downturn of her mouth.

"How do you know she's from the Pentagon?" Katja asked. She moved to pick up her pen from the aisle but it was several seats forward.

"Her business card."

"I see. What title did her business card list?"

Markus shrugged casually, but smacked himself internally for missing that detail.

"Well, it seems to me you might be overreacting. Maybe she cleans the gold-plated toilets or something equally glamorous?" Katja eyed the pen again, but she would have to get out of her seat to retrieve it.

"That's not the point."

"Then tell me, what is the point?" she asked, knowing damn well what the point was.

"Stop being daft. What if she knows Mom or Dad?" He lowered his voice, even though his parents were well out of earshot.

"It isn't a sewing circle, Markus, it's the goddamned

Pentagon. There are thousands of employees, most of whom have never met each other, and never will. You're being paranoid, but there is a solution."

"Which is?"

"Stop screwing random women," she replied matter-of-factly. Her focus shifted toward the pen again, as her hand raised slowly, almost imperceptibly.

"Don't even think about it," he warned. It wouldn't be the first time Katja tried to be sneaky about her telekinesis in public. But this sardine-can-sized fuselage, filled with nosy passengers, was *not* the place for such risks.

"Fine," she whined, and ventured out of her seat to fetch the pen the old-fashioned way.

"Think on the bright side," she added a few moments later when she had resumed her scientific doodles. "There's a whole bunch of chicks in New Orleans you've never banged before! Just try to make sure you're paying attention because we have an awful lot of cousins there..."

"Well, wouldn't that be an interesting way to try breaking the Curse?" he joked, but a dark cloud passed over her face at these words. He'd said something wrong, and he could neither imagine what it was, nor get her to explain. From long experience, he knew this without asking. *Kat, I wish you would talk to me, like you used to.*

He sighed and leaned against the window, realizing perhaps he was tired after all.

A few moments later, she reached out with her free hand and grabbed his. "Sometimes I wish we believed in God," Katja said, her tone and expression serious. He knew she was thinking about not only what faced them in New Orleans, but also her own future. "The comfort people find in knowing they're not alone, and that they have little control over all the bad things which might happen to them. All they need to do is believe, and God will provide. 'Give it to God,' people say. 'He never gives you more than you can handle.' How... *relieving* it must feel, to be able to pass your burden on to a higher power, and just... let go. I wish with all my heart I could believe."

"Me too, Kitty Kat," he said, patting her hand. "But since we can't hide from what's coming, why not face it head on, like our parents taught us?"

She stared down at her paper for several long moments, then looked up, meeting his gaze. "Amen."

OLIVIA

*O*livia Claiborne was tired. Of *what,* exactly, would depend on the exact moment you asked her.

If you asked this morning, she would have said she was tired of her husband's lack of backbone. His vagrant sister, Judy, was constantly asking for money, and he was always saying yes. In Olivia's opinion, which certainly had to count for something, Judy's inability to hold a job and support her three kids was *Judy's* problem to solve, not Greg and Olivia's.

If you asked her this afternoon, she would have complained how tedious some of her customers were. *You would think I'm running a daycare, not a high-end flower boutique,* she often griped to her husband. Her clientele were mostly blue-blood types from Uptown, and they came to her for big events, weddings, and the like. But they were so *picky.* At the end of the day, did it really require ten people, and four hours, to decide the difference between a gardenia, a lily, and a white rose? Really?

If you asked her last night, she would have said her mother, Maureen, was even more insufferable than usual. It started after she engaged in that silly fight with her crazy sister, Elizabeth. Her mother hadn't shut up since. She was constantly calling her to vent about the family, particularly Elizabeth, but also her other sisters, Colleen and Evangeline, who also believed in the incredibly base family superstitions. Her mother was threatening to move away and never speak to her family again, a worn out promise, and Olivia could only roll her eyes. She was tired of hearing about it. "You only feed into it, you know," she told her mother. "If you would shut up about it, they might too."

It was a sad truth that Olivia thought her mother was a complete moron. Maureen had become pregnant barely out of high school, by a much older man, and then basically sold off to him like cattle instead of being encouraged to build a future for herself. Olivia had loved her late father, Edouard, but that was entirely beside the point. She blamed the early marriage for her mother's inability to talk about anything that wasn't somehow tied to gossip or drama, having never matured much past that point.

But if you asked Olivia, at almost any given time of the day, what was tiring her most, she would reply her family in general. They were all superstitious assholes she couldn't relate to on any level. They continuously found ways, at every turn, to cause her misery. Most recently, her Aunt Elizabeth had disappeared and then turned up dead. By her own hand! Was there anything more selfish than suicide? Olivia's heart broke for Tristan, but she had trouble finding the compassion to pray for her aunt's soul. And then, Amelia had been hospitalized, and no one had any idea why. What good were doctors when they couldn't figure out how a perfectly healthy young woman suddenly stopped breathing? And wasn't Aunt Colleen supposed to be a dang healer? Hell's bells!

Of course, the first thing everyone said when these things happened? *The Curse.* The dadgum, stupid, nonexistent curse. People die! How were their family's experiences more special than any other family's? Why did they have to give it a fancy label? And what was worse, no one could point to any evidence except something her great-great-whatever-grandma had over-heard and passed on to her daughter. How this stupid idea had survived over a hundred years, Olivia would never fathom. The Deschanels might be wealthy, and educated, but they were all complete fools.

And now everyone was flying into New Orleans, as if it would help matters. More idiots banding together toward a common cause only resulted in idiots squared. It reminded her of one of the de-motivational posters she saw in her cousin Ashley's office: *Meetings- None of Us is as Dumb as All of Us.* Indeed!

Ashley was one of the few cousins she didn't find entirely obtuse. He was a perfectly reasonable, decent family man who, like Olivia, had better things to focus on than stupid notions. His wife, Christine, was lovely, their three kids well-behaved. Olivia imagined she would gravitate toward him when the family gathered, as she usually did, so they wouldn't feel so outnumbered in the swarm of mass insanity. He'd been spending his days at his sister's bedside. Olivia admired that dedication.

Olivia checked her phone for the dozenth time that evening, but still no call from her little brother, Alain. Something was up with him. She knew it. And he'd been avoiding her for days, which only heightened her protective instincts. There was a kindness and sweetness... a *vulnerability* about Alain that she felt responsible for preserving. He'd never had a serious girlfriend, and was never the first person in the room to speak. Quiet and thoughtful, he inherited a very keen artistic talent from their mother. It was Olivia who'd thought to put Alain in front of Greg early on, so he could turn those talents into something useful. Alain was an architect now, and worked for Greg's company. With his inheritance money, he'd bought a small storefront on Magazine Street and occasionally sold his sketches there, too.

Olivia was proud to be part of her brother's success. She thought if it were up to their inept mother, Alain would have ended up peddling his art in Jackson Square, penniless.

Other than her two-year old son, Rory, she loved Alain best in all the world. He was the exact opposite of her, but she tolerated his differences in a way she could not with others. The same qualities she criticized in her cousins, she embraced in Alain.

Which was why Olivia *would* figure out what was going on with him.

She locked the flower shop and glanced at her watch. The nanny would be expecting her soon, but she should stop by the hospital and look in on her cousin. Family idiocy aside, she was genuinely worried about Amelia.

Olivia rested her hand on her stomach, protectively. She was now past the three-month mark and it was safe to start being hopeful this pregnancy would end better than the last two. She waited to tell the family until last week; they would never know about the two she lost. Not to spare them sorrow, but because they would attribute it to the silly Curse. While she couldn't change their minds, she wouldn't allow such an affront to her own grieving.

She adjusted her purse, smiled, and walked to her car.

WHEN OLIVIA ARRIVED AT THE HOSPITAL, SHE FOUND ASHLEY IN the hallway on his cell phone, attempting to carry on a work conversation despite the bustle around him. He was a financial manager down in the Central Business District, and she could hardly remember a time when he wasn't engrossed in work, even at family events. He dressed in the expected suit and tie, but his shirt was unbuttoned a few notches and his tie lay askance. She wondered if he'd even left the hospital since Amelia was admitted.

He looked like the male version of his sister, Amelia: same pale hair and skin, from some nonexistent Nordic descent.

Ashley waved at her, smiled briefly, but kept talking. She patted him on the shoulder and stepped inside Amelia's room.

Amelia looked to be resting peacefully, except for her skin tone, which was even paler than usual. Jacob had her hands in his and had fallen asleep with his head on the bed. Olivia wasn't sure what to think of Jacob when he first came into her cousin's life, but over the years she'd come to see he absolutely adored Amelia. The only thing that would make Olivia like him more was if he had the power to convince Amelia the Curse was baloney so she could relax and have a family before it was too late. Amelia was one of the smart ones, and her belief in this crap was such a waste.

Perhaps Olivia should have seen all this coming. Her Deschanel gift was that of foresight; a seer. But watching Aunt Elizabeth completely lose her mind over the same "gift" was enough for Olivia to learn how to turn hers off. Besides, her mother had insisted upon it, years ago.

Olivia set the cheery bundle of pink lilies down on the desk next to all the other bouquets. She noticed Tristan, her Aunt Colleen, and Uncle Noah on a small sofa off in a dark corner of the room. Her aunt and uncle were sleeping, drained even in rest. They all looked horrible, really, but none worse than Tristan. She felt bad for him because none of it was his fault. The responsibility rested solely with Elizabeth, who'd been an A+ certifiable loony.

Tristan smiled thinly. Olivia knew he didn't like her, but that's how it was with the divide. Everyone in the family tolerated one another, but those who believed, and those who didn't, formed clear sides. Unfortunately hers was the slim side, but she took comfort in knowing it was the *right* side. She wouldn't give up motherhood, and other amazing experiences, like they foolishly had.

"How is she?" Olivia asked, nodding toward her cousin.

Tristan shrugged. "Doctors still don't know what's wrong," he said pitifully. "And Aunt C hasn't had any luck, either."

She nodded. "I'm so sorry about your mother. Depression is a tragic affliction in this family."

"Depression was only part of it," he countered, quietly.

Her eyes narrowed, knowing what he meant. "But it was most of it," Olivia insisted, wanting the last word.

Tristan laughed at her. She suppressed the urge to smack him. It wasn't the time. "When does Aunt Evie get in?" she asked instead.

"Tomorrow."

"Well, it's nice they could get away on such short notice," Olivia said, sounding as annoyed as she felt. She wished she could be *happy* family was coming in, but her responsibility to maintain sanity was only heavier when more Curse-crazed relatives were around.

Tristan opened his mouth to say something, but instead shook his head. Naturally, she had to be the bad guy. Another nail in her cross to bear.

Olivia decided to be the bigger person. "Has anyone else been by?"

"Almost everyone," he said, and she wondered if he was judging her for not coming by sooner. Not everyone could drop everything on a dime. "Even Nicolas came by."

That surprised her. Nicolas had always seemed to think he was too good for the family. Unlike others, for example Anasofiya, who at least tried to be civil, Nicolas didn't even bother pretending half the time. "How is Nicolas?"

He shrugged. "Fine, I guess. Busy at *Ophélie*."

Olivia didn't know why she was so bitter Nicolas inherited the family estate. His father Charles had, after all, been the eldest child, and heir. She thought maybe because he was so painfully indifferent about it. He treated it like any old house, while the rest of the cousins would give anything to own such an important part of the family heritage.

"Who's picking Aunt Evie up?" Olivia always had to know every detail.

"Aunt C, I guess."

Olivia stiffened, shifting. "Where are they staying?"

He sighed. "Shit, Olivia, I don't know. I've been a little preoccupied."

"Well, you don't have to get rude about it."

Tristan was clearly at the end of his patience with her and she'd only just arrived. "I'm exhausted. I'm sorry, I don't know our aunt's travel plans but you might check with your mother," he suggested, then closed his eyes, shutting her out.

"Hmph," she said, frustrated with his rudeness. "I think I will." She clicked her heels nervously and straightened her purse again, trying to decide if she should stay or leave.

Olivia shifted in awkwardness for a couple more minutes, and when no one spoke to her, she decided to go. She went to Amelia and kissed her on the forehead, then crossed herself, asking God for His mercy and healing grace.

She left feeling sufficiently dutiful.

COLLEEN

$\mathcal{C}$olleen hadn't left Amelia's hospital room since she was admitted a week ago, after getting the call from Oz. Thank God he'd had the impulse to check in on her... that the night of her collapse would be the evening he'd venture over for a drink and conversation. Colleen owed Oz a debt she could never repay.

Her husband, Noah, dutifully ensured her meals were taken care of, and the room was self-sufficient enough as far as her other basic needs were concerned. At first, he insisted they rotate, but when he realized Colleen wouldn't leave, even for a moment, he'd instead made it his goal to see her needs were met while she cared for their daughter.

She wouldn't have moved for anything. Amelia had never needed her more than she did now.

Ashley had taken up the adjoining rented family suite to conduct his business from close by. He was no more than a knock on the wall away if anything changed. Outwardly, she scolded him about being away from the office, but secretly she was unbelievably grateful for his presence.

Colleen's chair pressed up against one side of the bed. Jacob flanked sentry on the other side of Amelia, having been equally vigilant as Colleen in his watch. He hadn't said one word about the fight, or their breakup. The only thing that made Colleen's heart ache as much as seeing her daughter lying in such a state was witnessing the dedicated love radiating off the young man who'd do anything to save her. His head rested next to Amelia's on the pillow, her long white mane curling softly around his black hair, creating a somber halo. *Yin and yang,* people called them. She saw it now.

Both a doctor of medicine, and a healer of a more supernatural kind, Colleen had spent the past week searching for a solution to her daughter's condition. But no matter the angle, she continued to come up woefully short. Her conclusion, for once, matched the other doctors in the hospital: there was nothing physically wrong with Amelia.

The ability to help Amelia stopped with that revelation. There existed no healers, or doctors, who could mend the spreading blackness that afflicted the mind of an imperiled empath.

In the midst of it all, Colleen couldn't even take the time to grieve the death of her dear sister, Elizabeth. Whenever the weight of her passing threatened to take hold, she pushed it back down, where it would need to stay until she could mourn properly.

Her other sister, Evangeline, had flown in the night before. *Leena, go home and rest for an evening. Let us carry this burden for you,* her younger sister had said, with fear and love in her eyes.

It's no burden to love my daughter, Colleen snapped, immediately feeling shame for taking her pain out on someone she loved, but too tired to correct it. Apologies were not required in any case, as Evangeline was her dearest confidante. She understood.

Colleen heard a grunting stir, as Jacob woke. When he raised his head, she witnessed both the hollow detachment in his gaze, and the new lines in his face that had developed over the past week.

"Go eat," she encouraged gently. "I'll call if anything changes."

Jacob shook his head, squinting as his eyes adjusted to the harsh fluorescent lights. "It's okay, Mrs. D. I'm not hungry."

"Jacob, I've insisted you call me Colleen for years. And now, of all times, I will not have you falling back on formalities. In fact, you may as well call me Mom," she admonished, with hints of loving chastisement. If Amelia came out of this, Colleen would no longer let her daughter foolishly squander what she had with Jacob Donnelly. *Not if. When!*

A small, tight smile appeared. "I'm really not hungry, though."

Colleen frowned, looking at the clock. Five minutes until her visitor arrived, and she didn't want Jacob around when it happened. She couldn't guess the outcome of the meeting, but if it didn't go well, it would be best if Jacob never knew about it.

"Well, then perhaps you'll be a sweetheart and fetch me something? Noah is working late, and I skipped breakfast." Thinking again of the time, Colleen added, "Not from the cafeteria. What passes for food there is doing foul things to my constitution."

Jacob glanced down at Amelia, and opened his mouth as if to protest, but then simply nodded. "I'll drive down to the deli on Napoleon that Amelia always liked, if that's okay?"

"Perfect," she smiled. "And do take a moment to eat, too, please? Amelia will need you strong and healthy when she wakes."

"Yes, Mrs... *Mom*," Jacob replied with a sheepish half-grin, before he reluctantly shuffled out.

Colleen's own smile lasted only until she heard the soft click of the door. Heaving a sigh of relief, she tapped her foot, awaiting the visitor who may, or may not, make all the difference in her daughter's recovery.

Moments later, a man strongly resembling Jacob walked through the door. He looked uncertain, and she sensed his hesitance in responding to this meeting.

"Oz," Colleen greeted, as she stood and moved toward him. Unsure of his role, his hand went out, in dutiful observance of his lawyerly manners, but instead she pulled him toward her in a crushing embrace.

"You're practically family, are you not?" Colleen reminded him, forcing down the bubble of emotion threatening to surface. *Don't give in to your fears. And do not, not even for a minute, put all your belief in this solution.*

"My father would certainly say so," Oz agreed with a polite smile, but his eyes were on Amelia. In a mindless, but tender gesture, Oz brushed a stray hair off her forehead. *Their friendship goes back many years. If he can do what you ask, he will.* "I'm very sorry about Elizabeth. If there's anything at all I can do, maybe to look after Amelia's affairs even..."

"Anne is staying at Amelia's to care for her Siamese, Miss Kitty," Colleen informed him. "But thank you for the kind offer."

"Adrienne and I are happy to—"

"Oz, please, sit," Colleen insisted, gesturing toward the chair, still warm from Jacob. "You'll forgive me for getting right to the point?"

He nodded, taking a seat. "Of course. How can I help?"

Colleen folded her hands tightly in her lap, knowing her errant brain would cause them to fidget otherwise. She couldn't show weakness, not when she was about to dredge up a part of Oz's past likely buried quite deep.

"How much of your childhood do you remember, Colin?"

Oz's eyes were still on Amelia. "About as much as any child, I suppose. Why?"

"When you were quite young," she continued, carefully,

"your father came to me seeking counsel about a certain behavior you were exhibiting. Involving your dreams. Is this ringing any bells?"

"No," he said, but she did not miss the tiny gleam in his eyes.

"Specifically, your father claimed you were entering his dreams and those of your mother," Colleen explained, pausing to allow his memory to catch up. "At first, they thought they'd imagined it, or that it was a fluke. It's not entirely unheard of for couples to have shared dreams, and your presence in them might have been explained away. But, over time, they realized you were, in fact, inserting yourself into their dreams, so to speak. Visiting them, and engaging them. Naturally, they had no idea why this was happening. So they came to me. Not to understand the ability, but to squash it."

"Colleen, I'm sorry, but—"

"I refused to help them," she went on, ignoring his rebuttal with a dismissive flip of her hand, "because I don't believe any child should *ever* repress a natural ability. It is as much a part of you as your personality. And dreamwalkers are so rare..."

"Dreamwalkers?" Oz stared at her in clear disbelief. "Colleen, I know the past week has been unthinkably hard on you—"

"Colin Sullivan, if anyone knows how to put aside their stress and deal with the task at hand, it's me," Colleen admonished. It was not her imagination that he sat up straighter at the rebuke. "You were a dreamwalker. *Are* a dreamwalker. But it isn't a skill you've used in many, many years, because your parents asked you not to. They quite possibly convinced you to forget you ever could. It wouldn't surprise me if they ended up finding another Deschanel willing to do what I was not."

"You're not making any sense," Oz said, brushing his hands across his pants. Sweat started to bead at his brow, as fractured memories surged forward, confusing him. "You know I'd never

SARAH M. CRADIT

deny the things I've seen Deschanels do, but the Sullivans simply don't share your... unique gifts."

"A debatable argument," Colleen smiled. "Certainly you've seen unusual things at Sullivan & Associates. Things you can't quite explain, or that your uncles and cousins have sought to keep contained. But that's a discussion for another day. Your parents were quite convinced of your ability, and so was I. The only question is whether or not your censorship of the gift is permanent. If you can still find it within yourself to conjure up the experience."

A debate raged inside the mind of Oz Sullivan. Colleen was polite enough to let him continue it without her intervention. He was remembering; she was sure of it.

After several long moments, Oz finally asked, "Why are you telling me this? Why now?"

Colleen sighed, squeezing her hands tighter together. *This may be your only chance.* "Because, quite frankly, I know of no dreamwalkers amongst the Deschanels. If I did, they would have already been here."

"But why?"

Colleen's gaze traveled to her daughter. Beautiful Amelia, whose pale features were framed by the stark white sheets in a ghastly effect. *My only daughter. My firstborn. My dearest heart.* "In her current state, dreams are the only way to reach her."

"You're asking me to try and speak to Amelia through her dreams," Oz concluded slowly. His hand had folded over Amelia's earlier, and he now clasped it tightly.

"I am. I'm also a mother coming to you, as her only hope." *There are dangers in dreamwalking. Unknowns. But we mustn't think about those.*

Oz dropped Amelia's hand, as he looked down at his feet. His hands then shot up and tore through his dark hair, gripping it at the roots as his feet commenced in a rapid tapping against the fading linoleum. "Even if what you're saying is true, and I can't see why you would lie to me, whatever I could do when I was little stopped decades ago. I've never had anything like this happen to me as an adult. Not once."

"Whether your parents employed someone to influence you, or whether their pleading was sufficient, I believe they convinced you so fully of the wrongness of this ability that you blocked it completely," Colleen pressed. "But Oz, I've seen many, many children pushed away from their gifts. My niece and nephew, Olivia and Alain, were raised to believe their abilities were evil! Even Deschanels aren't immune to fearful ignorance."

"If my parents tried to get me to stop, it wasn't because they were ignorant," Oz defended hotly.

"Not in any kind of malicious way," Colleen agreed, her tone soothing. "It's natural to fear something you don't understand. Doubly so when that fear involves the welfare of your child."

"I would do anything to help Amelia. She's one of my oldest friends." Oz ended this with a fleeting look in Amelia's direction. "But there has to be another way. Even if I could get inside her head, what good would it do?"

"We don't know for certain," Colleen admitted, "but there's evidence that dreamwalkers have successfully pulled patients out of comas. Including imperiled empaths, like Amelia. Oz, I wish there *was* another way. The doctors will continue to spin their wheels in an attempt to solve this, but they won't succeed. They can't, because her affliction defies the conventions of modern medicine. And the extent of our Deschanel healers' abilities stops at the mind. We cannot breach her thoughts to reach her. There is only one type of individual who can," she added, with a pointed look.

She thought she heard Oz curse under his breath, and then, "I'm not saying I can do this. In fact, I'm convinced you're wrong. But, if you aren't wrong... I don't even know... how would I do it? I don't remember anything."

Colleen carefully concealed her own fears. All she knew

about dreamwalking she'd learned from books. Unreliable. Potentially dangerous. And not only for Amelia.

She released her knotted hands, feeling the tension rise up and away from her. It hadn't departed, but instead lingered, nearby. "I can show you."

Oz nodded, turning back to face Colleen. "I need some time to let the idea sink in. This is a lot, all at once. I'm sure you understand."

Colleen reached forward and grasped both of his hands in hers, startling him. "Oz, we don't have the luxury of time. Amelia is *dying*. I'm sorry to be so blunt with you, but we're long past the point of pointless platitudes. Amelia is your friend. She is your wife's cousin. And it's quite possible she might not survive the night."

Oz glanced down at her hands, then back at Amelia. His mouth hung open, slack with his loss for words. Finally, he said, "Give me ten minutes at least. Please. For all of our sakes."

Colleen released a grateful sigh. "I'll step out," she said kindly. "You're welcome to stay in here. I'll ensure no one interrupts you."

Oz offered a tiny nod, but did not look back at her as she left the room.

OZ

*O*z was frightened. Not since Adrienne's accident, a decade ago, had he ever felt quite so panicked.

He wished he could have refused Colleen, continuing to deny her bizarre and unwelcome claim. But he *did* remember. Not entirely, mainly flashes of words and admonishments from his parents. *You don't belong there, Oz,* from his mother. *Never, ever do that again,* from his father.

Oz, ever the dutiful child, had done as they asked. In any case, he'd been too little to understand the full scope of what he could do.

As he watched Amelia, his thoughts traveled to the many memories they shared, from childhood to teenage years. Amelia was magnolia blossoms on the eve of spring, and sweet tea on the river. Her presence was a touch of cool air on a humid day, and the voice of reason for a mind in peril. She'd tutored him in biology, won the class presidency against him, and was the fastest driver he knew. As he observed the slight flush in her cheeks, and the unnatural stillness of her resting features, Oz grasped he had underestimated her presence in his life. Her importance.

It was normal to take people for granted. He knew this. But Colleen's words from earlier, *she could die tonight*, constricted tight around his heart as he realized he really could lose her. They could all lose her.

He desperately wanted to help, but even if everything Colleen said was true... even if he *had* done those things as a young boy... who was to say he could do it now?

Oz remembered his separation anxiety as a child, when his parents first put him in his own room. He couldn't bear it, and he'd wished, more than anything, to be with them again. It wasn't terror, it was the fear of abandonment. Of waking up, and finding his mom and dad gone, leaving him completely alone. That was the catalyst to him seeing them in their shared dreams.

Oz didn't remember trying, exactly. He simply wished to be near them, and then he would find himself wandering their dreamscape. Too little to wonder at the strangeness of it all, his young world was unlimited.

But his feelings for Amelia were of a much more subtle nature. Her position in his life as one of his oldest friends was important to him, but he didn't pine for her, or wish to be close to her when she wasn't around. How could he possibly expect to find his way into her head?

"I'm sorry to interrupt your thoughts," Colleen apologized, as she re-entered the room.

Oz's heart raced so furiously even his hands were a bright red. *I can't really do this... can I?* "Tell me what you know. About what I need to do."

As it turned out, Colleen could tell him very little, as her experience was even more limited than his. "From what I know, it's as simple as wishing you were closer to the person. Wanting to be with them, even in their dreams."

"If that were true, I would have been in Adrienne's dreams constantly," Oz returned. "Or my children's."

"I think..." Colleen watched him thoughtfully. "I believe there may be a barrier you've constructed which has prevented that. A barrier created long before you understood how to control this ability. You'll need to break that down before this will work."

"But how?"

"How do we accomplish anything difficult, Oz? Focus."

Oz returned his gaze to the bed, and his friend. The thumping in his brain competed with the buzzing in his ears, and there was enough sweat at his brow to make him uncomfortable. He closed his eyes, and thought of his parents' words, as they pleaded with him to stop. Then, of how he felt, what his mind created to obey.

His skin was on fire, and Colleen's intent, hopeful stares were not helping. "Would you mind leaving us alone?" Oz ventured. "I'm not sure I can do this at all, to be perfectly honest, but I know it won't happen with you sitting there, staring."

A momentary wave of anger passed over her face, quickly replaced by understanding. "Yes, of course. I'll be right outside."

"Thank you."

Once the click of her heels faded into the distance, Oz looked down at Amelia and a piercing knot of abject horror clenched tight in his chest. *I'm less afraid that I can't do it, and more that I can.*

Closing his eyes, he tried to focus on the absence of Amelia in his life. Of not seeing her on her porch at nights, not sharing a drink and thoughts with her. He thought of the rush of adrenaline and wind as she drove them through the bayou highways in her vintage Porsche, handling the gearbox like a massage artist as he laughed in terror at her insane, but confident driving. Of how she always insisted on wearing sunglasses on poker nights, and conned him into taking her with him on his Saints season passes.

SARAH M. CRADIT

But minutes passed, and Oz remained firmly planted in the seat next to her, mind fixed on the outside world where it always was. With a grunt of frustration he shook his head, trying to squelch the voice telling him he could not do this.

Never, ever do that again, he heard his father say.

You don't belong there, Oz, his mother added, in perfect thematic synch.

You are *a dreamwalker*, Colleen concluded.

How did I start this as a child? First, he realized he hadn't done it from a hard plastic chair. It had happened while curled in his bed, where it was warm, and safe.

Glancing at the door, Oz slid his shoes off and then climbed into bed next to Amelia, as gently as he could. If anyone were to come in right then, they'd certainly have questions, but they could stand in line as far as Oz was concerned. "Sorry," he mumbled as his arm passed across her face, eliciting an autonomic gasp from her.

He rested his face near hers and closed his eyes once again. This time, he didn't think of how he missed her. He thought only of how sad he would be if she never came back. Of never again experiencing the thrill of being in her passenger seat, or observing the mischievous joy she couldn't contain when she swept them all at cards. The fever pitch of her enthusiastic "Who dat!" He saw her smile, which always made him think of warmth in winter.

Oz didn't recall the next few moments. He only knew when he opened his eyes, he was standing under a magnolia tree in what seemed like an endless field of brilliantly ornamented floral arrangements. As his eyes adjusted to the bright colors, and he allowed himself to find orientation, he realized he knew the location well: The Gardens. Colleen's home, and where Amelia had grown up.

It was not as he remembered it. The vibrant flowers were garish, colors quite literally *dripping* from the petals, like vivid

128

paint drops thrown against the foliage, in great, heaping globs. The sky had a greenish cast, and the magnolia tree hummed a low song that Oz recognized, but could not place. *All the plants are,* he realized. They were singing in unison, in their own, unique voices. *This must be as Amelia remembered it, from her childhood, with her big imagination.*

But there was also a suffocating stillness in the air. One which reminded him that he, and Amelia, were the only living souls in this version of The Gardens. Even if he walked for miles, he wouldn't encounter another.

"Amelia?" he called out. No response, other than the low baritone of the orchestral foliage.

As Oz carefully made his way through the living garden, the grass grew rapidly taller in each place he stepped, lightly whipping and curling around his ankles, releasing as he moved on. It felt like watered silk, spiraling in softness. He wanted to sleep in it. To dream in it.

A light breeze carried forth the scent of bubble gum cotton candy. "Amelia?"

"Hello?" a surprised voice called from off to his right. Oz followed the sound, as the flora seemed to carry him forward, pushing him toward the voice's owner.

After a much longer walk than he would have encountered in the real Gardens, Oz came upon a white, ornamented gazebo, covered in purple ivy and marigold bougainvillea. Inside, Amelia sat, as if on a throne, her snowy hair coming down around her white dress, and matching white gloves. She very nearly glowed, just as everything else in The Gardens did.

As she stood in shock, a great gust of wind carried through and the humming of the trees turned into a low, operatic song. "Oz!" she cried, attempting to launch herself forward. But as she approached the perimeter of the gazebo, her limbs were abruptly halted, in suspended animation, as though invisible walls enclosed the structure.

Oz ran to her, feeling keenly that all the living inhabitants of the garden wanted him to find her, to rescue her, and bring her home. It was only this gazebo, flashed in a deceptive white coat, which sought to imprison her.

He was surprised when he passed through the invisible barrier with ease. *So I can enter, but she can't leave. Is this a prison, or a fortress?*

Amelia's pale face bloomed in a bright flush as she took in the unexpected sight before her. Tears cut ragged zigzags down her cheeks. With a trembling hand, she reached out to touch his face.

"But... *how?*"

"I don't really know," Oz admitted, putting a hand over hers as he brought it back down to his lap. "Your mother..."

Amelia released a small laugh, swiping at her tears. "Well, now, that's all you needed to say."

Oz returned the laugh, but it quickly faded to a sigh. "She managed to get me in here, but I don't know how to get you out."

"You can't," she replied, with a sad shake of her head. As she did, her white hair shimmered, a slight rattling noise emanating from her, as it had with the plants. "I've tried. Everyone warned me... my mother... Jacob..."

"Warned you about what?"

"Not being better about shutting myself off from the world," Amelia explained. She gently pulled her hand back as she looked down at her lap, and the never-ending swirl of white taffeta. "As an empath, I don't only sense the pain of others. Sometimes I absorb it."

"And that's why you're sick?" Oz asked, not sure if that was even the right question.

"I'm past being sick," she replied. "I don't know how much longer I'll be stuck here, but my next destination won't be a return home. I will go wherever it is we go when our souls pass on. To heaven, I suppose."

"No," Oz said, furiously shaking his head. In a surge of purpose, he seized both of her hands in his again. "Amelia, I won't let that happen. I don't know how I'll prevent it, but I refuse to accept there's nothing we can do. You have way too much to live for. And you have so many who love you, and are waiting for you to wake up. Your parents. Ashley. Jacob."

Her blue eyes brightened. Outside, the plants stirred. "Jacob? He's there?"

"Why wouldn't he be?" Oz chuckled. "I think your mom sent him on an errand when she invited me in, but the man hasn't left the hospital before today. His chair was still warm when I sat in it."

"I did something foolish," Amelia admitted. "I planned to set things right, but fate took that chance from me." She paused. "How's Tristan? I feel so helpless, not being able to go to him. He's lost so much."

"Your family has him surrounded in a cocoon right now," Oz assured her. "And he's my cousin, too. I'll look out for him until we can get you home."

Neither of them said anything for a great long while, but the jasmine and wisteria began swirling, and floating through the air, separating as they reached the sky. A great flowery shower rained down around them, but inside the gazebo they were protected. The air remained still.

"I'm afraid," Amelia confessed. "I should be brave. I was raised to be strong. But even in my worst nightmares, I never imagined this."

Oz, who had always led with his heart, answered by pulling her into his arms, and his strong embrace. *I will save her. I will not let her, or her family, suffer needlessly.* "I can be brave for us both," he vowed, kissing the top of her head. *This is Adrienne's cousin. One of my dearest friends. I cannot abandon her.* "Let me carry that for you, Amelia."

He felt her soft hair on his lips one moment, and then in the next, he heard the ambient beeps of her heart monitor, and the low din of the bustle outside her room.

And then, strong hands on his collar as he was dragged roughly from the bed and dropped on to the cold linoleum. He heard Colleen's frantic voice trying to intervene, but it didn't stop whatever was happening.

"What the *hell* are you doing?" Jacob protested, standing over Oz with a look, which, on its own, could have very nearly stopped Oz's heart for good.

"Jacob, darling, will you please calm down and listen?" Colleen was saying, as she tugged on the angry man's arm.

Oz had never seen mild Jacob Donnelly worked up about anything, but he was quite sure he didn't want to see it even a moment longer. The Irishman looked as if he might draw down into his boxing roots. "I was trying to help her," Oz attempted to explain, placing his hands before him in defensive submission. "Colleen asked—"

"You, what?" Jacob snapped, dropping Oz the rest of the way to the floor as he turned toward a frazzled Colleen. "Is this why you wanted me to leave?"

Colleen hesitated only briefly. "Yes," she replied, squaring her shoulders as she straightened her posture. "I suspected you'd be uncomfortable with it, and I made a judgment call."

"You suspected correctly," Jacob answered, through firmly gritted teeth. But then the anger dissolved, leaving only the man's tormented helplessness as he swayed on his feet, turning back to Oz. "Can you? Help her, I mean?"

"I don't know," Oz admitted, tentatively sliding away from Jacob as he pulled himself to a standing position. "But I saw her. She wants to get out, but can't."

"Can't? Get out? Will someone please tell me what the hell is going on?" Jacob cried, eyes wide and red from exhaustion.

"She's stuck inside her own head," Colleen explained, her eyes watching Oz in grateful wonderment. And perhaps a bit of surprise. "Only Oz can reach her."

Oz nodded. "Now I have to find a way to bring her back."

ALAIN

*N*o matter how much Alain Blanchard wiped his hands against his slacks, he couldn't rid himself of the sweat greasing his palms. It further plagued him by pooling at his brow, and tormenting his neck, chest, and back. His nerves were a delicious wreck, his thoughts torn between excitement at seeing her, and horror of the same.

She'd be staying with him, at least. There was that. But, oh, perhaps it would be better if she didn't! Yet, they were in this together, for better or worse. To the detriment of society, and the betterment of the family. Maybe. No one knew. So much of this plan had been speculation, and guesswork.

"Alain, are you ill?" his sister Olivia demanded, snapping her fingers before his face as she appeared to be one moment away from pulling out the smelling salts.

"When is Alain not ill?" Maureen, their mother, cawed, as she barked orders at the maid, pointing out light swashes of dust missed on windowsills, and pillows not fluffed quite to her liking. She got this way whenever visitors came to stay, but *especially* when that visitor was one of her sisters.

"I'm fine," Alain grumbled. "I'm going for a walk."

"Now? But they'll be here soon!" his mother shrieked. "What is the matter with you? Yesterday you were excited to see Katja and now you're acting like you ate some bad boudin!"

Alain flashed her a guilty glance. If only she knew! But he wasn't accountable to her. He was a man long grown, twenty-six now, and had a right to his decisions and feelings. He didn't have to apologize for thinking independently, or drawing his own conclusions.

But an intellectual understanding didn't stop the guilt.

Nothing would.

"I'll be back before they arrive," he promised, already rushing toward the door, an escape to fresh air and perhaps a separation from the future discussion that might occur an hour from now when his cousins arrived. When Katja walked through the door, with her blushing pale cheeks, and the slight bulge to her small midsection.

No, he couldn't bear it without some time to himself first.

ALAIN STEPPED OUTSIDE HIS MOTHER'S LAKESIDE ESTATE, AND ventured into the tall grass bordering the property, edging Lake Pontchartrain. Toward the very place his life had careened entirely out of control.

Snaking through the grass, he let his hands take in the slight resistance of the blades as they passed across his fingers. He closed his eyes, surrendering to his sense of direction. And if he wandered right into the lake, so what? Maybe that was best.

It all started months ago, when Katja had shown up in New Orleans with an idea.

Alain had taken her to the lake, where the weather was still hanging on to the light wisps of winter, and the air was crisp and alive. He loved the Pontchartrain in late winter.

Of course, he hadn't had a clue what was on her mind. He never, ever would have driven her out there, to that remote location, had he possessed even an inkling of what her keen brain was mulling over and preparing to present.

Their communications started innocently enough...

Though Alain worked for Olivia's husband, Greg, as an architect, he was an artist at heart. His skills lay in sketching, and other precise forms of artwork, and as it turned out, Katja shared that aptitude. Tristan had told Alain he should reach out to their cousin and ask her how to sell his work, because hers had been featured on postcards, and in museums in the D.C. area.

"But she's only nineteen," Alain had protested.

"She's also a genius and a fucking amazing artist," Tristan countered. Alain went online and pulled up some of her stuff. He was impressed, and envious.

He hardly remembered Katja. Seven years younger, she wasn't ever at an age where he would've hung out with her at family holidays or reunions. And unlike her mom and brother, she hadn't been back to New Orleans in years. But he dropped her an email, and she responded almost immediately.

At first, they'd conversed back and forth about art. She gave him tips on how she found her mild success—mostly through her mother's prodding to actually reach out to people instead of waiting to be "discovered," something Alain felt a little ashamed at being guilty of—and he was surprised to hear she'd had private tutoring from an art instructor. "It's all a bit of a lark," Katja concluded, speaking as she sometimes did, as if her language had been developed in another century. "Something I do when I'm bored."

Eventually their conversations evolved beyond art, and a friendship developed. It didn't take long before their talks moved in the direction of family issues, and it was to her that Alain finally admitted—out loud—he thought the stories of the Curse might hold some merit, despite his mother's insistence to the contrary.

"I absolutely have no doubt in my mind they're true," Katja wrote back. "If you ever need convincing Alain, I make a pretty damned compelling argument on the subject."

Katja was good as her word. She'd done her research, and even hired a private genealogist to trace back records beyond what the family had saved. Her mother, Evangeline, also hired a biographer at one point, and they documented everything. In the beginning, Aunt Colleen and Aunt Elizabeth had been part of the project, but Colleen had become busy with things at the hospital and they slowly excluded Liz because her fixation had become unhealthy. Katja promised to scan and share everything when she had a chance—*"I seriously do not want to haul all of this crap to the school scanner, Alain, but if I have to, I will."*—but when she emailed him to say she was coming to New Orleans, she promised to bring it instead.

Alain wasn't sure if he wanted to see it or not. Mostly, he wished he didn't have to think about the family issues at all, particularly the Curse, which had torn his family apart in discussion alone. But he did want to see Katja, and was excited to talk about things in person.

That day, months ago, she'd texted him when the plane landed, and declared he should pick her up. She didn't really ask, she just told him what to do, and Alain didn't complain because his nature was filled more with indecision than argument.

The moment she got into his car, his heart stopped and he was very aware of the blush rising to his cheeks. She was, in a word, breathtaking. Resembling a queen of the North, an Alpine beauty, and a Swedish heiress all in one stunning package. Hair and skin like the blossom of a magnolia, blue eyes that radiated from perfect skin with a touch of pink in the cheeks.

Dear God. This was his cousin, and he needed to remember that.

"*God kväll*, cousin!" she'd declared, accompanied by a pat on his leg. When he didn't say anything in response, she laughed, and directed, "Well, shall we drive?"

Alain nodded and slowly looked ahead, realizing he still had said nothing. "Insert witty Swedish response here," he offered awkwardly, and put the car in drive.

"That's literally about all the Swedish I know," she admitted, tucking that soft white hair behind her tiny ears. As she swallowed, her milky neck ebbed slightly. "Well, I do know a few other things," she added slyly.

"I know some German," he mumbled. This was going to be a long night if he couldn't pull himself together. *Blood relative, Alain.*

"Ahh, *Guten abend!*" she exclaimed excitedly. In his peripheral he saw her clasp her hands together over her small mouth, smiling. "*Wie geht es dir?*"

Well shit, he thought. "Maybe I lied a little about knowing German."

"Fluent," she announced. "Also fluent in French and Japanese. *Konbanwa!*"

"Damn, Kat," he said, impressed, at the same time wishing she wouldn't make any more admissions that increased her unnatural attractiveness. "I wish my mother had pushed us into languages more."

"Yeah, yeah, but it's embarrassing that I'm half-Swedish, my dad was born and mostly raised there, and I only know how to say 'hello,' 'goodbye,' and 'tastes like chicken.'"

He laughed. "Does your mom speak Gaelic?"

She shook her head no.

"Apparently Grandma Colleen spoke it sometimes when they were growing up. My mom busts into it when she's pissed off."

"My mom starts solving quadratic equations," she revealed. "Gaelic, huh? Yet another language, of our own people, we don't know."

"Our people sort of suck."

"Sort of?" Katja joked. She started sifting through her saddlebag and pulled out Chapstick. He watched her apply it to her flesh pink lips and felt a chill run down his spine as the scent of strawberry wafted lightly. *This is why you need to get laid from time to time,* he could almost hear Tristan saying to him.

They made small talk for the rest of the drive. Alain had relaxed only slightly by the time they arrived at the lake. He pulled up to an abandoned park.

Leaving the car, he led the way down to the shoreline, settling in a grassy area near the knees of a Spanish moss-laden cypress. Katja sat next to him, and he got a wave of the heat radiating off her tiny frame. It was dark outside, and when he looked at his watch, he discovered it was past ten, though the humidity was still thick.

"This is nice," she said, leaning back on her hands. She tilted her head up and her long blonde hair cascaded freely, tickling the grass. He resisted the urge to reach out and touch it, but knew without doing so that it would feel like silk pulling through his fingers. Her eyes were closed and he could see every detail of her smooth skin in the moonlight. It was flawless, except for a tiny scar near the corner of her mouth.

"Yeah," Alain said, after a deep, steadying breath. "I found it by accident once, when I was a kid."

"Some accident," she responded. She removed her sweater then, to reveal a very thin, fitted camisole underneath. He was fairly sure she wasn't wearing a bra, but should be.

This was torture of the worst kind.

Katja pulled herself into a sitting position, facing Alain. The look she offered him was solemn.

"I've been trying the whole way here to figure out how to tell you this," she said. Her hands fidgeted in her lap, and she twisted a small silver ring around on her right hand.

"Tell me what?"

"First, you have to promise that, whatever you think of this, you won't think differently of me."

Oh, I already do, unfortunately, he thought, with rising regret. He felt the blood flood his face, and elsewhere, again. Shifting to bring one knee up nervously, he hoped she couldn't see. "Of course not."

Katja smiled, pushing her hair behind her ear. "Okay. You know I've been studying the family history." Alain nodded. "And I think I told you I've specifically been looking at ways we might be able to break this wretched Curse.

"Well," she continued, having paused only momentarily. "I think I found one."

He sat up straighter. In all his years of listening to his family rant about it, he had yet to hear anyone come up with a reasonable idea about how to fix it. "I'm listening."

She pulled a piece of laminated paper out of her satchel and laid it down in front of him. As she did, her blonde hair spilled over the front of her shirt and across her chest, forcing him to look away. "Have you ever wondered why we only have information starting from when the family came to New Orleans? Well, I went back beyond our New Orleans history, and looked at Brigitte and Charles' family trees. Or, the genealogist did, anyway. I found something sort of interesting." She started pointing to the top of the sheet. "Did you know Brigitte and Charles were first cousins?"

Alain shook his head. "No, but it doesn't surprise me. Doing it with your cousin wasn't exactly weird back then," he said, flinching at the irony.

"Actually," she corrected, with a touch of know-it-all in her voice, "you're thinking of further back. In the late 1800's, it was only common in rural areas that didn't have access to people outside their community. Charles and Brigitte both emigrated from Bordeaux." She started talking faster, growing more excited. "While it wouldn't have been illegal, it would have been morally frowned upon when they married. Which means it was either a secret, or they didn't care, right?"

She answered her own question. "Further back, it turns out their grandparents were brother and sister. And it continues a few more generations like that, from what we could find. We aren't sure because the records were spotty any further than that."

"I hope my future wife never hears this story," Alain said with a shudder.

Katja didn't laugh. "There's more. The biographer actually found some letters Brigitte wrote to her mother in France. They reveal all kinds of crazy shit, like the fact that apparently it was some big family disappointment she and Charles weren't closer relation than first cousins. Worse, she talked about how she wanted her daughter, Ophélie, to breed with her brothers Jean or Fitz, preferably Jean since he was the oldest and heir, but Charles absolutely forbade it." She pulled out copies of the letters, also laminated, and laid them in front of him.

"Good for him," Alain asserted, briefly scanning the letters, knitting his eyebrows. This was all incredibly disturbing, but she seemed less disturbed than excited.

"You would think so Alain, but here's the interesting thing. All this time we thought Brigitte was angry with Charles for what happened to Ophélie during the war, with the soldiers and abuse, right? Well as it turns out, the whole time she was actually angry with him over refusing to let his kids commit incest and carry on these disgusting traditions."

"Oh, come on. Even if all this incest stuff is true, there's no way Brigitte was more upset about failed inbreeding than her daughter being tortured and murdered."

"Of course she was upset about that," Katja countered. "She was still a mother, and Ophélie her only daughter. But she also bore the weight of the entire family's expectations on her shoulders. The whole reason she was chosen for Charles to begin with was that Charles had no sisters of his own. Everyone looked to her to carry on this important tradition. It had been going on for generations, maybe centuries. When Ophélie died, it was also a symbolic expression of her failure to deliver."

Alain frowned. "That's highly speculative at best."

"It would be if we didn't have Brigitte's letters to her mother, explicitly stating everything I just told you," Katja argued. "We have evidence of the close family inbreeding for generations, and Brigitte's own words voicing her distress over her failure. Unless you wanna go ask Jasper to channel her spirit, I think that's the most solid evidence we could ask for."

"But what about all those words about Charles 'paying the price,' and 'this midnight dynasty will fall' and stuff?"

"They make as much sense now as they did before. This family believed that in order to keep their bloodline strong, and to keep success in the family—remember, they were rich as all get out, even before they came to this country—they had to keep inbreeding. Not to mention all the crazy abilities Deschanels were gifted, which likely increase in strength with inbreeding. Charles was the odd man out, and believed they had come to the states to escape that crap and start a new life, a new destiny." She paused, catching her breath. Her throat throbbed with excitement, and small beads of sweat sat on her chest and the tops of her breasts. Alain wished she would calm down, for both their sakes. "And then Ophélie died. She was their only daughter, and their only chance at fulfilling the family destiny. Generations and generations of careful planning, broken, because of Charles going rogue. In Brigitte's eyes, any children produced from this line would only be further evidence of this failure."

The whole story was bizarre, but Alain had to admit any conclusion Katja had come to was probably not wholly wrong. Or at the very least, extremely well-researched. "Okay, so... what are you suggesting?" he asked.

Katja looked him square in the eyes. Her breasts shook slightly as she brought in a deep breath, and then placed her hand over his. He could smell the slight mint on her breath from the gum she'd been chewing earlier as she moved closer. "If Brigitte's only desire was for the family to continue tradition, then the family needs to... continue tradition."

"I don't follow."

She smiled and let out the breath she had been holding. "Yes, you do."

Alain thought maybe he did, but he couldn't quite believe she would even suggest such a thing. "No. I don't."

Katja sighed. She brought his hand up, and clasped it in both of hers. "We need to continue the family tradition by mating either first cousins, or brother and sister, together. Brigitte thought the family's ambitions died with her daughter, and so she cursed her descendants, whom she felt could never live up to what they'd created. I know it seems insane, but if the cessation of this tradition is what began the Curse, beginning it again should be the cure."

Yes... that's what he thought she might have meant. "You're serious?"

She clutched his hand tighter, eyes wild. "Alain, think about it! It makes sense. Nothing else has stopped it. We've gone generations far beyond the ones responsible for the crimes against Ophélie, and Brigitte can't really have meant for her family to completely end, right? She was waiting for someone to come along who would do the right thing—"

He pulled his hand away. "Katja, incest is *not* the right thing."

She was unperturbed. "Societally, no. Scientifically, the challenges only occur over multiple generations where autosomal recessive disorders, like cystic fibrosis for example, can suddenly start cropping up more aggressively because both parents are carriers. But we're a family of freaking *healers*, Alain! What's sickle cell anemia to a Deschanel?"

Alain was speechless.

"The fact is, Alain, I love my family. I love my brother especially, with all my fucking heart, and it kills me to see what he puts himself through, day in and day out, to fill a void he can't satisfy in any normal way. Tristan is the same. Amelia is the most amazing woman I know, and she'll never have children, out of fear. Nicolas—"

"Nicolas doesn't have children because he can't deal with people, not because of the Curse."

"...you. Me. Alain, you and I could do this. We could actually do this. We could break this Curse, and our loved ones could have the lives they deserve."

"You're insane!"

"The madness of the idea doesn't make it any less right," she insisted, not rising to his level of temper.

He put his hands up, frustrated, both pushing her away and blocking her unbelievable words. "Even if you're right, how could we ever tell anyone? How could we live with it? How could we function? What you're suggesting has a lot of damn holes in it, Kat."

"I didn't say it was ideal, I said it was a solution. A fix. A fix to something no one else in our family has ever figured out, until now." She touched his face, and he recoiled. "Alain, I don't want our family to keep living in fear. I want Markus to stop sleeping with skeevy jerks to fulfill himself, and for Tristan to stop having affairs with married women, bending his moral fiber. I want Amelia to have twelve children because she's so fucking awesome and if anyone should breed, it's her."

"How would our children go to school, or ever face anyone?"

"We could either move away, or even stay here. No one knows me. No one has to know we're cousins."

Alain snorted. "Please. The Deschanels are local celebrities. Everyone in Southern Louisiana makes it their business to know ours."

"And yet none of them know we're healers, telepaths, and empaths. Why do you think that is?" Katja tapped her chin, petulantly. "Oh, I know! We're professionals at controlling the flow of information, and always have been."

"Fine then. Even if we kept it a secret from the city, the family would know."

"The family would learn to live with it," she said angrily. "They would learn to live with it because you and I took one for the team and saved the family."

"This is some *Flowers in the Attic* bullshit, Katja!"

Katja rolled her eyes to the sky. "A work of fiction. And one you really shouldn't admit to people you've read if you want to be taken seriously in polite society."

Alain shook his head, inadvertently backing away again. "Even the ones who believe in the Curse would never understand or accept this. What you're suggesting is insane and could never, ever work in the real world."

She was frustrated with him, he could see it, but it didn't dull her determination. "Whether you're right or wrong, does it matter? As long as our loved ones could live without fear, wouldn't it be worth whatever they thought of us?"

Her point was valid; he would do nearly anything, and endure anything, to fix this problem in their family. But there had to be another way. "And what if you're wrong, Katja? What if we—uh, *do* this—and the Curse isn't broken? Then what? We would have committed incest, would have a child that could never function properly in society. Our family would never be the same. No, they'd be worse! You know I'm right."

"Alain, if I wasn't sure about this, I wouldn't be sitting in front of you suggesting it. I know the risks."

As crazy as her idea was, he believed *she* believed in it, and was fiercely determined to convince him. "And what of our children?" He couldn't believe he was actually asking her questions, as if this was even a serious discussion to be had. "Do they then have to mate? How long would this have to go on?"

For the first time that night, she looked unsure. "That part, I don't know yet. I don't know if we'd have to continue it, or if once would be enough. But even if we did have to carry on the tradition, then at least we could contain it on our line and, over time, figure out the best ways to handle it socially."

"It sounds to me like we would be getting rid of one problem only to take on another. What if you're wrong about genetic problems? What if they're worse than you think?" he demanded.

"I'm not," she said simply. "I'm a scientist in a family of scientists. I may not be sure about my feelings, but I am not confused about the facts.

"And Alain," she continued, "I'm not exactly jumping for joy over this either. But if there's anyone in this family I'd want to be in this situation with... it's you."

He blushed again, hating his inability to mask emotions. "You're my cousin and I just don't think about you like that!"

She pushed his arms down, and boldly placed a hand in his lap. "Don't you?"

He blushed even darker. He was hard as a rock. Had been since he picked her up. "You know you're pretty, Katja. Cousin or not, I'm still a man."

She placed both hands on his shoulders and climbed into his lap, straddling him. "A man who finds me attractive, could see past the burden of responsibility, and maybe actually enjoy this." She kissed him.

He abruptly shoved her off and she landed on her back in the grass. He saw the blaze in her eyes, and felt an equal fire stir within him. Without allowing himself further thought, he climbed over her, twined his hands in her hair, and kissed her.

"Fuck you, Katja," he said roughly, as he tugged at her shorts while she unbuttoned his jeans. He kissed her passionately, desperately, hating and loving every minute of it. She was right that he was attracted to her, and was wrong to exploit it, but he was letting her and letting himself.

"Yes," she whispered as he pinned her arms over her head. She bit his lip, drawing blood.

"Never again," Alain vowed, and then took her again moments later. He was going to hell, and so was she, but in this fucked up family, did it even matter?

Later that night, as he lay awake in his bed unable to sleep, with her at his side, he would remember that moment, and play it over, and over, and over again in his head. How differently things could have turned out...

"So now what?" he'd asked her on the drive to Louis Armstrong International. He wasn't sure if he was asking about the Curse, or about them, or both. He felt very unsure about so many things.

"Now we wait," Katja replied calmly. She touched her stomach. "You know, I never wanted kids. Curse aside, just never wanted them. No use for them with the things I wanted to do with my life. But now... now I'm sort of counting on one, you know?" She laughed but it wasn't the same excited one as earlier. Now she sounded resigned. Like a weathered adult. "To answer your question, Alain, we need to keep our heads clear and strong, hold our breaths for the next six weeks or so, and hope for the best."

"I can't believe this is happening," he mused, feeling more like he was watching the situation than floundering in the middle of it. He'd slept with his cousin. His *first* cousin. Multiple times. And it wasn't going to stop here. He didn't need her to tell him that, and he could try to convince himself it was for the Curse, but it was more than that. God help him.

"Believe it," she stated. "Life doesn't always turn out the way we expect it to, and sometimes that means improvising."

"Improvising is not the word I would use. We need to talk about what we're going to tell the family." He felt sick to his stomach now; the full weight of their actions hitting him fast. What if she did end up pregnant? What if what she suggested actually came to pass?

"One step at a time," she responded, sounding old and wise, like she knew exactly what she was doing. Yet he still heard the waver in her voice, and he realized she was staying calm and confident because she couldn't afford to doubt herself. Olivia once told him the reason she never cried was because she knew if she started she wouldn't be able to stop. Maybe it was a Deschanel thing, or perhaps a female thing. Katja seemed to know what she needed to do to keep her cool. He hoped he could do the same. It took many years for him to learn to control his temper—that terrible loss of control—and he feared what would happen if it somehow found a way back in.

ALAIN KNELT BY THE LAKE, AND VOMITED. IT WAS AS MUCH A physical release as an emotional one. Nothing could erase the memory of taking her. Not once, but many times, over the course of weeks, until they were sure she was with child. And even then, they hadn't stopped.

He loved her. He hated himself for it. There was no reprieve from this hell they'd created, together.

Alain let the cool freshness of the lake water run over his face one last time, and then stood, preparing to face the consequences of the decision he made by the lakeside, months ago.

OZ

*J*t was past midnight when Oz pulled his car up in front of his house on Seventh. The human inhabitants of the Garden District slept, but the night was alive with the trilling songs cicadas and other insects flying and buzzing around the banana leaves and magnolia blossoms. This, the witching hour, had always been Oz's favorite. He missed the days when he could lose himself to his thoughts, amidst the comforting lull of the sub-tropical jungle humming all around him.

By habit, his gaze traveled to the white porch across the street. Its owner's absence lay heavy upon his heart.

Since yesterday, the dream sequence was all he could think about. He'd stumbled home, exhausted, and there'd been no sleep to help dull his throbbing heart rate. Then this morning he'd shuffled to the office without even a shower and locked himself in his office for the duration of the day, feeling as if a lead weight was securing him to his chair, reminding him of the tremendous burden upon him.

You have to keep trying, Jacob had pleaded, once he realized Oz wasn't trying to molest his girlfriend.

I don't even know what I'm doing, Oz responded with a defensiveness that made him feel completely inadequate.

You will, Colleen assured him, in her usual, matter-of-fact way. Oz wished he could bottle even an ounce of that woman's confidence and consume it in moments like these.

And let's not forget the fact that apparently I have some incredibly rare supernatural skill my parents have always known about!

No, he wouldn't process that information. There wasn't any room for it in a mind already drowning with the weight of figuring out how to save his friend from herself.

Save her. *Save.* Four innocent letters, of which the sum of its parts bore tremendous power. All his life, Oz found ways of helping others in need. Nicolas called it his "tragic hero complex." But saving them? The difference between their physical survival, and the loss of life? Playing God?

He didn't ask for this responsibility. *But there it is, anyway,* he heard Amelia say.

Yes, there it was. And there it would remain, until he either succeeded, or failed at the cost of her life.

I have to go back. Not tomorrow. Tonight. I won't sleep until I've tried again.

Oz resolved to go in and change into something more comfortable. He hoped there were some clothes in the laundry room, as he didn't wish to wake Adrienne or the children.

As he loosened his tie, he saw Adrienne sitting on a barstool at the kitchen counter, her tired, drawn face lit by the tiny suspended lamp. All other lights in the house were off.

"Sweetie, why are you up?" he asked, tossing his briefcase on the kitchen table as he moved to embrace her.

"No particular reason," Adrienne replied, returning his hug. Her smile was one he'd known for many years; one she employed when troubled but trying desperately to hide it.

"Couldn't sleep, I guess." Her hands trembled in her lap, despite her efforts to squeeze them into submission.

"Tell me what's wrong," Oz pressed gently, taking a seat next to her.

Adrienne looked at him then, meeting his eyes for a long, heavy moment. In that instant, he thought she was about to confess something horrible. Something life-altering. Something bad enough to distract him from the business with Amelia. But then she said only, "I'm worried so much for my family right now."

Oz's heart melted at the sight of his wife's sadness, as it always had. Years ago, he would have crushed her into his arms, against his heart, and held her until the pain melted away. Now, he felt a distance between them when her sadness took over, and this gradual change was not one he consciously accepted. Only deep down, where he kept his darkest thoughts buried, would Oz ever understand his feelings for his wife had evolved. His innate need to protect her from the world hadn't waned, but the driving force behind that desire had shifted.

"Your family has seen more than its share of heartache," he comforted, placing a hand over hers. She said nothing, instead inspecting his hand.

"Aunt C called me today," Adrienne said, stifling a yawn. Her blue eyes were heavy with sleepiness. Oz suspected she was fibbing earlier about not being able to sleep. She had waited with a purpose. "She told me what you did for Amelia. This dreamwalking thing."

"Look, Ade, I was going to tell you—"

"Oz," she replied, smiling through her drowsiness. "I know you would have told me eventually. I only wanted to say thank you, and that I hope you'll keep trying. I don't know much about this so-called ability you have, or why. Maybe one day we can sit down and talk about it, but what I *do* know is you've always been my big hero. For over ten years. I'm more than happy to share my hero with someone I love. I hope you'll go back. That's all."

Oz didn't realize until that moment he'd been intentionally keeping this from his wife. Worried she might be jealous? Concerned? Not wanting to add more to her own perpetual stress? Possibly all of the above. Perhaps it was simpler. Maybe he wanted something for himself, to process and handle on his own, for once.

"I was actually going to change and go back now," he admitted. "I don't know if I can help her or not, but I couldn't live with myself if the possibility was there, and I didn't try."

"That's my Oz," Adrienne replied, smiling sweetly. She looked, in that moment, every bit the girl of sixteen he'd fallen desperately in love with. And, for a brief, split second, a conscious part of Oz realized how much his feelings for her had shifted.

And then it was gone.

"Now go change and get out of here. I think I really am tired, after all," she acknowledged with another large yawn.

WHEN OZ ARRIVED AT THE HOSPITAL, COLLEEN AND JACOB quietly excused themselves after a few tired pleasantries. This time, slipping into Amelia's dream state was easier. His sleepy mind was more susceptible to the surrender, and as soon as he began thinking about how desperately he wished to help her, the sterile room around him was gone, and he was standing in the middle of a street filled with loud, boisterous pedestrians. The scent of Guinness and wet cobblestones filled his nostrils.

Several young men stood together in the road, arms laced around each other in drunken sway, singing at the top of their lungs:

. . .

Come out, ye Black and Tans
Come out and fight me like a man
Show your wife how you won medals out in Flanders
Tell her how the I.R.A. made you run like hell away
From the green and lovely lanes in Killesahandra

LOOKING AROUND, OZ SAW BUILDINGS OF DEEP RED, GREEN, AND brown, with mastheads in broad Gaelic. The dank scent of water against stone. Signs for Temple Bar. *Dublin*, he realized. But where was Amelia?

He spotted her white hair up ahead, dangling over the arm of someone who was trying desperately to pull her back to her feet. As her head lolled back, Oz read the drunken laughter on her face, mouth hung open in a gleeful cry. Her savior was none other than Jacob, who was fighting between smiling and good-naturedly scolding her for her lechery.

Head still dangling over Jacob's arm, Amelia caught Oz's eye and winked. Oz broke out in a sprint toward her, but as her head came back up, both she and Jacob disappeared, as did the cobblestone streets, the bars, and the singing young men.

Now, he was in the backseat of a moving car. An uncomfortably tiny car, at that. The lane they drove down seemed no wider than the vehicle, and rolling green landscape passed by each window like waves. Scattered homes, and grazing livestock, were the only signs of life.

"When are you going to tell me where we're going?" Amelia probed Jacob, who drove with a stern, purposeful expression.

"We're almost there," Jacob replied, clearly dodging a more direct response to her question.

"Amelia," Oz spoke up. "Can you see me? Or hear me?"

She turned around in her seat, blinking indulgently. Now that he had a clear view of her face, he could see this was a much younger version of Amelia. Ten years, perhaps, back when she and Jacob were merely good friends. "Of course I can, Oz."

"Well, then is this a dream or a memory?"

"Both," she responded sadly. "Shh. Pay attention. We're here for a reason."

Oz reclined in his seat, biting back the remainder of his questions. Eventually, the landscape grew less sparse, and they came upon a tiny town. A village, more like. *Killianshire*, the sign read. *Population 950. Since 1339.*

Amelia and Jacob sat in the front seat, both quiet, both reflective. Oz attempted to pay attention, as Amelia requested, but he couldn't guess why they were here, or why it mattered.

The car slowed as Jacob pulled into a small cemetery. He drove through a gravel lane, past the older tombstones, and parked near a patch of graves that looked to be from the last century.

Amelia started to ask Jacob what they were doing, but he was already out of the car. Oz also climbed out, and saw the other man's eyes glistening as he beckoned Amelia to follow him.

Jacob knelt before a small gathering of headstones cornered together by a tired picket fence. He looked up at Amelia. "You once asked about my family. This is my family."

Together, Oz and Amelia took in the names on the head-stones, processing in unison: *Liam Donnelly, 1956-1986. Enid Donnelly, 1958-1986. Enoch Donnelly, 1970-1986. Maggie Donnelly, 1973-1986.*

Amelia silently put her hand out, and Jacob took it. Then, she knelt near him, as he said, "I was born here, Amelia. Not New Orleans. My father came home one day after losing his job and killed my mother, brother, and sister, and then took his own life. He shot me, too, and I almost died. I was ten." He raised his shirt up and revealed a small, round scar inches from his heart. She gasped and reached out to touch it, but stopped. Jacob took her hand and brought it to his chest.

"Jacob…"

"My mother had no people, and my father had only a sister in Dublin who wanted nothing to do with him. When she learned what happened, she came to the hospital to see me through my rehabilitation, then let me stay at home with her and her family long enough to arrange for me to live elsewhere. When I was well enough, she shipped me off to the states, to an orphanage, and that's where I was raised. In the Irish Channel."

As Oz observed this powerful exchange, he realized he was witnessing a memory important enough to Amelia that she bottled it up, allowing herself to escape here, in her turmoil. He still didn't know what it meant, or why she wanted him to watch, but it mattered. He understood that much.

"All this time, I've been crying to you about my family, and you've been through so much," Amelia lamented, shaking her head. "I'm so sorry, Jacob."

"How could you know? I didn't tell you. Didn't want you to know. At first it was because you had this amazing family, raised in a good home, and I was ashamed of where I came from. But later, once I knew you, it felt unfair to put this on top of your family's pain."

"That's—"

Jacob cut her off. "Then I realized you've been very brave to let me in on your family secrets, and I hadn't returned that trust. And I want to. I want to share this with you." Jacob took both of her hands in his. Both stopped trembling as they joined together. "Amelia, I want to share *everything* with you."

"Me too," Amelia responded quietly. She leaned in to kiss him, gasping at the moment of connection. "Marry me," she added, impulsively.

Oz's heart stopped at the gravity of the exchange before him, and for a moment he forgot he was observing something that had happened years ago.

Jacob laughed. "Silly *Blanca*, we haven't even dated." He wiped the tears from her cheek with his thumb.

"Really? Because I feel like the last year has been the most intimate of my entire life," Amelia replied, wiping his tears in return.

"Yes," Jacob replied, "I will marry you. I just wish you'd let me do the asking. It's a bit emasculating. I had a ring and everything, you know."

"In that case, I hope you won't be too emasculated when I ask you to take me to the nearest inn, promptly," Amelia challenged, sniffling.

Jacob's entire face lit up, and he opened his mouth to speak, but nothing came out.

"Donnelly, do try and look as if you've been laid at some point in the last two years," Amelia teased.

Jacob's eyes twinkled as he said finally, "Emasculate me, woman."

The landscape shifted once more and Oz was back in The Gardens. But he didn't need to search for Amelia this time. He already sat next to her in the gazebo.

"How did you do that? I thought you couldn't leave?" Oz asked.

"We've been here all along," she said. "I can show you the places I'm allowed to escape, briefly, but I'm tethered here."

"Why did we go there? Why did you show me that?" Oz pressed in desperation, feeling a strong pull toward waking. He wasn't ready, not yet, but he didn't know if he could control it to that extent...

"I don't know," she confessed. "My mind has been going back to that memory constantly since I slipped under. I feel like my brain is trying to protect me in some way, but I'm so tired, Oz.

Exhausted. Is that weird, to be tired when my body has been doing nothing but resting for a week?"

"I don't think I have much time left," Oz said. "Why is that memory important to you? Think. If it means something, the answer has to be somewhere in there."

"Isn't it obvious?" Amelia replied with a dejected sigh. "It was the moment I bound Jacob to me forever, promising him a life better than the one he'd been born into. Of course, in the end, I broke his heart."

"He loves you, Amelia."

"I know he does," she replied, looking down at her hands. "And look where that got him. After all this time, he has to sit and watch someone else he loves die."

Tears poured down Amelia's face as she sat shaking and sobbing in her big, frilly white dress amongst the bright wood-work of the gazebo. As he did the last time, Oz gathered her in his arms, letting the remainder of their time together be spent giving her some measure of comfort.

Oz awoke with a start. Colleen and Jacob were still mercifully gone, so it was only him and Amelia. He was afraid to look at her, for he now felt partially responsible for why she remained in this state. But he did look. And he saw the same tears from the gazebo, glistening on her cheeks.

His heart seized in his chest, as he reached a hand out and pressed it against her face. A soft shudder ran through her.

"I will save you, Amelia. No matter what it takes. I promise."

MARKUS

"It's nearly six. We're going to be late," Markus said as gently as he could, which was not very gentle at all.

"I want my father," Tristan protested into his pillow, a position he'd been in, in some form or the other, for days.

The room around them was filled with Elizabeth's things. This had been her room; not the one she shared with Uncle Connor, but the other, where she escaped when reality was too troubling. Why Tristan chose it to grieve was baffling to Markus, as it represented the place where she was at her worst.

"I told you, he isn't here," Markus replied, tugging on Tristan. He might as well have been tugging on a two-ton weight. "Everyone is expecting us in ten minutes. Aunt C is going," he added, hoping that might make a difference.

"She shouldn't, with Amelia on her deathbed!"

"Or perhaps she should for that very reason," Markus said, refusing to let the sight of Tristan's grief pull him down. Strength is what his cousin required, not commiseration. Markus' father, Johannes, was known as "The Unshakeable Swede," a nickname Markus was likely to inherit as he continued to mature. "What happened to your mom sucks, T, but there are other people in this family who matter to us. We have to figure out how to help them."

"You can do it without me," Tristan mumbled.

"Come on, son," Connor's voice called from the doorway. Tristan's red, splotchy face peeked up from the pillow, and Markus finally had to look away. No matter how he tried to be resolved and useful for his cousin, he couldn't erase the stark reality of the event that brought them to this moment. And if he were in this position, rather than Tristan, he wasn't confident he'd be so unshakeable anymore.

When Tristan seemed frozen to the bed, Connor did the most bizarre thing. He lifted his son from the bed, into his arms, and held him, rocking him as if he were a child, and not a fully grown man.

Markus knew this tender interlude was not for him, and he moved to leave, when Connor mouthed over his son's shoulder, *We'll meet you there.*

With a nod, he left.

THOUGH HE WAS ALREADY RUNNING LATE, MARKUS DECIDED TO walk to The Gardens, needing some air before being forced to sit in a crowded room full of frazzled relatives for hours. He supposed the Deschanel Magi Collective meeting was necessary, but it didn't mean he would enjoy it.

The rest of his nuclear family would be there, arriving separately. They'd scattered themselves all over New Orleans, rather than staying together. His parents were with Aunt Maureen. Not their first choice, but Aunt Colleen had been too distracted for guests, and Maureen was horrified at the suggestion they might instead grab a room at the Monteleone. Katja was staying with Alain, at his apartment in the Warehouse District, which made zero sense to Markus, but that fit well with his view of his sister in general, lately. It was as if he didn't know her at all, these past few months.

There was never a question Markus would stay with Tristan and Connor. Tristan needed him. He needed someone who could support him without the histrionics Tristan was used to from his mother, or the occasional-involvement-occasional-detachment support his father typically provided. Markus wouldn't say it out loud, but he was afraid for Tristan right now.

He walked down the upturned sidewalks of The Garden District, thinking of how different his life might have been had he grown up here, and not D.C. Life moved faster back home. Even in their large Alexandrian brownstone, he could rarely hear the sounds of tiny life outside his window. Conversely, when walking down St. Charles, even with cars going by, he could hear everything. Back home, they had politicians and intrigue. Here, they had banana leaves, bougainvillea, and heat reminiscent of the tropics. Thinking of his pale skin, he knew he wasn't made for this, but a part of him craved it, deeply.

A young couple approached, and Markus quickly, without thinking, sent them a subliminal thought: *This man blends in. Don't look at him.* This was how his illusions always worked. He didn't change his outward appearance, but rather, manipulated the way the world saw him. Now the action was so habitual he sometimes looked back and wondered why he'd bothered. Like this couple. What did it matter if they saw him as he really was?

But the answer required a reposing of the question: Who *was* Markus, really?

He wasn't sure he even knew anymore, if he ever had. Since he was a child, he'd thrown up walls of suggestion, intending for others only to see someone transient, and nonexistent. Any friends he'd made were friends of whoever he projected himself to be: the young Italian lover. The inscrutable book nerd. The callous jock. Once, he even pretended to be the object of his friend's crush, after she'd been heartlessly rejected by the real one. Another time, he lost a bet with Katja and was forced to walk around as Pope John Paul II for an entire day, blessing people's babies and feeding the poor. Homeschooling, and later a large college campus, gave him the freedom to be anyone. He chose to be everyone except Markus Gehring.

Approaching The Gardens, he caught the hum of conversation. Cousins, aunts, uncles all hovered on the steps, in the garden, around the porch. Talking, buzzing, in low, hushed voices.

One of his cousins broke away from the pack and jogged down the flagstone path, out the gate toward him. "Markus," Nicolas said, placing a hand on his shoulder. Nicolas, who'd never been an active part of the family, despite being the heir, was now one of the seven Collective Council leaders, walking around to greet his relatives.

How times had changed.

"Connor and Tristan will be here shortly," Markus replied, scanning the huddled masses. His parents weren't in sight, but he saw Katja standing on the porch, flanked by Alain. The latter had his hand at the small of her back, in a mindless gesture, then dropped it. Something about the protectiveness of the touch made Markus uncomfortable, but before he could sort it out, Nicolas was talking again.

"Everyone is here, pretty much. Jacob and Noah stayed with Amelia, so Aunt C could feel comfortable leaving for a few hours," Nicolas explained, with a few awkward shrugs. This role of leader and guide didn't suit him well, and it further emphasized Markus' vague sensation of having stepped into an alternate universe.

Nicolas continued, "Your mother is already in with Aunt C. Your father is wandering around, somewhere. I think we're about ready to get started."

Markus nodded, following his cousin, but his eyes didn't leave his sister and Alain. As he passed through the gate, Katja turned to look at him. Her eyes were wide, but lacking clear expression, and as she shifted, hand on her belly, Alain's solicitous touch returned.

Markus didn't hear anything Nicolas was yammering on about, for he'd finally realized what was bothering him about Katja and Alain. *It's the way he's touching her.*

Like a protective lover.

COLLEEN

*T*he long, formal dining room of The Gardens had never been so full of life. *Over a hundred,* Anne had dutifully come back with, when Colleen sent her off to do a headcount. A hundred! The Deschanels had never shown this much interest in family affairs.

Nearly all those present were afraid. Elizabeth wasn't the only death. Young Rene Guidry, Pansy's son, drowned two days earlier in the Pontchartrain after hitting his head when falling from a boat. He was barely nineteen. Then that morning, at the age of sixty-four, Broussard patriarch Cassius passed peacefully in his sleep, healthy as a horse. The family had predicted for years Cassius would outlive them all. Somehow, his death was even more shocking than young Rene's.

Colleen knew it wouldn't stop there. Elizabeth's visions had been horrifying enough to send her to her death. She wouldn't have given her life predicting the death of a Guidry cousin, or a Broussard. Only the loss of someone very dear to her heart would have driven her to such lengths. And that list was terrifyingly short.

Elizabeth wasn't the only one with visions. Colleen had

fielded call after call the past two weeks, cousins insisting terrible things were on the horizon, and the family needed to band together. The calls, emails, and visits peaked the day Elizabeth died, and Colleen, finally, called the family together.

As Colleen watched her many cousins huddled together, in small groups, comparing their notes and sharing grief, she pondered whether or not she had acted too late. Should she have called the family together sooner? Would it have made a difference?

"Stop torturing yourself, Leena," Evangeline scolded softly, wrapping her arms around her waist. *My dearest sister. My strength. I cannot get through this without her.*

"I'm not," Colleen lied, and craned her neck back to plant a gentle kiss on her sister's cheek. "You know how my mind races through the possibilities. Knowledge has never stopped any of this before."

"Elizabeth's visions were a curse all their own," Evangeline said, in a low voice. Her hair, typically wild and unchecked, lay strangled in a bun at her neck. Small, wiry tendrils peeked through, threatening to break free in revolt. This very nearly brought a smile to Colleen's face.

"I know," Colleen agreed. "You're right. What good is knowing the future when you cannot stop it?"

A formidable man, slightly younger than Colleen but nearly a foot taller, approached with heavy steps and expression. "It's time," Luther Fontenot intoned, offering a tight smile.

"Of course," Colleen concurred, going through the steps of mentally steeling herself. "Do you think they'll all fit?" she added, gesturing toward the waiting open door.

"They will," Evangeline replied with a flip of the wrist. "It's always felt like we were drowning in there. The room was made for an event like this. Maybe, for once, it will feel as it should."

"Nothing right now feels as it should," Colleen replied, and then nodded at Luther. "Go ahead and inform the ushers."

. . .

THE HUM AND BUZZ OF THE ROOM DIED TO A LOW DIN AS THE Deschanels filed into the second dining area. For some, it would be the first time, as the room was normally open only to Deschanel Magi Collective members. But in a time of crisis, meetings could be called to include non-members, and this was only the second-such meeting in all of Colleen's fifty-four years.

Markus, along with Remy Fontenot, Luther's son, acted as ushers, helping people find appropriate seats. The long table that spanned the length of the vast room was reserved first for the seven Council leaders, and then for the remainder of the Collective. Chairs, settees, and several cast iron garden benches were brought in to accommodate the influx of family members joining for the first time tonight.

All meetings could be this size, Colleen thought, as she watched the room slowly fill. *But so many choose the bliss of ignorance.*

Those who graced the velvet high-backed chairs sat with stoic faces, registering their shock, grief, and fear in a private way. For the newcomers, their attentions were drawn to the past magistrate portraits lining the edges of the tall ceilings, above the room-wrapping bookcases. Colleen's image would one day be among them, when her tenure was over and the role was passed to another. *I always envisioned it would be Amelia to take my place,* she thought, with an inward sigh.

When at last all were settled, Luther nodded to Remy, who closed the heavy oaken door and locked it.

"For our secrecy only," Colleen assured the shocked faces of those lined up against the bookshelves, suspicion written clearly on their faces, amongst the other emotions warring for dominance. "Nothing uttered in this room, leaves this room."

"Who would we tell, honestly?" Olivia piped up with a subdued annoyance. Her husband, Greg, sat at her side, staring at his feet with great interest. "The entire town already thinks we're complete nut jobs."

"A lot is discussed here that you aren't privy to," Evangeline scolded her lightly. "We have our traditions, and you are a guest. You're welcome to leave now, before the vows are said, but once we begin, you cannot leave until we all do." She looked around the room. "This goes for everyone."

Mumbling and shuffling filled the room, but no one moved toward the door.

Colleen drew in a deep breath, looking around the room at all the faces of her cousins, lit only by sconces, and candlelight from the chandelier. A story she once read, a biography of King Louis XVI of France, came to her. On the eve of the French Revolution, he, Marie Antoinette, and their children huddled in darkness and secrecy, living a life as outcasts rather than royalty. The Deschanels were no royalty, and no angry mobs awaited them, yet they stood on the precipice of destruction they'd somehow wrought on themselves.

"Repeat after me," Colleen began, folding her hands before her on the table. "In power, obligation," she paused, waiting for the room to repeat the vow back. "In obligation, commitment. In commitment, solidarity. In solidarity, enlightenment," she went on, pausing between each tenet to allow the room to repeat it back. Finally, she intoned, "And the Council also lives under governance, through enlightenment," as her fellow Council leaders repeated the final vow.

"Well then," she began. "A bit of housekeeping, to orient those of you who are new here tonight. The cousins wearing a crimson sash are Collective members. They all know our rules, and can answer basic questions should you have them. The seven of us wearing the crimson sash with gold inlay, however, are Council leaders. If you cannot see the whole room that would be: Luther, Evangeline, Pansy, Jasper, Nicolas, Imogen, and myself, finally, as magistrate. Imogen has only recently joined our ranks, replacing our beloved Elizabeth."

The room filled with mumbled utterances of blessings for Elizabeth's soul. Imogen smiled tightly. Colleen empathized it must be an additional burden for her to carry, being brought in under such circumstances.

"We ask," Colleen continued, "that you direct most of your questions to us, your Council. We are best equipped to guide you. We also ask that, whatever your particular ability might be, you don't exercise it in here. It will only cause unnecessary confusion, and distraction. Especially you fire elementals. There's an awful lot of paper in this room." She attempted that last as a joke, to lighten the growing tension, but everyone's expressions remained fixed, and stoic. "Finally, I also request that while all of us undoubtedly have much to say, we respect each other, and allow one voice at a time."

"Enough with the formalities!" Kitty Guidry exclaimed. "Can we talk about how to stop the rest of our family from dropping like dadgum flies?" Murmurs of assent rose from the perimeter of the room.

"Patience," Luther commanded, but Colleen patted his hand and fixed her gaze on Kitty.

"That's why we're here," Colleen agreed, smiling. "But if you came with the expectation we had answers, I'm afraid you'll be disappointed. We brought everyone together today because, quite simply, we have none. However, we're a resourceful clan, and together, perhaps we can come up with something our ancestors did not. This meeting has been a long time coming."

Kitty opened her mouth as if preparing another wisecrack, but then closed it again. A look of exhaustion overcame her, one that matched most of the room. "Where do we start?"

"At the source," Evangeline replied. "Elizabeth left the diaries of Julianne and Ophelia to Tristan. Tristan then passed them to the Council. All seven of us have been studying them, looking for anything which might tell us more about Brigitte, or her Curse." She then tossed a playful eye-roll at Nicolas. "Well, six of us, anyway."

"Hey, I told you I don't read anything without pictures," Nicolas responded with a light shrug.

"Maybe this all has nothing to do with Brigitte. It's probably more to do with this ridiculousness about our Empyrean heritage," Antoine Guidry interjected. His mother, Pansy, showed her first signs of life that evening by raising a quick finger, presumably to silence him.

"Empyrean? What the hell is this nitwit talking about?" Olivia asked.

"It's nothing we're ready to share with non-members," Colleen replied, with a reminder glance to the room. "We're here to discuss the Curse tonight. If any of you find membership is something you desire, we can talk after this meeting and work toward accomplishing that. For now, we must uphold our vows, and stick to the subject at hand."

"Everything we have suggests Brigitte was a loving mother," Evangeline steered the meeting back on track. "She was understandably angry at her husband, but she couldn't possibly have wanted everyone in this family to suffer for generations upon generations. Her love for her daughter makes no sense otherwise."

"Then why would she put this on us?" Tristan cried, voice cracking. The poor boy's eyes were rimmed in bright red. Connor's hand drummed methodically against his son's knee, in comfort.

"She's probably laughing at what fucking idiots her descendants turned out to be," Leander, Jasper's son, mumbled, loud enough for most of the room to hear. He crossed his arms, slumped down in his chair. Leander was normally a helpful member, and so Colleen tempered her annoyance by remembering he'd lost his grandfather that morning.

Tristan scowled at him. "Why are you here if you're just going to be a cynical asshole?"

Leander responded by pointing a thumb in his father's direction.

"There's zero point in arguing," Evangeline said sensibly. "And at this point, anyone who doesn't want to talk about this should keep their thoughts private, because we're not here to debate the realities, only to solve to them. You had an opportunity to leave."

There were more nods and agreements from around the room, but Maureen stood up. "We have a right to our opinions too, Evie. You might have an expensive degree, but it doesn't make you the authority on everything."

Colleen had to bite her tongue at her sister's outburst. Maureen's presence tonight was as irritating as it was surprising. She was unwilling to learn anything new, making decisions based on emotions. Logical response would be lost on her, and her emotional outbursts would delay them further.

"Maureen," Evangeline said, soothingly, "you also have a right to your beliefs. But our sister, Elizabeth, is dead. Our dear cousins, Rene and Cassius, are also gone. Our beloved niece, Amelia, may never regain consciousness."

At this, poor Ashley buried his face in his hands, and a small wind gathered at his feet. Colleen had one hand on his shoulder, the other resting against the table. *Calm yourself, my son. Your storm the night Amelia went into the hospital was enough.*

Luther added, "This is not a time to re-open old debates. We need to find a way to prevent this from happening to anyone else."

Ashley surprised everyone by speaking up. "Amelia wouldn't want us to fight," he said, his voice wavering. The wind near his feet subsided, but a small, noticeable breeze passed through the room. "I don't know what to believe anymore," he went on, "but I know I wouldn't wish this on any of you." He looked around the room. The expression on his face was enough to melt even the coldest heart. "So if it means listening to what they have to say, and doing whatever it is they say we have to do, I'll do it, on the remote chance they might be right and we can stop this." He caught his breath, unable to say more. Colleen watched him struggle to restrain his inner elementalist.

"Ashley's right," Nicolas chimed in. "I still don't know what I believe, but I'm tired of watching family members drop every time the weather changes. I care about the well-being of everyone here tonight. Even you, Aunt Mo."

Maureen looked away with a scowl, but said nothing.

"Does anyone know exactly what Brigitte said that night?" Markus asked.

"I have it here, though I'm sure many of us have it memorized by now," Colleen said. After pulling up the entry from Julianne's journal, she read it aloud: "*There is a price and Charles and his children will pay it. As will their children, and their children, and all children who attempt to profit from anything Charles has built. This midnight dynasty will fall, as Ophélie fell, and there will be no more. This I promise, on my mother, and on my beloved Ophélie.*"

Leander snorted. "Sounds pretty cut-and-dry to me."

"Of course it is, and we've rehashed this many times now," Jasper said. "No matter how many times we read it, it still doesn't sound like she was interested in negotiating. And I speak from years of experience when I say confidently that dead people don't continue to experience emotional growth the way live ones do," he added in earnest.

"We can't go back in time," Markus added. "But it seems to me the only fix for this is reversing the actions of the past or speaking to Brigitte. Since we can do neither, it seems we're at an impasse." Nods and murmurs of agreement.

"Indeed. I've tried," Jasper agreed. "Unlike our priestess, Marie Laveau, Brigitte seems unwilling or unable to be reached from beyond."

Leander slumped lower in his chair, horrified.

Alain stood abruptly, causing everyone nearby to adjust. Colleen's eyes scanned toward her shy blonde nephew who stood huddled in the corner, shoulders poised at odds with his fearful face.

His eyes darted across the room toward a very nervous Katja, who wore the panicked look of someone who would take a bullet before she allowed Alain to say even one word. The rest of the room sat silent, watching the nervous, nonverbal exchange between the two cousins.

Colleen's heart surged as she realized there was something critical, something absolutely imperative, going on. Something terrible.

Nothing amiss at all? she'd asked Evangeline, little more than a week ago.

Well, maybe you can tell me? She's traveled back to New Orleans four times in the past three months, Colleen. Has she seemed strange to you?

Katja? In New Orleans?

Alain said, quietly, "What if the answer isn't what we think?"

ADRIENNE

hile the rest of the family gathered in The Gardens' formal dining area, and Oz vigilant at Amelia's bedside, Adrienne stayed home with her children. Oz's mother would have happily watched the kids, but, knowing what she knew about her future, every moment with them was precious. It was a comfort being in their presence, even if they were simply off playing by themselves.

Naomi sat at the dining table drawing, while Christian was outside in the garden cataloguing plants for his cub scout troop. Adrienne longed to curl up with them both, blocking out the world while she breathed in their soft baby scents, and memorized the way their skin felt under her hands. But time was running out, and she had one chance to get this right. To give them a way to go on without her, and maybe even thrive.

When she heard the knock at the door, her heart leapt, and she quickly asked Naomi to go outside and play with her brother.

Big sigh, as Naomi dramatically flipped her dark curls behind her, with one tiny hand. "*Okay*, Mama."

Adrienne watched her scamper out the back door, and then turned toward the business at hand.

A curvy, blue-eye-shadowed blonde, not much older than Adrienne, stood on the porch. *She looks just like her mama, Pansy.* "Hi, Lougenia. Thanks for coming over."

Lougenia Guidry stepped through the doorway without waiting for an invite. Her big, wide eyes took in the sights around her, as she struggled in her six-inch heels. "This's a lot nicer than Mama said it was!" she exclaimed, apparently forgetting Adrienne was standing there. "How much y'all pay for this?"

Adrienne gracefully dodged the question, her expression turning solemn. "I'm so sorry to hear about what happened to Rene."

Lougenia waved her hand with an emphatic eye roll. "That cooyon was nevah right in the head. Fool even came outta the womb sideways. Fallin' off his own dang boat. Surprised he made it this long, hand-to-God."

Adrienne blinked at Lougenia's callous reception of her brother's passing. "Well how's your mama and 'em?"

"Oh, they jus' fine," Lougenia replied, still perusing the items in the room with little reserve. She picked up vases, turning them over, as if looking for an indicator of cost. "Mama's up in her important meetin' tonight, which y'all should be at too. Me, I ain't fixin' to waste my time listenin' to folks who think they important." She flashed a blue and gold vase at Adrienne. "Y'all got this at Ross, dincha?"

Adrienne bit her tongue, reminding herself Lougenia was a guest in her house... she invited her. She needed her. "No, I don't believe so," she replied, taking a deep breath to avoid making a scene. "So, about this 'transference.' Do you have to be in the room with the target—"

"Didja wire the money yet?" Lougenia interrupted as she set the vase down. She turned and looked at Adrienne, all business.

"Not that I don't trust ya or nothin', but I ain't fixin' to take chances neither."

"No, but I made the arrangements. I can't actually do it while I'm living, or it'll raise a lot of questions I'm not prepared to answer," Adrienne explained, wincing at how strange it felt to talk about her own death with such detachment. She handed Lougenia a manila envelope. "You'll find the documentation is all there."

Lougenia slipped the paperwork out, widened her eyes, then slid it back in. "I'm gonna have to trust ya, cousin, because this ain't nothing but a load a Greek to me." Narrowing her eyes, she studied Adrienne closely, scrutinizing. "You really dyin'?"

"Yes, I am," Adrienne said, wondering if simply requesting Oz do as she asked might have been easier than convincing her ridiculous cousin to help her persuade him. "And I really need to get this all sorted before I do." Quickly losing patience, she allowed her annoyance to steel the words.

"Ah'right, let's talk," Lougenia agreed and flopped down in an armchair. "So, what, you want me t'convince your man and some girl they should do the nasty?"

"Something like that," Adrienne frowned. Her heart sank as she watched the woman who sat in front of her, realizing her faith in Lougenia's ability to pull this off was negligible at best. But time was running out, and if the family seers hadn't started figuring out something was amiss with Adrienne, they soon would. "Look, this is a big deal to me. It's serious, and if you're not sure you can handle it, I need to know now."

Lougenia waved an overly-manicured hand at Adrienne, and crossed her legs. "I'd a done it for free. But, you see my husband got himself… well, nevermind. It ain't here nor there. You're family and you're in need, and I can help."

The tension, wound tightly throughout Adrienne's tiny frame, eased slightly. "So, tell me about transference. How does it work?"

"Weellll... you see, *transference* is what Miss Colleen likes to call it, with her fancy naming and whatnot, but I call it 'plantin' seeds.' Take that officer the other night'as an example. Wanted to ticket me for jus' taking a corner a smidge faster than the law allows. Well, I planted a few seeds in his head right then, and wouldn't ya know, he no longer wanted to ticket me?"

"So, you convinced him to let you go?" Adrienne affirmed.

"Didn't even hafta flash him the girls," Lougenia said proudly, crossing and re-crossing her legs. "But I do that kinda stuff all the time! That's easy. Little seeds are nuthin'."

"What about big seeds?" Adrienne probed. Her heart rate escalated once again, as she inched closer to the moment she would either take this path, or abandon it. "What's the biggest you've done?"

Lougenia leaned forward, her knees and elbows blending into one big salad of tanned limbs, as her bangle bracelets clanged together. "How'dya think I landed a man like Beau Frederick?"

Adrienne *had* always wondered about that. Beau was a local oil baron, from Saint Bernard Parish. Proud, distinguished. He was everything the Guidrys were not. And most importantly, "Wasn't he married when you met him?"

"Well, they were big seeds," Lougenia replied, with a knowing shrug.

Adrienne considered this news. "So, if it isn't too personal of a question, how does he feel about you now? I guess what I'm asking is—"

"You wanna know how deep dem seeds go, dontcha?" Lougenia asked with a wide beaming smile. "Let's just say I ain't hearin' any complaints, if you catch my drift."

Adrienne nodded, hoping Lougenia wouldn't elaborate. "I need you to..." she paused. Once she said it, would there be any going back? The words held a tremendous power. They'd danced in her head now for days, and once she voiced them aloud, they would transcend from theory to reality.

"You neeeeeed?" Lougenia repeated, leaning further forward.

I'm dying. I am actually going to die, and that won't change. It will happen whether I find the courage or not, so I must prepare my family. Sitting straighter, she said, "I want to leave Oz whole." No point in explaining what that really meant... how deep those words ran. Lougenia needed only enough to do what was asked of her. "He's been through a lot in the past decade, and I'm afraid my dying will destroy him." *Oh, what a presumptuous thought! How indulgent, to think I mean that much to him. But yet...* "If I asked him to move on, he'd never do it. But moving on, with someone healthy... someone who could love him, but also love my children, and raise them in the ways of the Deschanels..."

Lougenia nodded thoughtfully, rapping her long nails against the lamp table. "You want me to convince your man he loves someone else, then."

"More than that," Adrienne pressed on. This next part, for some reason, felt like an even bigger betrayal than the one she was forcing on Oz. "I need you to convince her that she loves him as well."

"That shouldn't be a real chore. Medium seeds, I think," Lougenia replied. "Who's the lucky girl?"

Please don't let this be what makes her say no. "Amelia. Our cousin," Adrienne answered, after a deep breath.

Lougenia frowned, and re-crossed her legs once more. "Ain't she with that Irish kid? Not that it's gonna stop the show, but bigger seeds might be needed."

"Not anymore," Adrienne answered. Oh, but was it the truth? Was it really? After a decade of devotion, a spat between Amelia and Jacob didn't necessarily spell out a permanent sundering of all they'd shared. Adrienne could justify leaving Oz whole, because she was causing his void to begin with. But was this fair to Amelia, who had always been so good to Adrienne?

"Well, I may still need bigger seeds, but it's okay though," her cousin responded, thinking. "You don't have to tell me or nuthin', but can I ask why you'd wanna see your man move on the second you kick the bucket? If I die, I'll be plantin' seeds from the beyond if I see Beau even *eyein'* a skank!"

"It's complicated," Adrienne said, and boy was that the truth! After all she'd put Oz through… first, when she was young, and then later, leaving him, toying with him. Putting his life on hold, and forcing him into a marriage he only half-wanted. Oz's passions went far deeper, far more intense, than an emotional fling with Adrienne had ever been able to fulfill. She'd given him moments. Big, powerful moments, but short ones. Bursts of life.

Seeing Oz with Amelia, a woman who was his contemporary, strong, mature, and thoughtful, reminded Adrienne of the woman she had hoped she would become, with time.

But she never did. And now, never would. Instead, she'd wasted Oz's prime years by placing him where he was too afraid to leave, and even more afraid to stay and confront reality. In her mind's eye, she pictured a future for Oz where he was happy to come home, with a wife who could be his equal rather than his ward. The complete family he'd always dreamed of, and never had, not really.

Maybe it's true after all, about my family being cursed.

"Well I ain't fixin' to get up in ya business. If this is what ya want, all I need is some time alone with each of 'em, and I'll take care of it," Lougenia said, with surprising warmth.

"How much time?"

"It depends on whether you want them seeds to grow all gradual like, or BAM, right away."

"How much control do you have over the speed? Do these seeds, um, have half-lives? I mean, could you plant some seeds now, and have it kick in all the way when I'm… well, when I'm gone?" Adrienne asked.

"Why, yes, I can do that. But that means he'll be lookin' at her all starry-eyed while you still breathin', so might wanna think real hard about whether that's what you want."

"It is," Adrienne said, in a rush of courage, though she was not sure at all. But she had no time to ponder, or weigh the options. This was her one chance to protect her family from the hurricane her death would rip through it. "When can you start?"

"How about now?"

"Now?" Adrienne's heart skipped.

"Well, ain't no busybody Deschanels around to stop us."

"But Jacob is there, at the hospital, with them…"

"So? All he gon' see is me bent over Amelia prayin' for the salvation o'her soul. And maybe prayin' about what a good man Oz is for being such a good friend and all that. Girl, I know what I'm doin'."

"You're really okay with this?" Adrienne probed, not sure whether she was stalling, or shocked this had been so easy.

"I told you how I got my husband," Lougenia reminded her. "'Sides, no matter how big these seeds are, they ain't gon' take hold unless there's already a foundation. And I'm guessin' you've seen potential and that's how you chose her, am I right?"

Adrienne nodded. The realization that, deep down, there was a foundation between Oz and Amelia weighed heavy on her heart. And it hurt.

"Then, I see this as Mother Nature jus' speedin' things up," Lougenia explained, then stood. "Now, let's do this cuz' I got shows to watch."

AN HOUR LATER, ADRIENNE SLOGGED BACK INTO THE HOUSE SHE'D called home for the past five years, drained entirely of anything resembling energy, or desire, to go on.

For whatever remained of Adrienne's life, she would not ever be able to let go of the images of Oz wrapped around Amelia's fading form as he, honorably, did exactly what she had asked of him. But yet, for a few moments after they entered the room, Oz's embrace was merely dutiful. Though Lougenia said the seeds would be gradual in taking root, Adrienne was positive she could pinpoint the precise moment when Oz's arms tightened around Amelia's chest, and his face pressed deeper into her neck. The beginning of real affection.

Adrienne dropped her purse and keys in the middle of the floor without stopping, moving straight toward the children's room. Solange, who lived nearby and was flexible about providing occasional help, watched the children while she was gone, and had efficiently tucked them off to bed. She kept the light off, and moved first toward Naomi's bed, gently scooping her into her arms, then carried her toward Christian's bed. Lightly climbing in, she cuddled both of her children, memorizing the scent of their hair, the softness of their baby skin. My babies. *Naomi might not have come from my womb, but she is no less my daughter.*

And I would do it again, in a heartbeat, over and over, to save her.

"Why?" she whispered, face full of tears, as she lay nestled between the two creatures her life revolved around. She hadn't lost Oz today in that hospital room. The loss of him had happened gradually, and without ceremony.

But her babies... they were entirely hers. Life had only brought them closer with every day that ticked by. And she'd be leaving them behind, with no choice, and no way to possibly prepare them for it. Somehow, the loss of Oz tonight made this more real than the moment the doctor pronounced her fate, or any moment since.

What she felt, right now... the soft tendrils of Naomi's black curls tickling her nose, Christian's hand twitching against her leg as he smiled in his dreams... very soon, she would never, ever feel these things again. One day, Naomi's curls would tickle her husband's nose, and Christian's hand would lightly shudder against the thigh of the woman who would bear his children.

But Adrienne would not be around to see it.

The heaviness in her chest was smothering. She opened her mouth wide and gulped the air, gasping, before burying her face in her daughter's soft hair and sobbing silently.

KATJA

$\mathcal{K}$atja watched everyone closely, memorizing every last detail. Every word, said and unsaid. Every gesture, down to the subtle body language. Every person who'd come tonight in hope of answers, or salvation.

All the Deschanels and cousins were here. Absolutely everyone, it seemed. Katja made a roster in her notebook, listing those present by family.

ATTENDEES:

Augustus & Barbara Deschanel (Someone must have drugged Uncle A to get him here)

Nicolas Deschanel (Guess he left that Mercy chick at home? Too soon?)

Anne Fontaine

(Where's Adrienne?)

Colleen Jameson (Noah at the hospital with Amelia?)

Ashley & Christine Jameson

Evangeline & Johannes Gehring

Markus & Katja Gehring

Maureen Blanchard (This should be interesting...)
Olivia & Gregory Claiborne (See above)
Alain Blanchard (Sigh)
Connor Sullivan
Tristan Sullivan (Someone please give him a hug!)
Jasper & Pandora Broussard
Leander Broussard (Aren't there other Broussard kids?)
Imogen & Harris Dubois
Violet & Leon (Is that right?) Dubois
Helene Broussard (Sad not to see her with Cassius any longer)
Eugenia & Wallace Fontenot
Luther & Josephine Fontenot
Remy, Fleur, & Teddy Fontenot (This family is too pretty to be borne)
Llewellyn & Sophie Fontenot
Charlotte & Annette Fontenot
Lowell & Julia Fontenot
Noelle Fontenot
A whole bunch of Guidrys I couldn't name if I was paid to.

NEARLY THE ENTIRE SURVIVING CLAN WAS PRESENT, MINUS THE little ones. Katja was shocked at the sheer number of relatives who'd showed, her interest particularly piqued by the appearance of some who had squarely positioned themselves on the "nonbeliever" side of the fence. Particularly her Uncle Augustus, who never engaged in any serious discourse on the Curse. Maybe he was there for his daughter, Anasofiya, who was off doing god-knows-what in Europe.

Katja was equally surprised to see Ashley. Ashley was a good man, and a solid supporter of the family, even if he wasn't a believer. But his sister was on the brink of death, so she supposed he was ready to listen to reason now. He looked like an apparition. One incorrectly placed word might send him over the edge—or whip up another storm Aunt Colleen would have to scramble to cover.

Her heart even ached for the abrasive Pansy, who was humbled in the face of losing her son, Rene.

Katja wasn't an emotional person herself, but she had compassion for her family's losses and hoped beyond hope that she and Alain could prevent further pain. Their grief served as a reminder, and would hopefully keep her strong and on course.

The deaths of Aunt Elizabeth, young Rene, and Cassius hadn't changed anyone's opinion on Brigitte's Curse. Those who believed before, believed even more vehemently now. Those who did not were traumatized, but didn't blame anything other than horrible luck.

Every time she caught Alain's eyes from across the room, her heart skipped slightly. Then they would quickly avert their gazes away from each other before anyone could take notice. His face remained blank, and nearly unreadable through the proceedings.

This went on for half-an-hour. And then, he spoke.

"What if the answer isn't what we think?"

Oh god, he's going to do it. He's really, seriously going to do it. Here, now, in front of all our relatives.

No, she wasn't ready! They hadn't figured out how to break the news. They needed more time!

"What do you mean, Alain?" Katja's mother asked, soothingly. In contrast, Alain's mother and sister had their arms crossed like a couple of petulant twins, daring him to continue.

Alain looked at Katja. There was a hardness, a resolve, in his face. She realized what she had been seeing in him all night was an emotional detachment. A building of courage.

He was going to do what she couldn't. *Sorry Alain, it took everything I had to convince you.*

Her heart threatened to leap from her chest in mutiny.

Alain looked toward her again, although not for strength. He was nodding at her saddlebag. In a daze, she lifted it from around her neck and handed it to him in what felt like torturous slow motion. His sweaty hand brushed hers in the exchange, his eyes peeled wide, as if he'd shuttered them open. She knew she should stand up next to him, but she was frozen in place.

"Aunt Colleen, has anyone ever researched more about Brigitte and Charles, or where they came from?" he asked. He was holding the folder of her research—oh, how proud she had been of her findings. Of contributing something no one else had!—and all Katja could do was stare helplessly.

This is happening.

"Of course. We have copies of their immigration records, and some mementos at *Ophélie*," Colleen replied. "Charles made it clear in the estate documents that anything before they came to New Orleans was unimportant, and wished only for the American traditions the family built to be upheld and practiced."

"I think," Alain started to say, but seemed to lose his resolve for a moment. The reality of what he was about to do had apparently caught up with him. Everyone stared, including Katja, who was still utterly incapable of action. He swallowed and continued, "I think the history before *Ophélie* is more rele-vant than what happened there."

The entire room was abuzz with whispers and exchanged glances. Aunt Colleen didn't look angry, exactly—Katja wasn't sure if she had ever even seen her actually lose her cool—but she did look caught off-guard and maybe ashamed, or uncom-fortable, that someone else knew more about the family than she did. She politely asked Alain to continue.

"Were any of you aware that Charles and Brigitte were first cousins?" Alain pressed.

A series of uncomfortable nods spread. "Yes, dear," Colleen replied. "A dirty family secret. Not one we discuss at reunions and holidays."

Nervous laughter rang around the table, until Alain quickly added, "Then did you know *their* grandparents were *brother and sister*? And if you go back at least four generations beyond that, you'll find more siblings mating?"

Well *that* shocked the room. Katja watched as their expressions ranged from disgust to shock to amusement. But, more importantly, it was a surprise to everyone.

"How... how do you know this?" Aunt Colleen asked, as she exchanged glances with both Evangeline and Luther, who wore similar alarmed looks.

Katja took a deep breath, and stood up. "I told him."

Before anyone could say another word, Katja pushed past her fear and walked to the head of the table where Aunt Colleen sat, taking up the opposite side of Alain. She asked if she could speak, and her aunt simply waved her approval and sat back, enraptured like all the rest.

Katja found her confidence as she spoke. She laid it all out for everyone, the same as she did for Alain that night by the lake. She presented her evidence meticulously, and without the complexity of emotion. There was hardly a sound in the room as she commanded it. Even Maureen and Olivia were unusually attentive.

Once she'd concluded, she felt the air sucked from her lungs. The anticipation was unbearable.

"So," Jasper finally broke the silence, "you're suggesting Brigitte was angry because Ophélie died before she could diddle her brothers? And that she cursed the family because of it?"

"Yes," Katja replied, unnerved. "That's exactly what I'm suggesting."

Nervous titters rippled through the room. Nicolas laughed under his breath. Maureen shook her head. Everyone else was looking at her thoughtfully. Katja couldn't guess what they were thinking, but she knew it couldn't be the weirdest thing they'd discussed in this room over the years.

"So, what then, child? Y'all thinkin' the cure is a good old fashioned roll in the hay between brother and sister?" Kitty jabbed, tilting her head in animated skepticism. Her sister Pansy, normally never one to miss an opportunity to further the ridicule, continued her silent grieving.

"I... uh, yes, I think that makes the most sense," Katja mumbled in response. *Where is my damn courage?*

Kitty rolled her eyes. "You're adorable, child. Really. But it's time to sit down and let the adults do the talkin'."

Katja prepared herself for battle against her older cousin, but then her mother surprised her by speaking up. "I came to the same conclusion with my research too, Katja." Markus and Aunt Colleen both whipped their heads toward her in shocked unison. "I believe you may be right. But I decided to abandon the theory, because we can't possibly ask this, or want this, of anyone. There has to be another way."

"No offense to anyone in this room, but I don't fancy you like that," Olivia announced, and the room erupted into nervous laughter.

"Well if we're taking orders, then I've got dibs on Anasofiya, and Katja," Nicolas said with a wink, to more amusement.

"We could draw straws," Leander joked.

"Rochambeau?" Antoine added.

"I'm sure the Guidrys would do it without much convincing," Remy cracked. "They're provocateurs of keeping it in the family."

This finally got a reaction from Pansy, who promptly slapped both hands down on the table, amid roaring laughter. "If you gon' act like a turd, Remy Fontenot, go lay in the yard!"

Go ahead and laugh. Maybe it will make this next part easier.

"Or," Katja began slowly. Her eyes fell on Alain, and he nodded faintly. "Perhaps there are two people in the family willing to take on this burden."

"I very much doubt that," Ashley said. "We all grew up together."

"Not all of us," she said, and her eyes fell on Alain again. This time, her mother caught the shared look, as did others in the room.

"No," Evangeline said, standing. It was simple, emotional. Visceral. "*No.*"

Katja felt Alain slip his hand into hers. His other reached across to spread protectively over her belly. Against their growing triplets. "Yes," she said, her voice choking. "I'm sorry, Mom."

Evangeline braced herself with the chair as her knees buckled out from under her.

AUGUSTUS AND HIS WIFE WERE THE FIRST TO LEAVE, BUT OTHERS followed. First in shell-shocked single-file, and then, after the first brave few, the rest moved toward the bolted door in droves. No one bothered to enforce the rule about leaving before the meeting ended. The astonishment in the room permeated like a heat wave.

As Katja watched her cousins leave, her feet felt as if they might crash through the floor. She expected judgment would come, but it didn't prepare her for this feeling of being completely ostracized. Of widespread disgust.

And then, one of the Broussard cousins stood up. Leander. The young man, who couldn't be much older than she was, approached Katja and embraced her lightly before taking a seat next to his father, who was among those remaining. A Guidry cousin followed suit, and then another. Before long, the dozen or so who lingered in the room were taking turns coming up to embrace the terrified couple, and show their support.

It wasn't until Markus pulled her into his steady arms that Katja finally lost it. Her rigid, solid brother was crying. "I wish you'd told me.... I wish you had *told* me," he kept whispering in her ear. *It wouldn't have stopped me,* she resisted saying, as she took comfort in his kindness.

Over her brother's shoulder, Katja's eyes caught the looks of horror and disgust on Aunt Maureen and Olivia's faces. Maureen looked downright ill, whereas Olivia appeared as if she had just witnessed a horrific car accident and her mind was catching up to her. *But they haven't walked out. This is Alain's mother and sister. They're here, and that has to mean something.*

Ashley motioned to his wife that they were leaving, but on the way out he squeezed the hands of both Katja and Alain, offering a small smile. Jasper and Leander sat quietly across the table. The older man offered her a small nod of support, and then resumed picking the lint off his jacket.

As Markus pulled away, Katja saw her mother excuse herself, face buried in her hands, and her father followed.

"I'm so sorry you're going through this now," Imogen said, breaking the tense silence. "But I appreciate what the two of you are doing to help this family."

The relief on Alain's face was instant. Maureen made an inhuman noise, a hyena-like cackle. "Are we all going to hug now that cousins are rutting like wild animals? Alain, I raised you so much better than this!" She pointed at Katja. "I might expect that from a child of Evangeline, but not from you."

"Fuck you, Maureen," Evangeline barked, emerging from the other room. "You know why our kids are in this situation? Because we, and I do mean all of us, failed to figure this out ourselves. I'm no happier about this than you are. I spent time nurturing my children's strengths so they could be amazing people and do amazing things, and now I'm wondering what Katja will do with her life when she becomes a mother at nineteen." Her eyes narrowed. "But I'm sure you wouldn't know anything about *that*, would you?"

Maureen's face was red as a tomato. "I would rather have

been branded a whore than have turned into a self-righteous, miserable bitch," she spit out. "And while we're slinging insults at our own children for heaven's sake, let's be honest. This idea came from Katja, not Alain. He would never have come to this conclusion on his own."

"You're right," Evangeline agreed, proudly. "My daughter was smart enough to use her resources, do her research, and find a solution. But I won't insult Alain, because he's a good boy and it took a lot of guts to do what he did." She looked at Katja, whose jaw hung slack. "What both of them did."

"Are you kidding? They're kids! A hole is a hole," Maureen said, flopping back in her chair in disgust. She squeezed her hands against the side of her head as if to crush the thoughts out if it.

"I'm not a child," Alain spoke up. His voice was steady, and strong. "And neither is Katja. I didn't ask for this situation, and neither did she, but it's here. You can say all you want, and think all you want, but if it wasn't us, someone else would have to. Every single person in this family should be thanking us."

"Yes, Alain, I *thank you* for being the biggest disappointment of my life by fucking your first cousin like a goddamned coonass!" his mother screamed.

"Stop it, Mom," Olivia pleaded. She seemed to have found her wits. "Please."

"Did you know about this?" Maureen demanded, spinning in fury toward her daughter.

"No," Olivia said quietly. "I wouldn't have let it happen. But this is something better talked about behind closed doors, don't you agree?"

"I would've expected this from Nicolas and Ana," Maureen said, with dripping derision. Nicolas met her gaze, unaffected. "Everyone knows those two have been up to no good. But Alain? And Katja? Jesus wept."

"Please, stop," Olivia pleaded.

"Are you condoning this?" Maureen shrieked. She sounded like a deranged bird. "You're saying this is okay, that we should just gloss it over and plan a damn baby shower?"

"I'm saying this isn't the place."

"Olivia is right," Aunt Colleen concurred. "This wasn't an easy thing for these two to tell us. Maybe we've learned enough for one night."

"Indeed," Maureen said and stood up, clutching her purse tightly. "Olivia, have Greg take me home. Alain, don't even *dream* of following me as I have nothing to say to you." She stormed out, with Olivia and Greg helplessly in tow.

Alain looked like a kicked puppy, as Katja held tight to his hand.

Nicolas cleared his throat and stood, stretching as if they'd simply been at the movies. "You two are welcome to stay with us at *Ophèlie*. I mean, if you're worried about what the assholes in town might say. We've got some crazy stuff coming up, but that might make you two look like the *Babysitter's Club*." He shrugged at the end, as if showing he cared would be a terrible thing.

Katja almost hugged him. "We need to talk, of course. We haven't thought that far ahead. But thank you."

Alain said nothing. He had no color in his face at all. Katja feared he might be violently sick at any moment.

"That's understandable. This isn't exactly a typical situation," Colleen said, with a dazed expression. "You are also welcome at The Gardens, as another option."

"You're welcome in our home, as well," Jasper chimed in. "Estella is still in Paris, and her room is yours, should you need it."

"Whatever you've... decided here," Evangeline added, "you need to think about your future."

"I can't think about anything else right now, Mom," Katja assured, a faint tremble in her voice. It had been easier to remain stoic when faced with censure. "I know I'm not going to drop out of college. I still want the same things. But... now there's this thing, too."

"Katja, we will help you with whatever you need," her father, who had been otherwise silent through the evening, clarified. "If you want to go to *Ophélie*, we will get you into college online for now. Whatever you want. You don't have to give up your future. Your dreams."

"Thank you," she acknowledged quietly. Katja realized this might be the queerest conversation of her life. They were talking about incest and curse-breaking as calmly as they'd discuss a slight change in the weather. *It might be surreal, but it's really happening, and when we leave the room and go back to our lives outside, it will still be real.*

"I'm pretty sure Olivia is going to be at my place when I get there," Alain said, sounding very unhappy about it. Although his sister had showed a modicum of support tonight, it seemed obvious to everyone it was more out of respect for decency.

Nicolas offered, "Stay in my Quarter flat tonight. Gives you some privacy to talk things out, and better yet, avoid Alain's crazy-ass family."

"Sure, thanks," Katja accepted, and Alain nodded. "And thanks to everyone for not chasing us out of town with torches. This was hard enough before anyone knew."

Markus smiled and put his hand over Katja's. Some of the other cousins and aunts reached forward to add their comfort as well. Even Nicolas.

"This situation is less-than-ideal," Jasper summarized, and those few remaining in the room nodded. "But I know you didn't come to this conclusion lightly, and we will all help, in any way we can. Why, I can even consult with Madame Marie for guidance. She often lights a way in the dark for me."

"We have time to sort out all the details," Alain deferred, ignoring the touch of craziness eschewed from his cousin.

"Katja isn't going back to school yet, and I can support us both for now."

"When will we know if it worked?" Leander asked. "I mean, how will we know the theory is right?"

Katja and Alain exchanged looks. "We're in a unique situation because Amelia has been afflicted by the Curse, but is still alive. So, hopefully, once Katja gives birth, Amelia should snap out of it. That will be our first big sign that we've broken it. If it weren't for Amelia's condition, then we'd have to wait on pins and needles for someone else to die, and even then we wouldn't be able to prove if it was a result of the Curse, or not. But I believe Amelia's recovery will confirm our theory is correct," Alain said. *Assuming she lasts long enough for us to help her,* Katja silently added. *Right now, all signs point to the contrary.*

"With all fondness here, I think you're fucking nuts," Nicolas asserted, looking at his cousins. "But let's say you're right. How long do you expect it will take, to correct things?"

"We don't know," Katja acknowledged. "This is unprecedented."

The questions eventually faded to exhaustion, and Nicolas declared his driver was out front. After saying their goodbyes, Katja and Alain joined him, sliding into the town car with relief.

No, relief wasn't the right word. It was more like acceptance. The adrenaline was wearing down, there were no more secrets, and now all that lay before them was the birth of their children.

It seems as if to avoid one tragedy we're creating another. If this does solve the Curse, another curse will follow us the rest of our lives.

And our children's lives.

OZ

*O*z kicked at the dusty sidewalk from where he sat on the old metal bench overlooking the Mississippi. It was late, and the tourists had all congregated back on Bourbon, or Frenchman. The occasional passers-by, and the fading sound of jazz from the nearby Quarter, were the only signs of life on this end of the waterfront.

"You invited me down here, for what, Ozzy? To watch you daydream?" Nicolas asked.

"I needed a break, and I knew you were in town for the family meeting," Oz replied. "But I need to head back to the hospital soon. It feels like we're running out of time."

"You look as shitty as I've ever seen you. And that's saying something," Nicolas observed. In the distance, a steamboat sounded its return to port.

"I feel pretty much how I look," Oz admitted, after a long sip off the bottle of Hennessy Nicolas passed him. He winced; even alcohol tasted different. Nothing was the same.

"Is it Adrienne?"

"Yes. No. Hell, I don't know," replied Oz. "Lately I haven't felt... no, I don't even want to say the words. And besides, all I can think about lately is Amelia."

"I heard about that," Nicolas said, eyes once again darting toward the amber liquid that had been a staple since his teens. He took the bottle back. "I heard about this dream shit, too. Are you sure you're not a Deschanel love child, or something?"

"I'm not sure of anything," Oz said, ignoring the tease. "My life doesn't feel like my own right now."

Nicolas pointed a thumb toward the west, where, an hour away, Mercy slept, waiting for him. "Fucking tell me about it. I don't even recognize myself. Domesticity is terrifying, Ozzy. Fucking nuts."

"It's good for you," Oz insisted.

"We'll see about that. So, this dream thing? What the fuck?" Nicolas demanded. "I can think of plenty of times in the last thirty years where that would have been useful information."

"I didn't know," Oz explained. A light breeze passed over the river, cooling the humid air. He closed his eyes to better appreciate it. "In fact, there's a lot I didn't know."

"Amelia is in good hands with you," Nicolas tried to reassure him, taking another swig from the cognac bottle. "I've never known a damsel to remain in distress for long when Oz Sullivan is on the job."

Oz finally raised his gaze, looking at his old friend. "Nic, there's a lot of messed up things going on in my head right now. I'm all twisted up."

"Is that supposed to be a newsflash from the 90's, Oz? No shit."

"I'm not kidding." Oz pursed his lips and released a long, measured breath. "I don't feel like myself at all. I've been having these dark thoughts about Adrienne. About how I feel about her, *really* feel about her, as if I didn't know until now. And then Amelia... she's my friend. One of my oldest friends, and I only wanted to help. But tonight, when I was with her..."

"Did you guys have dream sex?" Nicolas probed, not hiding his impertinent grin.

"No! Of course not!" His brow furrowed. "Can you do that?"

They both laughed, Oz's fading first. "Well, if I had your skills, that would've been my first order of business. But no one ever accused you and me of sharing priorities," Nicolas replied. "So, when you were with her, what happened?"

"It was different. It wasn't like drinking a beer on her porch, or bullshitting about whatever. I can't explain it. I don't know what the hell is wrong with me," Oz sighed. "No doubt it will pass, but holy hell."

Nicolas grinned. "I know exactly what's wrong with you. Colleen came to you and appealed to your unflinching hero complex." Nicolas began batting his eyelashes, and touching his hair, dropping into his best Colleen voice, "'Oz, only you can save us.' Then the hero alarm started whirling off the charts, springs coming loose, motherboard fried. Hell, Oz, I bet you can't even get hard unless there's tragedy involved."

"Shut up," Oz rolled his eyes in annoyance.

"Doesn't hurt she's hot. If she wasn't my cousin, I'd have put her on my 'would bang' list years ago," Nicolas added, finishing off the bottle without even a wince. "And don't give me that damn scandalized look. We both know it's true. You probably would have dated her if there'd been a crazy stalker she needed rescuing from."

"She turned me down in high school," Oz replied, then shook his head. "It doesn't matter if she's hot, or if, maybe, my 'hero complex' is drawn to her. What's going through my head right now doesn't feel like some heightened, transient emotion. It feels like..."

Nicolas leaned against the bench, eyeing his friend. "Don't refuse to finish a sentence just because what you're about to say is stupid. Say it."

Oz breathed out, setting his beer down. "These feelings don't feel new," he finished. "Whatever I'm feeling doesn't seem tied to recent events. It's like... okay, look, it's like someone flipped on a switch that had been dormant in my brain, and all these feelings came with it."

Nicolas pondered that for a moment, as if he might actually have some useful advice. "Maybe they aren't new? I mean, you've had your head wrapped around Adrienne for so long, I don't think you even remember what it's like to think straight. You said you used to go to Amelia's porch after late nights instead of going in and banging your wife. I'm sorry, but if I had a hot wife, I would not be hanging out with the neighbor, unless I was hoping to bang her, too."

"You called your sister hot," Oz observed, with a raised brow. "That's two relatives tonight. Should I be concerned?"

"I didn't say I'd fuck her, I just stated a plain fact. She *is* hot," Nicolas maintained dismissively. "Crazy, but hot."

"Adrienne is beautiful," Oz agreed. "And I love her. I've always loved her."

"You always did have a fucked up idea of love," Nicolas noted, pulling out a flask, and taking a long sip. "Not that mine is much healthier, but at least I understand relationships should be mutual. I wouldn't give all of myself to someone who couldn't give it back. But you're a better man than me, I guess."

"Was that ever up for debate?" Oz wise-cracked, but his heart wasn't in it. He snatched the flask from Nic's hand, and took a swig, then promptly choked as liquid fire burned his lungs. "This isn't cognac!"

Nicolas grinned. "Nope. Condoleezza's finest hooch, son."

"She's making moonshine now?" Oz shook his head, with a chuckle.

"Why wasn't Adrienne there tonight?" Nicolas switched subjects. "At the meeting, I mean. Almost all the local Deschanels were there."

Oz looked up. "She wasn't?"

"Uh, no. She wasn't."

Oz buried his face in his hands, wishing to block out not only his thoughts but also Nicolas, all of it really. What was happening to him? He didn't want the same apathy that infected his marriage to Janie to repeat with Adrienne. Had it been gradual? If he were to look back on the past months, or even years, would he see the path of trajectory and be able to identify it? To stop it?

Would he want to?

"I'm losing it," Oz lamented. "Really, finally."

"I have an idea," Nicolas responded, a thoughtful look growing. "Remember when I kicked your ass in Maine? For messing with Ana?"

"It took almost a month for my nose to heal. Yes, I remember."

"Well, you fucking deserved it. Enough that I don't regret it, but am now willing to step up and let you return the favor."

Oz snorted. "Excuse me?"

Nicolas stood up before Oz, slapping his cheeks as he bounced from one leg to the other. "Hit me. It will make you feel better. I can take it."

Oz laughed. "I've known you your whole life, and you have never, ever taken a punch well."

"Whatever, dude. At least I stay and take them instead of running like a little bitch."

"I didn't run," Oz maintained, as he stood to leave. "Did you guys get any closer to figuring things out, at the meeting?"

"Long story," Nicolas said, shaking his head, as he reluctantly returned to his seat. "Short term, no. And long term? Well, I still can't say I believe in a damn family curse. Sometimes bad shit happens. Doesn't require a fancy, supernatural explanation."

"I don't know why you keep acting like it's so far-fetched.

Your entire family believes it except the dumb ones, and even people who married into the family—like me, like my Uncle Connor—believe in it. Just because you can't see something physically, doesn't mean it isn't there. My father still crosses himself if he accidentally breaks a mirror, and he's the most pragmatic son-of-a-bitch I know, for God's sake. There's a lot of things in this world we can't explain, but that doesn't make them less real."

"Are you done?"

Oz shrugged and started walking toward the river, kneeling down. The moon's reflection transfixed him; he could stare at it for hours. Get lost in it.

"Sometimes life sucks, Ozzy," Nicolas added, more to convince himself it seemed. "There doesn't always have to be a colorful explanation for it."

Oz stood, blinking away the daze. "I have to go."

"To Amelia? Or to Adrienne?"

"Only one of them is dying," Oz said with a heavy smile.

WHEN OZ INSERTED HIMSELF INTO AMELIA'S DREAM STATE, HE once again found himself dropped into the middle of a memory.

He was in a small room, with sparse furnishings. The smell of aging birch and oak was almost overwhelming, and the rain fell in a steady patter outside the small window that reached to the ceiling. Wallet, keys, and passports lay hurriedly splayed on the tiny nightstand, the key barely hanging onto the edge. Beside a dusty lamp, a half-used pad of paper sat with the words, *Inn at Killianshire*, printed along the top.

This is a continuation of the prior memory, Oz deduced. *Picking up where we left off.*

On the small bed, Jacob lay on his back, gazing up in loving adoration at the nude figure of Amelia as she advanced upon him, her long hair tickling his chest.

"Amelia. I've loved you forever," Jacob whispered, in a choked voice. His hand stretched toward her face, cupping her cheek in his palm.

"Then love me forever," Amelia replied, as she maneuvered herself astride him, taking him in. Jacob's head fell back, mouth wide in a cry of ecstasy.

Oz turned to find a way out, but there were no exits. The boundaries of this instance were limited by what Amelia's memory had conjured. Making love to the keeper of her heart, Amelia's memory had no use for doors.

Realizing he was here until either the dreamwalking ended, or Amelia's vision shifted, he instead looked away to give them privacy. Never mind that this had happened a decade ago. To Oz, it was happening now.

But as the moaning swelled, Oz's eyes inadvertently traveled to Amelia's figure. Her smooth porcelain belly as it flexed with each movement she made. The hint of white fire between her legs, where Jacob's hand traveled, drawing pleasure. Her hair-like-snow, swaying back and forth over her small, perfect breasts.

The stirring between Oz's legs shamed him. He couldn't help but imagine it was he, and not Jacob, who lay underneath her. That it was his name, and not Jacob's, she cried out when she came. That it was he who wound her long hair through his fingers, clutching to hang on to a moment that would matter for the rest of their lives.

How had his feelings for her shifted so dramatically? Was this a side effect of the dreamwalking? Or something else?

It was not until he heard Jacob utter the words, "*Te amo, Blanca*," and he looked up to see Amelia resting in his arms, that Oz was able to steady himself.

"CAN WE TALK ABOUT SOMETHING OTHER THAN ME BEING HELD

hostage by my rogue brain?" Amelia asked, with a hopeful smile. They'd been sitting in the gazebo for several minutes, having been jerked rudely from her memory back to The Gardens. Outside the gazebo, the wind whistled lightly, and the blackness from before threatened the tips of flower petals and the trunks of the trees, reminding them it was not far away. "I need to think about something else for a while."

"We can," Oz said, giving her knee a light squeeze. The memory of watching her with Jacob was mercifully fading. "After a few minutes of me talking about my day, you'll probably beg for us to go back to talking about the creepy plants though."

"Well, how's Adrienne?" she ventured. The air around them had gone still, finally, and the colors returned to their vibrant state. The black, for now at least, was gone.

His face fell immediately. "She's different lately. I don't know what it is. I've been so busy with work, and now hanging out with you in Narnia, that I haven't really pushed her to tell me. Your mom has Anne looking after her, so I can focus on being here with you, but the truth is, I'm home about the same now as I ever was." He shook his head. "I really suck at being a husband sometimes." *Even more so now that I'm fantasizing about someone other than my wife,* he thought.

"You know that's not true," Amelia assured him. "Adrienne understands the nature of your work. And women are notoriously difficult about sharing when they're determined to keep something private. Especially Deschanel women. Besides, there's a very good reason for her to be out of sorts right now."

Oz looked at her, and understanding dawned. "Yes, of course. The family."

Amelia nodded. "It's a helpless feeling to see your family hurting and have no power to fix it. As a mother, watching other mothers lose their children, or children losing their mothers... well, it's enough to bring her to her knees, really."

A grin played at the corners of Oz's mouth. "Apparently your empathic powers aren't affected by the current state of affairs."

"Or, I could also be a therapist for a living. There's that," she reminded him, sharing her own smile. "Maybe... maybe take a day off from work, Oz. And from me. Have a family day with Adrienne and the kids. I think that could make you both feel better."

"Yeah..." Oz replied, but sounded entirely unconvinced. It was impossible to explain to Amelia something he didn't understand himself, exactly. How being around Adrienne reminded him of a past that was both amazing, and at the same time artificial. How he'd built his world around this fictional idea, knowing on some deeper, intellectual level it was flimsy at best and would crumble at the first sign of self-awareness.

It was not so much Adrienne's lack of growth over the years as it was his own forward propulsion. In hindsight, what he thought were mature decisions were idealistic and based on an obscured outlook.

The world, though, had not lived up to his hopeful optimism, and this was perhaps the single most important realization of his adult life. It was also dragging him down, and away, from his wife.

And seemingly *toward* Amelia, in a turn of events that baffled him even more than the de-evolution of his feelings at home.

"It will be okay," Amelia said, as if his emotions were blossoming on his sleeve. "Even if the world stopped turning, it wouldn't hinder your capacity to see the best in any situation. You've always viewed the world through the lens of sanguinity. You're a good guy."

"Even good guys can become disenchanted," Oz said, voicing aloud thoughts which, long dormant, now threatened to bubble to the surface in full disclosure. "And maybe I'm not a good guy. No, don't debate with me, I'm not fishing for compliments, Amelia. What really makes someone a good guy? Someone who will do whatever you ask? Who will take whatever is dealt, without complaint? I suppose, if that's the definition of a good guy, well, then I'm the freaking champion of the good guys. I could be their poster boy, and go on a world tour, preaching about the benefits of self-sacrifice. But if people saw the darkness in my heart? They might re-think that label."

Amelia watched him thoughtfully, unfazed by his confession. "We all have darkness in our hearts, Oz. People like to slap honorable titles on me, too, but then, goodness is relative, isn't it? Some would say goodness is acquiescence to all life throws at you. Others would say it's living by a moral code. Then there are those who would say goodness is only achieved through a life of charity and selflessness."

"What would you say it is?"

Amelia drew in a deep breath and closed her eyes. "I can't label others based on my own definitions. For myself, I divide my choices into two categories: those things I can live with, and those I cannot. I try to keep the scales tipped toward the former as much as I can."

"Does it work?"

She smiled sadly. "Usually. But not all of our crimes are equal. I believe crimes that hurt others weigh heavier than those which only hurt ourselves."

"Is there really a difference, though? In hurting others, we hurt ourselves."

"Well, yes. That's the definition of love."

Oz lay his head back against the wooden pillar, processing. Love. There were so many, often convoluted, definitions of the word. Was it love that prompted Oz to ignore the parts of his life that brought him disillusionment? Was it love that kept him from thinking too much about all the little things he swore didn't matter? The Oz of ten years ago believed love was the exercise of doing all you could for the keeper of your heart, no matter the cost, or effort. The Oz of today wondered if love wasn't more about putting someone's needs before your own, especially if their needs were at odds with your own.

But which Oz was the better man?

"No one ever wakes up and says 'I'm exactly who I wanted to be,'" Amelia broke the silence. "The sad part is most don't understand this realization is not always such a bad thing."

"You aren't reading my mind, are you? I mean, I guess I should know if you are, but my senses are all off in here," Oz teased.

"I wouldn't even if I could. That's your space," Amelia assured him, then sighed as she leaned to rest her head against his shoulder. "You have to go soon. Don't you?"

Oz laid his head against the top of hers. "I think so. I can feel the pull, and I don't know how to stop it yet. Plus, I think Jacob gets jealous when I'm here too long."

"Even his name makes my chest ache," Amelia whispered. He felt her grow stiff beside him. "You asked me if I was achieving my personal balance, of goodness? I've hurt the only man I ever loved, and so my answer is, right now, no. Right now I'm failing miserably."

"Amelia, I can fix that! I can tell him—"

"No," she replied, firmly. "Thank you, but it's something I have to do myself. I might take you up on it if things don't improve." As she said this, the breeze once again picked up, and the flowers sang their subtle, sad song. The blackness spread so quickly it was as if color never existed. "I suppose we'll know soon, one way or another."

The pull was strong enough Oz felt bile growing deep inside. He moved to touch her face, to try and impart some of his own strength to her before leaving. The unexpected sight of her tear-stained face nearly dissolved him. "Amelia..." he planted a kiss against the top of both her eyelids before pressing his forehead to hers. "I swear to you..."

The sound of light, steady beeps came into his hearing, as Oz was pulled away from Amelia, and back into the real world, her face damp on the pillow next to his.

OLIVIA

"*D*rop me off at the hospital," Olivia ordered her husband, as they sat in front of her mother's old Victorian. The drive over had been filled with silence. These were her first and only words following the unfortunate Magi Collective meeting.

"You don't want to stay with your mother?"

Olivia pivoted in her seat so her whole body faced him. "Hell's bells, Greg! Are you serious? I've had enough insanity for one evening!'

"Hospital it is," Greg muttered. "Do you want me to wait?"

"And leave Rory in the backseat in this heat? God knows you speak without thinking sometimes," she chastised. The acid in her tongue burned deeper than usual. But she couldn't be bothered to explain basic common sense after all they'd been forced to absorb this night.

"All right, I'll take him home," Greg replied, with a restrained head shake. She derisively noted he didn't have the *cojones* to try a full-blown one in her presence. Sometimes she wished he did. Now was not one of those times.

"Please," she added, the closest she would come to an apology. "I'll call a car to bring me home later."

She knew her husband was mildly afraid of her. Right now he should've been attempting to reason with her over Alain's decisions. To talk her down, to attempt to shine light on some hidden comfort she might draw from the situation. But Olivia would not only shoot down any consolation he tried, she'd punish him for offering useless solutions. He seemed to understand that.

Olivia had no time for empty gestures. But neither did she possess answers. Alain's predicament would have to wait until she could properly process it, and give it the attention it deserved, if she could ever bring herself to do so. Her own theory about this so-called Curse was developing, but her explanation was far less colorful than the ones her relatives had concocted: simply, the Curse was the Deschanels engaging in activities that made them their own worst enemy.

Though she thought the Curse was utter nonsense, Olivia had never doubted the abilities her family possessed. She was a seer herself, to her mother's dismay. Maureen had, since she and Alain were old enough to make sense of her ramblings, prayed loudly for them to be "normal," when what she really wanted was to not be the only one who wasn't special. Despite her pleas for divine intervention, Alain manifested his explosive ability when he was only an infant, sending his mother into a permanent bout of mania. When Olivia manifested, it was all over.

The first time, she was five. Her mother was watching John Lennon and Yoko Ono on the old boxy television. Olivia had pointed at Lennon and said, "That man is going to die, Mama."

"We're all going to die, Liv," her mother had returned, with her signature simultaneous head-shake-eye-roll.

"No, Mama. A man is going to shoot him very soon. He won't get Christmas presents this year."

Maureen had scolded her for watching too much television and letting her imagination run wild. But two months later, when Mark David Chapman pulled that fateful trigger, Maureen was terrified.

"Dumb coincidence," she'd muttered, though Olivia saw the abject horror in her mother's eyes. It was the same look she had whenever Alain accidentally blew up a light bulb, or broke a water main, when his moods got the best of him.

A year later, Olivia told her mother that their neighbor was going to sell his car for fifty dollars.

Maureen snorted. "Mr. Landry? That man has sworn for years he'd never sell that vintage Aston Martin. And fifty dollars? You're dreaming! That thing is worth more than your life!"

Four days later, Mr. Landry sold that old car for $50. He never explained why, but it didn't matter to Maureen, or Olivia, who were both flummoxed, for entirely different reasons.

The instances of Olivia's predictions increased over time— she could have told anyone who would listen that the Space Shuttle Challenger was not going to make it home, that Muhammed Ali would lose his last fight, and that they wouldn't find anything when they opened Al Capone's supposed grave on live television—but they came to a peak when she was eleven. A local news channel was running a special on hostage Terry White, the poor man who'd been a captive of Hezbollah for nearly seven years. Olivia declared, "He's coming home soon," even though all signs pointed to the contrary. "He's going to see his daughter for the first time."

Her mother had opened her mouth, then immediately snapped it shut. Likely she'd started to say, *That man is never coming home,* or *he's dead, we all know it.* But then, after a pause, she said, "You need to stop it, Olivia. Kill it. I don't care what you do, but never, ever do it again!"

Terry White's joyous reunion with his family was celebrated all over the world, but not in the Blanchard household. Instead, Olivia and Alain were made to promise they would quell their abilities. "They will go away, eventually, if you ignore them," Maureen promised, but neither child was so sure.

Both children had done as their mother asked, insomuch as they were able. Olivia ignored the tingling premonitions when she recognized them, and Alain did his best to control his temper so as not to blow up the house. But neither could entirely turn off their "gifts."

Olivia couldn't deny the magic running through all their veins. But how bold and presumptuous her cousins had been in their use of such power! Playing gods, weaving a false world around them. The Curse was not some ancient malediction. It was *them!*

Foolishness. And Aunt Colleen, the Queen of All the Great Fools. With a great clarity, Olivia now saw her family through exactly the lens they deserved.

Several had died already, and more likely would. Colleen and her lackeys simply couldn't help themselves in their bizarre fervor, whipping everyone around them into mass insanity. Olivia didn't possess the power to save them from themselves. All she could do was sit back and watch them be the architects of their own destruction. Pathetic.

In the silent car, an important thought began to grow. She realized there was one cousin she might yet be able to reason with. And if she could reason with Ashley... well, others might follow. Not many, probably, but enough. It would speak volumes if Colleen's own son stood up against her.

And if they didn't come to their senses? Well, she couldn't deny her flower shop had been a bustle of activity lately with all the funerals.

This Deschanel Curse wasn't good for much, but it was good for business.

. . .

AUNT COLLEEN HAD RENTED AN ENTIRE SUITE OF ROOMS IN THE hospital to ensure privacy. That much, at least, Olivia agreed was a wise decision. Ever since her Uncle Charles' family accident a decade ago, Southern Louisiana loved to swarm around a Deschanel tragedy, like rabid fruit flies in a freshly opened jar of honey.

She'd gambled on Ashley returning straight to the hospital. But the private end of their corridor was strangely quiet, as Olivia realized this might be one of the rare moments Amelia was left unattended.

Olivia liked Amelia. A lot. Maybe as much as she liked Ashley. Weird, of course, when you considered how little she regarded their mother. But Amelia was no fanatic like her mother, or the others. Olivia had a theory that Amelia was simply caught up in the webs woven by her mother, and she only needed the right influence to deconstruct them.

Having made up her mind to go have a private conversation with her unconscious cousin, Olivia hoped to set-up some subliminal suggestions. She'd never tried something like that before, but it couldn't be that hard, right?

As she approached the room, she found Jacob resting on one side of the bed. *Of course. This adorable man hasn't left her for a minute!*

"Jacob," she announced herself, with a beaming-wide smile for a man who was simply too sweet for words. A new thought occurred to her: *he might be an even better ally. If I can get through to him, maybe he can get through to Amelia. She's nearly as respected as her mother, and certainly more sane!*

"Oh. Hey Olivia," he replied, with a sheepish smile, as he stifled a yawn. "Sorry, I didn't hear you come in."

"Psh. You're exhausted. I'm the one who's sorry, for waking you."

Jacob waved away the thought, and gestured toward an empty chair. *Only a thoughtful man would think of others in their own time of need. Greg could learn a thing or two!* "You picked a good time to visit," he said, as she took the offered seat. "Everyone's gone."

"The meeting," she agreed, biting her tongue from saying more. She wouldn't think about the nonsense with Alain and Katja.

"Not that there's ever a bad time to visit. Or a good one, I guess," Jacob replied, gazing down at Amelia. *His charming Irish brogue is even more delightful when he's tired.* "She hasn't changed in over a week."

And she won't, as long as everyone feeds her these poisonous lies! "What about your parents, Jacob? Has anyone been here to support you?"

He flinched in surprise, releasing a tiny chuckle. "Me? No, I'm fine. And I don't have any family here, anyway. Only Amelia." Darkness passed over his expression. *Oh yes, that's right. He has no family, though no one's bothered to explain* why.

Olivia reached across Amelia's resting body, and patted Jacob's hand. "Don't worry. She knows you're here."

Jacob sighed, politely retrieving his hand. "I wish I could tell her. Sometimes I want to ask Oz if he'll pass a message to her, but anything I have to say to Amelia is deeply personal."

"Oz? What do you mean?"

He looked up. "Oh, you haven't heard. Colleen somehow figured out Oz Sullivan has this really bizarre ability... dreamwalking? Anyway, she talked him into trying to get into Amelia's head. It worked, I guess. He tells us she's okay. Knowing Amelia, it seems true. She's always been so strong. I can't begin to understand any of it, though."

Dreamwalking? And a Sullivan? Well, the latter part didn't matter. More important, what the Jesus, Mary, and Joseph was a dreamwalker? She had to learn more. But already, she strongly suspected this dreamwalking business was hurting Amelia, not helping her!

"What has Oz told you about this... dreamwalking?"

Jacob shrugged. "Not much. He's always exhausted when he comes out of it."

Exhausted, indeed! Those Sullivans...

"But what is it? Has he bothered to explain at all? Or Colleen? I've never even heard of a dreamwalker, much less seen one!"

"He never says much about it, other than to say she's okay, for now. I suppose I should push him more, but I don't really want to know about the adventures he's having with her while I'm stuck here. I don't get jealous easily, but..." he left it there.

"I can't say I blame you one bit, Jacob. I'm more surprised you're allowing this!" Olivia exclaimed, with no thought to how her outburst might be received by the grieving man.

"Nothing else was working, and Colleen suggested it. What was I supposed to say, no? Don't try something that might save her?" Jacob's tone lacked the enthusiasm of his words.

"I know, dear. All I'm saying is..." *To say it, or not to say it? To open Pandora's box, or leave it shut tight? Ah, who was she kidding...* "Oz Sullivan has a reputation."

Jacob blinked but didn't look up. "I've known Oz since I was a kid. Amelia has too. He's our friend. He's not in there taking her on a romantic picnic date, if that's what you're suggesting."

"Heavens, no! I didn't say he had a reputation for cooking did I?"

"Olivia—"

"Jacob, wake up! Amelia is in distress, and Oz loves a needy woman. I know you trust Amelia, and you should, because she loves you dearly, but I don't trust Oz as far as I can throw him."

"Well I do!" Jacob exclaimed, finally showing a peak in emotion. "And I trust *her*. If he's giving her some comfort when she's alone, and scared, what of it? I can't be there to do it, and it's *killing* me. Jealousy be damned, I don't want her to be alone."

This is going nowhere. He's in no frame of mind to deal with the truth. I'll have to show him.

"I'm sorry for upsetting you," she soothed, inhaling a deep breath as she stood and straightened her dress. "I want what you want, Jacob. I love her, too."

Jacob nodded, and then rested his head again on the pillow.

She was dismissed.

She would let it go, for now.

OLIVIA SLIPPED INTO BED AN HOUR BEFORE GREG'S USUAL bedtime, wanting to be alone. She switched the news on to block out her thoughts, but it was no use. Alain's nervous shifting, their mother's manic exclamations, the disgust of each departing Deschanel... all these thoughts forced their way to the front of her mind, practically insisting she reflect on all that had happened.

Fighting for equal importance, the nagging apprehension about what Jacob had revealed earlier.

Stop! You're doing exactly what Colleen and her groupies would want! Give no credence to it. Forget it. Forget them all. They've given no consideration to your feelings, so you owe them nothing.

Focus on the child growing inside you. On seeing him or her born, and healthy. Nothing else matters.

Greg entered the room with his toothbrush wagging from his mouth, as he shook his head at the current news feature. They were talking about the rampant abuse of FEMA loans after Katrina.

"This is why we vote Republican, dear," she assured him, with a pat of the hand.

Just as Jacob had dismissed her earlier with his silence, she now dismissed her overwhelming worries, deciding with a firm-set resolution not to give them even a moment more of her time.

God grant me the serenity to accept the things I cannot change, the courage to change the things I can, and the strength to tell all my idiot relatives to go straight to hell.

TRISTAN

"**W**hat do you want for dinner?" Tristan asked his father.

Connor sat in the leather armchair without any discernible expression. He'd returned to work right after the funeral, but no longer worked long hours. When he was home, he floated around the house like he was taking up the role of his wife's ghost. Tristan surmised he was feeling some remorse, for having given up on her, but Tristan was too guilt-ridden himself to offer comfort to anyone else. In fact, he was so overwhelmed with responsibility, and hopelessness in general, that he thought at any moment he might implode.

"We still have some of those casseroles," his father suggested helpfully, but his voice indicated he didn't care whether they ate casseroles or mud.

Tristan nodded and went into the kitchen. Markus was in there on his laptop, looking into options to do some of his coursework online. Tristan wanted to be selfless and encourage him to leave, go help his sister, but he couldn't bring himself to say the words. His father was too hurt to help him, and Tristan needed not to be alone.

Tristan slumped down into one of the kitchen chairs across from Markus, the pressing feeling in his chest had returned. The memory of the day he confirmed his mother was really gone came back to him constantly. It pounded on his thoughts relentlessly. The letter and the diaries, the policemen showing up at the door, removing any final doubt.

They needed someone to identify the body, and while it should have been Connor, Tristan wanted to spare his father, so he did it himself. As soon as they pulled the sheet back, he regretted it immediately. She had jumped from the plantation's third-level gallery, into the garden, her body twisted and crushed almost beyond recognition. Her back and neck had broken, as had several bones in her arms and legs. She resembled one of those bendable dolls Danielle used to love. The spring rains caused her corpse to bloat and distend in an inhuman way. This was not his mother, but unfortunately, this would be Tristan's last memory of her. It would haunt him forever.

The last time he'd seen his mother, his actions had distressed her to the point of driving her away. His last memory of his sister was just as bad. In both cases, he could have prevented their deaths. He knew it, deep within his soul.

Well, Mama. Danielle. I'll see you both soon.

Markus didn't ask him if he was okay. Instead, he closed his laptop and went to take care of dinner.

"Casseroles," Tristan whispered. He was out of breath, so only the first part of the word came out.

"The joys of Southern hospitality," Markus responded with a head shake. He pulled one of the rectangular aluminum trays from the fridge and turned it around, looking for instructions.

"It's not rocket science. Put the oven to 350 and throw it in," Tristan said, slowly returning to his senses.

"Right, because if it was rocket science, I wouldn't be having trouble figuring it out, now would I?" Markus retorted. Tristan smiled in spite of his mood.

With dinner warming, Markus excused himself, leaving Tristan alone with his thoughts.

He hadn't yet found the wherewithal to reach out to Emily about the baby. His mother's last request to him had been for him to raise it, but he'd been so preoccupied with her sudden death, and the arrangements, and his father, and all the grief... it had all been *so much*, that her situation had been the last thing he wanted to think about. And the more time went on, the harder it became.

And then the letter had come yesterday from Emily. That made two unfortunate letters to land on his doorstep in the span of a week.

Tristan,

I can't believe we've come to this. That I'm having to write you a letter because you won't return my calls, or my emails.

Rest assured, this was no plot on my part. I didn't expect to get pregnant, and God knows I didn't want to. Soon, it will be at the point where I can't hide it anymore, and I'll have to find a way to explain to my husband it's not his. When that time comes, he's probably going to kick me out. He has every right, and I would do it if I were in his shoes. He deserves better from me. But I deserve better from you.

I should be angry with you, but I'm more angry with myself. In retrospect, I should have listened to the voice in the back of my head telling me to stop, but I went with my heart instead.

I thought you were different. Your age was always in the back of my mind, but you led me to believe your maturity was something special. I should have known, all along, you weren't who you projected yourself to be. I could kick myself for loving someone who's apparently incapable of loving me back.

Since I will have little means to support myself once my husband and I separate, I will need child support. You don't have to be a part of

*the child's life, but you will be accountable for your end of the finances
in supporting him or her.*

Sorry for the inconvenience this has placed on your young life.
Regards,
Emily

Her words left him wondering if he and Emily had been existing in two entirely different relationships at once. In her mind, she'd apparently romanticized their arrangement to some sweeping love affair, persisting against the odds. From Tristan's side of things, Emily had only ever been an escape for him. One that always had a shelf life.

Tristan realized she probably hadn't heard the news about his mother, or she might not have sent the letter in the first place. Or, at least might have chosen her words differently. But her death didn't cancel out the situation with Emily. Grief didn't lessen his responsibility in the matter. He hadn't had time to think about whether or not he wanted to be in the baby's life, but he would do the right thing, eventually.

A half-an-hour later, they sat down at the dining room table to eat one of the last casseroles. They were a lively bunch: Connor staring lifelessly out the window spooning the food into his mouth in an automated fashion. Tristan gazing at his plate, moving the tuna and peas around in a semblance of organization. Markus checking his texts constantly, hoping for some word from his sister. It occurred to Tristan a joke might lighten the mood, but he couldn't bring himself to do it.

Moments later, Tristan's phone rang. He moved to reach for it and then thought better of it. He didn't feel like talking. Less than a minute later, Markus' phone rang, and he picked it up.

Tristan watched his cousin's face turn pale. Mark mumbled responses to whoever was on the other line, and then ended with, "We'll leave for Aunt Colleen's now."

"What? What is it?" Tristan probed. Connor perked up.

SARAH M. CRADIT

"Ashley's daughter, Katey, fell off the swing-set this evening. She broke her neck." He paused, swallowing. "She's gone."

No... no, this cannot be happening.

I need more time to figure this out. I'm grieving!

How many more have to die before you're satisfied, Brigitte?

ALAIN

*I*t was past two in the morning before Alain slid into bed beside Katja. He was careful not to disturb her. After three days and nights of talking nonstop about their situation, he had no words left.

All he could think about was death. Death in its many forms, and figures. There were physical deaths, which had manifested through his family over the years. Death didn't stop there, though. This decision he'd made, no matter the intent or the hopeful outcome, also marked the death of other things Alain didn't realize were important until he felt his grip on them loosen.

His idealism, for one. His innocence, which he'd not even understood he still had until he found out he'd gotten his first cousin with child. And, saddest of all, this was the death of the family as they now knew it. Even if the birth of these children saved them from future turmoil, a new tragedy would spring up in its wake. The triplets would forever be the physical manifestation of all the Deschanels had struggled to overcome. The victory would be bittersweet. There would be no celebration.

With one door closed tight against evil, a new one would open, and the darkness would further bloom.

Why had he listened to Katja with such comforting ease? Her confidence had startled him into submission, as he'd listened to her speak with authority on her research and assumptions. Not even once, in any of their conversations, had her voice wavered. Katja's nerves had been reserved solely for the reaction of others. Of her conclusions, she was sure.

But every minute that ticked by brought them closer to the culmination of all their plans. How much easier it had been to think about the future when Katja's belly had still been flat, and they'd simply been speaking in concepts.

Perhaps the children would even be born healthy, as Katja insisted they would. But what then? There was no polite society that would ever receive them. They would give up their social lives, their families. Olivia might come around, but it was unlikely Alain would ever share a meaningful relationship with his mother again.

And that was to say nothing of the dozens of cousins who'd left the meeting in disgust.

No matter what else happened going forward, the seeds had been planted and they would fester into snarling thorns. Ones that would surround and strangle Alain and Katja for the rest of their days.

And what of our children's children? Will they need to do this too? Alain had asked, when Katja first pressed these unthinkable plans toward him.

I don't know, she'd replied, and Alain had let that answer be sufficient, when it was anything but!

It was entirely possible they'd created a monster far worse, far bigger, than the one haunting their family now.

"Alain, try to get some rest," Katja whispered, surprising him. The clarity in her voice suggested she'd been awake for some time.

"I can't turn my mind off," he replied, staring straight ahead at the ceiling. He wouldn't look at her, or her growing belly. To do so would incite dark thoughts he was ashamed of.

"You have to try, or there will be many sleepless nights in your future," she gently replied.

If there were sleepless nights, he deserved them. Had earned them. Perhaps even welcomed them.

The throbbing in his head commenced, the pressure pounding at his temples in increasing rhythm.

In the other room, a glass shattered.

"What have we done?" Alain wondered aloud, as the first storm clouds passed across his troubled mind.

PART III
OMEGA

JULY 2006

"Heaven knows we need never be ashamed of our tears, for they are rain upon the blinding dust of earth."

Charles Dickens

TRISTAN

*T*ristan Sullivan was alone in the Collective chambers. Around him, velvet chairs sat vacant. Months earlier, the Deschanels had convened, hopeful they might finally, as a family, find a solution to Brigitte's Curse. The diaries his mother had left him, those belonging to Julianne Deschanel and her daughter Ophelia, lay spread open, the obscure contents taunting him.

It is time for me to read them, he had said to Aunt Colleen, who gave him permission to spend as much time at The Gardens as he felt necessary. She divided her own time between Amelia's bedside, and Ashley's living room, as both her children struggled through unthinkable suffering. Amelia barely hung on in her comatose state, and everyone knew this couldn't last much longer, while Ashley mourned the death of his youngest, and only daughter, Katey.

It was for Katey that Tristan now sat before these texts; Katey, even more so than his mother, or anyone else they'd lost. A deep, gnawing guilt pervaded Tristan's thoughts when he considered, had he not been so caught up in his own grief, he might have made progress that could have saved his young cousin.

Three months had passed. The initial shock faded, it was time to start thinking about how to fix this mess. The realization came like a swift kick in the rear, punctuation for the words, *NOW, are you ready?*

Aria, the head of Aunt Colleen's house staff, set some sweet tea before him on the table, without a word. He smiled gratefully, but she'd already turned to leave, understanding he'd come not for socializing, but privacy.

While he'd always known The Gardens to be one of the largest estates in New Orleans, it now felt vast and unending in its emptiness. Growing up, it was a place of laughter and lively activity. It acted as the center of the family sphere, more so, even, than *Ophélie*. But much had changed in the last year. The sound of Aria's fading footsteps sent ricocheting echoes across the marble and cypress for several long moments, speaking of the sorrow that now occupied the halls. A clock, lightly ticking in the next room, was Tristan's only companion.

He glanced toward the ceiling, where portraits of his ancestors lined the tops of the massive oaken bookcases. The table could seat close to twenty; the room could fit over a hundred. Somehow, Tristan found this comforting, rather than lonesome, as he sat surrounded by the venerable ghosts of this midnight dynasty.

Tristan started this exercise with no real expectations. He didn't anticipate some great revelation would jump from the pages, blessing him with the answers needed to save what remained of his loved ones. But doing *something* was better than doing *nothing*. Better than slipping further into the darkness surrounding his family. Better than waiting to die.

He began by piecing together what facts he possessed about his family's history, and the origins of the Deschanel Curse.

Opening this mother's moleskin journal, he started reading her notes:

Charles I, emigrated from France in 1844 with his young wife Brigitte. They purchased a significant quantity of land bordering the Mississippi River, near what is now Vacherie, and established a sugarcane plantation. Their first child, Ophélie, was born the following year, followed by a son, Jean, in 1846, and finally their last child, Fitz, in 1848. The Big House was finished after Ophélie's birth, and it was named for her.

The rest is a legend any Deschanel could recite in their sleep. The plantation was ridiculously successful before the war, and continued to prosper during and after because of Charles' quick thinking. Unfortunately, some of his dealings backfired, resulting in the brutal death of his daughter, Ophélie, which later prompted Brigitte to administer her now infamous Curse.

Between Ophélie's death and the end of the war, Charles' son Jean married Julianne Bonapartie. During the War, Julianne remained at home with her own parents (a mercy, as she would have very likely been given the same treatment as Ophélie if she'd lived under her husband's roof). Once Jean returned from battle, she moved into Ophélie, where she would spend the rest of her life.

Julianne had kept a diary since she was a young child, and continued the practice into her marriage and time at Ophélie. Her entries were often short, and spoke more of contemporary issues, but they also shed light onto the situation between Brigitte and Charles. From Julianne's entries, it's clear she had one of the best vantage points of anyone in the family. She also brought a fresh perspective, coming from a perfectly normal family (when compared to the colorful and powerful Deschanels), so her belief in all she saw held that much more weight. Julianne moved into Ophélie at sixteen-years-old.

In one of Julianne's entries, she describes waking to the sound of Brigitte speaking to herself. In a rare moment of lucidity, while Julianne was feeding her dinner one evening, Brigitte spoke what sounded like a curse against her husband's family. Only a few days later, Brigitte's youngest and third child, Fitz, died in a boating accident with his wife Sandra and their toddler son, Charles. It was a clear day, and Fitz a skilled seaman. Everyone thought the circumstances were strange, and suspicious, but none more than Julianne.

In her diary entry, Julianne makes it clear she believed this to be no accident, and more specifically, that she thought Brigitte was responsible.

Julianne worried for her husband, Jean. From the way she describes their marriage, he wasn't the best husband, but she cared a great deal for him. Their marriage soured when she failed to immediately produce children. Julianne hinted she believed Brigitte was somehow responsible for that, too.

When Julianne shared her perspective of all she'd witnessed with Brigitte, and her beliefs about the death of Fitz and family with others, most tried to reduce her fears by reminding her Brigitte was grieving. Certainly she did wish harm on Charles, and even his son, perhaps. But an actual curse? One with the power to carry out her wishes? Julianne was undeterred. She knew what she saw, and what she believed. Merely anxious about it before Brigitte died, by the time she passed, Julianne was absolutely convinced of the powers Brigitte wielded, despite the cynics. So convinced she later made her only daughter, Ophelia, promise never to have children.

Julianne had two surviving children; not many for the time, but she didn't have her first child until she was twenty-seven. She hinted several times in her diary that she was afraid to conceive, so sure was she of Brigitte's curse potency. Julianne never said it directly, probably because she knew Jean could find and read her writings at any time; to wish herself barren would have been blasphemous. Having children was really the only role she was expected to serve.

Her son, Charles, was born in 1875, and Ophelia three years later in 1878. Julianne's stories of Charles are mostly factual: milestones of his life, details of his meals, marks in school. Her stories of Ophelia are much more colorful; she clearly cherished her daughter.

Julianne died in 1896 at the age of forty-eight. She left years and years of diaries behind to her sixteen-year-old daughter, who continued the tradition of journaling, taking over where her mother left off.

Julianne did not, in her lifetime, ever witness the Curse in action. The death of Fitz and his family pre-dated the Curse, and Julianne's own barrenness could have been pure coincidence, or a result of her late blooming. The fact that she believed so strongly in the Curse, without evidence, illustrates the impression Brigitte's behavior left on her. Ophelia, on the other hand, never met her grandmother but observed the Curse's tragedies first hand, which she chronicled.

From 1901 to 1903, Ophelia's brother, Charles, and his wife, Amelia, had three children: John, Jean, and Elizabeth. Ophelia's journals are filled with stories of their development and her time with them, as she vicariously experienced a family life she could never have herself. Amelia became pregnant again in early 1905, but that year there was a terrible outbreak of yellow fever in the city. All three of their beautiful children died of the disease that summer, and she gave birth to her fourth child, August, while their graves were still fresh.

In 1906, Amelia and Charles brought their last child into the family. A daughter, Blanche, who was beloved but, as a girl, could never carry the Deschanel name forward.

Amelia would die only five years later at the age of thirty. The doctors could find nothing wrong with her. Ophelia's journals indicate she believed her sister-in-law "died of a broken heart."

At the time of August's birth in 1905, there were only a few male members left of the Deschanel family. Charles I, who, perhaps due to the cruelty of the Curse, had survived to ninety-five and watched the destruction of his family. Jean was fifty-nine and had outlived his wife and three of his grandchildren. Charles II was thirty and had outlived three of his children. With the other men too old, the burden of replenishing the family's fortunes was all on August.

Ophelia was very protective of her niece and nephew. With their mother dying when they were toddlers, she was essentially the only mother he and Blanche ever knew. Her brother, Charles II, did not believe in the Deschanel Curse, despite what had befallen his family, and forbade Ophelia from filling the children's' heads with nonsense.

World War I came and went with little impact on the family; Jean and Charles II were too old to fight, and August far too young. In 1920, when August was fifteen, Ophelia managed to convince her brother to send August to Boston for his education, where his sister, Blanche, was already studying. Ophelia's true reasons—wanting to see him far from Louisiana, and danger—were revealed in her diary (which was more candid than Julianne's, as she had no husband to fear), but she sold it as a boon to August's experience and education. A lot was riding on his ability to see the family through to success and he needed adequate preparation. He returned home five years later in 1925, at the age of twenty, married to a Yankee girl named Eliza Gass.

Although the Great War had been over for sixty years at that point, tensions had not completely dissipated in the South, and the marriage was not well-received by local society. Within August's own family, though, this was not exactly shocking or strange given their long associations with the North, and August himself had grown up in a much different time. August was happy, and in love, which worried his aunt. She wished more than anything that he could be happy, but worried endlessly that it would not end well. Unfortunately, Ophelia's fears were well-founded.

Eliza was pregnant a year into their marriage, but it resulted in a stillbirth. The second year she had an early miscarriage, and later that year she suffered yet another. The third year of their marriage she birthed another stillborn, and by the fourth year she was believed to be suffering from some sort of disorder of the uterus (the family referred to her as the Deschanel's version of Catherine of Aragon, Henry VIII's first wife who'd also had a string of unlucky pregnancies despite an heir being imperative for England's success). Eliza was never able to get pregnant again.

August's grandfather, Jean, urged him to consider taking another wife. Although the family had become genuinely fond of Eliza, and found her suitable for August, her inability to have children posed a real problem. Jean himself was in his early eighties, and Charles II his fifties. Neither would be able to take a new wife and try again. By this time, Blanche was on her second husband, a Guidry this time, but her children would not be Deschanels.

August had a responsibility, fair or not, and nothing would change that.

Unfortunately for Jean and Charles II, they both died without knowing if August would be successful. Charles died of a heart attack in 1930 at the age of fifty-five, and Jean the following year at eighty-three. Ophelia, August, and Blanche were the only Deschanels left.

In stark contrast to the lack of security in the family breeding stock, their financial fortunes flourished over the years. Charles I had been successful in business back in France, before he had even come to the States, and his associations with the North during The War had allowed him to focus on his investments during a period that meant great difficulty for most of his local peerage. His wealth had skyrocketed during Reconstruction, where he benefited immensely from the suffering of his friends, and he had investments all over the southern states. His son Jean had learned his father's knack for business, and young Charles II had as well. Charles I had built an empire that was now at risk.

August was not entirely like the three men before him. He had inherited their sense for business, but not their dispositions. He was quiet, kind, and thoughtful of others. His devotion to his poor wife, Eliza, showed his truest nature, refusing to leave her even if it meant the ruination of the family. When she became ill in 1948, and then died in 1949, he was prostrate with grief. As she was dying, he vowed never to marry again, but in a twist of irony, he fell to the unintentional seduction of Eliza's seventeen-year-old nurse, an Irish *girl named Colleen Brady. Although completely ill-suited to be his wife, he married her within a couple of months of Eliza's death. Ophelia said her impression of the situation was that he married her as an expression of the family fortunes so far, and that he "might as well marry the help, in any case."*

Ophelia believed what happened next was proof Brigitte's Curse had a sense of humor. While August had been childless with his beautiful, highborn Yankee wife, his servant-class underage bride started producing children like a factory.

Charles III was born barely a year after their marriage, in 1950. Augustus came along in 1951, followed by Colleen in 1952, Madeline in 1953, and Evangeline in 1954. In '55 there was a miscarriage and then in '56 Maureen came along. Two more miscarriages in '57 and '58, and finally Elizabeth in '59. Altogether ten pregnancies, seven children, and a Hail Mary save of the Deschanel clan. Tiny little Irish-born Colleen had re-energized the near-extinct family.

August was thrilled. Where he had loved Eliza as his partner, he cherished Colleen as the one person who could assist him with a responsibility that had been placed on his shoulders many years ago. Blanche had moved her family to Tammany Parish, wishing to be far from the craziness of the dwindling Deschanels and their Curse.

Ophelia remained the well-loved, albeit somewhat kooky, aunt and played a very active role in the lives of her great-nieces and nephews. Colleen and Evangeline were her favorites; these were the two to whom she passed all of her knowledge and history of the family, including the Curse. Both girls were exceptionally bright, and logical almost to a fault, so it is surprising in some ways that these two—and not the more flighty, impressionable ones like Madeline and Maureen—were the ones to believe so deeply. Elizabeth showed an early interest, but given her proclivity for unhealthy obsessions, Ophelia worried about her mental health and seldom shared any stories with her. Charles and Augustus were too pragmatic, taking not so much after either of their parents, but after their grandfather and great-grandfathers.

Ophelia was growing old. She had witnessed the Curse manifest itself in many ways... through deaths, through barrenness. She had watched her family dwindle down to nearly nothing, only to spring back into a robust, healthy, and happy clan again. Generations had passed since the Curse had been laid upon the family. Time had separated the guilty from the innocent. She prayed nightly for the safety of her nephew's family, but secretly feared this "lull into false comfort," would only result in more tragedy. Her journal entries took on a happier note in her senior years, but occasionally she would slip into her old fears, and the melancholy would overtake her. Her generation slowly dwindled to an end.

August and his family lived a mostly idyllic life. Their children were all happy, healthy, and were some of the most gifted Deschanels to date, both in their special abilities and their academic pursuits. Charles and Augustus both had inherited the strong business sense of their male ancestors, with Augustus having the added power of persuasion. Colleen and Evangeline were strong in the sciences, Colleen in biology and Evie in physics, and both grew into powerful healers. Madeline was an artist, and Maureen, while not the strongest student, was gifted in music and could play almost any instrument. Elizabeth was very bright like her older siblings, but easily distracted by her abilities, and struggled in school. She was a talented writer, though, and her writings as a child were both expressive and concerning. Even her dark moods, however, did not take away from her mostly happy childhood and her strong sense of family. It's unfortunate she was unable to carry that forward when she started her own household.

Only three unhappy events occurred, and none were considered to be related to the Curse.

The first was the passing of August in 1961 at the age of fifty-six, after a two-year battle with cancer. The whole family was heartbroken, but none more than Ophelia, who saw her nephew as the best of all the men who had come through her family. Although he had never shared the same connection with Colleen as he had with Eliza, *he was a great husband to her and a doting father to his children. Most important of all, he had succeeded in breathing new life into his family.*

Then in 1970, Madeline was tragically killed in a car accident at the age of seventeen. Other than August, this was the first Deschanel death since 1931. While the thought of the Curse playing a part did enter into Ophelia's mind, according to her diary entries, it was mostly chalked up to a coincidental, tragic accident that could happen in any family. All families experience unexpected loss.

In 1975, on Christmas Day, Ophelia passed away at the age of ninety-seven. Her last journal entry indicated the family should remain vigilant and aware, but that she believed the Curse had dulled and possibly disappeared completely over the years. The Deschanels who lived now were all innocents, and surely even Brigitte's sense of revenge had an expiration? Ophelia passed hoping she had seen the worst her family could go through; that she was now leaving it in better circumstances and could go in peace.

Her death marked the end of an era for the family. The new one, the one starring the children of August, began.

Charles was the first to bring in the new generation with his son, Nicolas, followed by Augustus' daughter, Anasofiya, months later. In the fall, Maureen gave birth to Olivia.

Next came Colleen's children, Amelia and Ben, in '76 and '77, and then Charles' daughter, Nathalie, later the same year. 1978 saw Colleen's youngest son, Ashley, born, as well as Charles' third child, Giselle; his fourth, Lucienne, would come in 1979, and then his last child, Adrienne, in 1980. That same year Maureen gave birth to her last child, Alain. In '82, Elizabeth had her daughter, Danielle, and then her son, Tristan, in '85. Evangeline, who waited until her thirties to have children, had Markus in '85, and Katja, the youngest of the cousins, in '87.

All in all, the generation produced fifteen children. If August had reinvigorated the family, his children succeeded in growing it by leaps and bounds. *Almost forty years of relative peace had prevailed by the time the last of August's grandchildren were born.*

Unfortunately, Ophelia's sixth sense regarding the false security was correct. In 1996, the Curse swept through the family once more.

Tristan added this note to his mother's:

Whether you believe in the traditional view of the Curse being vengeance for the violence against her daughter, or Katja and Alain's take on things being about some ancient need to inbreed, one thing is definitely true: it all comes down to the words Brigitte spoke as she lay dying.

Known Curse victims/patterns:

1865—1875- Julianne's early infertility (with Ophélie and Fitz both dead, Julianne and Jean were the only couple capable of carrying the family name forward)

1905- John, Jean, Elizabeth (Charles II's children) perish all at once

1906- Charles II and Amelia have their second surviving child, but it is a girl. Much like Jean, this leaves only one person (August) to carry the family name.

1925—1949- Eliza's infertility

1996- Almost fifty years of peace and then nine people die in a single year (Charles III, Cordelia, Nathalie, Giselle, Lucienne, Benjamin, Laurel, Colby, Danielle)

Tristan updated the note below, on behalf of a mother who never had a chance to.

2006- This time, only a decade before the next big massacre. So far, 5 victims: Elizabeth, Rene, Cassius, Annette, Clothilde's miscarriage. Amelia may make 6.

No matter how many ways I attempt to look at this, I cannot pull out any discernible pattern. In the early years, infertility seemed to be the way the Curse kept the family numbers from growing. 1996 and 2006, then, almost feel like a cleansing. Like Brigitte wanted to lull us into a false sense of safety, only to pull the rug out, reminding us we will never, ever stop suffering for the sins of her husband...

Tristan hadn't realized he'd fallen asleep on the pile of journals until he awoke to the sensation of someone standing over him. Aunt Colleen.

"Learn anything today?" she asked, though the question felt more polite than inquisitive. She sunk down into a chair across from him, looking at least ten years older than she had before the world went crazy.

"No," Tristan said, gazing with disdain at the old books before him. "There's nothing here I didn't already know. Lots of mindless ramblings, mostly; that and dry historical crap. What was my mother thinking, leaving these to me?"

Colleen smiled thinly, blinking her tired eyes. Her usual tightly-bunned hair wisped around her lined forehead. "Perhaps she thought your young mind might grasp something she couldn't. In any case, the Council pored through them as well, and came to your conclusion."

"So, what then? Is this it?" Tristan asked her, looking to his wise aunt for some shred of hope, as he always had.

"I don't know," she said, wincing as the admission was clearly painful for her, someone who prided herself on always knowing what was best for the family. *If anyone feels as guilty about Katey as I do, it's her.* "Katja and Alain..."

"Do you really believe it, though, Aunt C? What kind of family would perpetuate incest? It's completely insane!"

"We don't have to understand it to believe it could be true," Colleen replied, voice heavy. "I don't know if the children Katja carries will solve this Curse. But I do know my dearest daughter, my heart, is dying, and my surviving son recently buried his only daughter. Your mother is gone. Many of our cousins, taken from us as well. When does it end?"

Tristan stared in helpless disbelief as the strongest woman he knew dissolved before him.

"If they're wrong, then all hope is lost, Tristan. If they're wrong, we really are cursed to watch everyone we love taken from us." Colleen buried her face in her hands for a moment, running them down her cheeks and neck as she looked at Tristan, red-faced and pitiful.

"So, I choose to believe in their theory. Because, right now, Katja and Alain are the only hope we've got."

COLLEEN

*C*olleen sat in the living room of her son Ashley's townhouse, her heart divided between her daughter laying in a hospital bed across town, and the son sitting devastated across from her. He clutched his two sons and wife as if waiting for them to be cruelly ripped from his arms the way his three-year-old daughter, Katey, had been.

Alexander and Ben, six and five years old, bore the confused looks of children who'd experienced a loss but hadn't yet figured out the breadth of it, their reactions of sorrow more in response to their parent's mood than their own understanding. Christine, Ashley's wife, stared blankly at the wall, her arms limp.

Colleen had, at first, tried to connect with her son by relating to his loss, having lost her own son nearly a decade ago. But no two losses could be compared, and so instead she'd taken turns holding the boys, or Ashley, over the past few months as she attempted to absorb some of their grief, despite her own crumbling heart.

I couldn't bear the loss of my own child. How do I tell one of my children it will be okay? That they will endure? How do I look Ashley in the eye and tell him life will go on, when I'm not at all confident it will? When his sister lays near death, and his other children could be next?

Christine stood suddenly, swaying on her feet as both Ashley and Colleen rushed forward to steady her. "Don't touch me. Either of you. This family has taken everything from me!" The young woman shook them both off and then ambled into the bedroom like a zombie, stumbling into walls as she went in search of escape.

"I'll take the boys. You go to her," Colleen offered, but Ashley shook his head, clutching his sons tighter.

"How's Amelia?" he croaked, as he rocked Alexander and Benjamin in his arms.

"No change," Colleen said quietly. "Oz is still doing everything he can, but I'm not confident it's doing much, other than wearing him out."

"Go back to her, Ma. I'll be all right. I'm going to lay the boys down for a nap, and maybe try to take one myself."

Colleen waved away the suggestion, though half her heart longed to be with her daughter, who stood on the precipice of life and death. "Your father will be here soon, and then I'll go. Amelia has both Oz and Jacob for now. Their presence likely does more for her than mine, anyway."

Ashley forced a tight smile, but said nothing. His soft, baby-like angelic face had developed deep grooves in the past months, and the stubble on his chin was the first facial hair she'd seen on her normally clean-shaven son. His pale hair, nearly white as Amelia's, had taken on a dishwater hue.

The night of Katey's death, a rare F3 tornado swept through the Central Business District, causing over a million dollars in property damage, in the immediate vicinity of Ashley's office. The occurrence was so unusual the city immediately sought national meteorologists to make sense of it. Colleen had pleaded with her brother, Augustus, to use his illusionist power of persuasion to influence the city so they'd let the investigation go.

But since then, Ashley's grief had stirred up several, smaller storms around the city, and it was growing harder to hold off suspicions.

"Chris wants to take the kids and leave. Leave *me*," Ashley revealed, his voice hollow. He could have been talking about anything. "I want to stop her, but how can I blame her?"

Colleen's heart caved in her chest, as it had a thousand times over the past month. Tears flooded her eyes, spilling down her cheeks as they cut a furious path. And then the anger... the rage! How could this happen to good people? How could it happen to *her* people? "She won't. She can't! You two need each other right now, Ashley."

"She doesn't see it that way. She blames me for all this. Or I guess she blames the family, which I'm a part of. I'm not sure she's wrong, either."

Colleen gulped a deep breath. "If I could take every ounce of your pain, Ashley—"

"Ma, I know. I love you. Don't take this the wrong way, but you saying that makes it harder." She almost heard him add in his head, *I can't deal with your grief, too.*

Her mind searched for comforting objections, but Ashley added, "Please, go to Amelia. If you want to give me peace of mind, that will do it. I need to know someone is with her because... because... I can't be." And then her son's expression crumbled as he buried his face in Benjamin's blonde hair and quietly sobbed.

The doorbell sounded, startling them both. Ashley moved to answer it, but Colleen stayed him and went instead. Opening the door, she found Noah on the other side. She resisted the temptation to throw herself into his arms and demand the comfort her husband would be eager to give. The family still needed her strength, and once her real grieving started, it would not be sated or stopped.

"Go, darling, I'll stay with Ashley now," Noah said, laying a gentle hand against her face, intuitively understanding she wouldn't want more. She allowed herself one moment of departure as she closed her eyes and welcomed the embrace.

Planting a kiss on her husband's cheek, she tucked her purse under her arm, and went to comfort her other child.

COLLEEN STEPPED THROUGH THE DOUBLE DOORS OF THE HOSPITAL —once familiar to her only as the place of her occupation, but now for so many other cruel reasons—and headed in the direction of Amelia's room. As she rounded the long hallway toward the suite, she was startled to see her cousin Luther leaning against the wall, eyes closed in quiet contemplation.

"Luther," she called, as she approached him. "It's nice of you to come by." *Especially since today he deals with his own loss. The Curse claimed his niece, Annette, just shy of her twentieth birthday. Llewellyn's daughter.*

"Colleen," he replied, taking her hands in his as he raised them to his lips in a soft, tender gesture. "How are you holding up?"

Colleen shook her head, words failing her. Quickly, she pulled her hands back, afraid the tenderness would break the dam holding back her tears. "Surviving," she said finally.

"Surviving," he repeated, his lips twisting. "Doesn't feel quite like that, but I second the sentiment nonetheless."

"I was so sorry to hear about Annette," Colleen comforted. Showing empathy to others was a safer place than receiving it. "How are Llewellyn and Sophie? And Charlotte? I feel terrible I haven't been by."

"Charlotte is returning home from Yale tomorrow for the service," Luther replied, his jaw tight as he shifted. "My brother isn't taking calls, so even if you hadn't been dealing with your own troubles, he wouldn't have received you. There's no need for guilt at a time like this."

Colleen nodded. "Every branch in this family, someone is grieving. No one has escaped."

"Jasper thinks he's next," Luther replied, with a tight, ironic smile. "He always was dramatic."

Colleen sighed and shook her head in response. "In any case, everyone should hold their loved ones close until the storm passes."

Mentally, Colleen ticked off the losses, once again. First, her sister Elizabeth. Then, Amelia fell ill. Young Rene Guidry drowned soon after, followed by the heart attack of Cassius Broussard. Then, darling Katey, followed by Clothilde Guidry's miscarriage. And now, sweet Annette. Seven thus far.

When would it end? Last time it had taken nine. Would this culling be worse?

"We can't dwell on the unknown, dear one," Luther said, laying a hand against her arm. This unexpected gesture from her cousin startled her into soothing relaxation. "I know what you're thinking, but you must let it go. We're not fighting a tangible opponent. This isn't a fair game. All we can do... all we *should* do... is pray."

Colleen bit back the choking tears lingering at her throat, nodding as she looked away. "I know. I know."

"I came to pray over Amelia. She may yet overcome this, Colleen," Luther went on. "She's strong, like her mother."

A quarter of a year Amelia has been like this. If not for Oz, she'd already be gone. But there's a limit to what he can do to sustain her, and I fear we're reaching it.

Colleen smiled through her bleary eyes. "Strength doesn't stand up well against this invisible menace."

"Pray Katja and Alain's sacrifice will be our salvation, then,"

Luther responded, as he moved to embrace her. "I will continue to lay my faith in God as well."

She watched as Luther walked back down the hallway. His brief and unexpected presence had been a comfort to her, but more importantly, had reminded her not to let grief consume her strength. Amelia needed her. Ashley needed her.

And she needed herself.

KATJA

*K*atja expected to feel antsy about getting back to her studies, but she'd been surprisingly satisfied with the internet, and the library in Nicolas' Quarter apartment, where they'd been staying since the night of the Collective meeting.

Nicolas explained most of the books had belonged to Katja's mother, Evangeline, and her Aunt Colleen, from their days growing up at *Ophélie*. *I moved them here for decoration, so when I brought chicks home they'd think I was a genius,* he explained, but seemed genuinely happy Katja had found some use for them. Some of the texts were slightly out of date, roughly two decades old, but web resources provided a solid counterpoint as to current developments and methods.

It was now July. Three months had passed since she and Alain stood before the entire family and bravely announced they were going to start a family together, in an effort to break the Deschanel Curse once and for all.

The fact that these children—triplets, how was that even possible?—would be born of incest was only one piece of the trial they were about to face. She, Katja, was going to be a mother in a couple of months, before turning twenty. She didn't know how to digest this. Time had done nothing to ease the shock of the coming reality.

Amelia hadn't risen from her coma, so they could only surmise that a healthy birth would be the catalyst for bringing her back. It felt like such a long time to wait. They wouldn't have the triplets in their arms until late fall, and a lot could happen between now and then. Katja's new doctor worried that, due to her petite frame and age, there could be complications. The stress alone posed significant danger.

Her parents continued to be supportive and seemed to have advanced beyond an emotional response, to a scientific one. They helped her plan her future instead of crying over its loss.

Alain's family, in contrast, had not come along at all. His brother-in-law, Greg, wrote him a very nice letter of recommendation so he could find a new job, but had done so in secret, fearing Maureen's disapproval.

When Katja considered Olivia and Maureen's reactions to this situation, she thought, despite the fact that mother and daughter *seemed* aligned, their reasons for turning Alain away were actually quite different. Katja interpreted Olivia's reaction as guilt for failing her brother, whereas Maureen couldn't get past how this made *her* look, and chose to manifest that through unshakeable disgust and shame toward her only son.

Things might have been simpler had she and Alain stopped sleeping together once she conceived, but it was becoming clearer to Katja she didn't *want* to stop, and that her feelings for Alain reached far beyond duty. She loved Alain, and was past the point of caring about right or wrong. Her hope was she would spend the rest of her life with him, in whatever corner of the world they could feel normal and welcome. Provided these children turned out healthy, they might not be their last.

We're going to hell anyway, right? Alain had joked, though over time it felt less and less funny.

They rarely left the small apartment on Frenchmen. Alain spent an increasing amount of his time in the courtyard, painting. He told Katja they needed money, and painting was his only source of income now—Greg's well-intentioned letter collected dust in a desk drawer—but Katja knew better. They'd never stressed about money in this family.

The more time he spent in the courtyard, the more Katja worried about him.

Alain had been of fairly average build before, but he now bordered on lanky. Dark circles cut wide arcs around his eyes and his skin had lost its healthy glow. Katja didn't know how to fix whatever was troubling him. Primarily because he wouldn't talk to her, and while she was certain it was mostly regarding his family, she couldn't help but wonder if he was starting to feel a sense of shame or disgust about his part in their choice, as well. Alain had been close to his mother and sister his whole life, and their disapproval was too much.

Katja had never experienced her parents' disapproval on anything, because they trusted her, always encouraging her to make decisions that were best for her. Even with this situation, they'd quickly moved past their initial fear to emerge as the couple's biggest supporters. Katja was surrounded by love and support on all sides—her parents, cousins—and Alain was only buffered on one. All but one of the people who really mattered to him had abandoned him, and the one remaining was a constant reminder of why the others had walked away.

As time wore on, he sometimes took to sleeping elsewhere. She'd wake in the middle of the night and find him either sitting on the balcony, or on one of the living room couches, staring at nothing. Sometimes he noticed her and other times he didn't seem to realize she was there at all. As June wore into July, she thought she might be losing him, and nothing she did was working to re-engage him. He assured her he loved her, with words, but his eyes said differently.

She mentioned it to Markus, who told her, "When women say they want to be alone, they rarely mean it. But when men say it, they do. Pushing him will push him away."

"I don't think leaving him alone will help. He's getting worse, and he's going to keep getting worse as long as his mother and sister keep acting like self-righteous assholes."

"You need to talk to Olivia," Markus advised. "Maureen won't be reasonable, but Olivia might. She's a miserable bitch, but she loves her brother and if you appeal to her with how he's been acting, she might be able to get past herself and talk to him."

It was a prudent idea, although she didn't look forward to talking to Olivia. She'd put it off for weeks, but couldn't wait any longer. Alain was slipping further away by the day and it had become clear to her that fixing him was beyond her ability.

So she sucked up her selfish dislike and called her cousin. When Olivia didn't answer, Katja left her a message, and then fretted over whether or not she'd get a call back. She left two more messages, and nothing. About a week after her first attempt, Olivia returned her call.

"Thanks for calling me back," Katja said graciously.

"I didn't do it for you," her cousin answered.

"Alain is suffering," Katja replied, ignoring her barb. "And regardless of how you feel about what's happening, he needs your support."

"Of course he's suffering, Katja! He made some rash decisions and now he's feeling the full consequences. It's a wonder *you're* not suffering more!"

"I'm not suffering as much as Alain because my family hasn't abandoned me," she said squarely.

"*He* abandoned *us*," Olivia objected, but the words had the empty sound of someone reading from a script. This was a refrain Olivia had repeated for months. "My poor mother—"

"Is being a selfish bitch," Katja finished. "This isn't about her.

Or you. You can't pick Alain's path in life, but you can sure as hell respect the one he chooses, whether you like it or not."

"How am I supposed to respect this? It's not as if he was doing... heroin or something. We could help him with that. But this? He'll never, ever be able to get over sleeping with his cousin, and now that you are... *pregnant*... he'll have to live with the consequences the rest of his life. Tell me, Katja, how do we support such an unnatural thing?"

"You just do," Katja said, wearily. "You can't change what has already been decided, but you can decide whether or not his choices also mean you losing him forever. It took a lot for me to call you, Olivia. Please, talk to your mother. And then call Alain." She paused, and the silence felt deafening. "We're having these babies with or without your support, but for your brother's sake, I hope you can get over your issues and come be by his side. I'm throwing a small party for his birthday next weekend, and we would love to see you."

There was more silence on Olivia's end, and then, "I'll talk to my mother, but I make no promises." She hung up before Katja could thank her.

Katja's heart sank. She didn't have much hope of Olivia coming through, and she was running out of ways to soothe Alain. No matter how much he assured her he was fine, he was very clearly *not* fine.

If her instincts couldn't be trusted, then surely their slowly dwindling supply of non-broken dishes, and potted plants, was all the indicator she needed.

ADRIENNE

*O*ver the past few months, Adrienne slowly packed some of her belongings away. Not enough Oz would notice, especially with his mind completely occupied on work and Amelia. But enough that, when Adrienne breathed her last breaths, it would be easier for him to erase her memory and move forward.

He spent his days in the office, and his nights by Amelia's bedside, keeping her company in her dreams while trying to find a way to get her out of them. Adrienne couldn't complain about it because she'd pushed him to do it. Both in ways he knew about, and those he did not, and never would.

But she couldn't deny how unbelievably hard it was to watch her husband slowly fall in love with another woman, even if Adrienne had designed the path for him.

There were a million reasons why she had chosen Amelia to replace her. Amelia was smart, and kind. She had a logical, reasonable head on her shoulders, and would do anything for family. Most of all, she was stable, in a way Adrienne had only aspired to be.

"It's awful generous of you, to loan Oz out like that," her

sister, Anne, observed, as she came in from the kitchen and handed her a glass of sweet tea. Overhead, the fan was moving so fast, the resulting high-pitched whir sounded like it might take off. The New Orleans summer was sweltering; more so than usual.

"She's family," Adrienne said with a shrug, not wishing to discuss the unnatural triangle with Anne. She'd invited her half-sister over with some trepidation. There was no love lost between her and Anne, and the bad blood in the space between them had never truly dissolved. Adrienne was determined to make amends, and warm some of the cooling between them, before she died. Colleen had, conveniently, assigned Anne to take care of Amelia's household, which meant she was always only a few steps away.

"Still," Anne said, with a slow shake of her head, clearly not picking up on Adrienne's hesitation. "I wonder what they do in her head..."

"So! Are you seeing anyone?" Adrienne probed, forcing the change of subject.

Anne blushed, dropping her lashes like a schoolgirl. Adrienne resisted the urge to roll her eyes—it wasn't Anne's fault these things seemed so trite to Adrienne now—as Anne said, "Well, yes, kind of. I mean, after Finn married Ana, I didn't think my heart was ready..."

Oh boy, thought Adrienne. *She never even so much as dated Finn. You'd think I was talking to a teenage girl.* "So, you are?"

The crimson in Anne's cheeks deepened. "You know him. Liam, Oz's cousin? The French one? He's helping Nicolas with the annual estate audit at *Ophélie*, and we've been talking..."

"Talking?"

"Oh, stop looking at me like that! It's not serious or anything." Anne looked down at her hands, as if she'd said something scandalous.

Adrienne was growing further annoyed, despite her best

efforts. "Not serious? What, like you've held hands, or have you let him make a few turns around the bases?"

"Adrienne!"

"Look, Anne, I'm not a mind reader."

"Liar. We all are," Anne said with a broad smile. "Anyway, no, we haven't... well, been *together*. We haven't done anything, really, but the sight of him makes my stomach a big, fluttery mess. I've never felt this way before, and I don't know what to do about it."

I seriously don't think I can take this right now. I can't listen to her banal ramblings about puppy love with some guy she probably hasn't even held hands with, while I've sent my husband off to his future without me. I really, truly cann—

"Adrienne, what's wrong?" All the coquetry and playfulness disappeared from Anne's face, as she set her glass down and leaned forward. "Why did you really invite me over?"

"We never spend time together. I thought it would be nice," Adrienne muttered, holding back the tears that tortured her, always, threatening to force her into a complete loss of control.

Anne's gaze was suspicious. "I'm glad you did, but it's not like you usually want to see me. I've been across the street at Amelia's for months, and we've hardly shared a dozen words." She reached a hand out and laid the back of it against Adrienne's forehead. "You look like you've seen a ghost. No, you look downright ill. Adrienne, what is going on? You can tell me. We may not be close, but we're sisters, and I love you."

The sobs deep in Adrienne's throat bubbled to the surface. "The things I've done... if Oz knew..."

Anne touched her arm. "The things you've done? What does that mean?" Her expression was serious as she added, "Whatever it is, I can help, and I won't judge you. I promise."

Adrienne almost told her. It had been so terribly difficult keeping all this bottled up, in the midst of dealing with her pending mortality. She prepared to open her mouth and let the whole thing come tumbling out, just as the front door opened. A very tired Oz walked through, and dropped his briefcase on the floor. *He never does that. Not ever.*

Adrienne rushed to his side, eager to push past the moment where she'd almost spilled her heart to her sister. "Sweetie, what's wrong? You're home early."

"I'm going to kiss the kids goodnight and get to bed," Oz replied, every word sounding like a great strain. "We can talk in the morning. It's the weekend."

Adrienne's heart dropped to the floor. "Amelia... she's not..."

Oz shook his head, as he ran his hand through his wife's hair in mindless comfort. "She's not gone, but she's fading. I don't think I can save her. I'm sorry, Ade, but I can't talk about this tonight."

Adrienne nodded, kissing him before watching him walk up the stairs. She wondered, briefly, if she'd pushed him into a situation where he would lose two women at once.

No, that won't happen. I can save Amelia. I can absorb her hurts, as I've absorbed my children's. I'd hoped for more time, but...

She felt Anne's presence behind her, as her sister laid her face against her shoulder. "How about I stay the night? We don't have to talk, if you don't want. I did bring over some terrible films I found in Colleen's movie closet."

Adrienne turned and embraced her sister. "That would be nice," she whispered, realizing perhaps, after all, she *would* like to hear about the hopefulness of young love. Maybe an escape, for one night, wouldn't be so bad.

ANNE WAS GONE BY THE TIME ADRIENNE AWOKE TO THE SUN streaming through the sitting room blinds. Upstairs, the children squabbled over their toothbrushes, and she smelled bacon cooking.

Entering the disheveled kitchen, "I can't remember the last

time you made breakfast," Adrienne said, as she kissed the back of his neck. Her head was killing her this morning. More so than usual. Every sound, every beam of light, felt like a thousand needles.

The frequency has increased. It isn't like before where you could pretend you might have a month or two. Weeks is more like it, maybe days, and if you aren't careful, Oz will figure it out.

Oz's exhaustion from the night before had apparently faded with rest. "Good reason to make it, wouldn't you agree?" he said with a lighthearted pat to her ass. She winced involuntarily as her head throbbed.

"Hey now, I didn't hit you that hard," he teased, planting a kiss against her pained forehead. "Did you have fun with Anne last night?"

Adrienne nodded, stealing a piece of bacon cooling on the towel. Oz moved to swat her hand, but she quickly danced away, making a point to show him her exaggerated enjoyment as she tore off bites and chewed. He feigned throwing the tongs at her.

"Mhm," she replied, through a mouthful of bacon. "Not that I'm complaining, but I'm surprised to see you home. If you're not at work, you're usually down at the hospital."

Oz's smile faded as he put down the tongs and pulled her into his arms. "Those things are important, Adrienne, but not as much as you and the kids. I know I haven't been here as much as I should, and I plan to change that."

When she said nothing, he pressed his lips to hers and whispered, "I love you, Ade."

Adrienne nearly lost her breath as her heart pounded in her chest, aching with years of love for her husband. Oh, this had been so much easier when he'd been pulling away! It had given her the strength to think, maybe, he would survive her absence. That, maybe, she could get through the next few days without breaking down.

He held her close. The sound of tiny feet scampered down the stairs and into the kitchen, as both Naomi and Christian slammed in to share the hug.

"Our turn!" Christian exclaimed.

"Ouch, you're on my toes!" Naomi shrieked.

Adrienne cried into her husband's chest, the illusion of comfort she'd crafted finally unraveling around her feet as she realized the enormity of what it would mean to die and leave them all behind.

AMELIA

*A*melia leaned back into the gazebo, exhausted. She and Oz had run through the Jacob Ireland sequence for what felt like the hundredth time, and the only purpose it seemed to serve was ongoing torture. Meanwhile, the world her mind had constructed was fast crumbling. The safety her gazebo provided from the encroaching mental darkness would not last much longer.

Your mother believes the dreamwalking is why you're still here, Oz told her. *That it's somehow sustaining you. Maybe keeping you grounded. I don't know if it's true, but I'm grateful you're still here. And I'll keep coming until we can bring you home.*

Equally unhelpful was the confusion brewing in her mind over how she felt about Oz's presence. Over the past few months, something beyond friendship had taken root and grown.

Whatever it was, Amelia refused to entertain it. She would either survive this and make amends with Jacob, or she would die with her heart belonging to him.

Natural, understandable, she'd surmised, in the endless hours she had to ponder things like this. *He's the only person I've had contact with since spring, and my fear and loneliness are reaching out to him as my only lifeline. If a patient came to me with this scenario, I would tell them what they're feeling is perfectly normal.*

But it didn't feel normal. Nor did it feel new. It had the familiarity of an old and powerful love, spanning longer and deeper even than what she shared with Jacob.

I won't feed it. No matter what happens. But I will, somehow, repay Oz for this kindness he's shown me. We'll forever be bound, if I survive this.

"I finally took your advice. About Adrienne, I mean," Oz ventured. "About spending more time with her."

Amelia socked him on the upper arm so hard he flinched. "Slacker. About damn time."

Oz massaged his deltoid, shaking his head. "Damn you hit hard, even in here."

"Man up, Sullivan. Besides, it's all in your head." She smiled.

His return smile read as fun laced with... something more. Much more. Her heart skipped, and she stood, forcibly leaving the moment behind.

Amelia watched as Oz picked up the rising melodic notes of the floral song playing through The Gardens. Sometimes it was subtle. Other times, like now, it rose to levels rivaling a live orchestra. "That song... you can hear it too, right?"

Amelia nodded, still facing away.

"It's so familiar. I even find myself humming it at work, or at home, but my mind can never quite grasp the words. For months I've been thinking about it, and I never thought to *ask* you. Do you know it?"

She turned, leaning against the railing. "It's an old folk song from the 19th century. I don't know the actual title, but we sang it all the time as girls, mostly in my chorus group. We called it the Spider's Web song, though I'm sure it has a proper title. All the girls, myself included, used to beg to sing it. Something about how haunting the melody was, and how sad the words were. There was a mystery about it, you know? One with the power to draw all of us in. And so Mrs. Siebold would save it until the end of practice as a reward if we finished our curriculum. Secretly, I think she loved it as much as we did."

"Sing it to me."

Most girls might have giggled, or feigned embarrassment at the request, but Amelia was not most girls. Never had been. She simply closed her eyes, and her pure alto voice carried across the air:

Down in the valley, there is a mission, down by the old oak tree. Down by the mission, there is a fountain, where my love told me:

There's a web like a spider's web, made of silver light and shadows, spun by the moon in my room at night. It's a web made to catch a dream, hold it tight 'til I awaken, as if to tell me my dream is all right.

I met a stranger, his name was Danger, we rode side by side. Way down in Santa Fe, I killed a man they say, Danger told me, "Ride!"

There's a web like a spider's web, made of silver light and shadows, spun by the moon in my room at night. It's a web made to catch a dream, hold it tight 'til I awaken, as if to tell me my dream is all right.

And now if I return, they will hang me, high from the old oak tree. Down by the mission, down by the fountain, where my love told me:

There's a web like a spider's web, made of silver light and shadows, spun by the moon in my room at night. It's a web made to catch a dream, hold it tight 'til I awaken, as if to tell me my dream is all right.

"Wow. How did I never know you could sing like that?" Oz professed, blushing.

Amelia shrugged. "Why would you?"

"I should have. I'm glad I know now," Oz stuttered. "I suppose the song is no accident, though? Like everything else here."

"It definitely left an impact on me all these years," Amelia agreed. The conversation was veering away from whatever grew between them, and she felt safe taking a seat next to him again. "I used to read the Laura Ingalls Wilder books. Do you remember those? *Little House on the Prairie* and all that?"

"I never read them, but yeah. All the girls in our grade school devoured them."

Amelia went on, "I first heard this song when I was engrossed in the series. Fourth grade, I think. Even though her books weren't all sunshine and rainbows, there was always a steadfast hope about them. You knew Wilder's life turned out okay, so the stories had to also, right? Manifest destiny at its finest. But this song... the words were so deliciously creepy. My friends used to speculate on what the ending meant, assuming some big romantic tangent that continues after the end of the song. But I never imagined a happy ending for the writer. It always conjured up images for me of *Little House's* darker side. The parts she couldn't write about."

"That's messed up," Oz said, then laughed.

"I suppose it is," she agreed, laughing with him. "Anyway, to come back to your question, no, I don't think it's an accident. And just like when I was a girl, I don't think it's here for any happy reason."

Oz contemplated this in silence. Amelia had months to think about the significance of everything in this strange world, but she understood Oz was the kind of man who needed answers, and meaning. He'd been so kind, visiting her like this, it was only a small inconvenience to share her thoughts if the knowledge brought him a modicum of peace.

"I've been thinking about what you said months ago," Oz

ventured. "About how you much you loved Jacob, but ended up hurting him anyway."

"Oh?"

He dropped his head. "I once, not so long ago actually, did something much worse to Adrienne. Something I wish I could take back. She doesn't know, and I don't know if I should tell her. At times I think, yes, she deserves the truth. But then I can't help thinking she's been through so much, and this might break her. Of course, maybe that's just me justifying my guilt."

Amelia suppressed a grin, knowing exactly where he was going. "You wouldn't be talking about the one-nighter with Anasofiya, by chance?"

Oz whipped his head up, stunned. "What? Who told you? Nic?"

"No, Adrienne did," Amelia replied, releasing her smile. "Though I knew something was deeply wrong with Ana when she left New Orleans in such a hurry. Eventually my mother also figured it out."

"No, there's no *way* Adrienne knew or she would've killed me!"

"Actually, you've got it all wrong," Amelia explained, glad to be able to offer him some peace on something that had evidently haunted him for a long time. "Adrienne is capable of a lot more than you give her credit for. She figured it out on her own, by the way. You can't get anything past a Deschanel, even one who isn't wholly clear on how to tap into her sixth sense. But she wasn't mad, Oz. Adrienne, in her own way, understands she's taken more than she's given in your relationship. She told me she knew about the tryst, knew it was eating you up, and she'd already forgiven you."

"Why didn't she tell me?" Oz lamented. "Why has this never come up?"

"I think she saw it as your freebie, in a manner of speaking. Like your transgression evened the playing field a bit. Though, she *did* say if you dallied again, she would cut your balls off, and then let Anne loose on you with her legion of plants," Amelia grinned.

Oz returned the smile, but his mind was elsewhere, likely reliving every conversation he'd had with his wife since the affair, looking for any signs he might have missed.

"Whether she knows or not, or cares or not, I'll spend forever making it up to her," he put words to his thoughts. "And Ana, who I also hurt in that mess."

"Ana is fine," Amelia countered, thinking of the last time she saw her cousin, in a vision, the ethereal radiance with which she glowed. "For the first time in her life, maybe. She's moved past the transgression, and so should you."

He nodded, and his face clouded over. The pull was coming; after all this time, she could now read it in his expression. He'd learned to better control the departure, and so delayed his leaving a few more minutes.

"Amelia, maybe it's time for me to tell Jacob how you feel," Oz suggested warily, as they watched the once-beautiful flowers outside the gazebo shrivel and drip into large black puddles. Before, the colors would return. Now, the world around them rotted into decay, with no recovery. *Soon. Even the dreamwalking can't work miracles.*

"I think we've been at this long enough where you don't need to tiptoe around me anymore, Sullivan," Amelia teased, forcing a smile she did not feel. "What is my mother saying?"

Oz looked down, but placed a warm hand against her knee. "They want to move you home. Where you can be comfortable."

"Ahh," she replied, not really surprised but still shocked to hear it said aloud. "They've given up."

Oz whipped his head up and looked straight into her eyes. Her soul felt the impact. "Amelia, *I* haven't given up. Jacob hasn't given up." His hand trembled as he tried to grip her knee.

"I know," she whispered, placing one hand over his, before

reaching her free hand out to wipe away his tears. *I'm not the only one confused by all that's happened in here.* Oz's heartbeat thrummed hard through his hands. "I need to think about what to say to Jacob."

She didn't add she was beginning to wonder if she'd been misinterpreting the Jacob memory all along.

Originally, she'd held on to the idea it represented the moment she was first bound to Jacob, through the revelation of his family's fate, a secret he'd shared with no one before her. That the moment was also illustrative of Jacob placing his heart in her hands, and Amelia's vow to offer him a better life. She believed this memory was meant to show her how that love could save her, as she and Jacob had saved one another ten years ago by opening their hearts, shutting out all the outside pain.

Oz had agreed with this theory, though neither of them could understand how to connect this experience with pulling Amelia out from her coma.

Now, though... as the world died around her, and her mind slowly succumbed to the blackness, a part of Amelia wondered if that moment in time had instead been the beginning of the end. Bringing Jacob into her family had caused him nothing but heartache as he gave all of himself to someone who could only give a grievously small portion back in return.

Was letting him go, then, the answer?

"You've had so many visitors," Oz ventured, as he leaned his head back against the post. "I sometimes forget how big the Deschanel family really is. All those cousins..."

"Mom and her Magi Council all meet regularly, but getting the rest of the cousins in a room is like passing an act of Congress. I guess widespread tragedy will do it, too," Amelia replied. "How are Katja and Alain holding up?"

"I haven't seen them," Oz admitted. "Your mother said they hardly leave the flat these days. But Katja is due in a couple months, Amelia, so we just need to—"

Amelia shook her head and stood, gripping the posts as she watched the escalating rot outside. "We don't have a couple of months. And anyway, I don't think their theory is correct."

Oz stood and joined her. She felt his warm breath against her neck as he practically exclaimed, "But you said—"

"I know what I said," she sighed, turning back toward him. His wide eyes reflected his fear: her admission had not only stunned him, but dulled his confidence. "I love my cousins, and my heart breaks for the sacrifice they're making. I wanted to believe... I forced myself to believe... for their sake. But I think the Curse started long before Brigitte and Charles. I think it may have begun when Aidrik mated with our ancestor and created a family of hybrid Empyreans. Maybe there are even other mixed families out there with similar problems."

Oz watched her closely, as he processed this. "Have you ever told anyone else this theory? Your mother?"

Amelia shook her head. "To what point? At least when the Curse had a purpose, people could search for ways to end it. If simply existing is what causes this malediction, then what hope does that give anyone? I support Katja and Alain for the simple reason that they've given this family new hope. Perhaps it will last another ten years or so. That may be the best we can hope for."

Oz was shaking his own head, "No. I hear you, but no. I'm not wired to lay back and take whatever fate decides to dish out. My wife and son are Deschanels, so I refuse to."

"Is that what you think I'm doing?" Amelia replied, with a small smile. "There's a fine line between acceptance, and defeat. Understanding the nature of your enemy, and realizing that nature is unchangeable, isn't defeat. It's enlightenment."

Oz grunted, looking away. "You sound like your mother."

"Who a lot of people respect, including you," she countered.

He looked out, his gaze moving right and left across the fields of black, as he leaned against the railing. "I never believed in this silly idea of a Curse. Not even when Adrienne's near entire family died, or your brother, or Danielle. Cursed like the Kennedys maybe, with perpetually bad luck, but some sort of ancient blight? My logical mind doesn't work that way, despite all I've seen growing up around your family."

Oz wandered to the other side of the gazebo and sat, motioning for Amelia to join him. "But I do believe something is very wrong. And if I can't believe there is also, somehow, a fix? How do I go on? How do I accept that, knowing my wife, my children, everyone I love could be ripped from me without notice? And to lose you..."

Oz let the words die between them, and Amelia chose not to acknowledge the unspoken declaration. Moments like this would creep up, unexpectedly, and they both understood that to pursue the emotions was dangerous ground.

"All families, cursed or not, face this risk every day," she reminded him gently.

"I don't accept inevitability," Oz said, as he lowered his face into his hands. "I'm sorry, but I won't. And even if your theory is right, it doesn't mean we can't overcome the consequences some other way."

Amelia smiled, drawing in the putrid floral air. "Adrienne is lucky to have such a brave knight at her side. And maybe you'll solve our mystery, Oz. I hope you do."

Without words, Oz pulled her into his chest, as he always did when his time in the dream world was fading, and allowed their final moments together to be ones of quiet comfort.

OLIVIA

*O*livia had genuinely tried to stay out of Jacob's business. She truly had. Ever since that first conversation with Jacob, she hadn't so much as *mentioned* her concerns about Oz's dreamwalking nonsense. Her visits to see Amelia had been perfectly respectable. Her conversations with Jacob, utterly benign.

And besides, she had pressing matters closer to home. Her child would be born in a couple months, which took up most of her time. And this was to say nothing of the quickly approaching due date for Katja's blasphemous triplets.

The conversation moments earlier hadn't been her fault at all. Oz had been there—of course, the man never left!—doing whatever it was he was doing with poor, invalid Amelia. Jacob rested, trustfully. Olivia had made her usual small talk with the nurse, but then on her way out, the darndest thing happened. Oz came out of his stupor, and his face was bright red. Entirely, full-on flushed, as if he'd recently finished doing something indecent.

"Mind telling us what you've been up to?" she couldn't stop herself from asking.

Perhaps the arms crossed defiantly across her chest had spurred on his defense, but Oz immediately began blubbering about how it was none of her business, and she couldn't understand. "I would agree, I cannot possibly understand the mental rape of a woman unable to defend herself," her fiery-tongue had shot back, and then Jacob awoke.

"Are you on about this *again?*" Jacob muttered, slowly returning to consciousness.

"I'd forgotten all about my concerns, but now I see it's even worse than before," Olivia returned, gesturing toward a red-faced Oz.

"It's exhausting, Olivia," Oz replied, running hands over his strained face. "I'm trying to help her, and ignorant accusations only set us back."

"You're not making this any easier," Jacob added, though Olivia didn't miss the troubled look on his face as he eyed Oz. "I know Amelia appreciates your visits, but I'm really going to have to ask you to keep these opinions to yourself. This is hard enough. Please."

Oz watched them both for a few moments, before excusing himself, mumbling something about getting home to his wife and kids. *Oh, I'll just bet! Flock back to the family with your guilt!*

"The last thing I'd want to do is upset you," Olivia tried to soothe, kneeling near Amelia as she watched Jacob from across the bed. "Truly. I'm only looking out for Amelia. And for you."

Jacob raised a pertinent eyebrow, but quickly dropped his gaze, exhausted. "You can help by never mentioning your suspicions again."

"I'll do you one better," Olivia said, brightening as a brilliant solution came to her. "I won't bring it up again unless I have proof I'm right!"

Before Jacob could respond, she strode from the room with the first real sense of purpose she'd had in months.

. . .

OLIVIA LOATHED THE FRENCH QUARTER. HALF OF IT WAS A FILTHY cesspool of disease and debauchery, the rest a commercial nightmare. The historic gems within were overshadowed by disgusting tourist shops selling overpriced beads, and masks, and things no one generally had any business needing or buying. One such shop belonged to her cousin, Jasper Broussard.

Olivia's opinion of Jasper didn't fall far from her general view of the district he chose to occupy for his ridiculous "profession." He and his wife, Pandora, had once pursued the occult in a scholastic manner, opening up a museum for genuine artifacts. Apparently realizing there was no money to be made in preserving the boring, they course-corrected and instead began peddling services and wares of a less legitimate nature. The Soothsayer's Coffer was filled with love potions, books such as *Voodoo for Housewives*, and promises to cure any ailment, or ignite any heart. Jasper and Pandora had become the very things they most despised. Worse, they'd become filthy rich from their misleading endeavors.

Olivia had little respect for either Jasper's original intention, or his adjusted plans, finding both to be ridiculous and unseemly. However, she couldn't deny the man's knowledge of all things supernatural.

Using her handkerchief to open the door to the Soothsayer's Coffer, Olivia was first greeted by the deep intonation of Marie Laveau: "Step forward, my child, and enter a world of wonder!" and then the scowling face of Jasper's son, Leander, who slumped behind the counter looking as if his employment was a form of torture.

"What wonders can I uncover for you?" he barked in monotone, rolling his eyes toward the ceiling. As his gaze fell on her, though, he offered a half smile. "Oh, hey Olivia. You lost?"

Olivia tightened her purse across her chest, straightening. Her eyes fought not to take in the ridiculousness around her, such as the Eyes of the Old Crone, or the Raven's Beak. To her left, Jasper's smiling over-tanned face beamed from a poster where he sat next to his latest book, *One Man's Conversations with Marie Laveau.*

"I was looking for your father," she replied, ignoring Jasper's unnaturally white teeth sparkling from the glossy print beside her.

Leander nodded his head toward the back of the store. "He's in his office. Make sure you knock first. Never know what that man is up to."

Olivia shuddered, then thanked her cousin, making her way through the dangling skull beads and whiffs of ten different cloying incense. *Lwa Broussard,* the door sign read. Olivia didn't know much about occult nonsense, but she remembered the word *lwa* referenced some sort of voodoo deity. *Of course. The man genuinely believes Marie Laveau talks to him. Why should this surprise me?*

Jasper answered the door and his face spread into a surprised, but amused, smile as he took both her hands in his. "What a pleasure," he declared, kissing each cheek. "To what do I owe it?"

Olivia bit back her annoyance and followed him in. "I was wondering if... if you might be able to tell me about an ability."

"Oh? I rather thought after the Collective meeting you might never want to talk to any of us again," he surmised, with a haughty chuckle. "Though of course, I'm more than obliged to help you."

Don't smack him in the face, don't smack him in the face, don't smack him in the face. "That's so kind of you," she replied with a saccharine smile. "What can you tell me about dreamwalking?"

Jasper's expression immediately plunged into deep thought. "You're not the first to ask. I don't suppose this has anything to do with the recent discovery of Oz Sullivan's ability?"

I don't suppose it's any of your business. "Do you know anything about it, or not?"

As she hoped her comment would inspire, Jasper's ego overwhelmed his curiosity at her intent, and he stood, searching the vast, crumbling bookshelf behind him. "Of course. Many, inside and outside the family, consult me about rare supernatural abilities and occurrences on a regular basis. If anyone will know about it, I will."

Olivia rolled her eyes at his back. "I figured as much. So, what can you tell me?"

Jasper plopped an old book in front of her that looked suspiciously like propaganda. *ABILITIES, UNLEASHED!* the cover read, and inside there were advertisements for male enhancement, and weight loss supplements.

Olivia patiently waited as Jasper found the passage he was looking for. "I know this looks dubious, but if you know how to read these manuals, they're a wealth of information," he assured her. "Ahh, here. This is what I was looking for." Then, he marked the page with a piece of notecard, and slammed the book shut, startling her.

Waving her hankie ineffectively at the moldy poof of dust, "Aren't we going to look at it?"

"There's a story within that I want to share with you. But first, let us talk about dreamwalking, or as some call it, dreamscaping."

"Dreamscaping?" It sounded like something you might hire a contractor for. Or grooming a woman-of-the-night might do to make herself proper for a client.

"It's a derivative of telepathy," Jasper explained, poised with one hand against the book ladder. "Some would even say it's a bastardized version. Like a bad mutation, so to speak. The strongest telepaths, as you may know, can not only read thoughts but are capable of inserting themselves into the thoughts of others. Those who can do that and assume control take the ability a step further, becoming illusionists. Your Uncle Augustus, for example, is an illusionist with a specialty in influencing others. That's a strong form of telepathy."

"So, what's your point?"

"I'm getting there, dear. To understand the connection to the point, you have to appreciate the journey. If an illusionist is a rare kind of telepath, then a dreamwalker is an even more rare form. You would think the mind is especially vulnerable while dreaming, right? That it would be unguarded, and therefore ripe for the picking."

"I hadn't thought about it much at all," Olivia replied drily, dangling her leg over her knee in obvious annoyance.

"Well, it's not," Jasper clarified. "In fact, the mind is a veritable Fort Knox while sleeping. Our brain has natural defenses to protect from subconscious attacks. And so, even the strongest telepaths cannot breach a dreaming mind."

"Except dreamwalkers," Olivia said, pushing her cousin toward the elusive point. "They can do it."

"Precisely. They can. Though very few have the knowledge to control it." Jasper peered at her from across his unnecessarily ornate desk. "It's like having raw, unharnessed energy in your hands. Without training, it becomes unruly. The universe is always seeking to maintain balance, and so any great power comes with some governors. Most dreamwalkers either suppress this ability, out of fear, or they pursue it blindly and become destructive."

Olivia perked. Now they were getting somewhere. "Destructive, how?"

"Though a mind is guarded from attack while dreaming, it must do so because of the pure vulnerability of the mind during this state. It's like… how do I explain this… once the heavy iron gate is pulled up, there are no other safeguards. The mind is entirely bare. You can imagine the damage one could do with such access."

Yes, she could. "So, what kind of damage *could* someone do?"

"Well, all kinds," Jasper explained. "Anyone untrained in swimming through another's subconscious could do any number of injuries, and most completely inadvertent. Memory tampering. Emotional subterfuge. Oh, and I even read a case once where a dreamwalker accidentally erased someone's knowledge of motor skills from their frontal lobe, with just one wrong step! A rewiring of the synapses gone wrong."

Jasper rambled on with more examples, but Olivia's mind clung to something he'd said early on. "Tell me more about the emotional subterfuge," she pressed.

"There're all the unintended things you'd expect, such as accidentally impacting someone's emotional state or feelings for another," Jasper replied. "Which is not unique to dreamwalkers, by the way. Illusionists can sometimes plant those suggestions as well, if they're strong enough." He waved his hand. "Anyway, the most common emotional side-effect of dreamwalking is the connection formed between parasite and host."

Olivia wrinkled her nose. "Parasite and host?"

"Science jargon, dear. The parasite being the dreamwalker, and the host being the dreamer. You see, there is a raw, unchecked intimacy that comes with the bond formed in a dreamwalking session. If done once, or briefly, the impact is minimal, and often reversible. But if performed over time, the tether grows and takes firm hold over both souls. An intimacy that transcends anything physical you or I could ever imagine. If the parasite and host are already closely bonded in the real world, this can strengthen that bond. If they are not, it can create one where none existed."

"Sounds romantic," Olivia quipped, though it did not sound romantic at all.

"It can be," Jasper agreed, smiling. "Though more often than not, it is entirely devastating. Quite far from romantic, in fact."

Olivia leaned forward, listening closely.

"This is the account I bookmarked," he said, re-opening the gaudy tome between them. He pointed toward the story, and moved to explain it before she could read. "A man and a woman. Their names are protected, but this book calls them Aaron and Abigail. Their friendship goes back years, though Aaron, a dreamwalker, has kept his ability secret from Abigail all these years. They grow into adults. Abigail ends up in an abusive relationship, and Aaron decides to break his vow of silence and enter her dreams, with the honorable goal of helping her. To give her a safe place to talk. This continues over the course of six or seven months, and during that time Abigail's situation at home grows worse, while she becomes emotionally closer to Aaron. What neither realizes is that they've become joined, on a level no one can comprehend in the conscious world. They've grown possessive of one another, and are sick in the absence of the other. In essence, through this bond, one can no longer survive without the other. In a fit of jealousy, Aaron murders Abigail's fiancée, and she subsequently tells him she never wants to see him again. Unable to live with himself, but unwilling to live without her, Aaron asks her to take his life. Abigail complies, then takes her own."

"Sounds like Romeo and Juliet," Olivia said skeptically. "Also seems like they were both unsettled to begin with."

"You may be right," Jasper agreed, nodding. He flipped the page. "But here are fourteen more stories, all nearly identical. You'll find dozens of similar accounts around the world. The cast is different, the circumstances varied, but the end result is the same."

"They all die?"

"Die, end up in prison, spiral into depression. On only rare occasion, they end up together," Jasper said with a slight smile. "For some, I suppose, it's not an entirely terrible phenomenon."

Olivia's worst fears were not only confirmed, but enhanced. Oz had been in Amelia's head for months. Months!

She stood abruptly, knocking a handle-less mug of pens to the floor. "Thanks for your time, Jasper."

"Well now, you're in quite the hurry all of a sudden! Did I answer what you came here for?"

Olivia turned briefly at the door, smiling in tortured gratitude. "And then some. Good day."

OLIVIA'S FISTS FELL HARD AGAINST THE OAKEN DOOR OF THE Jameson house. She knew her aunt was home, because Noah was on Amelia duty. And if she was home, she would be alone.

Aria answered the door, but Olivia marched past her before she could say a word. "Aunt Colleen!" she yelled, pacing the foyer to project her voice throughout. *"Aunt Colleen!"*

Her aunt appeared from the back door, untying a gardening apron. "Olivia, what is it?"

Olivia's breath caught in her throat, choking back a forming sob. She wouldn't let it. She could not. "You knew all along, didn't you? *Didn't you?*"

Her aunt's hand reached out to steady her, as she attempted to guide Olivia toward the sitting room. But Olivia planted herself firmly, refusing to move. "Tell me!"

"Darling, I have no idea—"

"The side-effects of dreamwalking! You knew and you let Oz do it anyway!" Olivia shrieked, ripping out of her aunt's grasp. "You let him do this to your daughter!"

Colleen's eyes widened briefly, and then her face settled into a firm, resolved expression. "One day, when Rory is older, you may be faced with a similarly unsavory situation. I pray you won't. But if you are, you'll remember this discussion, Olivia. Amelia is my daughter. There are no consequences worse than her death."

Olivia looked down at her hands, realizing she was trembling. She clasped them quickly together, steadying herself,

SARAH M. CRADIT

though she could not stop the turmoil inside. "That was not for you to decide," she said, slowly. "You've always interfered with everyone's lives. And you always have a damned excuse for it, too." Olivia bit her lip to stop the anger from overflowing. "If Amelia does wake up, I hope she sees you for who you really are."

For the briefest of moments, her aunt looked shaken. And then, in her even, controlled voice, she instructed, "Aria, please see my niece out."

TRISTAN

*T*ristan hadn't meant to ignore Emily for so long. She'd been on his mind, but it was a space shared with a list of unspeakable horrors. The loss of his mother had brought him to his knees, and all that happened since kept him there.

You cannot ignore this responsibility, both Aunt Colleen and his mother had said, at different times, with different meanings and intentions. He'd understood all along they were right, and now he was ready to face the music.

And who knows, maybe Katja and Alain really would break the Curse, and he would no longer need to look over his shoulder, wondering when the boogeyman was going to come for him and his family. Maybe he and Emily could even make an attempt at something normal.

Well, except for that husband of hers. There's that to deal with.

So Tristan faced his fear and reached out to her.

First he tried texting, and then calling. Every attempt went unanswered. He considered calling her at work, but then realized, with some shame, he didn't even know which school she taught at. There was so much he didn't know about her, and she was carrying his baby.

SARAH M. CRADIT

"Go see her," Markus recommended, as he watched Tristan furrow his brows at his cell phone.

"She's married! I can't just waltz up to her front door and discuss this over tea."

"You said the guy works all the time. So go when you know he won't be there," Markus suggested with a shrug.

"That's a huge risk. What if he's home?"

Markus closed his laptop and peered levelly at Tristan. "Look. She's at least five months pregnant. Maybe more. He already knows something is up. He might kick *your* ass, but you'd deserve it."

Tristan opened his mouth to object, but Markus was absolutely right.

"But first, figure out what your agenda is. Don't walk up there like an idiot," Markus continued. "Better understand what you want."

"I want what Emily wants, I guess," Tristan hedged, looking down at the table.

"Don't be a pussy. Emily is only half the equation. Do you want to be a dad, or a sperm donor who sends a fat check each month?" Markus pressed, throwing his palms up in frustration.

"A... a dad," Tristan stammered, as the realization spread through him. He wasn't ready, not by any stretch of the imagination, but now that the opportunity was here... now that he'd had some time to digest the reality, and set aside the other chaos in his life...

"Hey, that's progress. Do you want to be a weekend and summer dad, or do you want to somehow convince this chick to leave her husband and be with you?"

That answer wasn't so simple. "I don't know," Tristan admitted.

Markus waved his hand in the air. "Doesn't need decided today. Get in the car, we're going over."

"What! To her house?"

"Where the hell else? Now let's go, before your balls crawl back up and stay there."

EMILY AND HER HUSBAND SHARED A SMALL CREOLE COTTAGE ON the outskirts of the Quarter, south of Rampart. The once-bright colors peeled rebelliously in large curls, and the garden was completely untended, branching wildly into the neighbor's yard. He remembered her husband was supposedly quite successful, and realized this likely wasn't true. They'd both crafted their share of lies. Tristan realized anew what a mystery this woman was to him.

"If you're scared, I can throw up an illusion and make her think I'm you," Markus offered. "Of course, you might not like what I tell her."

"No. I need to do this myself," Tristan replied, though the suggestion was tempting.

Markus waited in the car as Tristan made the agonizing walk up the small wooden stairs and knocked on the door. He glanced back at his cousin, who offered an encouraging nod. Tristan turned back toward the door with a deep breath...

...and found himself staring at who he presumed to be Mr. Emily.

Tristan stammered to find words, as the man said, "I know who you are. Leave."

"I need to see Emily," Tristan managed to spit out. *My child. I have a child. Me! Somewhere beyond that door he's growing, and he's going to know his father. I swear on my mother's tortured soul I will not let this child grow up without me.*

"And I need you to leave," said the man, requiring no formal introduction as Emily's husband.

Tristan found his voice, channeled through his anger at the man's rudeness. "I have some things I need to say to her, and I'm not leaving until I do."

Emily then appeared behind her husband, small and timid compared to his towering frame. The bags under her eyes hung dark and heavy, her expression betraying how worn out she was.

"We need to talk!" Tristan shouted, looking past her husband. "I'm sorry for how I acted, and I can explain it if you want, but we're going to have a baby, and I'm ready to help you!" *I don't know if I love you, but I could. I could love the woman carrying my child.*

Emily shook her head, stepping out from behind her husband's shadow. Tristan's eyes dropped down as he watched her run her hand over her flat stomach. Very flat for someone five months along.

Realization dawned on him.

"You see, after a short visit to the clinic, you two have *nothing* to talk about," her husband said and slammed the door in his face.

Tristan managed to keep his composure all the way to the car, but when he slid into his seat, he buried his hands in his face as the horrified gasps of hyperventilation began.

"We don't have to do this here," Markus soothed, as he threw the car in gear and peeled out from the curb.

I had the power to prevent this. I could've said something. Anything at all. She wanted my help, and my support, and I ignored her. I did this.

That's three deaths on my conscience now.

I need to get far, far away from everyone I love.

ALAIN

*A*lain considered the paint-splattered canvas before him, wondering where the last hour had gone. Who painted this? And where had he been?

He leaned back in the metal chair as a banana tree frond tickled his forehead. Yes, he was in the courtyard. The rich scents of Frenchmen Street wafted in, followed by the low sounds of tourists ambling around the bars below. For a brief moment, he considered wandering down to Cafe du Monde for some *cafe au lait*, but then remembered it was Saturday and the lines would be clear back to the Pontalba buildings.

The distinct creak and smack of the screen door filled his ears, and he sensed Katja approaching. His fingers tensed on the dripping paintbrush, as he drew in heavy, ragged breaths.

Go away.

I hate you.

I need you.

"Sorry to disturb you," she started, with a timidity completely unlike her. He didn't turn. He couldn't bear to see the summer sun shining down on her blossoming form.

"It's okay," he responded, setting the brush down. "Everything all right?"

Katja's voice choked. "They're talking about taking Amelia home."

Alain stared straight ahead, glaring at the shadow Katja's growing frame made on the flagstones. "I'm sorry to hear that," he replied, evenly. He couldn't think about Amelia dying. It reminded him of his pregnant cousin standing several feet away, and his role in creating that.

Katja's frustration with him burst to the forefront of her own anguish, "Alain, it means they're talking about letting her die! Doesn't that bother you?"

"Of course it does," he replied, and it did. But what was one more loss, in a sea of them? What more could he, Alain, do that he had not already done? He'd already given them everything.

But he could say none of that, so instead he prompted, "You should go see her, Kat."

"I intend to!" Katja nearly shrieked, as her shadow danced before him. "But so should you. Amelia has always been kind to everyone, and Aunt Colleen needs the family to rally around them right now. They've suffered worse than anyone, what with Ben passing the last time around, and now Ashley's daughter. We should all be there."

"I can't—"

"And what's more, I think we should consider inducing the triplets," Katja interrupted. He couldn't stop what happened next, how she flounced around from behind his chair to now stand entirely before him. The sun beat through the break in the trees, casting a line of light right on to her belly, as if to taunt him through this tangible juxtaposition of light and dark. Good and evil.

But her words jarred him even deeper. "Are you crazy? They could die!" he exclaimed. But he wasn't nearly as sad about this fact as he should've been. It was the fear of seeing them before he was ready which provoked the outburst.

"We come from a family full of goddamn healers!" she cried, arms flying in animation. "Alain! A slightly premature delivery is nothing science, or our family, can't handle. But we cannot lose any more of our people. I can't bear it!"

No, none of this could be endured. But it must. "This is a decision we should make together, and I'm sorry, but I don't think it's a good idea. I love Amelia, too, but we can't put everything at risk for one person."

Katja gulped in a mouthful of air, no doubt preparing to assault him with a barrage of rebuttals. Then instead, her face fell entirely as she watched him. The sense of loss on her face caused him a moment of regret.

"I'm going to the hospital," she said tightly, and marched off.

WHEN SHE WAS GONE, ALAIN COULD FINALLY BREATHE AGAIN.

He felt trapped inside his own head, held hostage by his decisions, which grew increasingly, more apparently, wrong as time went on. When Katja had first come to him, it seemed very clear what they needed to do, and in the first few weeks following, he had even come to a point of being comfortable and—at least kind of—happy with the decision. He loved her, even now when he couldn't stand the sight of her or her ever-increasing belly. But in the moments of clarity where the fog would leave his thoughts, he saw their choices through clean eyes. A growing dread, and hopelessness he couldn't shake, filled him.

He saw what his behavior was doing to Katja, and the part of him that loved her felt genuinely terrible for having caused her pain. But the darker part of him wondered if, as her stress level rose, she might lose the abominations that grew within her. He knew he could never talk her into abortion, and he could never physically hurt her to cause an accident... but he couldn't help it if he hoped one would happen anyway. Those thoughts were plaguing him, along with a thousand sets of hands crushing his skull. He was damned, no matter the outcome.

Alain knew she had tried to get his family to come see him; that she believed it was their behavior driving his melancholy. But she was wrong. His family's attitudes were mostly a symptom of the bigger problem. He couldn't blame them for what they thought, for he'd come to the same conclusion on his own. In fact, to see them would only make him feel worse. He couldn't face them until he had resolved this twisted dilemma, and he hadn't figured out how to do so, yet.

His small birthday celebration was nice, and Alain enjoyed himself in spite of everything else. Evangeline, Johannes, Nicolas, Mercy, and Markus came to share a classic comfort meal prepared by Condoleezza: jambalaya, cole slaw, and *creme brûlée* for dessert. Nicolas contributed an aged bottle of something strong for the obligatory birthday toast. His mother and sister didn't come, of course, and this disappointed Katja, but Alain was relieved. How could he tell her he didn't want his family to be there, but wouldn't mind if she took an accidental fall down the stairs?

Only two more months and the triplets would be here. So many choices to make, so much anticipation. Sometimes he would watch Katja and wish she wasn't his cousin; that he was free to love her and the children growing in her. She was amazing... perfect. Exactly what he wanted. But that was the cruel joke of his fucked-up life, dangling that which he wanted most but should never have.

Time was running out to resolve things, but he would, because he had to.

MARKUS

On the way back from Emily's house, Markus stopped the car twice for Tristan, who claimed he was going to lose his lunch. All that emerged were desperate, choking sounds, and incoherent curses aimed at the universe. After the second time, Markus redirected the car toward the river, and parked in an empty lot near Jackson Square.

"Where are you taking me?" Tristan croaked miserably against the window.

"For a drink. You can't go home like this." *Not with your father one foot off the deep end already.*

"I can't go anywhere," Tristan replied, his breath fogging the glass as Markus switched the car off. "Everywhere in this city reminds me of her."

Markus didn't know whether the "her" Tristan referred to was his mother, Emily, or a combination of both. It didn't matter.

"Come on," Markus ordered, as he ripped the passenger door open and lugged Tristan out. Tristan stumbled into his cousin's arms and then righted himself, before ambling into the side of the brick building with a thud. "Easy," he added.

"I need to do something, Mark. I need to do something *now*. Jump in the river and swim until I drown, or drown until I swim. Run through the cemetery until time runs backwards and my mother is here, and my baby is still mine and all my cousins... all my cousins..." Tristan slumped to the dirty alley floor as his rambling continued.

For the love of neuroscience, he hasn't even had a drink yet. "Come on, Tristan. Let's go inside."

"...And I would tell Brigitte to have some fucking *foresight* and think... *think*... about what she's doing because a lot can change when wars end and smoke clears..."

"Tristan—"

"Do you know she visits me? Not Mom, Brigitte, I mean. But she's usually talking in French and I don't understand a shitting single word in that language, some Creole I am..."

He's really leaving me no choice. Markus lifted a hand and slapped Tristan across the face, hard enough for the slumped man to whip his head up in anger.

"Sorry. Now, please, let's go inside before the tourists start throwing beads and taking photos," Markus mumbled, pulling his cousin to his feet.

THE BAR WAS NEARLY EMPTY. IT WAS STUCK HALF DOWN AN ALLEY, out of the way of the tourist throngs, and held no immediate appeal to a casual passerby. It looked like the average neighborhood pub in a small town: nondescript, but plenty to drink.

Tristan was unusually quiet once inside, saying nothing until after his third shot of whiskey. Senses sufficiently dulled, he said, "I don't know if I loved her. I've been trying to sort it out in my head, but I really don't know."

"Emily?"

Tristan nodded. "She was always kind to me. Pretty. And until everything exploded she never put any pressure on me, you know? What I can't figure out is, if I wasn't a Deschanel, would I have even given her a second thought?"

Content Tristan was calm enough he wasn't going to bolt, Markus signaled for his own drink. "If you weren't a Deschanel, you'd have been dating an unmarried woman your own age."

Tristan shook his head. "No, that's not what I mean. You're right, but that's not where I'm going with this. I'm searching for whether I had real feelings for her, or if I really just used her, entirely, completely."

"I don't think it matters," Markus replied, with a sigh born of pragmatism and a need to see the world in a far more black and white spectrum than Tristan was playing in now, "because she used you, too. You think you're the bad guy, for fucking a married woman? You didn't rape her. She didn't have amnesia. And you know, I didn't see her leaving that husband of hers, either."

Tristan lifted the shot glass, reflecting the overhead light off his amber drink. "But she might have, with the baby. That changed everything. Maybe that's what she was trying to tell me."

When the bartender came back around with Markus' drink, Tristan ordered another three for himself.

"We're not in a hurry," Markus remarked, but did nothing to amend the order. Tristan was safe with him, and he wouldn't let anything happen. For his own part, Markus rarely drank beyond a light buzz. He preferred all his senses about him.

"Oh, I am," Tristan replied, with a bitter laugh, as he finished his drink.

"Why do your feelings for Emily matter?" Markus asked. "You wouldn't have had to marry her to get the kid."

Tristan looked ahead at the glittering bar. "Because I'm so numb right now, from everything. Everywhere. But then the pain sneaks in, and it's so acute, and so widespread, that I can't even pinpoint the source. I don't know what hurts the most. Did

I love her? I have no idea. But the child..." Tristan lifted his hands in the air, forming a small ball. "Markus, I can't describe it to you, the knowledge my cells, parts of me, were growing to form a person. A real person." He dropped his hands, smacking them against the bar. "This is my fault."

"Oh, fucking hell, it is not," Markus protested. "She could've made the same fucking choice, even if you'd gone to her and professed your love and promised the world. You understand that, right? It was her decision to make. Her body."

"It isn't that simple, and you know it," Tristan barked.

"Oh, it is. It certainly is. You think returning her messages changed the fact that she's married? She can't be a complete idiot," Markus returned. "Her husband likely would've left her with nothing, and legally he'd have been within his rights. And her trade-in would be a boy barely out of his teens who doesn't even live on his own."

"You don't have to insult me."

"Reality check is all. Emily wasn't going to leave her husband. He never would have allowed her to stay and keep the baby. In hindsight, I don't see how this ever had a chance of ending differently."

Then there was silence between them, the only sounds around them coming from faded speakers overhead, and the two ceiling fans nearly whirling off their chassis.

"I never had girlfriends in school," Tristan broke the calm. "It was too much of a hassle, with mom always up my ass about being careful. When I got into college, I got drunk at a frat party and slept with some girl I didn't even know. She was my first, and I don't even remember the act. I found her panties in my pocket when I got home. What I *will* always remember is how *empty* I felt. I threw her underwear in the trash. And I never touched another woman again, until Emily."

Markus didn't respond. They were both coping with the same problem in different ways.

"Every single day I was with Emily, I convinced myself I felt nothing for her. The sex was great, she was a fun companion, and she was safe. Completely safe! When you tell yourself something long enough, you start to believe it, you know?"

Markus nodded.

"Self-delusion is a skill I learned from my mother," Tristan went on. The whiskeys he'd ordered minutes earlier were gone, replaced by three more. *I'll need to stop him soon. I don't want our next destination to be Touro Infirmary.* "What's real? What I told myself, or how I felt when she fell asleep against my chest? I don't even know what love is. A happy, warm feeling? Devotion? Right now, I feel nothing. Nothing at all."

"Well, you're drunk."

"Nothing," Tristan repeated, lifting a new shot of whiskey before him. "Nothing for months. And I don't think my feelings are coming back."

"Time," Markus said, though he wasn't convinced time did anything other than dull a sensation. If something was important enough, your feelings for it never truly went away. "You've had far heavier shit to deal with in the last three months than most people cope with over a lifetime."

"Sometimes I hated her. I thought, a woman who would cheat on her husband is worse than the scum under my feet. But then, I guess I hated her for the same things I loved her for. For curing my loneliness. Fucked up, huh?"

"Come on, let's get you home."

Tristan lifted the final two glasses in unison, pouring them into his open mouth as the whiskey ran down over the stubble on his chin, and out the sides of his mouth, joining with the fresh tears streaming down his cheeks. "Take me to a bridge, any bridge," Tristan slurred, as he stumbled into the wall behind him. "I want to see if I can fly!"

"Here's a spoiler: you can't."

Tristan slid to the floor and looked up at Markus with wide,

SARAH M. CRADIT

searching eyes. "Well, then I'll see Mama and Danielle again. And that won't be so bad now, would it?"

Markus knelt and lifted Tristan's weight as he helped him back to the car.

I'm not going back to D.C. Not now, or likely ever.

Katja and Tristan need me. And I need to make peace with that, because it's not changing anytime soon.

ADRIENNE

*A*drienne inhaled the late summer scents of crepe myrtle and verbena, as she sat with her husband and children under the oaken canopy in City Park. A light breeze passed through, providing temporary relief from the enveloping humidity. But Adrienne's heart soared with love for her small family, and she wouldn't have noticed a hurricane, so enraptured she was with the magic of the day.

A few feet away, Naomi and Christian kicked a soccer ball across short distances. Christian would scold Naomi for kicking it in the wrong direction, and in return she'd kick it hard enough to send him chasing after it, then turn to her parents and giggle.

"She's mischievous, like her daddy," Adrienne noted, with a wink toward Oz.

"Or maybe she's had enough of your influence. I seem to recall a young girl with a ton of spirit, who used to run circles around her whole family," Oz returned, pulling Adrienne toward him with a gentle squeeze. He planted a kiss on her forehead as he held her.

"It's not my fault no one shared my imagination!" she

declared in mock protest. "I saw the entire world as my playground."

"It was a compliment," Oz assured, kissing her again. For a moment, the years faded away and they were the Oz and Adrienne of a decade ago, their love swallowing whole everything around them. "I fell in love with the girl and her huge imagination. I'm happy it's rubbed off on Naomi, too."

"You are not even *trying*, Na!" Christian declared, hands on hips. "The goal is *here*," he added, drawing an invisible but dramatically pronounced line in the air behind him, "and you have to kick it *here*. *Heeeeerrre*. Got it?"

Naomi nodded, squaring up as she bit her lip in mock concentration.

"She's toying with him still," Adrienne whispered. "Watch her kick it into the pond."

Naomi's eyes never left the invisible goal as she ran toward the ball, releasing her foot in a powerhouse kick. But a small smile played at her lips as her foot hooked toward the left. The ball shot up into the air and plopped down into the small body of water.

"That was not the goal, Na!" Christian shouted. He huffed and puffed in the direction of the pond, as Naomi giggled into her hands.

"How did you know she was going to do that?" Oz asked, smiling.

Adrienne laughed gently, watching her children argue. "Because it's what I would have done."

Adrienne leaned back on the blanket, gazing up at the bowing branches of the oak. Earlier in the day, they'd taken the kids to Cafe du Monde for beignets, and then to the Aquarium of the Americas, where both children stopped bickering for a whole hour as they took in the inhabitants with wondrous awe. They had a picnic in City Park, followed by a quick tour of Storyland, which Naomi found fascinating and Christian complained about the whole way, exhibiting his frustration through the precise kicking of rocks. Oz had promised to make oyster po'boys while they played baseball in the backyard, to close out the evening.

She couldn't imagine a more perfect day, nor remember the last time they'd done so much together as a family. And the whole thing had been Oz's idea.

I've been so busy, but that shouldn't come at the expense of my family, he'd said. *I want to make up for that, Ade. Not only this one, but every weekend. Sundays should be our family day, and we'll always make it special.*

Adrienne had swallowed back the lump in her throat then. Nothing sounded better to her in all the world. She prayed that when she was gone, which would not be long now, Oz would remember this wonderful feeling and continue the tradition with the children. And Amelia.

Amelia... Adrienne had gone a whole day without thinking about her. It was a strange feeling, to both wish another woman could love your husband and also to despise her for the same thing you wanted her to do. There was no woman in the world better suited to take care of her Oz, and her babies. It was the single comfort Adrienne had left as she prepared to depart the world, and leave her family behind. But time was running out.

"Are they still bringing Amelia home?" Adrienne ventured.

Oz's face fell. "Tomorrow. I don't want to think about that today though, okay? I'll go see her tomorrow, but today I want to enjoy my family." The smile on his face was forced, but also genuine.

Adrienne nodded, leaning into his chest. "Okay, sweet-heart." But she'd asked for a reason. It was now apparent Amelia wasn't going to pull out of this, either on her own or with Oz's help. Adrienne had never really believed much in the family curse, so she wasn't looking to this cousin baby to solve anything. Though a small part of her, one almost too small to acknowledge, still held on to the possibility of a reprieve.

If Amelia was going to survive, it would require a miracle. And it just so happened, Adrienne had the ability to deliver one, which would be a lot easier if Amelia was across the street, rather than across town.

Once I take it from her, what happens next is completely unpredictable. I might die on the spot. It might fester in me for minutes, or hours. But I can't wait. As soon as she's home, I must do this. I must. I can't risk her dying and all this being for nothing, only to buy myself a few more hours or days.

And I have to call Lougenia. She needs to plant one last, powerful seed in them both.

"It's funny," Oz said, as he watched the children play, "though Naomi was Janie's, she reminds me so much more of you."

Adrienne held that compliment close to her heart. She'd never once looked at Naomi any differently than she did Christian. That Naomi's father would sense Adrienne's influence was the sincerest praise imaginable. "I hope Janie rests easy knowing her little girl is well-loved," she whispered. Her voice cracked. She had to be careful. "Christian, though. He is all his father."

"Do you mean to say I'm bossy and have a low tolerance for imperfection?" Oz teased, craning his head down toward her.

Adrienne giggled. "You said it!"

"Then he'll make a great lawyer someday. Sullivan, through and through!" Oz declared. His expression shifted as he watched his only son play. "I'll love him no matter what path he chooses, though."

"What if he marries a crazy woman, like his dad?" Adrienne asked. The tease was only half-hearted. Adrienne understood Oz's life could have been far different had he married someone whose head was on straight. Someone like Amelia.

"Then he'll be most fortunate," Oz smiled. His eyes took on a hazy look as he pressed a hand against her face. "I wouldn't do anything differently, Adrienne. Not a thing. All the heartache was worth it, because, in the end, I'm the richest man alive for all I've ended up with. Two beautiful children. You. I wouldn't change any of it. And I wouldn't change you."

Adrienne could no longer restrain the swelling sobs in her chest. Maybe she should tell him... maybe he deserved to know, to not be caught off-guard, to understand what she'd done...

For one moment, I could almost believe in this Curse, because to believe in the Curse means to believe there could yet be a cure. Oh, God, what I wouldn't do to reverse this!

"I love you, Adrienne. And if Christian finds a woman like you someday, he will be a lucky man indeed," Oz added.

No, I can't tell him. This is it. The last time we'll share a moment like this, and be together as a family. I won't taint their memory of this day with sadness. I can only pray that later Oz understands my betrayal is the last and most important gift I can give him.

"I wouldn't change it either, Oz. You have always been, and always will be, my big hero," she whispered through her tears.

"All right, all right," Oz said, wiping at her tears. Overhead, the sun began to disappear behind a row of oaks. "Those po'boys aren't going to make themselves, right?"

"Last I checked, you didn't exactly possess the skills to make them either," she teased, sniffling. "But I'm hungry enough to eat just about anything."

Oz ruffled her hair and stood, "Come on, kids!"

As they scrambled to follow their father out of the park, Adrienne hung behind and watched the three of them. Naomi jumped on Oz's back, feet swinging, while Christian swatted at her legs, weaving back and forth. Soon, this is how it would always be.

But not tonight. Tonight they were four, for the last time.

COLLEEN

"It's not over!" Jacob yelled, once they were outside the room. "I'm not giving up on her, and I don't understand why you are!"

Seeing Jacob's pain was nearly as heart-wrenching as the decision Colleen had come to, finally. "Jacob, darling. I *know* how you love her, how much you love her, but I don't think you've ever quite understood the magnitude—"

Jacob dropped his voice, as he eyed Colleen steadily. "You might not let me play in your sandbox, Colleen, but I know who Amelia is, and what she's capable of. I know her better than anyone."

Denial was a powerful thing, and Colleen couldn't proffer comfort to him until he moved past it. "I understand you think you know Amelia as well as you can. And you do, as well as anyone who is not a Deschanel could. She has loved you as much as she can allow herself," she said. "But she has kept from you the extent of her abilities. Her empathic nature is less a strength, and more a weakness."

"I already know that," Jacob insisted, growing further impatient.

"You *don't* know," Colleen replied, evenly. "At least, not all of it. Her empathic connection can kill her. It *is* killing her. And none of us have the power to reverse it." She paused, allowing him to digest that.

"You think I'm being ridiculous, or daft," Jacob accused, turning to look at Amelia through the glass. "But I can't accept what you're saying. Not that her ability has put her in danger, but that it's over." He pressed his forehead against the window. "If only she'd explained this potential to me, I could have protected her better."

"Allow me to try," Colleen said gently as she placed a soothing hand against his back. "Perhaps perspective will help. When a normal person, such as yourself, reads the news or watches television, you're subjected to all the world's grief. Murder, rape, senseless violence. You might shake your head, or feel sadness, maybe even shed tears. It might stay with you, for a while. But you move on. You let it go." She drew in a deep breath, and removed her glasses, fogged from the developing tears. "Amelia is incapable of letting it go. The pain stays with her, festering, eating at her. I trained her to stay away from the news, but she can't avoid emotional situations entirely. Life doesn't work that neatly. When Tristan's pain hit a peak, Amelia not only felt it but absorbed his shock and agony. Emotional distress, as much as physical, can shut the body down."

Jacob swallowed hard, but his eyes never left Amelia. Colleen realized, not for the first time, what a strong young man Jacob Donnelly was. His smiles and laughter hid a much deeper resolve that he'd kept with him since his troubled child-hood. "And you believe Amelia's body has shut down."

"I know it has."

"And you also believe nothing can heal her. Not the medicine of man, or whatever it is you Deschanels can do," he deduced, months of realizations seemingly hitting him all at once. "Because this is a malady of the mind, not the body."

Colleen steadied herself, reaching around to take Jacob's trembling hand in hers. "Yes, this is what I've been trying to tell you, Jacob. I can't save her. I cannot save my own baby girl."

It was Jacob's turn to be the strong one, as he wrapped Colleen in his sturdy arms, running his hands over her back in comfort. Her tears consumed her, finally, as the embrace brought the reality of all they faced into brutal clarity.

"The power we have over what happens to our loved ones is limited. This isn't your fault," Jacob said, as he comforted her. She knew he was thinking of his own family back in Ireland, all lost to senseless violence. "If you think moving her home is what needs to happen, then we will do it. But it should be our home. Mine and Amelia's."

Colleen nodded, drawing inwardly on her steel center to pull herself back together. "Yes," she replied. "That's what Amelia would want."

Jacob moved again toward the glass, watching his love. "I wish I could do what Oz does. Talk to her in her dreams. I would do anything to say goodbye to her properly. Our last words together..."

"Are not words meant to be taken to heart," Colleen assured him. "She knew you loved her. It was that love which gave Amelia her fire."

"My white witch," he whispered against the glass, laying his face against it with a stilted exhale.

"I'll go speak to the doctor," Colleen concluded.

A FEW MINUTES LATER, SHE RETURNED TO FIND JACOB CURLED IN the hospital bed beside Amelia.

"Tonight," she told him, running her hand across his back. His body shook with his sorrow, and her heart caved deeper. "Noah and Ashley will be here soon. You'll ride with Amelia in the ambulance, and we'll all follow."

"How... long... will..." Jacob struggled to breathe. "How long, once she is home?"

"Not long, darling," Colleen said, as she found her own comfort through offering what she had to him. "Not long."

KATJA

$\mathcal{M}$onday came with the news that their cousin Kitty, from the Guidry branch, had suffered a heart attack. She was in her early fifties, and in fairly good health. Miraculously, she'd survived. Katja couldn't even recall who Kitty was, beyond a few words at the Collective meeting, but that didn't make it any easier. The pressure was mounting.

The night before, Amelia had been moved to her home on Seventh. *To die in peace,* people were saying, but what peace could be found in such a senseless loss?

Katja went briefly to visit. The air in the cottage felt warm and still, as cousins collected in every room, whispering in somber tones. When Katja entered the doorway to Amelia's room, Amelia almost *did* look at peace, in her own bed, flanked by the two men who'd done everything they knew to save her. Oz, on one side, resting his eyes. Jacob, on the other, already mourning the loss. Amid the coverlet's jumble, she nearly missed Amelia's Siamese, Miss Kitty, determinedly curled up in a tight ball between her mistress' feet.

Off to the side, Colleen and Noah sat with Ashley. They'd

thanked her for coming by and paying her respects, but none had the energy even to stand.

In the end, Katja had simply kissed Amelia's cheek and sent her love quietly.

"I'M GOING TO DO IT," KATJA ANNOUNCED TO ALAIN, WHEN THE driver dropped her back off at the apartment. "I know you said the decision belongs to both of us, but I don't care anymore, Alain! I'm *not* going to watch more people I love die!"

Alain's back was to her when she entered. Now, he spun his chair slowly to face her. Shadows danced across his face, producing a look that was utterly sinister. Chills traveled down her spine.

"You. Will. Not," Alain answered in a voice she didn't recognize.

"I will," she challenged bravely, coming closer but carefully. "You can't stop me. I won't allow the suffering to continue!"

Alain stood, his stiff movements resembling a reanimated corpse. As he approached her, she backed away instinctively, sensing a new danger from the man she loved.

With a thud she smacked against the wall, but Alain continued toward her. Suddenly, his face was inches from hers, his hot, heady breath swirling before her. "You will *not*," he repeated.

"Stop," she pleaded, turning her face. Over his shoulder, she watched splinters tracing through the center of the mirror, as the glass cracked.

His hand swung up and grasped her neck in one, quick move. She wheezed as the air was robbed from her lungs. "I will kill you if you do," he seethed as he crudely turned her neck to the side so he could repeat the threat directly into her ear. She gasped for air but his hands crushed her windpipe. "All four of you."

In that moment, Katja believed him. Whoever had his hands at her throat, holding her life at his fingertips, he was not Alain. Not the man she'd lain with, and whispered her fears to. He would never, not ever, do this to her.

Spots peppered the room as she began to lose consciousness. And then he dropped her. She sank to the floor, one hand clutching her belly protectively, the other raised high, opening her airways.

Katja gasped huge heaving breaths as she watched Alain turn and walk away from the room, with the same collected posture. *Alain... Alain what's happening to us? To you?*

She slipped her hand into her pocket, and, finding her phone, she went to dial her mother. But as the rings resonated against her ear, she realized if she told her parents, they would have Alain arrested. And Markus would flat out kill him, no hesitation.

Katja ended the call and closed her eyes.

ADRIENNE

*I*t was time. Amelia was home, and the family collected for their goodbyes.

If I don't get the courage now, I'll never find it.

She'd sent the children to Oz's mother's house. Catherine hadn't even questioned it, knowing Oz and Adrienne were dealing with the Amelia situation. *She'll question it later, though. I only pray she doesn't blame herself for not noticing something was amiss.*

Next, Adrienne picked up the phone and dialed Nicolas. Condoleezza answered. "Would you please put my brother on the phone?" Adrienne asked.

"Of course, dear," came the response.

Moments later, Nicolas was on the other line. *My brother. My only brother. I love you, and I wish I'd said it more. I wish we'd done more together.* "Can you come over? Please?"

"Uh, right now?"

"Yes, right now. Please. It's important," Adrienne responded. She fought back the pleading in her voice. This wasn't news to be shared on the phone, and she didn't want him wrecking his car trying to get there.

Nicolas sighed. "Okay. I'll be there in an hour."

"Wait, before you go. I need you to promise something for me."

"What?"

"Don't tell Oz," she said. "I'll explain when you get here, but I need to talk to you, alone."

Nicolas' tone shifted. "Okay. Okay, Adrienne, I won't. I'm coming now, all right? Stay put."

"Thank you, Nic," she whispered as he hung up the phone.

It was real now. Nicolas was coming.

She only hoped she could make it that long.

THE FRONT DOOR TO AMELIA AND JACOB'S HOUSE WAS OPEN, AS she expected. Dozens of Deschanel cousins assembled throughout, clinging to faith. *We've all lost so much. They're holding on to the remote possibility Amelia might beat the odds and give them a fresh hope. When she survives this, likely they'll assume it's some divine sign the Curse has ended. Maybe it's better they believe that.*

One face after another nodded to Adrienne, running their hands over hers, as she passed through. She smiled, offering comfort in return, but moved quickly toward the reason for her visit.

As she ascended the stairs, the sound of tears filled her head. *Am I too late? Please, God...*

Entering the room, she watched as Ashley escorted his mother out, followed by Noah. Only Oz and Jacob remained in the room. Oz looked up at her in surprise, then understanding.

"I tried," he said, defeated. But he wasn't talking to Adrienne. His words were meant for Jacob. His eyes didn't even rise toward his wife. *Guilt, on many levels. I suppose Lougenia was able to come back by, after all.* "I thought we had it figured out, I really did..."

"I know, sweetie," she consoled, eyes on Amelia. "Would it be okay if I had a moment alone with her?" When Jacob's eyes widened with fear, she added, "Only one. I promise. I have some things to thank her for; things that are just between us girls."

Jacob nodded slowly and rose to leave. As Oz followed, his eyes only briefly met Adrienne's, but she knew his thoughts: his heart was breaking for Amelia, who he'd finally realized he had deep affection for. And his wife served as a reminder that the loss would be a deep one.

Lougenia's work was even stronger than I thought.

Adrienne sat at Amelia's bedside once she heard the door close. She smiled, noticing the small brown and cream cat curled loyally at the foot of the bed. "I don't have long, Amelia, dear. I wish I did, but that's life, right? Here's the thing. I'm going to give you your life back. It's a gift not only for you, but for my husband, and my children." She took Amelia's hand in hers. *Don't hesitate any longer. Say what you need to say and go.* "I love him, Amelia. And I know you do now as well, even if those feelings don't make sense to you. But I'm going to ask, in return for this gift, that you embrace these feelings. Take care of Oz. And take care of my babies. With me gone, there will be no better person for the job."

Adrienne then closed her eyes, and narrowed her focus down to the darkness ailing Amelia. It didn't take long to find it. It was massive, consuming, swirling around inside her cousin like a colossal, black hurricane.

Then, as Adrienne had with her children, she concentrated on drawing that force away from Amelia and into herself.

It nearly knocked the breath out of her, as the energies transferred. Several times it resisted and she used all her strength to regain her hold, as she heaved it back toward herself. When at last she finished, a great black void consumed her, and Amelia coughed as the last of it left her body.

"Sleep," she soothed Amelia. "When you wake, it will be all better." Her cousin remained silent, but Miss Kitty stirred from her post.

Adrienne barely held it together as she stumbled out of the room, following the cat, gripping the doorframe. "You can go back in," she said, and both Oz and Jacob raced to return, barely acknowledging her in their rush to Amelia's side.

She felt a momentary flash of guilt, for what this would do to Jacob. But Jacob was young, and didn't have a family to worry about. He would move on.

As she staggered down the stairs toward the front door, Lougenia reached out and grabbed her arm. "Adrienne! Ya look like ya gon' pass out. Let me help ya."

She looked up at her cousin, gratefully. "There's only one way you can help me, Lou."

"Then rest easy, darling," Lougenia responded as she escorted her toward the door. "It's all done. He gon' survive this, and he'll do it with her at his side. I made sure of it. And if he starts actin' out, I'll make doubly sure of it."

"There's one more thing," Adrienne panted, her full weight resting on the doorframe. "There's something Oz did last year. Something he's tortured himself over for too long. I need you to help him let go of the guilt."

"You mean that thing with him buggerin' Anasofiya?" Lou asked.

"For the love of *God*, does the whole town know?" Adrienne exclaimed, wincing as a new wave of pain rippled through her.

"Naw, I caught it when I was in his head," Lougenia assured her. "And you jus' consider it done, Ade."

"Thank you, Lou. Sincerely."

"It ain't nothin', Adrienne. You want me to come home with ya? It's happenin', soon I mean?"

Adrienne shook her head. Even the weight of the air was

very nearly too much. "Just help me across the street. My brother is coming, so I won't be alone."

As Lougenia gently nudged her up the stairs, she said, "Ya be brave now, Adrienne. God be with you."

TRISTAN

$\mathcal{T}$ristan's building agony was so great he nearly fell out of Amelia's house. On his way, he passed a very exhausted-looking Adrienne, who hardly noticed him.

"Where are you going?" Markus asked, catching him by the arm.

You're not my keeper, dammit! Tristan wanted to scream. "For a walk," he barked.

"All right. Let's go," Markus replied, as Tristan yanked his arm away.

"I need to be alone," he insisted. When Markus eyed him skeptically, he added, "I'm fine. Really."

Markus watched him walk away looking unconvinced, but mercifully didn't stop him.

Tristan moved at a leisurely pace until he was out of sight, then broke into a sprint in the direction of St. Charles Avenue.

He arrived, panting, as the streetcar pulled up. Agony, fear, sadness, pain, and agitation all fought to take over as he nearly jumped off again, wondering if he could run faster than the streetcar could carry him. He planted his feet firmly against the car's floor, tapping his hands against the seat as he closed his eyes, searching for patience. For words.

Eventually the car came to the end of the line, and Tristan flew off, switching to the Canal Street car. The ride was shorter this time, and he again found himself sprinting, panting, gasping, until he was standing before the neglected cottage south of Rampart.

He raced up the stairs, pounding on the door. "Emily! Emily, come out and talk to me! Emily!"

Backing down the stairs, he paced the upended sidewalk, searching for any signs of her in the house. "Emily! I love you! Emily, please! I need you! I need to talk to you, to see you! To touch you! *Emily!*"

A neighbor poked her curler-covered head out a window, shaking the assembly, making the pink plastic tubes bounce. Tristan ignored her censure.

"Emily, I know you're in there and I'm *begging* you!"

When at last the door opened, Tristan rushed up the stairs, but it was not Emily standing before him. Her husband's face boiled with rage, as he swung the baseball bat.

Tristan had no time to think before the wind was knocked from him, as the bat connected with his torso. His lunch churned, lurching back up his throat as he flew down the small staircase, rolling on to the sidewalk. He raised his hands in defense as the bat came down on his arm, followed by a loud crack. *My arm. The bones in my arm.*

"Stop!" Tristan cried, curling into a protective ball, but one blow after another was struck, landing on his legs, his back, arms, and neck. The pain was blinding, and one glimpse at his attacker's face told him mercy would be unlikely. *He intends to kill me, and no one's going to stop him.*

"John!" Emily's voice called, as tiny footsteps pattered down the stairs. "Stop! You'll kill him!"

"He's on my fucking property! It's self-defense," John raged, moving to strike again when Emily reached up and grabbed the bat in mid-swing, stopping him.

"He's unarmed," she said calmly, taking the bat from his hands.

"You're going to defend him now?" John demanded, throwing a swift kick at Tristan's face as he writhed on the ground.

"Not him, honey. You. Do you really want to go to jail for this piece of crap?" Emily soothed, rubbing her hands over her husband's shoulders in some messed-up form of marital comfort Tristan couldn't begin to understand.

John shrugged her off and stormed away, leaving Emily and Tristan alone.

Who are *you?* Tristan wanted to ask, but his mouth filled with blood, and his head swam with stars and confusion.

Emily knelt down, and for a moment Tristan filled with hope she might help him. But then her eyes narrowed and she said, "You make me sick, Tristan. You're a child, trying to play grown-up." She glanced at his hand, which clutched his belly. "Does that hurt? Well, let me tell you about pain, you son-of-a-bitch. Try being abandoned by someone who swore you could trust him. Try having your husband drive you, at gunpoint, to an abortion clinic, telling you, 'Someone's going to die today. You, or the baby.' Try having to then live with that husband because you have nowhere else to go, and a life full of regret. No, you don't know pain, Tristan Sullivan."

She stood then, towering over him. Tristan squinted his eyes, making out only her frame against the dazzling sun. "If you're not gone in two minutes, I'm going to call the cops and tell them you attacked John. Then I'll tell them you raped me. I'll tell them whatever I have to, to ruin your life the way you've ruined mine. So go, you ridiculous boy. Get out of here, go back to your charmed little world of gated mansions and afternoon tea."

Tristan closed his eyes and focused his telepathy. He didn't care if it was a violation. He had to know. *I hope you die, Tristan. I hope you choke on your own vomit and patheticness and fall into the river and drown. I hate you for all you did to me. I hate you for making me hate myself. And I swear if you don't get up in ten seconds I'm going to take this fucking bat and finish you myself, you miserable sack of shit.*

Tristan mustered all his strength then to stand. Emily backed away, flinching, as if he was somehow going to attack her in his weakened state. *I'm not your husband, lady. I'm not like that.*

"I'm sorry for what happened between us. I'm sorry for what he did to you. I won't bother you again," he said, spitting a mouthful of blood at his feet. "But if your husband ever lays another hand on me, or even so much as looks at me, I'll send the fucking fury of all the Deschanels upon him. And trust me, he won't much like what they will do to him."

"The Deschanels?" she called after him in fear-filled wonder, as Tristan limped away from her, toward the very river she hoped would drown him. "I thought you were a Sullivan."

Tristan turned only briefly, laughing through his blood-stained teeth. "Lady, there's a lot you don't know about me!"

Tristan ambled toward the river, ignoring the rest of her words as she called after him with more questions, piecing things together in this, the final moments of their knowing one another. But Tristan had no words for her in response. He had nothing. Everything had been taken from him.

This hopeless realization emitted a huge rolling bout of laughter as he nearly collapsed in his fit of sudden giggles. He had nothing! Nothing! He was alone in this world, and that was *fucking hilarious!*

Tristan laughed all the way to the river, broken arm crudely flapping, ignoring the gaping expressions from the passersby who couldn't decide whether to run away or help him. When at last he reached the levee, he climbed up and over it, and slid down toward the bank of the Mississippi.

Laughing still, he knelt and lapped the water at his face, splashing it all over his clothes and up into his shoes, with his good hand. Above him, people were shouting for him to come back up, that the current was heavy, that he was going to hurt himself.

Finally, some brave bystander did drag him up, amid Tristan's crazed laughter, which was quickly fading to colossal, racking sobs.

"Son, can I call someone? You're badly hurt," the man asked, as a crowd nearby watched, whispering, gaping.

Tristan reached across his body, into his pocket, wincing, as he pulled the phone out, and handed it to the kind man. "Can you call my dad, please? Connor Sullivan? Tell him I need him." And with that, Tristan passed out.

OZ

*A*s soon as Adrienne left, Oz knew what he had to do: visit with Amelia one last time, and hold her as she passed, so she could go in love, and not fear.

Love. He was consumed with it. He felt it in the air surrounding her, passing through his skin any time he touched her; saw it in the rise and fall of her breaths. It stole his breath away, it was so powerful. And as it grew, his guilt slowly faded, one emotion drowning out the other, confusing him further.

Soon it will mean nothing, he told himself. *She can't survive this, no matter how badly you want her to. And if she somehow did, you could never, ever be with her.*

He could only surmise this flood of tender emotion originated from their experiences together over the last three months. Where else? Oz loved Adrienne more than anyone in the world, except his children, but when he was with Amelia, now, what he felt eclipsed any love he'd ever known. It made everything he and Adrienne endured over the last decade feel like nothing more than a fling, though he knew that feeling was blasphemous, and wrong.

SARAH M. CRADIT

But intellectual knowledge changed nothing. Not his heart, or his fear of losing it when Amelia's ceased to beat.

He no longer asked Jacob's permission to visit with Amelia. He'd earned the right to be there, with all he'd done. In fact, Oz tried to talk to Jacob as little as possible. Speaking to the man enhanced his guilt, while ignoring him made it somehow less tangible.

Oz entered the dream world to find the entire setting in complete disarray. Hurricane-force winds blew through the garden, with plants, vases, and wood planks flying through the air. Amelia had her head buried between her knees, hands over her head, as the gazebo came apart around her, flying white daggers ripping through the foliage.

"Amelia!" he cried, shielding his face as he dodged begonias and shards of glass pots. "Hold on!"

When at least he reached her, she peeked her face through her hands at him. "This is it. The end of everything," she cried, as her hair whipped around her in furious blows.

"Amelia Marie, look at me," Oz called out, above the rising tenor of the destruction. "Look at me!"

Amelia raised her head. Her eyes were bloodshot red, but she glowed with strength and bravery. She was so unlike his Adrienne, who needed the strength of others to find her own. Amelia was prepared to meet her doom all on her own. She squared her shoulders and inhaled.

Oz pressed his forehead against hers, tenderly rest both hands on the sides of her face. "I promised you we would find a way! I'm not giving up." *I love you. God help me, but I do, and I can't watch you die, even if it means I can never have you. Even if it means putting that love in a box and forgetting it.*

"Oz," she said, kissing his cheek, "it's over. I'm done trying to make sense of things. The visions of Jacob were nothing but my mind going through the paces. And it's okay. Some things in life are irreversible."

"*I'm* not okay! I can't lose you!" he cried, realizing the tears falling in his lap were his. Above, the top of the gazebo flew off, disappearing with a flash into the fading distance. There was almost nothing left of the garden, or the small prison Amelia had lived in for months.

Amelia pressed her face into his chest, breathing gently against him in submission. *She's not defeated, only calmly accepting a fate she's been preparing for all along. She's stronger than me. I can't bear it.*

Oz whipped his head around in panic, searching for something, anything, for his mind to hold on to. A hint, a suggestion, anything. *Think! Think! The visions! The visions have to mean something. Why would the mind of someone so strong be giving her a lifeline for it to mean nothing? Think!*

A conversation from a few days ago occurred to him. *I wonder if the visions aren't telling me to hold on to Jacob, but to let him go,* Amelia had said.

At the time, Oz thought the notion was ludicrous. But as the world now crumbled around them, and Amelia's remaining time dwindled, the only thing more absurd would be giving up. It was the one thing, the only thing, they hadn't pursued.

"Amelia," he said quickly, raising her face to look at him. Her lower lip trembled as she dropped her eyes. She didn't want Oz to see her final lapse in bravery, and he loved her all the more for her weakness. "Remember what you said before? About maybe the visions being exactly the opposite of what we thought?"

She nodded, but her eyes kept drifting toward the flowers flying past, as the last of her stronghold dissolved. A sob rose in her throat, but she choked it back. Oz squeezed her hand. "Do it, Amelia. Let him go."

Amelia turned back to him, eyes wide with a thousand emotions. "Jacob?"

Oz nodded furiously. "I know you love him, and he certainly

loves you, but it's the one thing you haven't tried. To let him go. To set him free, and in turn free yourself of the guilt you've felt all these years."

Amelia suddenly bent herself over, head through her knees, as she gasped at the disappearing ground. Oz rubbed her back, aching to see her like this, and to ask this of her. *Because if she survives, she'll be all alone. If she releases Jacob, she can't turn to you. You can't give her the contents of your heart when they aren't yours to give.*

And then his Amelia sat back up and placed one hand against his face. In the silence between them, a forbidden love grew and took an irremediable hold. Neither said the words, but Oz saw, through her eyes, the nature of her returned love for him.

The gazebo then exploded in a thousand pieces, as the last blades of grass shrieked in the agony of a dissolving earth. Oz's instincts flowed forward, as he pressed his lips to Amelia's, unknowingly sealing the bond Lougenia had laid foundation for.

Amelia nodded, pulling back as she twined her arms around his neck. The look in her eyes said she didn't believe it would work. Her surrender to Oz was only a final comfort. "You tell him... you make sure he knows..." her voice choked, as she finished, "... how much I love him."

"I will," Oz promised.

Amelia kissed him this time, harder and even more desperate than the one Oz had given her moments ago. "Thank you, for everything," she whispered between his lips, as they closed their eyes against the destruction. The bench they sat on, the only thing left in this dream world, blew away, and it was just Oz and Amelia, locked in terrified embrace, as the world ended.

And then it stopped.

The wind died, the chaos stilled.

Amelia was the first to pull back as she gaped at Oz in awestruck panic. Around them, only a stark whiteness remained, as if they stood upon a blank canvas.

"Am I dead?" she whispered, turning around on the blank page, searching for signs of anything, as he did the same.

"If so, we both are," Oz marveled.

Then, Oz was overwhelmed with the rising pitch of excited voices around him, as he slowly came to, processing the new emerging landscape.

"Oh *mi bruja blanca*, my God, you're awake, you're awake, oh God," Jacob cried out from the other side of the bed, leaping out of his chair. Oz saw Noah take his son in a tight embrace as they cried together in tears of joy. Colleen was pushing everyone aside, declaring she needed to get in, needed to see.

Amelia's panicked eyes flitted across the room, darting back and forth as she registered that she was alive, and had made it out. Oz had not yet fully taken this in until her eyes fell on him.

She allowed her family, and Jacob, their embraces, all the while a look of acute panic plaguing her expression.

And then she was pushing her mother away, pushing Jacob away, as she climbed into Oz's arms, where she'd been safe for so long.

Oz held her tight, feeling both their heartbeats thrumming uncontrollably in unison. *She's alive. My heart. No, I can't have her. But oh, how I love her. How I need her. For just this moment, this last moment...*

As he rocked Amelia in his arms, he regretfully observed the looks of shock, panic and accusation from Jacob, Colleen, and the rest of her family.

ALAIN

*A*lain had been inching toward the limit of what he could take for weeks. Months. The sight of Katja's growing bump, even her kind, understanding smile, sickened him. It was not a lack of love, but rather his *immense* love for her that fed this cancer eating him from within. His love for her was unnatural; the children, worse: monsters. He had done this to her, and he couldn't undo it. He couldn't put her back to her former, innocent state.

This was irreversible, but it was fixable.

Katja no longer tried to get his attention, or to cheer him up. She seemed to be finally realizing what he had known long ago: that all the sweetness, pleasantries, and posturing in the world wouldn't reach him. There was nothing to be reached. He was simply a vessel now, one required to end this mess.

Split from deeply within, he no longer felt much of Alain left inside of him. He could access Alain's memories, and even some of his feelings, but it was as if he were sitting beside his body, watching events play out on a television. He observed hollowly as he nearly strangled the life from Katja earlier, without feeling a thing. He couldn't remember what it was like to be happy or carefree, though truth be told, he'd never been much of either. But he *had* experienced emotion. He had not always had this vacancy inside. One that had been consuming his soul since the day Katja learned she was having their child.

Three abominations. How was this possible? And one boy, two girls. Of course... Brigitte would want it this way, so that the very same boy and one girl would later couple together and create more purebred Deschanels. Probably their son would couple with both of his sisters. It was so clear, and so terrible.

With the perspective of time, and now well-apart from his misguided lust, he did not see this the way Katja and others did, that it was an end to a curse. No, he knew it would end one but bring on another... of brothers bedding sisters. Corrupted hedonism that may have been acceptable in Brigitte's time but would drive them from society now. There was no way to win at this game, but he wouldn't allow his children, or anyone he loved, to succumb to such wicked and disgusting terms. Eventually, Alain even started to believe his family deserved this curse; that perhaps total extinction was preferable.

A part of him still loved Katja with all his heart. The memories that were strongest for him were the first few nights after she came to New Orleans. She was fresh-faced and beautiful, full of crazy ideas that he'd eaten up, just as he had absorbed her, completely. In those days, he had believed, like her, they could stop all of the family's pain and over a hundred years of malediction, by simply loving and creating a new world for their family. What a fool he had been. Not a fool to think it would work because he still believed it could, but a fool to believe that this was the best way. A fool to believe that it wouldn't come at the cost of their souls, that there was any conclusion which brought redemption.

He knew now what he had to do. He'd known for a while, but knowing and obtaining the courage to follow-through were not the same. It had taken even more time to build up the determination, but he had it now. There was still some nostalgia in him that made him want to cuddle up next to her one last time, to feel her soft pale hair across his arm, the warmth of her milky skin next to his. He couldn't risk the effect of it on him, though. He knew right this moment that he could do this, but what if that changed after touching her?

No.

He had never owned a weapon before. So when he found Nicolas' gun, he'd had to look up on the internet how to properly load, chamber, and fire the compact pistol. It was easy enough. He tried to imagine firing it into a person, and while that was at first repulsive, it slowly, over time, started to seem easier, and even natural. He could envision the act of contrition as if he'd already done it, a thousand times over.

Over the six months of her pregnancy, he had stopped seeing Katja as a person, and started seeing her for what she really was: a vessel for evil.

On the night of his deliverance, he didn't worry so much about closure. He could have written notes to many. Sister. Mother. To Nicolas, who'd given them a home in spite of their disgusting ways. Others maybe, even Tristan or Amelia. Markus. But none of them had come to his realizations yet, and maybe never would.

Instead he wrote only a very short note, by way of explanation to others.

"We cannot sacrifice our souls for the redemption of our bodies. This is done." He signed it: *The Alpha and the Omega.*

He left the note on the kitchen table, where it was sure to be found. He knew how Tristan's family had felt when Elizabeth took her life, and this compassion was perhaps the last part of the real Alain remaining. He wouldn't write them a biography, but they would understand *why*.

The clock caught his attention. It was very late in the evening, or early in the morning, depending on how you looked at it. Three. He felt no guilt over what he was going to do, but he did feel some at leaving the mess for Nicolas to stumble upon later.

Unlike the night he'd choked her, or all nights leading up to this, there were no explosions triggered by Alain's troubled mind. Tonight, his mind was clear, and resolved. Clearer than he'd been in so very long.

He loaded the gun and released the safety. He didn't bother wearing gloves, as there would be no mystery about who'd done this. Heading up the stairs, he counted them one-by-one to keep his mind focused.

One.

Two.

Three.

Four.

Five.

Six.

Seven.

Eight.

Nine.

Ten.

Eleven.

Twelve.

He wished he had a silencer, but thought vaguely that only people in the movies had those, and they were illegal.

Katja's door was cracked open. She always left it open, as if waiting for him, but he never came. She lay on her side, her belly exposed.

Her blue eyes flew open, first filled with happy surprise. Then, a terrified understanding. "Alain," came her whispered plea, as they watched each other. Two lovers whose story would come to an end this night.

Alain fired into her stomach, twice. Her eyes opened wide and then closed, as the blood rushed away from her body in a quickly spreading crimson blossom. He had only a moment to feel sadness at her life—and the lives of his children—draining away before he put the gun to his temple and pulled the trigger a third and final time.

I am the Alpha, and the Omega.

A flash, and then, darkness.

NICOLAS

or ten minutes, Adrienne explained to him she was dying. Not eventually. Not years, or months from now. But now. Tonight. Her illness was incurable by doctors, or family healers, and she'd called him here to be at her side when it happened. She wanted to die in her own bed, in the home where she'd raised her family, where she had loved and been loved. And she wanted Nicolas, her brother, to be at her side when the moment came, not Oz. For Oz, his final memories would be from the day earlier, of laughter, and happiness.

"Is this some kind of fucking joke, Ade?" Nicolas exclaimed after she finished her twisted story, backing away from her in a horrified dance. Her ashen skin, and sunken eyes, verified the truth, but if he pushed hard enough, maybe she would buckle and tell him it was some sick gag. Make-up or some crap. Then Oz would pop out and punch him, and Nicolas could tell him what a bitch he was.

"Nic, sit down, please," Adrienne pleaded, then erupted in a fit of coughing. Blood gurgled out over her fingertips.

"Jesus Christ, Adrienne." Annoyance forgotten, he rushed back to her side, ripping Kleenex out of the box as he knelt before her. He wiped tenderly at her mouth, and she smiled, grateful.

"I wanted my big brother here," she said, straining as she reached a hand toward his. Shaking, Nicolas clasped it in both of his, staring in utter bewilderment.

"Why? How?" What was his question, even? He had no idea what to ask, or where to start. Adrienne, dying? It couldn't be. After all she'd been through, that she should now die of an incurable disease, in a family of healers, seemed a cruel joke. And poor long-suffering Oz deserved lifelong happiness, not a handful of years. A widower, twice.

"I have so little time left. Even if I told you everything, none of it matters," Adrienne explained, watching him as she wasted away. *Am I fucking seeing this? She's changing before my eyes. Dying right in front of me. Jesus motherfucking Christ.*

"Why on Earth would you not want Oz by your side, Adrienne? I understand the kids not seeing this, but Oz? He's never going to get over not being here!" Nicolas had half a mind to go get his friend anyway, but feared leaving her for even a moment. He'd never forgive himself if she died alone while he was off betraying her wishes.

"Oh, Nic, you know why," Adrienne smiled. It was a crude gesture, like a skeleton grinning, and it made him sick to see it.

He did understand, but that didn't mean he liked it. Oz would never forgive him, for not calling, even though being here would likely have been what finally ended poor Oz's grip on sanity, once and for all.

"He loves you, Adrienne. You know that, right? He's a self-sacrificing son-of-a-bitch who can't resist saving someone, but that doesn't mean his love for you isn't real," Nicolas said, biting down his lip to stop the vile tears threatening.

"I know," Adrienne replied, coughing again, this time so hard she threw up in the garbage can next to the bed. The bile mixed with her blood was horrifically vivid. Nicolas was no expert at watching others die, despite having lost most of his family. This wasn't like the movies, and nothing could have prepared him for the stark finality. "He loved me too much, maybe. That's where you can help, big brother. He needs to move on. And we both know he's no good at it."

"Fucking understatement," Nicolas muttered, as he again helped clean off the blood at the corners of her mouth. *This isn't real. An hour ago, Adrienne was fine. She had to be.*

"Amelia," she croaked. "She's good for him."

"Ade, no, are you seriously playing fucking matchmaker for your husband? That's just wrong," Nicolas scolded. He spotted a glass of water across the room, on the dresser, and brought it to her. Her hands were too shaky to hold it, so he rested one hand against the back of her head, and lifted the cup to her lips, allowing her to drink.

"I didn't ask for your opinion," Adrienne said after she swallowed, wincing, "and anyway you're not exactly the love guru."

"Only you would attempt to trade one dying woman for another," Nicolas mused, shaking his head. Adrienne had always been like this, going about things all wrong. Great intentions, shitty execution.

"Amelia is going to be fine," Adrienne assured him. "She'll be waking soon. And when she does, Oz will need her, and she him. And if you love your old friend, and your sister, you'll encourage the relationship."

"And how do you know she's going to wake up?" Nicolas prodded, ignoring the rest of her statement. "Are you a psychic now, too?"

"Hush. She will. I didn't invite you here to argue. If you love me, you'll do as I ask." Her eyes implored him. "You do love me, don't you? Despite all we've been through?"

"God, Adrienne, only you could ask such a thing at a time like this!"

"It's my last time to ask such a thing," she reminded him.

"Fuck's sake, of course I love you, you silly twit. You're my sister. I know that never meant a whole lot growing up, but we made up for it later, didn't we? In spite of our parents' selfishness, we found our way. I wish it had happened sooner, but I guess wishes are like assholes."

"I'll miss your gift of language," she teased. He gripped her hand tighter.

"And I'll miss your special brand of crazy," Nicolas replied, and this time he did cry.

"Come, lay with me," she offered, opening the blankets. "I'm getting too tired to talk."

Nicolas hesitated briefly, and then carefully climbed under the covers. She lifted her head, an invitation for him to slip his arm under, and then she settled against his chest.

"This is really going to happen, isn't it? We can't stop it," he said, drawing in a terrified breath. "How do I prepare for this? I can't... you can't... I'm not *ready*, Adrienne! Sorry. You have far too fucking much to live for, and I can be a better brother. Goddamnit, will you let me at least try? To heal you?"

Adrienne's breaths grew slower. "If it makes you feel better."

With absolutely every ounce of energy and desire Nicolas Deschanel possessed, he focused on seeing his sister better. On feeling her cells grow together in harmony, and cohesiveness. Every fiber of his being worked to block out the blackness, which he could not see, but could certainly *feel* spread all throughout her.

But the blackness didn't shrink. It never moved even an inch.

"Fuck," he whispered, trying again, to the same results.

"I told you. Now, shh. I'm so tired, Nic, and I want to hear the summer rain outside. Is the window still open?"

"Yes, darling," he replied, pressing his lips against her forehead as her breaths slowed further, rasping as they went from autonomic to a great effort. Her lungs wheezed as his spirited baby sister attempted to hold on to the final moments of her life.

"I love you, Adrienne Leigh. Let go, little sister. I'll take care of your family. You don't have to fight this."

Adrienne's gasping breaths gained strength and volume as she craned her neck up at him, mouth wide with effort. Her face was so pale it took on a bluish hue, but her eyes... *her eyes*... they were still full of life, as his sweet sister had always been. Still on fire.

Time ticked slowly. First there were seconds between breaths, and then he could count the space between them. Finally, Adrienne went entirely still.

Nicolas lay in silence, holding her, as he listened to the summer rain for both of them.

OLIVIA

"Greg, I am so far from kidding right now!" Olivia exclaimed as she threw clothes from her closet, to her bed, in a haphazard heap. "We can't stay here. I won't have Rory brought down by this family!"

Greg had his hands folded over his head, a clear sign he had no fathomable clue how to talk to his wife when she was in one of her moods. "We're not leaving. This is our home, Liv. Both of our families are here." Timidly he added, "And mine is quite stable."

Olivia spun on him, fire lighting her eyes and cheeks. "You don't get to judge my family!"

"But you yourself said—"

"And it's my *right* to say it! Not yours."

He approached her with trepidation, looking ready for her to strike. "Come to bed. We can talk about this rationally, tomorrow. I'll even make crepes for breakfast. Your favorite."

He said this last in the deliberate tone of a parent appealing to a child, an effect which was not lost on Olivia. "I don't want your damn crepes, Greg. What I want is for Rory, and this child growing inside me, to have a normal life, with stable influences.

They can't have that here, can they? And don't you dare answer that with anything substantial or I swear to heaven I'll throw this shoe."

Greg watched her for several moments, and then with a shake of this head he snatched a pillow from the bed. "I'll sleep on the couch."

"Do that," she snapped back. She waited until he was gone before she let the tears flow.

Olivia didn't know *what* was going on with her anymore. Maybe it was the baby hormones giving her absolute fits, day and night. Or maybe it was the newly developed stress over its well-being. Nightmare after nightmare haunted her dreams. Blood—but whose?—ran with impunity, nearly driving her to lunacy. The tickle of her seer abilities, whispering at her to listen. *Come on, Olivia. You know you want to. Aren't you even the least bit curious?*

She was, and that was the problem. She absolutely, positively, could not give in to this madness, which had consumed everyone else in the damn family.

But she also couldn't risk staying and putting her baby in danger. The stress alone would be enough.

As if sensing she was the subject of her mother's thoughts, the baby kicked, enough to force Olivia into a sitting position. "Shh, Adeline, it's okay now, darling," she comforted her daughter. She knew, without a doubt, she was having a girl, though no tests had confirmed it. Maybe she'd dabbled in her ability, after all. It was hard to resist, even after all these years.

Earlier, she's received word Amelia had been taken home to die. And no one, not a single person Olivia appealed to, cared a whit about what she'd learned from Jasper. They all accused her of meddling where she didn't belong. *If loving my family, and wanting them to be safe, and okay, is a sin, then I will gladly live in turpitude the rest of my days.*

It was time to get out of New Orleans. She wanted Greg to

come, she really, truly did. Despite his lack of gumption, he was a good man, and he was her husband, and Rory's father. A part of Olivia loved even his weaknesses, because they laid the foundation for his big heart. But Rory and Adeline came first. And Alain, if it wasn't too late to save him.

She believed it wasn't.

AN HOUR LATER, WHEN GREG WAS SNORING LIKE A CHAINSAW IN the living room, Olivia quietly snuck out of the house, Rory in one arm, and a suitcase in the other. *Goodbye,* she whispered, in her mind, unable to risk rousing him with words. *I wish you would have come.*

She used the manual release on the garage to avoid the churning noise of the door motor. Rory stirred only slightly as she secured him in his child seat, tenderly tucking his favorite blue fleece blanket with cheery yellow ducks around him, and then she slid in the driver's seat.

Her plan was simple: Go to Alain's, and appeal to him to leave with her. The family could take care of Katja and the children. Olivia couldn't leave him behind, no matter how much she might wish to flee this godforsaken city.

"Simple, right, Rory?" she cooed at her sleeping young son in the rearview mirror, as she backed out, resolute.

OLIVIA HEARD SIRENS IN THE DISTANCE, BUT THOUGHT NOTHING of them. This was New Orleans, and they were a staple background noise. Never in a million years did she think they would end up at Alain's apartment, only minutes after she did.

She'd never visited Alain, though Katja's appeals *had* moved her. But on several occasions, Olivia had driven by, and looked up, hoping to catch a glimpse of her brother. She never did, but she knew which unit was his. Many years ago, before she'd been forced into the role of family voice of reason, Olivia had hung out with Nicolas in the same apartment, drinking cognac and laughing at tourists.

It seemed an eternity ago.

In his car seat, Rory slept. She hated to disturb him, but she couldn't possibly leave him down here, unattended, in the middle of the night.

"Come on, kiddo," she whispered, hoisting him up against her shoulder, blanket draped over the top. He didn't even notice.

The wrought-iron fence ahead opened for residents only, so Olivia buzzed Nicolas' flat, heart racing. What would she say? She hadn't thought about it, really.

When there was no response, fate intervened in the form of an old woman, who spotted her from the courtyard behind the locked gate.

"I'm visiting my brother, Alain Blanchard," Olivia told her, readjusting Rory. "He's expecting me, so I don't know why he isn't answering."

The old woman unlocked the gate without further trouble. *It's the baby. Not that I'm picky about her reasons for taking pity.*

Olivia thanked her, and knocked on the door. Just as with the buzzer, there was no response. Olivia, though, was convinced he was home. Alain never left, according to Katja. *Guilt is a powerful weight.*

She was surprised when she tried the door and it was unlocked. Their mother had been the type to double-check every lock before retiring for the night, even the little ones, on the windows. It was a habit that rubbed off on her children.

Right away, Olivia sensed something was wrong. More than the metallic scent drifting through the flat, but also another thing, deeper down, which was no longer a tickle but full on scratching. *You should have listened, you should have listened, you should have listened...*

The main level empty, Olivia carefully settled Rory, swaddled in his blanket, on the recliner, and moved slowly up the stairs to the second floor.

First was a bathroom. Empty. The second was the spare room, also empty, though it was being used by someone, evidenced by the dirty clothes all over the floor. She closed that door, and then moved toward the other one, the one that lay cracked, a sheath of moonlight sliding out into the hall.

Olivia's heart pounded so hard her shoulders ached. *A heart attack?* No, not likely, but something else... that other thing... *You should have listened, you should have listened...*

With a trembling hand, she nudged the door open.

It didn't register.

Not at first.

And then, it did.

"*Alain!*" she howled, the guttural, keening cry of an animal baying in pain. The sound of regret, shame, and tremendous loss rolled into one, horrible sensation. The sound of *you should have listened, you should have listened...*

— She couldn't look at the hole in her brother's face. She couldn't. No. *She couldn't.* Wouldn't. She couldn't see it, couldn't comprehend the pieces of his brain—his beautiful artistic mind—now splattered on the stained cypress behind him.

But she could hold him. Heedless of the gore, she pulled his limp form into her arms, pressing him close the way she embraced Rory when he was sick, or distraught. "Alain, I'm sorry, I'm so goddamn sorry, my baby brother..."

You should have listened. The answer was there all along. You could have saved him. You should have listened. You should have paid attention. You should have... should have...

Olivia's sobs turned to screams as her heart twisted with the regret of someone who had been so right, and yet so wrong. "No, Alain, not you. Not you. *Anyone but you.*"

The sirens' wailing grew closer, but even then Olivia didn't make the connection. She knew her brother was gone... and on the bed...

...on the bed, a small gurgling sound tickled her ears. At first Olivia thought she imagined it, and then it happened again, coming from the scene she had all but ignored in the shock of seeing her brother dead on the floor.

"He...hel...p..." she heard, and then knew it was not her imagination at all.

She gently—reluctantly—released Alain and stood to see Katja struggling to speak. She lay in a pool of blood, forming a sick halo around her belly. All of a sudden, Olivia saw with perfectly clarity what had happened: her brother had done this to Katja, and then turned the gun on himself.

Olivia rushed to Katja's side, reaching forward to touch her face. "Katja, can you hear me?"

Katja nodded, blood trickling out of her gaping mouth. "Livvy."

I have been so unfair to her. She's just a girl! And she was carrying my own blood, and now... and now...

"Shh, Katja. I'm here. It's going to be all right," Olivia whispered, as she fumbled in her pocket for her phone with her free hand. She didn't know if Katja was going to be all right. She certainly didn't look like she was going to be all right. Dawning in Olivia, at this moment of understanding, was an unshakeable desire to help Katja in a way she was not able to help her brother.

"My babies..."

Olivia couldn't look down. Not when, inside of her, a child was also growing. One which would be born in another few months, as these triplets should have been. *Their blood is on my hands, too.*

Before she could call 9-1-1, help arrived, barreling through the apartment in a blur of uniforms, and yells.

"Hold on," Olivia soothed Katja, as she realized she could never, ever leave New Orleans now. "I won't leave you Kat."

The strong arms of a police officer embraced Olivia from behind, and she turned dissolving in his arms.

TRISTAN

*C*onnor helped his son into the backseat of the car, where he lay curled, unable to move. Tristan heard him thank the man for his help, before getting in behind the wheel.

But instead of driving, Connor sat staring ahead for several moments.

"It's okay, Dad. I'm okay," Tristan mumbled through his sore jaw. And the crazy thing was, he believed it! He recognized the hour before, when he sat washing his sins in the dirty river, that moment had been his rock bottom. He couldn't be brought any lower than cleansing his filth with more filth. "You hear that, Brigitte? Fuck your Curse! I'm still here, you vengeful bitch!"

"We need to get you to a hospital," his father replied, finally starting the car. In Tristan's pain-filled stupor, he could have sworn his father was crying. But his father never cried, so that was impossible.

"I don't think there's any permanent damage," Tristan sang from the backseat, feeling near delirious in his newfound euphoria. "And if there is, we're Deschanels, right? We can fix that shit right up!"

Connor said nothing in response. From his vantage point in

SARAH M. CRADIT

the backseat, he could see his father's knuckles bone-white as he gripped the wheel.

"Okay, well *you're* not a Deschanel, but I'm sure Aunt C won't mind a quick drive-by healing. She's just sitting around at Amelia's."

"Not anymore," his father responded tightly.

Tristan's heart sank. "Then Amelia..."

"Amelia is going to be fine, thanks be to God," Connor replied, with a shaky, wavering voice.

What is going on with him? Do I really look that bad?

"Wow, I'm so relieved to hear that," Tristan sighed, wincing as the strong exhale pierced his ribs. "I thought when I saw her earlier I was saying goodbye."

"We all did."

Tristan got a brief glimpse of his father's jaw set tight in the rearview. "Look, Dad, lighten up! I really am okay. Could use some damn *morphine* right about now, but I'm gonna survive. I'm gonna survive everything, actually. The Deschanels and Sullivans are resilient as hell, and I'm fortunate enough to be both."

He thought about Emily, and her revelations to him regarding the abuse she'd suffered at her husband's hands. Tristan wondered at how he'd never known any of her horror at home. But what if he had? Would he have rushed in to save her, a barely-out-of-college kid with no place of his own, and hardly any world experience? He felt sorry for her, that she'd chosen such a dismal life, but he couldn't save her. A person was only responsible for saving themselves, when it came down to it.

It was strange to him, how he could sleep with someone for a year, share his evenings with her, and yet know nothing about her.

"Son," Connor said finally, as he shakily veered the car into a small lot on the edge of the Central Business District. "Tristan, I need to tell you something, but I'm not sure how..."

"Just say it, Dad," Tristan encouraged, realizing then that his father was, in fact, deeply troubled about something. With some trepidation, Tristan attempted to raise himself on an elbow, so he could face him. "Tell me."

How was he to know those words would be an invitation to shatter his new, protective bubble? How was he to ever have guessed that earlier was in fact *not* rock bottom? That things could get worse... so much worse...

MARKUS

$\mathcal{T}$here was a word that Markus thought described what had happened to them, but he struggled to find it.

He recalled the times, during his youth, when his parents would take him and Katja to the beach. They would drive down to their summer house in Hilton Head every year, and spend a month in what felt like an entirely different world. Everything in Hilton Head was different; it was a class of people who seemed to want for nothing and need for nothing. While Markus and his family fell into that category too, they had always lived somewhat modestly. He and his sister had never been spoiled. Everything they wanted, they'd been taught to work for.

The Atlantic was cold near home, but in South Carolina the sands were warm and the ocean felt kissed by the sun. When they arrived, after suffering through a slathering of sunscreen from their mother, Markus and Katja would race down the beach to see who could hit the ocean first. Katja had been quicker for years, but as Markus grew taller and leaner, he began to beat her. They'd play for hours, bags left unpacked until the next morning. Evangeline and Johannes loved this tradition as much as the children.

They were often allowed to play unattended, but Evangeline made them promise one thing. "Never turn your back on the ocean," she cautioned. "Waves are unpredictable, and can knock you off your feet and pull you under."

One year, when Katja had been eleven and Markus thirteen, they were playing in the ocean while their parents cooked dinner in the house. Markus was body boarding when he realized he hadn't seen Katja in a while. Unable to find her with a quick search, he panicked and called for his parents. His father had flown through the sand and into the ocean, diving immediately to look for her. Moments later he returned with an unconscious Katja. Johannes began pumping the water out of her lungs, Evangeline sobbing from the sidelines. Markus had never been so scared in his life. An eternity later, Katja started coughing.

"A sneaker wave," Markus overheard his father saying to his mother later that night.

Yes, there was the word. What had happened to their family this week felt like a sneaker wave, coming up from behind and out of nowhere to completely pull them under.

MARKUS HAD SPENT SO MUCH OF THE PAST MONTHS IN HOSPITALS, there was something vaguely soothing about the incessant beeping, quiet rumblings, and smell of sterility mingled with decay.

Beside him, his mother rocked herself back and forth while his father looked on helplessly. They were broken, both of them. For how long, Markus did not know, but he hoped it wasn't permanent.

But she lived, he thought. *Katja is still with us. By some miracle of science. Now it's time for us to work our own miracles.*

Inside the ICU room behind them, Katja slept. Her condition kept the visiting hours to a minimum, but they were allowed to sit outside the room, and watch over her.

One floor up, two of Katja's triplets, Stella and Sebastian, lay in the NICU, holding on valiantly. The third had died when Alain's bullet tore through Katja's belly. It was a miracle the second bullet had passed clean through.

It's too early to know anything concrete, the doctor had said earlier, after Katja had been stabilized and moved to the ICU from Emergency. *The bullet shattered her spine. It's unlikely we can fix that entirely. Her body is fighting the antibiotics, and we struggle to calm her when she's awake so we've given her heavier sedatives. We won't know anything for a few more days, but there's a strong chance your daughter can survive this. And her babies.*

Across town, the situation was stripped of this hope. Maureen was having her son's wake, for tomorrow was the funeral. Custom dictated he should be buried in the family tomb in Lafayette No. 1, with the rest of the Garden District Deschanels, but Maureen had lost her mind, vowing it was those same Deschanels who'd killed her son. She declined to tell anyone else in the family where Alain's final resting place would be.

Maureen refused to acknowledge Alain's child who also died that night, calling the lost girl an abomination. So Markus helped his mother plan a private burial at Lafayette, where they laid little Nora to rest.

Too many funerals. Tomorrow would also be Adrienne's funeral. That one had caught them all off-guard. While the rest of the family went nuts over the various messed-up situations, Adrienne passed away from an illness she shared with no one, not even her husband. Oz was understandably angry. At the world. At her. It was Nicolas she'd called to her side in her final moments, not her husband.

Markus couldn't make sense of it. And really, there was no

point. Several of his cousins were dead. A niece he'd never meet. His sister clung to life several feet away. The situation was incomparably mad. Every empire must eventually fall. Was this the fall of the Deschanels? Finally?

Somehow, the most surprising of all was Olivia's presence on the bench across from them. She'd ridden with Katja in the ambulance, clinging to her son with one arm, and Katja's hand with the other. Her husband had picked up Rory, because Olivia refused to leave, not even for Alain's wake, muttering, *I promised Katja I wouldn't leave her.* She sat ashen-faced, staring at the room, saying nothing unless asked, leaving only to occasionally check on the twins upstairs.

"I can heal her, if only they'd let me in!" his mother had exclaimed, for the entire hospital to hear. They didn't need to worry about their family secrets being exposed, though. The staff assumed she was insane with grief.

"They will soon, Mom," Markus soothed, saying the words but feeling nothing. "Let them do their work."

"Why did I go home? Why didn't I stay with my baby girl? I let her take this burden entirely unto herself, and oh, how long was she suffering? Katja never complains about anything!" His mother's body shook with grief.

"Evie," Johannes answered, touching her arm lightly. "Please don't. You know better."

Markus couldn't bear the oppressive burden a moment longer. Everyone in this family was coming apart at the seams. His parents, his aunts, his cousins. He had no one, and while that was normally fine by him, right now he needed an ally. Someone he could speak to rationally, and formulate a plan with. It wasn't enough anymore, to sit back and benignly accept this was their lot in life. Soon, there wouldn't be enough Deschanels left to figure things out. It was incumbent on Markus to do it, but he needed another head in the game. He couldn't do it alone.

Only one person came to mind. Despite all she'd been through, Markus suspected she'd still maintained her healthy sensibility. And if she hadn't... well, then he really would be alone in this.

But he would try, for there were no other options.

EPILOGUE: AMELIA

Amelia still couldn't quite believe she'd spent three months unconscious. As a student of medicine, she understood what happened to the brain and body when a patient was unconscious for long periods. After three months she would have expected she might need to learn to speak again, and possibly retrain other motor skills, like eating or holding on to things. Walking should come at some difficulty, and her memory would have some damage.

But none of these things were the case. Amelia simply woke, to a room full of surprised, but relieved, faces.

She had no questions for the doctors who flocked to her house, because it was apparent they'd be able to answer none of them. In fact, they wanted to ask *her* about the last few months. What did she remember? Was she in pain? Was she aware, when she was under? The words "imperiled empath" would only raise further questions, so no one revealed the origins of her crisis. *Augustus will need to come do his work on the staff, I think. They aren't going to drop this,* her mother had lamented. *Everything about this defies rational explanation, and they're going to insist on studying you.*

They wanted to bring Amelia in for a few nights of observation, but she passed all their reflex tests with flying colors. Her mother, who all the doctors in the hospital looked up to and trusted, promised to stay at Amelia's for a few days and watch over her personally. At that, they finally relented.

Once the doctors were gone—for the moment—her mother went to retrieve Jacob and the others, but Amelia stopped her.

"No, please don't."

Her mother sat at her bedside. "Would you like to rest first, dear?"

Amelia shook her head. "Mom... so much happened, when I was under." She swallowed, letting her heavy lids close. "I kept seeing all these beautiful memories of Jacob and me, back in the beginning. I thought they meant his love was what kept me alive. But it wasn't until those final moments, when Oz told me to let Jacob go, that all the craziness stopped, and I woke."

Colleen's eyes narrowed. "Oz told you to do this?"

"It was one of many theories that I considered over the months I was trapped. He merely reminded me in the end."

Something momentarily flashed across her mother's expression—guilt? fear?—and then it was gone. "It doesn't work that way, darling. I don't know what miracle brought you back to us, but it wasn't that."

"One minute the world was dissolving around us, and the next I was awake. I know it sounds insane, but we both know our minds craft various ways of bringing us to terms with difficult realities." As she absently petted the stretched-out cat beside her, Amelia's eyes caught sight of the dozens of bouquets filling the room. They were for her family, not her, she realized. No one expected her to make it. "My love of Jacob was selfish. I always knew it. He went from one tragic family to another, and he doesn't belong to our world, Mom."

"He is central to our world, and to yours," her mother admonished, taking Amelia's free hand and pressing it between hers in desperate love. "I still remember the day I first met him. Eighteen, knuckles scarred from years of schoolyard fights, eyes full of unmet passion. Then I watched him blossom in your presence, Mia. His scars healed, and he found an outlet for all the love bursting inside of him. There's nothing selfish about your love for Jacob. You saved each other with that love."

Amelia's eyes filled with tears, as her mother's words permeated. Logic from both sides tore at her mind, overwhelming her.

"But now isn't the time to sort this out, dear one," her mother quickly added, laying a kiss on her forehead. Amelia again saw the guilt in her expression, but she couldn't put together where it was coming from. "I'll let them know you need some space, and rest."

"Thank you, Mom."

When her mother stepped out, Amelia closed her eyes to shut out the world, and all the pain with it. She wouldn't think about the unused plane tickets to Ireland waiting in the drawer, or the priest waiting to seal her commitment to Jacob, in marriage. Sister Agnes, Jacob's adopted mother, would be so disappointed. That all felt like it happened in another life, and if she was to survive this decision, that's exactly how she would need to think of it.

Then there was Oz, her knight in shining armor. Her protector. Beyond her initial awakening, where she'd allowed him, and not Jacob, to hold her, and comfort her, she'd not so much as glanced in his direction.

She would forever be in his debt, but she could never, ever risk being in a room alone with him, again.

"A lot happened while you were imperiled," her mother said, when she brought her some food later that evening. "Things I must tell you about my dear, but not yet."

"No need, Mom," Amelia replied, placing a hand on her mother's arm, "Oz told me. I know everything."

But that wasn't exactly true, for moments after Amelia's awakening, she'd sensed Adrienne die quietly in Nicolas' arms. And then Alain took his own life, after putting two bullets in Katja and her unborn children.

"Stop thinking about it, Amelia. Block it out. I won't have you getting sick again!"

Amelia would follow her mother's advice. She had to. All that death... the look on Jacob's face when she told him it was over, really over... whatever the hell she was feeling for Oz, after all they had weathered together... no, she would think of none of it. Thinking about it would kill her.

She was actually quite exhausted. The doctors branded it a coma, for lack of a more cohesive explanation, but Amelia understood her mind had been instead on overdrive, never stopping. Tormenting her, attempting to push her until she finally relented. In the end, she did relent, but instead of giving her body, she gave her heart.

Jacob, I loved you well.

Several days later, after all the wakes, funerals, tears, and more family gatherings than she thought she could handle, Amelia returned to the office. In order to move forward, changes were needed, to push her more decisively from the past and into the future. It would need to be a brand new future, one that didn't resemble her old life in any significant way.

As she packed up her belongings, she looked up to see Markus in the doorway.

"Mark. I'm so sorry—"

"I went by your house, and you weren't there," he quickly cut her off. "Why are you packing?"

"I'm leaving the practice," she answered, carefully wedging a framed picture of her and Jacob in the box, between two books. *Stop. Don't think of it.*

"Why?"

She sat down, motioning for him to do the same. "Nicolas has asked me to come help with his project at *Ophélie*. Given everything, it felt like a good decision. I might sell the house too, but I haven't thought that far yet."

"I'm considering offering my help, too," Markus said. She'd never seen him look so nervous, and she wondered what his real reason was for coming. "How is Nicolas? He wasn't at the wake, or the funeral."

"You know Nic. He's in denial, like he was when his parents and other sisters passed. He put it on a shelf, where it will stay, most likely," she said, with a sad shake of the head. "But when he asked me to come help, I understood that was his way of reaching out to family. Even if he hadn't asked, I might have offered."

"And Oz?"

Amelia looked down. Oz had suffered a complete mental break when he learned about Adrienne, and had to be sedated for days. Once he came to, his grief seemed like a distant memory, and his emotional fixation transferred to Amelia. This put her in a terrible position, to turn a friend away in his misery, but she knew later he would thank her for it. "I don't know." *I don't want to confuse matters. For him, or me.*

"You know I don't care much for gossip, but you might want to know what everyone is saying. I would."

Amelia sucked in a deep breath and raised her eyes again. "No one else could understand what happened while I was under. Oz and I will always share that. But that's it. That's the whole of it, and there's nothing juicy, or interesting to tell." *Nor will there ever be.*

"Have you spoken to Jacob?"

Amelia, I have loved you forever.

Then love me forever.

"No," she replied.

Markus nodded thoughtfully, but it seemed like he was somewhere other than in the room.

Amelia set down the book she was holding. "What's on your mind, Markus?"

Markus ran both hands through his pale hair, then drug them down and over his face in one long, pained move. "Three more cousins died last night, murdered in some restaurant in Terrebonne Parish. Maple, Candi, and Reba Benoit? Maybe you heard. It was all over the news, and the family can't shut up about it. 'All hope is lost' seems to be the new Deschanel battle-cry."

"I heard. It was idealistic to expect that would fix things," Amelia sighed, then reached across the desk, laying a hand over his. "I'm sorry. That was insensitive, given what happened."

"I'd rather hear the truth than useless sentiment," Markus replied, squeezing her hand briefly before reclaiming his. "So, you have a theory, then?"

"It's abstract," she answered. "But maybe. I think we were cursed long before Brigitte made her pronouncements. If we had better records from France, we might have known that before. It wouldn't take much to get them with our connections. I don't know why we never did."

Markus snorted, but he was listening. "So, what then? Some other crazy bitch?"

Amelia shook her head. "I think the answer is less elegant than a curse. Maybe our bad luck has more to do with our hybrid blood. My belief is that it started when Aidrik fused his blood to the Deschanels, and made us part Empyrean. Aidrik told Nicolas that the Eldre Senetat strictly forbids mating between their race and ours. Maybe for good reason."

He looked openly surprised. "I don't know if you're right, but the idea of a curse never made much sense to me." Markus sat forward in his chair, leaning over the desk. "You asked what's on my mind. This. All of this. The fucked-upness of our family, and our lack of power over it. I'm done with the whole mess. I intend to solve the mystery and put an end to it once and for all. I could use some help."

"We can't change who we are," she contended, but even as the words escaped, her mind returned to Oz's desperation to fix her, and his complete unwillingness to give up. *It's not in the fabric of who I am.*

"You're going to *Ophélie* to help," Markus pushed on. "So am I. We'll be surrounded by Empyreans. Full-blooded ones. Why couldn't we, as an aside to whatever else we're doing, also use the time to study? To learn?"

"Ever the scientist, Mark," she teased, a smile playing at her mouth.

"I'm very serious." He leaned back in his chair, folding his hands across his chest. "I can't go home. I can't be idle. This time, it all hit way too close to home."

Amelia nodded in sympathetic understanding. "We've all lost too much."

"Maybe you're right, and we can't change who we are." Markus stood, as he pushed the chair back in. "But what if we could?"

What if we could? The words hung in the air between them. Markus' flushed face, and his rising pitch; his rapid breathing and elevated heart rate. The light tick of the desk clock. The box before her containing the remnants of her sincere attempts to help others.

What if we could?

Amelia couldn't begin to absorb all her family had lost. All *she* had lost. But what was painfully evident was the family's inability to weather any further tragedy. The thin thread they walked along was frayed, threatening to snap. She couldn't repair the damage already done, but if there was even a chance she could stall further destruction...

She watched Markus' wild expression as he awaited her

response. She moved around the desk until she faced him. Then, she thrust her hand out.

"A friend reminded me hope is all we have," she said. "We are Deschanels. We survive."

Markus looked at her hand in brief disbelief, and then took it in his own. "To hope," he said.

For Benjamin. For Colby. For Danielle. For Charles, and his girls. For Elizabeth. For Katey. For Cassius. For Rene. For Annette. For Adrienne. For Alain. For Nora.

"To hope," she replied.

Amelia has never known heartbreak like losing Jacob, but she'd do anything to protect him—all the while, growing closer to Oz, the only one who knows what she experienced. What happens, though, when Amelia and Jacob's love is more than what they think it is? When destiny reaches across the centuries?

Don't miss a minute. Download *Asunder* today.

Want a glimpse into what comes next? Read further for an excerpt.

ASUNDER EXCERPT

Amelia had to get out of the house. Specifically *this* house, which now felt like a macabre gallery of her past, every item narrating its own unique story to torture her.

It was her home, and the setting for the fondest of her adult memories. But it also served as a constant reminder of everything she'd given up. Of Jacob. And of all the ways she tried to justify this crippling heartbreak, in an attempt to move on and start a new life without him.

If Jacob's memory—the light scent of his sweat, his ringing laughter—wasn't haunting her thoughts, then the lit porch light across the street served equal torment. Oz kept it on, hoping she would find her way to his door. *To talk,* he assured her, when he once managed to grab her attention. *I need to talk about this with someone. With you. You're the only one who understands.*

But Amelia wouldn't. How could she? Months of him dancing through her dreams had left them both confused, and desiring something they had no business even giving passing thought to. Meanwhile, her heart ached in the absence of the one man she'd ever loved, while Oz mourned the unexpected loss of his wife.

"It's all so much. So much. I can't fathom this loss. It's not real to me, not after everything she and I went through. But you, Amelia... you are so vivid. Alive. I can't... I won't... but I need to make sense of this. I love you, and God help me, I don't know how to turn off the emotions and wanting screaming through my every pore."

She had tried to support Oz through his grief, until he said those words. "Oz, my mother said this is an expected side-effect of the dreamwalking. It will go away. And even if it doesn't—"

"Amelia, I can't eat! I can't sleep! I can't think about anything except how powerfully empty I feel when you're not around. When I close my eyes, I long to be in your mind again, where I can be close to you. I'm not in control of myself, and you're the only one I can make sense of this with!"

Having recognized his unrestrained wanting, Amelia had blocked his attempts to re-enter her dreams. She would never tell him she understood, and perhaps even felt the same way. For whatever love had formed in those months of dreamwalking, it was not *right*. Not *okay*. And despite that it *felt* real, there was no way it could be. Had she known this could happen, Amelia would have pushed him from her head the first time he showed up. Even if it meant her demise.

She slipped down into the old recliner, as Miss Kitty, her Siamese, hopped in her lap for affection. Even her beloved kitty reminded her of Jacob. They picked her out together, at the animal shelter in Metairie. It was Jacob who named her, declaring, *She has a sassy look about her. Like, if she introduced herself to another cat, she'd get all puffed up and say "That's MISS Kitty to you, pal."*

Tears threatened at every moment of every hour, it seemed. Her stomach refused food, and her body, having slept for almost three months, insisted upon being conscious through every painstaking emotion her mind put her through. She had to fight it, to not give in—it was dangerous, and deadly—but she was so *tired*.

Something had to change. And only Amelia had the power to change it.

The sound of the door chime woke her from a sleep she hadn't realized she'd fallen into. Miss Kitty bolted for the door, something she only did when she was sure who was on the other side. *Jacob,* she realized, taking a quick glance at the clock. Somehow she lost several hours.

With a deep breath, Amelia opened the door. Her heart stood before her, his disheveled look a mirror image of her own. *"Blanca,"* he greeted, in a low voice. He wouldn't meet her eyes, but had he tried, she probably would have looked away. His eyes might be enough to make her doubt the courage of her convictions. His voice already nearly was.

"Hi," she replied, opening the door wider to allow him entrance. The second he stepped into the foyer, the room lit up with his presence, as if to say, *Ahh, this is more like it.* So did Amelia, though it wasn't a feeling she could allow herself. "I was going to make some sweet tea, but I fell asleep. I have some bottled water, though, if you're thirsty." *Of course, he knows there's bottled water, because he bought it.*

Though the sweat beaded at his brow from the sweltering August heat outside, Jacob shook his head. "Naw, I'm fine. Are you okay, Amelia? I mean, overall?"

Her heart surged again. Oh, how she longed to tell him, *No, no I'm absolutely miserable without you. I'm lost. Devastated, and broken in ways I can never repair. I struggle even to breathe.* But instead she said, "I'm holding up. My family needs me right now. Especially Ashley, now that Christine took the boys and ran off."

Jacob shook his head. "I heard. Tell him… well, I mean, you don't have to tell him. But I'm so sorry."

"I'll tell him," Amelia promised. Jacob and her brother had always gotten along, despite having little in common. Ashley was very nearly as disappointed as their mother when Amelia decided on a life without Jacob.

But neither of them understood what Amelia had been through, when her mind locked her in a prison for three months. None except Oz, and he was the last person on Earth she wanted to see.

"So... you said you had the rest of the boxes packed?" Jacob ventured, looking around the room in what seemed a mixture of awkwardness, and longing.

"Oh! Yes, let me get them," she said, and started up the stairs, toward the room they'd shared for years. She was surprised to hear his steps following her, but she shouldn't have been. Always a gentleman, he never would have let her bring them all down on her own.

As they turned the corner into the room, all at once his strong arms came around from behind, gently encircling her. His breath was hot at her neck, as he entreated, *"Blanca... why?"*

Amelia stared straight ahead, rigid, though her heart raced as hard, if not harder, than his. "This was always the ending, Jacob. We just didn't know it."

"The only ending I ever envisioned was one with us growing old together, bickering over who was picking dinner," he teased, though his voice was solemn. "Nothing you've said has convinced me that can't still happen."

As much as she knew it would hurt to face him in the middle of such a discussion, she couldn't say it to a blank wall, either. Amelia turned, and looked directly into his eyes. "You'll never know what I went through. Even if I tried to explain it, you will still never, ever know. And I wouldn't want you to." *For your sake.*

Jacob's lips tensed; a familiar sign he was trying hard to

conceal his emotions. "Is it Oz? If it is, I don't want to know the details. A nod will be sufficient."

"No," she replied, quickly. Maybe too quickly. "Absolutely not! It isn't like that." *Oh, but it was. Not by any choice I made, or would make, but still.*

"He saved your life, so I can't hate him for that, but I know there's something between you two..." The undercurrent of his words was a dare to convince him he was wrong.

"It isn't what you think," Amelia reassured him. "We went through something unspeakable together. But I've never... would never..." Her voice choked up.

Jacob looked as if he might have a witty, cutting retort loaded, but his kindness overcame him. "I believe you." His hand went up to touch her face, and for a moment, she closed her eyes and allowed the old comfort. "And you're wrong, you know."

Amelia looked up. She couldn't hide the tears, but it didn't matter. She had made no secret of her pain.

"The night you woke up, you said to me that you'd destroyed me. That when I told you what happened to my family, you swore to give me a better life, but instead you'd ruined it. But you didn't destroy me, Amelia."

Now his other hand held her face as well, as he kissed her trembling mouth. "You saved me."

He left Amelia standing there in stunned silence. It was not until she heard the front door close that she realized he'd left without his boxes.

Pick up your copy of *Asunder* now, and have it ready to curl up at your next reading session!

1970

1972

1973

1974

1975

1976

1980

Vampires of the Merovingi Series

The Island

Crimson & Clover Lagniappes (Bonus Stories)

Lagniappes are standalone stories that can be read in any order.

St. Charles at Dusk: The Story of Oz and Adrienne

Flourish: The Story of Anne Fontaine

Surrender: The Story of Oz and Ana

Shame: The Story of Jonathan St. Andrews

Fire & Ice: The Story of Remy & Fleur

Dark Blessing: The Landry Triplets

Pandora's Box: The Story of Jasper & Pandora

The Menagerie: Oriana's Den of Iniquities

A Band of Heather: The Story of Colleen and Noah

The Ephemeral: The Story of Autumn & Gabriel

Banshee: The Story of Giselle Deschanel

For more information, and exciting bonus material, visit www.

sarahmcradit.com

DESCHANEL CURSE TIMELINE

1844-1848

Charles Deschanel I, and his young wife Brigitte, emigrated from France and purchased a plot of land along the Mississippi River in Louisiana. Their children, Ophélie, Jean (the Deschanel heir), and Fitz, are born within the first few years. Charles names his plantation after *Ophélie*.

1861-1862

Civil War tears the country apart. Charles shrewdly makes back channel deals with the Union, which saves his property when New Orleans falls early. He is branded a traitor by fellow Southerners, but is one of the few of his peers to emerge not only intact but with even stronger prospects.

1863

Ophélie is brutally murdered by one of the Union soldiers, after months of abuse.

1865

Civil War ends. Both Jean and Fitz fought, and survived. Charles continues his associations with the same Union men who murdered his daughter. This infuriates Brigitte, who plans her revenge.

1866

Brigitte finally gets her revenge when she takes her own life, cementing the Curse against Charles and his descendants. This is witnessed by her son Jean's wife, Julianne, who writes about it in her diaries. Later, she will convince her daughter Ophelia of the Curse potency.

Later that year, Charles and Brigitte's son Fitz, along with his wife and son, are killed in a boating accident, presumably the first victims of the Deschanel Curse.

1875 & 1878

Charles II (grandson of Charles I) and Ophelia are born to Jean and Julianne. These are the only two children they will have. Charles II becomes the Deschanel heir.

1896

Julianne dies, leaving all her diaries and recollections of the Curse to her daughter, Ophelia. Ophelia carries these beliefs with her all her life, never marrying.

1901-1903

Charles II and his wife Amelia give birth to three children: John, Jean, and Elizabeth.

1905

A yellow fever epidemic sweeps New Orleans. All three of Charles II and Amelia's children perish to it. Later that year, Amelia gives birth to a son, August, who will become the Deschanel heir.

1906

Amelia gives birth to her only other surviving child, a daughter, Blanche. Blanche will go on to start the Broussard, Guidry, and Fontenot dynasties. Current descendants refer to Deschanels as either "descendants of August," or "descendants of Blanche."

1908

Charles Deschanel I dies.

1925

August, at the age of 20, returns home from boarding school married to a Yankee woman, Eliza Gass, whom he is very much in love with.

1930 & 1931

Charles Deschanel II dies, followed by his father, Jean Deschanel, leaving August as the only surviving heir.

1925-1949

August and Eliza try repeatedly to produce children, resulting in a series of painful stillbirths. Eliza falls ill and dies in 1949. With no heirs, and August coming into middle age, the future of the Deschanel family is uncertain.

Within days of his wife's death, August marries his deceased wife's nursemaid, a young Irish woman by the name of Colleen Brady. It was said he married her as an expression of the family's ill fortunes thus far, and that he "might as well marry the help, in any case."

1950-1959

In a felicitous twist of fate, August and Colleen go on to conceive ten children, six of whom survive into adulthood: Charles, Augustus, Colleen, Evangeline, Maureen, and Elizabeth.

1961

August Deschanel passes away, leaving his son Charles III as the Deschanel heir.

1975

Ophelia Deschanel passes away at the age of 97, the last of the older generations. She passes on all her notes, and legacy, to August's daughters.

1976-1987

The sixteen grandchildren of August Deschanel are born. At this point, there have been no major tragedies in many years, and the Curse begins to fade into history.

Children of Charles: Nicolas (1975), Nathalie ('77), Giselle ('78), Lucienne ('79), Adrienne ('80), Anne ('81)

Children of Augustus: Anasofiya ('75)

Children of Colleen: Amelia ('76), Benjamin ('77), Ashley ('78)

Children of Evangeline: Markus ('85), Katja ('87)

Children of Maureen: Olivia ('75), Alain ('80)

Children of Elizabeth: Danielle ('82), Tristan, ('89)

1996

A series of tragedies strike the family. Colleen's son Benjamin, along with his wife and child, perish in a house fire. Charles Deschanel, his wife, and three of his daughters (Nathalie, Giselle, Lucienne) die in a bayou car accident. Later that year, Elizabeth's daughter, Danielle, is struck by a car and killed on Christmas.

2006

Current Time

ABOUT THE AUTHOR

~

Sarah is the *USA Today* Bestselling Author of the Paranormal Southern Gothic world, The Saga of Crimson & Clover, born of her combined passion for New Orleans, and the mysterious complexity of human nature. Her work has been described as rich, emotive, and highly dimensional.

An unabashed geek, Sarah enjoys studying obscure subjects like the Plantagenet and Ptolemaic dynasties, and settling debates on provocative Tolkien topics such as why the Great Eagles are not Gandalf's personal taxi service. Passionate about travel, Sarah has visited over twenty countries collecting sparks of inspiration (though New Orleans is where her heart rests). She's a self-professed expert at crafting original songs to sing to her very patient pets, and a seasoned professional at finding ways to humiliate herself (bonus points if it happens in public). When at home in Oregon, her husband and best friend, James, is very kind about indulging her love of fast German cars and expensive lattes.

www.sarahmcradit.com